THE BEACH

Genie stopped and pointed to a ditch under the fence. She slid her surfboard under the chain link barrier, and scrambled after it; within seconds she was inside, waiting for me. In the sun with the surfboard under her arm, she seemed so vital, so firm and ripe that I thought of her as a human mango and I wanted to eat right there, on the spot.

I pushed my board under the fence, dropped to my belly, and dragged myself after the board, inside the perimeter of Camp Pendleton. I was on U.S. government property, the Marine Corps training base. I was trespassing, breaking and entering, perhaps an attempted robbery in the eyes of the law; maybe even part of a Soviet espionage scheme. If we were caught, all my life would be reduced to zero. The long-suffering professional would become a worthless, unemployable convict housed at government expense in a federal penitentiary. All because of my desire for my friend's seventeen-year-old daughter.

STRANGE AILMENTS; UNCERTAIN CURES

"Fresh and funny."—*Kirkus Reviews*

"Deals with the sexual modes and obsessions that make life interesting, adventurous and troublesome."—*Publishers Weekly*

Strange Ailments; Uncertain Cures

Bruce Goldsmith

BANTAM BOOKS
TORONTO · NEW YORK · LONDON · SYDNEY · AUCKLAND

I would like to express my appreciation to Warren Cook for his unshakable enthusiasm and prodigious efforts on behalf of this work.

This is a work of fiction. Names, characters, places, and incidents are either the product of the author's imagination or are used fictitiously. Any resemblance to actual events, locales, or persons, living or dead, is entirely coincidental.

*This edition contains the complete text
of the original hardcover edition.*
NOT ONE WORD HAS BEEN OMITTED.

STRANGE AILMENTS; UNCERTAIN CURES
*A Bantam Book / published by arrangement with
Mercury House*

PRINTING HISTORY
Mercury House edition published July 1986
Bantam edition / September 1988

The extract from California Girls *by Brian Wilson, © 1965 by Irving Music, Inc. (BMI), is reprinted by permission of Almo Publications.*

ISBN 0-553-27617-4

Published simultaneously in the United States and Canada.

Bantam Books are published by Bantam Books, a division of Bantam Doubleday Dell Publishing Group, Inc. Its trademark, consisting of the words "Bantam Books" and the portrayal of a rooster, is Registered in U.S. Patent and Trademark Office and in other countries. Marca Registrada. Bantam Books, 666 Fifth Avenue, New York, New York 10103.

PRINTED IN THE UNITED STATES OF AMERICA

O   0 9 8 7 6 5 4 3 2 1

To Sally

1

Even today, I don't have the faintest idea how long I stood staring in through my living room window at Genie. Probably it was only a minute, but it seemed like hours. I had come up to the house because a car was blocking my driveway. It obviously belonged to a friend of the baby-sitter. But what I saw through the window made me forget everything, even the long and tiring drive home from Escondido.

There in my living room was seventeen-year-old Genie Cotler, our baby-sitter, stark naked, on the couch straddling a long-haired surfer named Nick who sat with his back to the window. Genie squatted over him, drenched in sweat and passion, balancing herself with her legs wide apart and her feet planted firmly on my Indian cotton sectional sofa. Genie's eyes, so lovely in an almost Oriental way, were closed. Her sinewy fingers clutched her own kneecaps so tightly that her knuckles were white from the tension. The only point of contact between Genie and Nick was where her blonde pubic mound enveloped his erection. There, in a slow undulation of power, delicacy, and torturous pleasure, Genie drew herself up and down, squeezing him with movements from the center of some brute prehistoric animal within her. What I was watching was not sex, but lust incarnate.

Genie was only seventeen; I was thirty-four. I was twice her age and yet at that moment I realized I had never experienced what she obviously knew and felt on that couch. Sure, I'd seduced women. And sure, my wife Marilyn and I had what anyone would call a reasonable sex life. But what I saw here literally blew open a long-atrophied core area of my brain. I wanted what I saw with an urgency I'd never known. I couldn't take my eyes off the window.

Genie was working hard, closing in on her longed-for release. I was so aroused, and at the same time so terrified of the powerful feelings emerging from within me, that I stood paralyzed, barely breathing. Suddenly, from the driveway, not thirty feet away, came the shattering roar of Marilyn's BMW airhorns. My wife was reminding me to get moving. Genie, hearing the noise, glanced up. Our eyes locked and she watched me watching her. I felt horrible, ashamed to be caught spying, particularly on something so pure. But I was so drawn to what I was seeing that I couldn't turn away. What further amazed me was that, knowing I was watching, Genie closed her eyes and continued to thrust against Nick. Quickly she lost herself in her climax, working Nick like the beast she was for all of her pleasure. Then she collapsed, out of sight, on the sofa. The horn honked again. I moved back out of sight of the living room window, took a couple of deep breaths to calm myself, then tapped on the front door.

"Genie," I called, "would you please have your friend move his car out of the driveway." The voice that emerged from my throat sounded strangled and feeble.

"One second, Mister Marcus," Genie called back confidently.

I returned to the BMW and Marilyn, who sat in the passenger seat writing up voluminous notes on her micro-lit clipboard. We had spent the weekend in Escondido, looking at health resorts (or "spas," as the Europeans call them). Such places as The Golden Door, the Grotto, The Whole Earth, and a new one called simply, and pretentiously, The Pacific Ocean. They believed in salt water cures and did a lot of swimming at that last place, as if one couldn't have guessed. Each spa had a unique gimmick to lead its clients down the road to health. Marilyn had what she called a dream. To me, it was no dream, but an obsession—something neurotic. Over the last year, the "dream" had changed her into a driven, humorless, high-strung, uncharacteristically angry woman.

I loved Marilyn, but that love only made it harder for me to deal with her health-resort mania. Marilyn was a brilliant woman with a highly focused mind—a quality I had liked and admired in her from the beginning. When we first met, we were overjoyed to have found in one another a kindred spirit, a haven of sanity in a world we both felt, as a result of our tormented upbringings, to be unstable and destructive. I had no idea then that her warm, loving, outgoing personality would evolve into all-out fanaticism.

Marilyn wanted to throw away her career as a doctor, a successful obstetrician and gynecologist, and flee to the country to pursue her compelling vision of creating a resort community devoted to health, fitness, and lifestyle. She wanted to heal the world. Marilyn fervently believed that our society was moving faster and faster into the business of creating illness through pollution, social violence, incomprehensible modern stresses, and widespread corporate greed. She was convinced we were a society in chaos, without direction, verging on anarchy, and that she, I, and our daughter Rebecca were living in the center of a time bomb from which we had to escape. And quickly.

Just two days before our trip to Escondido, Marilyn had been jogging on the grass strip dividing San Vicente Boulevard when a mugger began to chase her. Marilyn was in good enough shape to run a marathon and took off, sprinting at full speed. She easily outdistanced the mugger, who probably went into cardiac arrest trying to catch her. But the experience quite rightly terrified her. She actually came home crying. I say "actually" because it was the first time in almost a year that Marilyn had given in to feelings that made her appear vulnerable and frightened; in other words, human. My pleasure in comforting her was short-lived; in no more than an hour she had turned the situation around and was using it to argue how vital it was for us to get out of the city, fast, and build the health resort. Not even something apolitical and benign, like jogging, was safe anymore.

Marilyn had already been researching the project for months, trying to pin her fantasy down into dollars and cents. She had compiled comparative information on everything from health instructors' salaries to exercise programs, construction costs, Nautilus machine financing, various holistic health schemes, and overall profit projections at differing occupancy rates. She even went so far as to research the tax benefits of locating the resort in an agricultural region and growing food organically, thereby controlling pesticide contamination and, at the same time, qualifying for U.S. Agricultural Department farm subsidies. She plugged every bit of this information into the computer at the hospital and ran program after program in an effort to optimize the size of the resort, maximizing economies of scale yet keeping it manageable with a small number of investors. I had to admit she was thorough. Everything was down on paper. Our weekend in Escondido had been an attempt to compare her ideal resort with those already in existence. The result of the weekend's tour was absolute. In Marilyn's mind there was no comparison; her resort won, hands down, over everything we had seen.

I got back in the BMW and waited for what seemed like another eternity. How long could it take Genie and Nick to put their clothes back on? Marilyn was anxious to get in the house. The mood in the BMW was tense. I ignored my wife's impatience and tried to mull over what we had accomplished on our two-day whirlwind research tour. But I quickly realized that I couldn't concentrate; as soon as my mind even attempted to examine some aspect of The Golden Door, it would go adrift and I would begin fantasizing about what I had just seen on my living room couch.

I felt like I was suddenly going crazy. On one hand I was an adult, a father, with a lovely, brilliant, thirty-year-old wife and an adorable, smart, well behaved four-year-old daughter. On the other hand, I was acutely conscious of myself as a voyeur, lusting after a seventeen-year-old baby-sitter. In my erotic fantasy I became terrified that the pretty picture of my marriage to Marilyn was crumbling like a jigsaw puzzle in an earthquake. Hurricane Genie was tearing up my inner life. I knew only two facts for certain. One, I had hated the weekend in Escondido and wanted nothing to do with fat farms, health resorts, or spas. And two, I couldn't take my mind off of Genie's nubile body. I wanted her. Which was impossible. Genie was only seventeen. I'd known her since she was twelve. Her father, Ed Cotler, was one of my closest friends. If I touched her, he'd kill me. But so what, I thought, touching Genie would make the risk worth taking. This, I realized, was crazy. I had to drive the idea from my mind. I reached for the steering wheel and pressed long and hard on the horn.

Moments later the front door of the house opened and Nick ran out. Without even acknowledging me, he jumped into his VW dunebuggy and gunned the engine. I started the BMW and backed into the street. Nick threw his dunebuggy into reverse, accelerated out of the driveway, spun around in a U turn, and roared off into the night. I pulled back into the driveway, let Marilyn out by the front door, then drove straight into the open garage and unloaded the suitcases.

By the time I got inside the house, Genie had been paid for her two days of baby-sitting and was ready to go home. I avoided looking at her. Not that she seemed ashamed; I was the one who was embarrassed. Genie politely said goodnight and left. Marilyn had no idea that anything unusual had gone on. The living room appeared undisturbed; Genie and her friend had covered their tracks perfectly.

Upstairs, Rebecca had been awakened by the honking horn and the commotion. By the time I had hauled our suitcases up to the bedroom, Marilyn was already sitting on our daughter's bed, kissing her and scratching her back, which was Rebecca's favorite pleasure. She was like a cat who could sit for hours while Marilyn or I scratched her skin. The sharper our fingernails, the better.

"Hello sweetheart," I said to my daughter as I kissed and hugged her. "I'm so happy to see you; daddy missed you very much."

"I missed you, daddy. Don't leave me again, promise?"

She squeezed me very hard and looked me straight in the face. Her eyes were clouding with tears.

"I didn't think you were ever coming home," she added.

This was the first full weekend we had ever left Rebecca, and she wasn't making me feel any better about it.

"We missed you very much, too," Marilyn purred. "We thought about you all the time."

"You did?" Rebecca inquired.

"You betcha," Marilyn emphasized. "We brought you lots of presents."

Rebecca waited. This interested her.

"Do you want them now?" Marilyn asked. "Or tomorrow?"

"Now."

"But you're supposed to be sleeping now."

"What did you bring me, mommy?"

"If we give them to you now, will you go back to sleep?"

Rebecca nodded enthusiastically. She was wired, fully awake. What else would she answer?

"Where's the suitcase?" Marilyn asked me.

"On our bed."

Marilyn left the room.

"Did you have a nice time with Genie?" I asked.

Rebecca nodded.

"What did you do?"

"We went to the zoo."

"What animals did you see?"

"Monkees."

"Anything else?"

"Effelents."

"Which did you like better?"

"Monkees."

"Why?"

"Cause they look like daddy," Rebecca giggled.

"Thanks a lot," I told her, pretending to be hurt. "Why do you say that?"

"Cause they do."

I squatted on the floor and hung my arms down to my feet, imitating the posture of an ape. No one else might have admired my imitation, but my daughter always thought it was terrific. I hopped around the room like a monkey as I talked.

"I don't think I look anything like a monkey. I don't know why you say that. How would you like it if I told you *you* looked like a monkey?"

Rebecca giggled, amused by my ape dance.

"You're not answering me, Becka. What if I told you you looked like a monkey; would you like that?"

"But you do look like a mon-kee, daddy."

"I don't." I pretended to be hurt.

"You do," said Marilyn from the doorway.

"Both of you need your eyes checked," I said as I scratched my armpit in the best movie monkey tradition. Rebecca laughed with enthusiasm, then caught a glimpse of the two wrapped packaged Marilyn was holding. Her interest in my monkey act vanished.

"Boy, oh boy," she giggled greedily.

"Here you go, sweetheart. You see, daddy and I thought about you all weekend." Marilyn handed Rebecca the gifts.

Rebecca struggled with the wrapper on the first box and eventually pulled out one of those toy birds that endlessly dip their beaks in a water glass, seemingly powered by magic.

"It's Big Bird," shrieked Rebecca.

"Let me show you how it works."

Marilyn set a glass of water by Rebecca's bed and plunged the beak of the bird into the water. Almost immediately the bird began bobbing up and down as if it were drinking by itself. Rebecca was fascinated.

"Open the other one," I encouraged her.

Rebecca tore the wrapper off the other box. Inside was a sweatshirt with the word "Health" printed all over the back in every language from Japanese to Hebrew.

"You see what it says here," Marilyn pointed to the embroidered name on the front of the shirt. Rebecca scrutinized the writing.

"Ra-bekka," she squealed with delight.

"Very good," Marilyn encouraged her.

"You're a real smart girl," I added.

She immediately pulled the shirt over her head. Marilyn had to help to keep her from getting her arms tangled. Finally it was down over her little body.

"It looks great on you," Marilyn cooed. "Doesn't she look cute, Michael?"

"You look very beautiful, sweetheart," I responded on cue. Rebecca beamed with pride.

"Now it's time to go to sleep, Becka," Marilyn told her.

Immediately my daughter's eyes clouded with tears.

"No."

"Yes, sweetheart. It's very late, way past your bedtime."

Rebecca looked to me for help.

"It's very late, Rebecca. Your mommy is right."

"No, I don't want to sleep." She started to cry.

Marilyn held her.

"Come on Rebecca, you promised, remember? You said if we gave you your presents, you'd go to sleep, remember?"

Rebecca ignored Marilyn and continued to cry.

"Give mommy a kiss goodnight."

Rebecca ignored her and kept crying.

"Rebecca, be a big girl."

It was no use; she kept crying.

I felt an elbow in my side. It was Marilyn, gesturing for me to sing. Music, if you could call it that, often helped put Rebecca to sleep.

Marilyn led the song.

"Goodnight ladies, goodnight ladies, we're sad to see you go."

I joined in, off key but loud.

"Merrily we roll along, roll along, roll along.

Merrily we roll along, across the deep blue sea."

Rebecca stopped crying and made a face.

"That's a bad song." She turned to me. "Sing the 'girl song,'" she commanded.

I had teased her a couple of weeks before with a personalized

version of a song from my high school days, the Beach Boys'
"California Girls." For some reason she couldn't get enough of
it.

"Yeah," added Marilyn, affectionately teasing me, "sing the
'girl song.'"

Marilyn was sometimes very sweet in the way she encouraged
me to sing. She knew that one part of me was embarrassed at
warbling in public while another part of me got a real kick out of
singing for my daughter. My voice wasn't great. But then again
the neighborhood dogs didn't howl when they heard me, so I
couldn't be too bad. Certainly I had never in my life sung in
front of other people until I married Marilyn. One day she heard
me crooning in the shower and told me I had a very good voice.
She wondered why I had never been in the grammar school glee
club or the temple choir. No one had ever encouraged me in that
direction, certainly not my parents. Art and esthetics hadn't been
a part of my upbringing. In my childhood the only choices open
to me were the professions: law, medicine, dentistry, pharmacology. Singing was for poor Italians from New York, not for the
Marcus family.

"Sing the 'girl song,' daddy," Rebecca commanded again.

"If I sing it, will you promise you'll go to sleep?"

Rebecca nodded enthusiastically.

"You too?" I asked Marilyn.

"I'll promise you anything to hear you sing," my wife said
affectionately.

I had to admit that without Marilyn I would never have been
freed up enough to sing to my daughter, much less even to have
conceived a daughter. Marilyn had wanted children. I had liked
the idea of a family, but the reality of it had frightened me.
However, her confidence and dedication to the idea had won out,
thank God, and overcome my fears. As a result, I was able to
live out parts of myself I had never known existed. With
Rebecca I could be silly. I could be a child again. I could slow
down the relentless onslaught of time by seeing her grow. I could
even learn to play like a child with my child. That night I could
sing to my daughter and my wife without shame. Who would
have thought a grown man, a pharmacist, would sing a sixties
Beach Boys' hit to his four-year-old daughter and thirty-year-old
wife on a Sunday night at eleven-forty? All this pleasure I owed
to Marilyn.

"Well East Coast girls are hip,
I really dig the styles they we-ear," I began.
"And the northern girls with the way they dress,
They keep their boyfriends warm at night.
The Midwest has the sunshine
And the girls all get so tan,
And the southern girls, with the way they talk,
They knock me out when I'm down there."

At this point I smiled at my daughter, who giggled, anticipating what was coming. Marilyn moved beside me, put her arm around me, and joined in on the refrain.

"But, I wish they all could be California,
I wish they all could be California,
I wish they all could be California Girls,
Dah, dah, dah, dah, dah dah dah,
Wish they all could be California Girls."

"I'm a California girl, daddy."

"You are, sweetheart, and I love you." I kissed her. "Now it's time to go to sleep."

She nodded and kissed me back. I set her down on her pillow. Marilyn gave her a big kiss.

"Sweet dreams, Becka; we'll be right next door if you need us."

" 'Nite, mommy."

Rebecca closed her eyes and was almost instantly asleep. Marilyn and I tiptoed out of her room. Moments later we were in our own bedroom, preparing for sleep.

"You're very cute when you sing, you know that?" Marilyn told me as she unpacked her suitcase.

"You tell that to all the boys, don't you?"

"Only to my husband."

"Oh, you're married, are you?"

"Very much so."

"Then what are you doing in my bedroom?"

"It was your voice; I'm a sucker for singing."

"You're a groupie, is that it?"

"You won't tell anyone, will you?"

"What's it worth to you?"

"Blackmail, huh?"

"It's a tough world; a man's got to make his living somehow."

"I thought you were a druggist."

"I thought you were a gynecologist."

"It all seems to be changing, doesn't it?"

I hoped our amusing little repartee would lead to lovemaking. Instead it led to the bathroom where Marilyn, with another agenda in mind, talked as she washed. What she wanted was for me to sell the pharmacy and use the proceeds to finance the down payment on her health resort. Instantly all affection between us vanished. I was enraged, and we argued. Over seven long years, I had built the pharmacy from nothing into a success. I loved that place. It was mine. Marilyn couldn't understand the fact that I had not one iota of interest in giving up my business to go live in the boonies on a diet of bean sprouts and carrot tops. I had absolutely no burning wish to transform the arteries of mankind from sewers clogged by cholesterol and jelly doughnut fat into roto-rooted, vegetarian, aerobic marvels of modern medical hydraulic renovation. No, it was tedious enough spending my days filling prescriptions for Valium; I was not going to make health, with a capital "H," the fundamental and obsessive focus of my life.

We ended up going to bed angry. I lay under the blankets for what seemed like hours, unable to sleep. I thought about the weekend and tried to find something positive in what had gone on. But my mind kept returning to fantasies of Genie. Beautiful Genie on my living room couch, desecrating that sofa with her remarkable body. I'm normally a very timid person when it comes to talking about women or sex. I'm not one of those guys who runs on and on about "the shape of Linda's tits," or "the ass on Vikki Owens." That kind of conversation disgusts me. From certain men, like my business partner Jerry Herrman, I had to listen to such bullshit all the time. I figured they didn't have such a good sex life at home so they had to excite themselves by making everyone else think, at least for the moment, that they were real connoisseurs of the female species, and thus studs to be admired for their extreme masculinity. I never bought that act. But that night, as I lay in bed, all I could see in my mind was Genie's anatomy. Those impeccable breasts damp with a mixture of sweat and that shithead of a surfer's saliva. The taut neck, aching to be kissed and bitten. Full lips, pulsing with blood, crying out to be sucked. And her muscles—everywhere she had definition, as they called it in the health spas. She was leonine, like a jungle creature. And her thighs, connected to those perfect, juicy buttocks. I just wanted to plant myself inside of her forever. Most awesome and what I couldn't get out of my head was the concentration that she focused on her own passion. She felt sex so deeply; her movements were so obviously unself-conscious and pleasurable. She was supple like a yogi, yet taut like a gymnast. I lay in bed with an erection.

Feeling guilty, I looked over at Marilyn, who was asleep. Why couldn't my hard-on be for my wife? Why was I suddenly so aroused by a seventeen year old? I mean, I didn't know Genie at all. She was simply the young, very beautiful, very underage daughter of a friend. I loved my wife, I told myself, and I didn't even know this girl, really. My erection seemed to go against everything I believed in: family, wife, community, business, and general national stability. It was good for nothing that I held sacred. Yet I lay in bed and there it was. I couldn't deny either the hard-on or the source of the hard-on: Genie.

It was as if an act of subversion had suddenly engulfed my subconscious. If I had been a staunch Republican, I might have been able to describe it as a Communist plot—some kind of personal, psychological, internal, terrorist subversion, as if a right-winger's brain had been suddenly taken over by the mentality of Ché Guevara. A real Republican might attribute it to the food at the liberal-pinko health resorts we had visited that weekend. Maybe some sort of chemicals had been laced into our yogurt which altered brain cells, thereby undermining the western world through the destruction of erotic complacency in normal, well-adjusted marriages. Since I wasn't a serious Republican, I attributed my erection to Genie's beauty and my own recent frustrations with Marilyn. There's only so much conflict even a good marriage can survive; thanks to her health resort obsession, we were closing in on that limit. The issue between us just seemed unresolvable. I lay there that night afraid the health resort was putting our marriage in real jeopardy. I felt I had to do something, and fast, to diminish the war between us and reconnect our affections. It occurred to me that maybe the erection could help.

I slid across the sheets and curled around Marilyn's back, cocooning her with my belly. She didn't move. I kissed the nape of her neck, lightly biting her as I knew she liked. She didn't stir. Marilyn was an extraordinarily beautiful woman. My guess is that most men would find her physically more beautiful than Genie. Marilyn had the classic black-haired look of elegance, with flawless white skin, aquiline nose, Navajolike cheekbones, long, thin, strong fingers, swimmers' legs, lithe, thin torso, and small, firm, erect breasts. In every way, Marilyn was a beauty. Except that there was an edge to her that made her seem impenetrable. When I had first met her, I had liked this quality because it seemed a challenge. Could I ever get to know this woman, I had wondered. Would we ever get close? She was a very independent person, and very private. I'd been married to her for five years and I still wasn't sure that I knew her. Yet there I was, trying to arouse her in the middle of the night with an erection that I was afraid was a betrayal of our marriage. What I wanted was to be inside my wife and to use my renegade erection to renew and revive our love for one another.

But Marilyn didn't stir. I tried fondling her nipples. No dice. I scooted down under the sheets, slid my head between her thighs and began to caress her with my tongue. She was as dry as a bone. It was hopeless. After ten minutes of real work with my mouth, tongue, lips, and fingertips, I gave up. She must have taken Valium or a sleeping pill.

The problem was, what to do with my erection. It wouldn't quit. I felt like I was fifteen again. And in fact, I rather liked that feeling. I tried thinking about other things—finances, health food, movies I'd seen. But everything seemed to lead inexorably back to thoughts of Genie, and the erection returned. I considered the old cold shower routine. But since that had never worked when I was in high school, why should it work now? I got out of bed anyhow and went into the bathroom.

I saw myself in the mirror, just as I had seen Genie through the window. I was naked. She had been naked. I had an erection, just as Nick had had an erection. I wanted Genie urgently. I shut the bathroom door, lubricated my cock with soap from the sink, and began to stroke myself, fantasizing about Genie sitting on me, so wet, so passionate, so eager. I was a married man, I thought, but look at me. I was disgusted with myself. It felt wonderful.

2

To say that the next day was unusual would be an understatement. I arrived at the pharmacy by seven-fifty. As always, I was the first one in. However bad my life seemed, I was invariably hit by a surge of pride the moment I unlocked the doors, shut off the alarm system, turned on the lights, and entered my drugstore. From wall to wall and floor to ceiling, every shelf, every bottle of deodorant, every magazine, and every prescription vial was something for which I had sole responsibility. They were all mine, even the video games I'd installed by the candy counter. I had done it. I alone had made this business a success. It was a great location on Westwood Boulevard just a few blocks south of UCLA and Wilshire. I'd gone into debt up to my eyeballs to buy the business. At the time I bought the store, everyone had told me I was crazy. But I had made it work. No matter how badly the rest of the day went, I always felt a thrill as I entered the store early each morning. And, given the way the last few months had been going, I really needed that thrill.

That morning started out like every other June morning in Southern California. The sun finally came out, burning its way through the omnipresent dawn fog. The streets filled with cars, bumper to bumper, each transporting its owner to work. Southern California traffic must be the ultimate wet dream of Saudi Arabian oil sheiks; our gross waste of fossil fuels makes the Christian's biblical concept of manna from heaven a smalltimer's fantasy. No wonder the Arabs are Moslems; who would want to be a Jew or a Christian when all Moses and his starving desert people received from God was a bit of bread? The Arab Moslems, if they wanted to, could buy all the bread in the world with the oil money their God pumps them.

That morning, as every morning, my employees drifted in slowly. Harriet Drake, a grandmother in her sixties, was the first to show. She worked the cash register by the makeup, magazine, and greeting card counters. In between customers, this nice old lady analyzed the daily racing form before placing regular bets with her bookie. The next in was old reliable Milt—always on time, and always, I was sure, a little boozed. But I never caught him at it and didn't want to, as long as he made no mistakes. Milt nodded good morning to me, took off his sport coat, buttoned up his white tunic and began filling prescriptions. Al Holster was the next pharmacist to come in. He was a dead ringer for the trusting local druggist I saw every night on TV advertising hemorrhoid suppositories. Al's passion was Las Vegas and gambling. His game was craps. I got a real kick out of that. Las Vegas was missing a good bet not having the man from the hemorrhoid commercials doing a TV spot for its tourist bureau on the joy of craps.

Audrey, my concession to female pharmacists, rolled in at eight-ten. She was a cold fish—she came in, did her work, said virtually nothing, and left at the end of the day. I had no sense whatsoever of the life she led outside the drugstore. I didn't even know if she was married or single. But I really didn't care; she did her work and was efficient, and for that I was grateful. The last pharmacist in was, as he always put it, my "good buddy," Adam Kauffman of the hippie generation, complete with neatly trimmed black beard. I was sure this thirty-two-year-old ex-radical was regularly performing pharmaceutical experiments on himself with highly controlled substances. But as with Milt and his boozing, I didn't really want to find out. Adam did his job, and a lot of the older customers liked him and asked for him by name. I guessed that the drugstore and their need for it reminded the older folks of their age and slow physical disintegration. They didn't enjoy being reminded of their dentures, hemorrhoids, and penchant for eighty proof sedatives and found Adam's energy and humor something of a relief.

Late as always was Mary, the pharmacy's cashier. Miss Prude. I was sure that I could get my condom sales up two hundred percent if I could find someone else to work the register. But Mary was honest and she could count. And in this day and age, those two qualities are almost irreplaceable. So I sacrificed condom sales for balanced books. Next in were my UCLA stock boys, Jeff and Ted, and then finally, his usual half hour late, Herbie the maintenance man. As usual, Herbie had had trouble starting his Cadillac. Where else in the world do maintenance men have trouble with their Fleetwoods?

The day began normally enough. Patients phoned in requests for prescriptions. We called their doctors for confirmation. Old Mr. Eberhart confided to me that he wanted something to perk up his love life with his wife. I suggested he talk to his physician. But Eberhart wanted my feelings on vitamin E. What could I say? The man wanted vitamin E. It wouldn't hurt him, I told him. Which is probably what he wanted to hear. So Eberhart bought vitamin E. I probably should have sent him to the magazine counter for a copy of *Penthouse*. "Take one tablet and study the centerfold,'' I could have typed on the vitamin E label.

Housewives came in for greeting cards and perfume. And Harriet let us all know she was having a hot day with her bookie. By the sixth race she was ahead $272, which put her in a good mood to handle the aggravation from the local high school kids, which was already starting. Their behavior was always the same. It was almost unbelievable. From year to year, the only thing that changed about them was the tint of their hair. This year purple and green highlights were the fashion. They came in after school to play the video games, buy whatever candy they couldn't steal, and sneak peeks at *Playboy, Penthouse, Gallery,* and *Rogue.* We had to watch them every minute.

For most of the day, I tried to stay hidden in my little cubbyhole of an office behind the pharmaceutical storage shelves. The second quarter of the year was over and I was faced with the loathsome problem of calculating the store's financial situation and distributing forty-nine percent of my hard-earned profits to my legally silent but personally very vocal partner, Jerry Herrman. Certainly he was entitled to his share; it was his attitude toward life that made me sick. I busted my ass working like a damn little beaver to make money, and he sat back and not only scooped the cream off the top, but gloated about it. Jerry was a pig and I resented feeding him, even if he was legally entitled.

Anyhow, I sat there in my office entering figures into my calculator, trying to make sense out of the second quarter. I had a difficult time concentrating. Marilyn and the health farm kept intruding, and I could see no solution to our conflict. The more I thought about it, the more depressed I became. Inevitably I was led back to my fantasies of Genie, which at least provided some relief from my anguish. The more the financial date bored me, the more I knew I wanted that gorgeous seventeen-year-old girl to squat naked over me like she did over that slob of a surfer. I looked at the work I had accomplished and realized I wasn't making progress. If I didn't get down to it and start concentrating, I'd soon have to face Jerry with an incomplete accounting. That would mean question after question—his version of the Inquisition, an activity in which I had no interest in participating. I tried to force both Genie and Marilyn from my mind.

But at three-thirty my phone buzzed with some far too exciting information: Harriet, at the cash register, was calling to tell me

that a young girl named Genie Cotler would like to see me.
Harriet wanted to know if she should send her back to my office.
What a question!

My little cubicle was a mess, with boxes of financial papers
stacked over not only virtually every square inch of the desk, but
on every horizontal surface as well, including the floor. A
romantic office, this was not. The only personal decor was on
the wall beside the desk—a photograph of Marilyn holding
Rebecca on my daughter's first outing to the Beverly Glen park.
Both Marilyn and Rebecca had seemed so euphoric that summer
day. We were so happy then. If Marilyn knew what I felt toward
Genie, she certainly wouldn't be euphoric now. I had an impulse
to pull the picture off the wall. But that was ridiculous, a betrayal
of almost cornball proportions.

Before I could move anything, I heard a knock on the door.

"Come in," I called, and then was embarrassed by the sexual
connotations of what I had just said. But who, I asked myself,
other than me at that moment, would interpret that invitation as
anything other than an innocent formality?

The door slowly opened. It was Genie. A different Genie.
Today she was wearing a skin-tight black leotard, jogging shoes,
and an oversized, stylishly ragged cotton sweatshirt—a bewitchingly
sensual combination. This girl had, as we used to say in high
school, "pecker power."

"Hi," she smiled shyly. She was obviously nervous.

"Hi," I answered, trying to smile back innocently and not
betray the fact that I was so drawn to her I could barely speak.

She looked around the office for something. Perhaps it was
just to size me up. I couldn't tell her reaction.

"I need to talk to you. About last night," she spoke quietly
and hesitantly. "This a bad time for you?"

I shook my head no. "It's fine," I told her.

"Thanks," she said as she closed the door to the pharmacy.
Obviously she wanted privacy.

"Let me move this so you can sit down," I told her as I
cleared a box of invoices from the seat of the only other chair in
the room. Genie sat down, not four feet from me, crossing those
beautiful thighs of hers, which rubbed the legs of her leotard
together and created the most sensual noise I could imagine—a
symphony better than anything by Brahms. I tried to drive such
thoughts from my mind while I waited for her to speak, but it

was hard because for a long time she said nothing. Obviously what she had come to talk about was difficult for her to face.

"Would you like a cup of coffee?" I asked, pointing to the Mister Coffee machine at the end of the desk behind the box labeled "Accounts Receivable."

"Thanks," she said, "normally I don't drink the stuff; it's not good for you. I only drink espresso, 'cause it's pure. But a cup right now would be real nice."

I got up and poured her a cup.

"Sugar or milk?"

"Milk. If it's real. I can't stand the fake stuff."

"I've only got Coffee Mate."

"Black, then."

I handed her the cup, and with a quiet sucking noise she took a sip. How I envied that coffee. At that instant my only aspiration was to be that black fluid being drawn so delicately through those plum-colored lips.

"It's not as good as espresso, but I try to use good coffee; is it okay?" I said lamely in an effort to force the sensual thoughts from my brain.

"It's great. Thanks."

Again we stared at each other in silence. Finally she got up her courage to talk.

"I guess you're wondering why I'm here."

"I figured you had your reasons."

"You have any idea why I'm here?"

What a seductive question. Did she really expect me to confess my desire for her?

"You told me it had something to do with last night."

"Yeah. But it really has to do with my dad."

I nodded for her to continue.

"I know you're a good friend of his, so what I'm asking isn't exactly fair." She studied my reaction.

I said nothing and simply waited for her to continue.

"You're a friend of his. And I'm his daughter. How long have you known me?"

"Five years. Six years?"

"Are you a friend of mine, too?"

"I'd like to think so."

"But not like you are with my father?"

"Well, it's different isn't it? He and I have spent a lot of time together. Done things together. We have certain things in common. And some legal dealings. You and I, well, we haven't had the time alone to develop such a relationship."

"But you still consider us friends. Can we really be friends if you don't know me?"

She had a good point. Why she was pursuing it was still beyond me.

"I'd like to think," I told her, "that friendship is something that's a feeling that's almost undefinable. A bond. I know that for one reason or another I feel that bond toward you. Why, I don't know. But I don't, for example, feel it toward the cashier, Mary, outside. You understand? In my eyes, you're a friend. Mary isn't."

Genie thought this over; it made sense to her.

"Are you telling me that, as a friend, I can trust you?"

"Of course you can trust me."

"Even if it means telling you something and your keeping it a secret from my father?"

Suddenly it was clear. And just as suddenly I realized that this was the opportunity for Genie and me to get closer. Sharing secrets—the favorite occupation of teenage friendships. Could I turn down such a chance?

"Genie, whatever you tell me is between us, I promise you. Not only do you have my word on it, but think about it—how would me going to your father with a confidence you and I shared make me look in his eyes? I'd be a wimp, wouldn't I?"

"He might think of you as a loyal friend."

"Well, I wouldn't do it. That's not the kind of man I am."

She studied me carefully before speaking.

"You know, I believe you."

"Thank you," I told her.

"Okay, I told you I was here about last night."

I nodded.

"My dad is a real rigid guy about some things, wouldn't you say?"

"He would say he has his principles," I offered in Ed's defense.

Genie frowned. Obviously she disagreed.

"Principles. . . ." she muttered.

I nodded again.

"Do you agree with all his principles?" she asked.

"Some," I answered. And I was being honest. Ed Cotler was a brilliant lawyer—a litigator—who saw himself as a bastion of logic and reason. He went after issues propelled by a moral force, almost like a character out of the Old West. I had first met him in a professional capacity when I was being sued by some crank from Beverly Hills who claimed I had sold him a tainted prescription. The story was complete bull, simply an attempt to extort money from me. It was just after I had bought the drugstore and I was barely making ends meet. I didn't have the time or the resources to face a lawsuit. My insurance company recommended Ed Cotler. We hit it off immediately and he took the case. Within a month, the lowlife lawsuit against my store quietly disappeared. By that time Marilyn and I had already begun our dinner and bridge evenings with Ed and his wife, Anne. What Genie didn't realize was that my friendship with Ed was exclusively social. As individuals we were highly disciplined, hard-working traditionalists who shared an interest in political debate. But did I know him as a man? In fact, as Genie's question implied, what did I really know about him? How much did one person ever truly know about another? For that matter, what could one person really know about himself? Endless, eternal, perplexing questions without answers.

"Have you ever seen him get angry?" Genie asked.

"Yeah. Over legal issues. Or political debates. He's pretty passionate sometimes. Why?"

"That's not the kind of anger I'm talking about. What I mean is, have you ever seen him lose his temper and go crazy, you know, like blow his cork?"

"No," I told her honestly.

"Well, you're lucky. It doesn't happen often, but when it does, it's maniac time. Terrifying. Even the dog hides."

"You're kidding," I muttered.

"I wish. You get in his way at the wrong time, you get hurt. A year ago I misread his mood, argued with him, and he slapped me so hard I thought my nose was broken."

"That's horrible."

"Tell me about it. That's why I'm here."

"How can I help you?" I offered.

"You really want to help me?"

"I do."

"I really can trust you?"

"Absolutely."

Genie thought it over for the final time then apparently decided I was being honest.

"Okay, here goes." Genie began. "Nick, the guy you saw with me in your living room, my father hates. I'm not allowed to speak to him or see him. So for the last couple of months I've been getting together with him secretly. What can I do? Every guy I ever go out with my father finds a reason to hate. It's true. In Nick's case my father may be right. I mean, Nick is a lot of fun, a real exciting guy, but he's also very crazy. And he wants too much from me. The way he's been acting the last few weeks scares me. Last night I told him I didn't want to see him anymore. He didn't take it too well. But at least it's over now. What you saw through the window was the sad end. I was trying to make him feel better so he wouldn't take it too hard. I feel real bad about doing it in your living room. I mean, if I hadn't thought I had to do it then, I never would have done it. I owe you an apology. But with Nick, he's so nuts, sometimes, that you never know what he's going to do. That's why I had to let him down easy. I'm telling you this so you'll understand the favor I need from you."

"Shoot," I told her. I was astounded by her directness. Perhaps "overwhelmed" is a better description.

"Don't tell my father you saw me with Nick, okay?"

"That's all?"

"That's plenty."

"I never met the guy; I don't even know who he is."

Genie smiled.

"You know, Mr. Marcus, you really are a nice man. I mean it. Thank you."

"Mister Marcus was my father; my name is Michael. Can you say that?"

"Michael?"

"Very good."

"Michael, you're making this very easy. But what about your wife; will she tell my mom?"

"Marilyn and I were having an argument in the car while we were waiting for you. I don't think she knows what Nick looked like. If you remember, it was night and you forgot to turn the driveway lights on, so you don't have anything to worry about.

Go home. Forget the whole thing. Don't drive yourself crazy about it.''

"Michael, you are terrific. Thank you.''

"Hey, stop thanking me. You deserve it. You're a remarkable girl. It took a lot of courage to come here and tell all this to me. I know, because when I was your age I figured all adults hated me. I didn't realize then it was just my parents dumping their own pain my way. I longed for one adult to be my friend and tell me I was okay. That's why I want you to know that if you ever feel the need to talk to me, you have a friend here who cares. I mean it.''

"Thank you. You know, I was worried about how you'd react to what I had to tell you. I don't really know any people your age. But you made it easy for me.''

"Genie," I teased her, "if you do want to be friends with me you have to do two things: first, you've got to stop thanking me, and second, you can't refer to me as if I were some Civil War veteran. You know, I'm not quite old enough to have heard Lincoln deliver the Gettysburg Address.''

She grinned that lovely grin again, then blushed.

"I didn't mean it that way.''

"How did you mean it?''

Genie studied me for a moment, trying to decide if I was serious. I felt a strong surge of desire between us, which scared me. I wondered if she had recognized my hunger when she saw me watching her through the living room window. Did she have any idea how aroused I was at that moment, just being alone with her in my office? I had to shift my weight in the chair to keep my erection from hurting me. There I was feeling like a sixteen-year-old kid while trying to keep a straight face and act like an adult.

"Now you *are* kidding me.''

"Very good," I encouraged her.

"Oh my God," she said suddenly, glancing at the clock. "I'm late—I have to get home.''

Genie jumped to her feet and held out her hand for me to shake, which I did with a horrifying amount of pleasure; for one, brief, ecstatic moment my entire life consisted of the feel of my fingertips against the baby-soft flesh of her right palm.

"Michael, thank you again.''

"Remember what I said about saying, 'thank you.' ''

"I remember. But I do thank you."

I nodded modestly.

" 'Bye," she murmured, then turned and slipped out of the room, leaving the office door ajar. Suddenly the drugstore with all of its sounds stomped out my brief fantasy of paradise with Genie. I heard the customers and the cash register. Druggists on the telephone. I was back in the real world, and back too abruptly. My heart was pounding like the bass drum in a John Philip Sousa march.

It was at that moment that I heard a deep male voice shout angrily across the drugstore. And just as suddenly, all the normal noises outside my office door went silent. I knew immediately, without question, that it was a robbery. My first reaction was to trip the silent alarm button on the floor. This would notify the police, but from past experience I knew they could take twenty minutes getting to the store. We could all be long dead by that point. What should I do? The answer came from the drugstore in the form of the robber shouting orders to the druggist.

"Give me the money, all the morphine, amphetamines, and dilaudid you got, and do it quick or I'll blow the girl's head off!"

The son-of-a-bitch was using Genie as a hostage. I went crazy. Robbery was one thing, but using a young girl as a tool to get money was so brutal and traumatic for Genie—this was the behavior of scum. The man outside in the drugstore with the gun was slime. And for that, in my eyes, he deserved to die.

3

My reaction was instinctive. I slid open my desk drawer, lifted out my Smith and Wesson .38 revolver, and flipped open the cylinder: all chambers were loaded. I had been preparing myself for this situation during the last three months, since my previous robbery. I was determined, after the last holdup, not to let myself be a victim anymore. The police had taken eighteen goddamn minutes to show up, by which time we all could have been killed. That would never happen again, I had promised myself. The next day I had gone to the gun store and ordered my pistol.

Twice a week on my lunch hour, without telling anyone, I had been sneaking off to the local range and learning how to use it. Even Marilyn didn't know about the revolver. If she wanted to avoid the horrors of modern life by running to the boonies, that was fine. But I was determined to make myself strong enough to face anything that might come in my front door, without help from undependable outsiders like the cops.

I closed the pistol's chamber and flicked off the safety. Frightened but ready, I dropped to the floor. On my hands and knees, I crawled infantry-style out through the open office door, below the sight line of the robber, who stood on the other side of the pharmaceutical counter. The druggists, on my side, were frozen in fear, staring over the counter at the gunman and his hostage. This suited my purpose perfectly. The pharmacists didn't move as I crawled around their ankles like a commando. What I was doing was not a question of courage, nobility, or heroism. No, I was responding to the most basic of impulses: the life of a young woman who enthralled me was jeopardized by this revolting asshole. I had to save her.

To the druggists I would have been a bizarre sight crawling between their ankles behind the counter. But, thank God, they were all too terrified to look down, so they never saw me and thus never gave me away. At the end of the counter, I slithered for protection up against the formica corner and peeked out for an instant into the aisle facing the druggists. It was just as I had feared.

The robber was a skinny black man in his early thirties, a junkie if I ever saw one. The scumbag had one arm around Genie's neck and with the other hand held a pistol to her head. She moved stiffly, obviously terrified, as the junkie wheeled her around in circles, yelling at the customers in the store.

"I want everyone down on the floor, face down, now!"

The customers obeyed and dropped to the ground. This was a bad sign, I felt. Fifteen men, women, and children lay face down on the floor. It was like something out of Auschwitz, except that the person in charge was a crazed junkie who was certain not to endanger himself by leaving any living witnesses. And everyone in the store, druggists included, had gotten a good look at the man. That left me as the only one who could stop this gun-toting maniac because I, too, had a pistol. As sick as it made me feel to consider using it, I had no choice. Without me, there would be a massacre. I had to act. And soon.

"Spread your arms and legs," he yelled, "and don't anyone move. Anyone moves, I shoot!"

I didn't hear a sound from the drugstore floor. Obviously everyone took the man seriously.

"Put the money in the bag. And get me the morphine, dilaudid, amphetamines and get it in the bag, fast, you hear me honkie!"

"Yessir," I heard old Milt answer.

This was my chance. With the junkie facing the druggists, I slipped from my hiding place, crossed the aisle, and ducked below the adjacent counter. I was protected from the junkie's vision by a shelf stacked full of America's entire line of deodorants.

I crept silently down the aisle until I got to the end, where I was behind the junkie, yet still protected by the physical barrier between us. The junkie was waiting for Milt. The store was incredibly quiet. Where was our famous police force? When you needed the cop, where the fuck was he?

"You gotta have more money than this," the junkie barked at Milt.

Now was my chance. I charged out from behind the counter with my pistol pointed straight at the junkie's head. Milt suddenly looked up, past the junkie, directly at me, giving me away. The junkie turned and swung his pistol around in my direction. It was either his life or mine. No more than one foot from the robber's head and clear of Genie, I pulled the trigger of my .38. For an instant nothing seemed to happen; time stood still. Then I heard the explosion. Was it a cannon? No, it was my revolver; the bullet had been fired. The junkie looked at me. He seemed very surprised. A druggist with a gun, coming at him from behind and firing, was obviously not something he had figured on. But my .38 had done its job, regardless. The side of the junkie's head turned red. He let go of Genie, touched the blood pouring down his face, looked at his crimson fingers, then collapsed on the floor like a sack of potatoes. Bright red blood poured from his head onto the floor. His pistol clattered across the aisle and bounced off a can of Right Guard by my feet. I looked at the gun and couldn't believe it. The thing was plastic. The dumb son-of-a-bitch had been trying to hold us up with a water pistol.

Genie looked very pale; her face glistened with perspiration. Suddenly she began to wobble. I grabbed her. She was shaking, faint, in shock.

"Milt, smelling salts," I yelled, not feeling so good myself.

Milt seemed to move in slow motion. I picked Genie up and carried her around the counter to my office, where I sat her down in my chair. Milt handed me the smelling salts. I broke the vial under Genie's nose. The scent jolted her upright. She threw her arms around me and began to cry. I held her tight, stroking her hair, comforting her.

"It's going to be all right," I told her quietly. "You're safe now. It's all over."

She held me close and continued crying. Outside I could hear sirens. The police and ambulances had arrived, I guessed.

"Mr. Marcus?" a voice called to me from the doorway.

I nodded, still comforting Genie, who continued crying.

"I'm Lieutenant Fred Peterson of homicide. That was nice work you did out there. You okay?"

I nodded again. Genie, I was worried about. But her hysteria did seem to be diminishing. Lieutenant Peterson just stood patiently and waited. I found out later that he had recently been promoted from bunco work and was aggressively trying to make his reputation as a detective. He was twenty-nine years old, five-foot-six, balding, an immaculate dresser with big ambitions. He just happened to be driving near the drugstore when he heard the call over the radio. He had come in with his gun drawn only to find his job already done for him. But it was his case now, and he had many details to clear up—all the bureaucratic complications that go with robberies and shootings. Everything would have to be photographed, documented, measured, and fingerprinted for courtroom posterity. I was a witness, as was everyone else in the store. What worried me was Genie and the effect hours of questioning would have on her. But there was little I could do about it.

Outside the store I could hear sirens and more sirens. At the time I couldn't understand why they needed to make so much noise when the party was actually over. But I learned later that, for the police, the fun had only just begun. So many squad cars ended up parked in front of the pharmacy that it probably looked to passersby as if the drugstore were hosting the Los Angeles police convention. One ambulance just wasn't enough, so we had six. The junkie, whom the police identified as Robert Allen, was rushed to the hospital. It was amazing to me that with a bullet through his brain and all that blood lost, he was actually still alive. If the junkie had been the pope instead of a scum, the fact that he wasn't dead would have been celebrated around the world as a miracle. As far as I was concerned it felt more like a curse. One part of me was glad I hadn't taken a life, but another, more practical part began to wonder whether the junkie would recover and come back for revenge. The last thing I wanted was to worry for the rest of my life about some lunatic popping out of nowhere and shooting me or my family. My .38 hadn't done what it should have. I wondered if I should go down to County Hospital and shoot the man again, putting him, me, and our community out of our collective misery. I could only hope that nature would take its course and do the job for me.

It must have been a slow day for news because all the local television stations and newspapers sent down camera crews and reporters to cover the robbery. Of course, they had to wait while the police methodically wrote up their investigation. As soon as I was excused by the detectives, the media types descended on me like vultures. Incredibly, they viewed me as an authentic hero for saving Genie and the other potential victims of the junkie. One wag called me the "John Wayne of Westwood." I couldn't figure out if that was an insult or a compliment. They wanted statements and interviews. I wanted to comfort Genie, but she was still being questioned by the detectives.

Left to deal with the reporters, I played it straight and modest, explaining that after my last robbery, I knew I had to learn to protect myself—events happened too fast in the world to allow the luxury of relying exclusively upon the police. "I am not a hero," I told them, "I am simply an ordinary citizen who refused to be a victim any longer." They liked this line a lot and asked if I had been inspired in my action by the recent Community Watch campaign, which had been originated by the mayor, Anthony Malcolm, as a result of Proposition Thirteen's budget cuts into the Los Angeles Police Department's funding. The mayor was in favor of citizens accepting a role in community crime fighting. The police, however, vigorously opposed any intrusion into their territory. The conflict between the mayor and the police department was a big issue now, less than five months from November, when the mayor hoped to be re-elected. I told the reporters that my action was a personal one, but that I supported the mayor's idea; there was no other alternative.

Lieutenant Peterson, I could see, wasn't crazy about my support of the mayor's position. The police obviously don't want the average citizen running around carrying a gun and shooting people. So ask a cop about citizens protecting themselves and the answer will always be, "Leave it to us, the professionals." But ask them again, would they give up their own personal guns, as they would like other citizens to do, and see what kind of an answer they give. I have yet to meet a cop who doesn't have pistols of every sort stashed all over his property. The truth is that the police don't want to give up their power. If they have all the guns, then they have all the authority. We, the citizens, have made them the arbitrators of life, death, and the enforcement of the law. No policeman is going to give up that heady role to be just another citizen with a gun.

Lieutenant Peterson listened to what I told the reporters. A part of him respected what I had to say because it was what he would have done. Another part of him hated what I said because it was a threat to his status. If only they knew why I really did it. I could hardly tell the world about Genie, her sensuality, and my unending erection.

I didn't get out of the drugstore until almost seven, by which time Genie had recovered enough to drive herself home. Between the reporters and the police, she and I never had time to talk alone, although I had been aware, off and on, of her staring across the room at me as I gave interviews. But every time I gazed back at her, she looked away. What was she trying to figure out about me, I wondered. Obviously I had aroused something in her. But what?

I sincerely loved Marilyn, who was a wonderful woman and a terrific wife. Yet her obsession with the health farm was really getting to me. I couldn't help asking myself, as I saw Genie sneak looks at me between interviews, where it was all going to lead. And where it *should* lead. What actually was right and proper? I was talking about a passion, a passion I had long buried in myself that was now suddenly emerging full blown. It was a passion searching for a place to express itself, which it certainly wasn't going to find serving bean sprouts in Escondido. I couldn't direct the passion at blowing away more junkies. That left Genie, which both worried and excited me.

4

"Michael, I'm frightened," Marilyn told me at dinner. "What if you had missed him? And what if he'd had a real gun? Right now your mother and I might be down at the morgue identifying you."

My mother Gloria, who happened to be over for her weekly dinner, nodded in agreement. She was a short woman, with curly hair and a shapeless body that was always overweight. She blamed her weight problem on her genes. I attributed it to her compulsive binge eating. Food filled a great emptiness in her soul.

"Do you see where this is leading?" Marilyn continued. "There will be another robber. Then another. Will you shoot them all? Or will you make a mistake with one of them and miss? And then Rebecca won't have a father anymore."

"So, my only alternative is to sell the pharmacy and move to the health resort in Escondido, is that what you're telling me?"

"Michael, darling," my mother chimed in, "the world has gone crazy. What Marilyn is saying is very sensible. You've always been such a reasonable person. But what you did today, this is crazy. Owning a gun. Shooting someone. You're not Superman; bullets won't bounce off your chest, you know. It reminds me of how your father behaved right before one of his episodes. Have you seen a doctor lately, Michael?"

"Mother, this has nothing to do with my father, so let's leave him out of this, okay?"

Her statement enraged me. It was a very low blow. My father, God rest his tormented soul, had been a source of enormous anguish for my mother, my brother Joe, and myself for as long as I could remember. With everything that had happened among all of us, I knew I still hadn't sorted out my feelings toward my father. He had been dead for more than four years, but the contradictions and paradoxes of his life still possessed me, perhaps even more than when he had been alive. Somewhere deep inside of me I was still in his grip, as if his hand reached out to me from the grave and wouldn't let go.

My father had long ago been diagnosed as schizophrenic. For

months, sometimes even for years, he'd behave normally, go to work, be the good dentist he was, and come home to his family every night. Then whammo, out of nowhere, suddenly one day he'd flip out and involve himself in some outrageous escapade, usually involving women and gambling. Booze always played a part. I'll never forget the time he became convinced he had a system that would beat the pants off of Vegas. He borrowed $20,000 by taking a second mortgage on the house, chartered a small plane, and flew to Nevada to challenge the powers that be at the Tropicana. I wish I had owned stock in the hotel so that I could have enjoyed his spree. I mean, he must have had a good time during the four straight days he stayed up gambling away the mortgage money. The weird thing was, we were told when we finally caught up with him in the Las Vegas jail, that at one point he had been over $200,000 ahead.

When my mother and I got to him in the jail he was still drunk and, of course, enraged. He was convinced that the Tropicana had cheated him out of his winnings. The Las Vegas police very nicely let us take him back to Los Angeles, where the doctors, long familiar with his case, brought him back to earth with their usual course of high-voltage electroshock therapy. The psychiatrists at the Neuropsychiatric Institute were convinced that something he'd seen during his World War II stint in the South Pacific periodically triggered the schizophrenic episodes. But of course no one could prove this so the Veterans Administration wouldn't assume responsibility. Not only would my father be out of commission for months during these "episodes," as my mother called them, but we'd then be responsible for his gigantic hospital bills which put the whole family in financial jeopardy.

The odd part about the electroshock therapy was the aftermath. The bolts of high-voltage juice through his brain actually did seem to sizzle out the bad memories and restore him to reasonable behavior. But they also made him dull and, for a time, almost zombielike. I know my mother preferred him that way. Then he could go to work, treat his patients, and return home in the evening like a normal family man. In my heart of hearts, and I never admitted this to my mother, I liked my father best right before the episodes, when he got that crazy look in his eye and tried to engage me in his latest scheme. There was life in the man then, an energy that both excited and frightened me and, when I thought about it later, I knew I envied.

That passion for life was something I don't think I ever allowed myself to feel. The reason was obvious. The cost of my father's excitement to my mother, my brother, and myself was just too horrendous. No matter how charming my dad had been before the episodes, by the time he got through with his escapades and hospitalizations, all of our lives had been traumatized. My mother always seemed to go crazy herself, trying to cover the fact that her husband had been put away in the looney bin. And as the older son, I was thrust into the role of keeping my mother calm, being responsible for Joe, and in effect becoming the head of the family at age nine, twelve, fifteen, and so on, sometimes for months at a time. I drove myself to become the most reliable, most reasonable, even-tempered, calm, orderly, responsible person possible. By the time I was sixteen, I knew that I had to carve out for my own family a life of quiet stability so that my children would never grow up in such a crazy situation. I resolved to be a good provider and a respectable member of the community. And, up to the moment of the robbery, I had succeeded perfectly in fulfilling my commitment.

That is why my mother's accusation that I was behaving as my father did before one of his episodes so enraged me. Not only was it untrue, but it was crazy, virtually an obscenity, given my commitment to my family. For her to start that kind of nonsense meant that she had entered into her own hysterical mode and the discussion, as far as I was concerned, was over at that point. I ignored her comment.

But Marilyn picked the ball right up.

"Sweetheart," she smiled at me, "I didn't tell you I was frightened just to annoy you. I just want you to look at the facts. I do love you, you know."

"I know."

"The guy you shot," she continued, "what if he decides when he recovers that he wants revenge? Against you. Or Rebecca. Or me. What will we do?"

Marilyn went right for the jugular. I had to admire her for that; she was one smart cookie.

"I talked to Lieutenant Peterson and he said that he'd never seen such a thing happen unless the robber knew the victim and the crime was something personal, which this wasn't."

"There's always a first time," my mother said.

I again ignored my mother.

"Fact number two," Marilyn continued in her organized, professional manner, "you're going to get a lot of public attention. On the news. In the papers. Don't you think other criminals are going to see this and assume that you have something worth stealing? You're going to become a prime target for God knows who else."

"I assume," I answered her, "that they would figure it'd be easier to rob someone else, someone who didn't protect himself; no one wants to get shot."

"My point is, sweetheart," she flashed that patient smile of hers, "that they'll see you have something worth robbing, and knowing that you have a gun, the next time the robber will shoot first and then grab what he wants. He won't take the chance of letting anyone go."

"You think someone's going to come into the store and shoot twelve people for a few cc's of morphine? Please. No one's that crazy."

"Michael," Marilyn pleaded, "I'm scared. Honestly. You know that. This isn't the way we should be living. This isn't the way Rebecca should be growing up. We didn't grow up this way. This is terror time, Michael, can't you see that?"

"She's right again, Michael, you should listen to Marilyn."

It was easy to ignore my mother. It was harder with Marilyn, who so obviously was sincere and cared so much about me.

"You know," Marilyn continued, "maybe I should take you with me to the hospital for a few days. People are dying there every minute. I think you've forgotten that when people are dead they don't come back; it's all over for them at that point. If a robber shoots you, you're gone. One tiny little piece of lead goes into your brain or your heart, and the whole body stops. It's amazing; nature works for millions of years to create a lovely specimen like yourself and a tiny piece of metal ends it all. I love you and I don't want to see that happen. I'm married to you. I have a daughter by you. I want to live to a ripe old age with you. We can even get senile together—whoever is less crazy can take care of the other, I don't mind. But if you keep playing with guns in your store, it'll never happen. They'll get you, Michael, and I don't want that to happen. Do you believe me?"

I nodded.

"And if you're not killed by one of those bullets, but just shot in the spinal cord, you'll end up paralyzed. Do you know how many quadraplegics I saw during my intern days who'd been put in their wheelchairs by gunshot wounds? You're thirty-four, Michael. An active man. How would you like to spend the next forty years being spoon-fed while you're, pardon me Gloria, shitting into a cellophane bag?''

"Marilyn," I told her calmly, "you've made your point quite clear, thank you."

"I want to make sure you've heard me."

"I have. I know you care. And I appreciate it."

"If you truly understood what I was saying you'd never have bought that gun."

"It saved Genie's life, didn't it?"

"The guy had a water pistol, Michael."

"I had no way of knowing that."

"I want you to promise me you'll get rid of that pistol."

"Sweetheart, if these robbers come after me like you're afraid of, do you want them to have weapons and me to have nothing?"

Marilyn stared at me for the longest time. Then she spoke very quietly, as if in pain. Obviously I was causing her to suffer.

"You haven't heard a word I've said. I'm trying to save your life; I don't want you to die. The world has gone crazy. It's a jungle out there. You've done very well with the drugstore; it's worth a lot of money. Let's take that money and use it to buy a healthy life. Michael, sell your half of the store to Jerry. Let him have the whole thing. Then we can build that spa in Escondido and we'll be safe there. Rebecca can grow up in a good environment, without all this craziness. Maybe in a few years, things will straighten out here and we can come back. We have an opportunity to get ourselves out of this sewer. Don't you realize how lucky you were today? Look at what happened with the junkie as a warning. The message reads, 'get out or die here.' Can't you see that?"

Before I could answer her, the phone rang, startling all of us. I welcomed the excuse to get away from the dinner table and answer it.

"Hello," I said into the receiver.

"Hey, is this the hero of Westwood?"

Coincidence of coincidences, it was my business partner Jerry Herrman. He was, as usual, exuberant. I heard in his voice that either he'd just made a great deal for himself screwing some poor sucker out of some real estate, or else he's just finished banging some cutsie blonde on his Chris Craft down at the Marina while his wife Margaret was attending a PTA meeting.

"So you heard about it," I said glumly.

"Shit yes! I'm down here on the boat and saw you on cable news. I'm real impressed, you fucker. I didn't know you had the guts to do something like that. Hell, I didn't even know you owned a gun. You're a fucking genuine, authentic, real American hero. And I am god-damned proud of you."

Obviously he was trying to impress the blonde he was banging.

"Do you realize," Jerry continued, "that you and the drugstore are going to be in every paper and on every TV channel tomorrow? Why, I'll bet people come in from all over the city just to shake your hand. Hell, it was high noon in the drugstore and you came out with guns blazing. Like John Wayne. You mark my words, the next couple of days are going to be the biggest we've ever seen. If you play your cards right you can use all this publicity to really build the business. Prepare for the rush. Think franchising!"

"Jerry, truthfully," I told him, "I was just sitting here happy to be alive, you know what I mean?"

"You're still shaken up, huh? I guess it's like killing your first deer. I remember that feeling."

This was my partner's attempt at sensitivity. I was not impressed.

"Thanks for calling, Jerry. Let's talk tomorrow. And don't worry, we'll be able to handle the rush," I told him sarcastically.

"Michael, the reason I called was only to find out if you're okay, you know that?"

"Sure Jerry. Thanks, I appreciate it."

I hung up and turned to Marilyn.

"That was Jerry. There was a story about the robbery on cable news. He wanted me to know he thought it'd be good for business," I said with a mocking tone in my voice.

"Good old Jerry," Marilyn picked right up on it, "always full of ideas. Wait a minute!" she said with sudden inspiration, "if that's what he thinks, maybe you should call him back and talk to him right now about buying the whole drugstore. I mean, wouldn't such an increase in business raise the value?"

It took every ounce of self-control to stop myself from yelling at her. God, she made me angry. When I finally calmed down, I spoke to her quietly and methodically.

"Understand," I addressed Marilyn, gritting my teeth, "that

if Jerry thinks I've lost my nerve and have to sell out quick, he'll give me fifty cents on the dollar, just like he did when I had to raise the money to pay my father's hospital bills. If you remember," I added sarcastically.

Both Marilyn and my mother remembered only too well and wisely said nothing. Maybe it was because they could see I was beginning to lose my grip on my rage. What had happened in the store was extremely important for me. For the first time in years, I had acted with passion and succeeded. Yes, it was dangerous. Yes, shooting the junkie was crazy. And yes, what had happened to the robber was terrible. The look on his face as blood spurted from the side of his head was still in my mind as I faced Marilyn and my mother. I felt guilty and sick. Nothing would have helped me more than to talk about it. But given the circumstances, that was impossible. I, the world's nicest guy, had shot a man in cold blood, and the vivid memory of it revolted me.

On the other hand, Genie and fifteen other human beings were still alive, thanks to my action, and I wanted Marilyn and my mother to appreciate that side of things. I had taken a chance, put myself on the line, and performed brilliantly. It was my first pure moment of absolute physical and emotional bravery since my early teenage years when three or four times a week, winter and summer, I escaped my family at six in the morning and was out on the ocean, riding the waves, developing my form, in training for the then new sport of competitive surfing. The board, the wave and I had formed a coordinated perfection that I hadn't felt for almost twenty years. As terrible as it sounds, it took shooting the junkie to remind me of that feeling. No matter what Marilyn or my mother or even Jerry thought about what I had done, no one could erase my satisfaction at having saved fifteen people's lives. I alone had stopped the junkie. That moment was as real and memorable as anything I had ever experienced, and I had absolutely no interest in anyone demeaning it or me one bit further.

5

The rest of the evening was crazy. After the television news story, the phone didn't stop ringing. Everyone I ever knew seemed to have been watching the TV and felt compelled to call to congratulate me on my heroic behavior. Even Hal Beckman, the head of the Southern California Pharmaceutical Association, who never in the past would have given me the time of day, phoned to invite me to speak at the monthly meeting on the subject of "self-protection." Quite unexpectedly, my little drama at the drugstore had made me a big deal in the community. I had touched a nerve and was transformed from the shy, anonymous pharmacist into a public figure.

The more calls I received, the more upset both Marilyn and my mother became. Even though I tried to downplay my role in the robbery, the very fact that I was getting so much attention confirmed to both my wife and my mother that I had somehow betrayed their expectations. Marilyn withdrew to her study, as she so often did in the evenings, to read the latest copy of the *OB/GYN Review* and the *New England Journal of Medicine*, which had arrived in the mail that day. My mother, however, sat in the living room with me, listening to and disapproving of my phone conversations. Between calls she tried to sell me on her eternal pitch, her fantasy of a happy reconciliation between myself and my brother Joe. That night, her way of promoting my younger brother was to try to interest me in his latest business venture, which I knew had to be just another one of his illegal get-rich-quick investment schemes. Why my mother so adored Joe, I'll never know. The scumbag had cost both my mother and myself thousands of dollars in legal fees to keep him out of jail. And the anguish he caused her; I couldn't understand her devotion to him. She had to know he was gay. She was so sympathetic to his being "misunderstood." The only thing I could figure out was that she felt terribly guilty for Joe's troubles and somehow twisted that guilt into a kind of blind love for the bum. For years, Joe had cost me incredible pain, as well as money. And he had never been there for me when I had needed him. In my mind Joe was a user and a taker, nothing more. If my mother wanted to invent fantasies about Joe, that was her business; I just wanted to be left out of it. Fortunately the continuous stream of phone calls finally frustrated her. She gave up trying to talk about my brother and went upstairs to kiss her sleeping granddaughter good night before going home to bed herself.

As the evening wore on, and the calls began to taper off, I had time to wonder about many things. Genie hadn't phoned, which I thought was strange. Nor had her father, which I found even odder. Marilyn remained in the study, reading, leaving me time to reflect on her arguments at the dinner table. There was a growing gap between us, a disharmony of lifestyles and sensibilities that threatened to become an unbridgeable emotional chasm. Whatever conflicts we had, I loved Marilyn. What could I do, I asked myself, to prevent our problems from polarizing us even further? In spite of everything, I was committed to Marilyn and committed to making our marriage work.

As I got ready for bed, my worries began to multiply. Foiling the robbery and saving Genie began to seem less important, while my fears about the future increasingly dominated my thoughts. Marilyn was right; I certainly was no John Wayne. It seemed almost inevitable that if I continued defending myself in the store with my gun, the odds would eventually catch up with me and I'd be one dead pharmacist. And all that excitement about Genie, I thought, what was that about? It was simply a temporary lust, the fantasy of a middle-aged druggist. How many marriages had I seen destroyed by such things? I thought of my parents, my father. Lust. In the long run, I philosophized as I washed my face, what good did all the lusting actually accomplish? How long did the lust last? How often was the man any happier after the lusting had run its course? Usually the men were left even more unsatisfied. They had given up complex relationships for simple affairs. When the affairs were over, they found themselves middle-aged men living alone in apartments down by the Marina, boozing and wearing gold chains in an attempt to rekindle love in singles bars on Friday and Saturday nights. That is, if they weren't too tired from working all week. No, I realized as I brushed my teeth, I had to follow the advice of Harry Truman, who told himself early on in his life that he had to master the call of the flesh if he wanted to succeed in his career. It was either that, or end up like my father.

As long as I could remember, I had been afraid of becoming like my father. Part of this fear was consciously shoved down my throat by my mother, who obviously had her own ax to grind. The bulk of my fear came from the pain my father's "episodes" had inflicted on everyone. I was terrified of the schizophrenia, afraid it might be genetic. I read everything I could find on the subject, but no one seemed to know for sure. The old wives' tales maintained that insanity ran in families. I was afraid that I was like a Doberman pinscher—friendly, loyal, and obedient, until one day, for no apparent reason, I would turn and viciously attack those I loved, as I felt my father had done. All through pharmaceutical school I had been like a Doctor Jekyll, who went about his business, sure that one morning he would get out of bed and find himself reborn into a monster. The more I thought about my behavior in the store with the junkie, the more I began to believe that the Mister Hyde, the monster, the father in myself, the schizophrenic, was finally emerging. My lust for Genie. My pleasure at shooting the junkie and saving her life. All of this seemed part of the pattern. I was going crazy. I couldn't let this happen, I told myself.

I studied Marilyn at the sink as she cleaned her face with her expensive French cold cream. Marilyn's fingers massaged a cotton ball in meticulous little circles, covering her face in a grid pattern that eventually cleaned every square inch of her face and neck. Marriage was being able to watch one's wife cleanse very pore on her face exactly the same way every night, and not tire of her. Stability and regularity were the name of the game. This had been my creed for years. Yet I had jeopardized everything in the drugstore with my gun. Marilyn was absolutely correct about that.

I began to wonder about her obsession with the health resort; maybe she was right about that, too. Maybe I was being too rigid about Escondido. What kind of life did I really want, I asked myself again. I had always told myself that I wanted a nice, quiet, prosperous, day-to-day routine; I had no need for glamor—big cars, wads of dough, fancy clothes, enormous houses, the whole upper middle class lifestyle meant nothing to me. No, I wanted stability. Calm. A life for my daughter unlike what I had had growing up. With the health resort, Marilyn was offering all this to me. True, it was packaged differently from what I would have chosen. But it basically resembled what I told myself I wanted. So then why was I so resistant to her dream? Why did a life in the country sound so boring? That night I tried to convince myself that Marilyn's dream was no more boring than what I did every day. That's what I wanted to believe.

At that moment, cleaning her face, Marilyn seemed extremely remote, which frightened me. Naked as she was, and as beautiful as she was, distance was not what I wanted between us. Under the bright bathroom light, her skin appeared even whiter than normal. Her muscles were those of an athlete. She looked so healthy and so physically perfect, why didn't she seem sensuous to me? She was a picture of all the qualities most men would find desirable. It had to be the anger, I told myself, combined with her normal highly independent and self-sufficient nature. I had a great need to be close to her. Impulsively I slipped behind her and, as she was wiping the last square inch of her forehead, wrapped my arms around her from behind, pressed my belly against her taut buttocks, fondled her breasts, and began nibbling delicately at her neck. But she didn't respond; she remained distant and continued cleaning her skin. It was as if I weren't even in the room. I let go of the human marble statue I had attempted to arouse and watched her for a few minutes in the mirror. Marilyn was starting with a new chemical on her skin, inch by inch, making little circle with cotton balls.

"So, you want to talk about it?" I asked.

"I didn't think you thought we had anything to talk about."

"Marilyn, give me a break, huh? I'm obviously here to talk to you."

"But are you here to listen? You didn't seem too interested at the dinner table."

"You're wrong; I heard every word you said. You just don't understand the difference between listening and agreeing."

"If you listened carefully to what I said," Marilyn spoke with sudden affection, "you couldn't help but agree."

"That's your opinion."

Sometimes the woman was so impossible I wanted to strangle her. To engage her in a debate was always a disaster, yet somehow I regularly fell into that trap. I took a deep breath before continuing. It was important to change the momentum of the conflict.

"Marilyn, believe it or not, I thought about what you said at dinner, and, this is difficult for me to admit, but you may actually be right. What do you think of that?"

Marilyn set down her cotton ball and observed me closely. Did she think I was lying?

"Right about what?" she asked.

"The gun. The drugstore. Modern life. Maybe even about the fat farm."

"Health resort," she corrected me.

"Resort, sorry."

"How do you mean I'm right?"

"Notice who's listening now; I said '*may* be right.' "

"Okay," she said patiently, a little more warmly, "*may* be right. Why might I suddenly be right?"

Of course I didn't mention my fantasies about Genie, but I did tell Marilyn virtually everything else I'd thought of in the last few hours—my fears of doing to my family, to her and Rebecca, what my own father had done to me. Pleased by my revelations, she even smiled.

"Are you saying," she inquired, "that you're going to put the pharmacy on the market and that we should seriously start looking for a resort site to buy?"

"No. I said that you may be right, but I need some time to think it through. This is my life we're talking about, you realize?"

"I understand," she continued, "but the trick with things like this is to give yourself a deadline. You're never going to feel one decision is absolutely right; what's important is to make a choice. Just tell yourself that two weeks from tonight you and I will sit down and you'll tell me what you decided."

"How about not giving me a deadline, huh? Isn't it enough that I'm considering doing what you want? Be generous and give me some time. Is that too much to ask?"

"Michael, darling," she smiled sweetly, "if you wait to make a decision until after some other junkie shoots you, the opportunity is going to have passed you by."

This was the part of Marilyn that I couldn't understand; she had once been such a generous person, but now she only seemed to see herself and her own needs. I was just supposed to be a rubber stamp, and that depressed me.

"Marilyn," I said quietly, "tell me the truth. Other than selling jogging suits to fat ladies, or running a fruit juice blender making health drinks, what am I going to do with myself day to day at our health resort? I'm a city kid. I like my business here. I'd go nuts out there in the country."

"Michael," she said in that patient tone, as if she were talking to a child, "living in Escondido is going to be such a rich experience; there'll be a million things for you to do."

"Like greasing the Nautilus machines?"

"Why are you being so petty? We're going to be running a resort and an agricultural enterprise. A farm. It's going to be a huge operation. Five years from now you're going to really laugh when you think about this conversation. There's more to do than you can possibly imagine."

"Marilyn, tell me something. Have you ever milked a cow?"

"No, but. . . ."

I cut her off.

"No buts. I've milked a cow and it's hard work. I have no interest in getting up at four o'clock every morning and milking cows. Or driving tractors. Or leading exercise classes. I hate calisthenics. And I have no desire to be a desk clerk. 'Good afternoon, Mr. and Mrs. Fairway. We have a lovely suite waiting for you. May I carry your bags?' What am I going to do there, Marilyn? Please, I'm not kidding. I need to know."

"What you're going to do is to stop being so difficult, so rigid, and take a chance. Michael, you've lived almost your whole life within a ten-square-mile area. You're just afraid of change. Trust me, Michael; it'll do great things for you."

She had made this point to me before, over and over, as if somehow the distance, in feet, from my mother's house to the drugstore confirmed that I was a country bumpkin who knew nothing about life. We were back into the debate syndrome and I knew it was useless to continue arguing. Sure, I could bring up my years at the University of California at Berkeley. My summer spent hitchhiking through Europe. My trips east to various pharmaceutical conventions. But I knew she would stay fixated on the distance from the store to my childhood home.

"Marilyn, this may come as a shock to you, but do you know that I actually love you?"

She was confused by what she thought was a sudden shift in tactics. In fact, I was sincere.

"What I want to know is," I continued, "do you still love me, I mean, in spite of this difference of opinion?"

"Of course I do," she told me without hesitation.

"Then give me some time to think."

Marilyn thought for a moment. "Okay. I'm easy. Think." She grinned.

It was almost one in the morning by the time we went to bed. Marilyn, whose hospital rounds began at seven forty-five, set her alarm for six. I set mine for six-thirty, then shut off the light and snuggled close to her. It was late, we were both tired, and yet we had not really resolved our conflict. For months we had gone to bed angry; I had to change this and find a way to connect with her again. If I didn't, I was certain we'd drift farther and farther apart. Sex and romance appeared to be the only options open to me and I knew I had to reach her with those feelings. But how? It seemed strange that every day Marilyn could be professionally in touch with the product of love, lust, and passion between men and women an still be so detached from it in herself.

Not that Marilyn was sexless. She got excited and she certainly had orgasms, although not always, and not without a lot of work; but I felt she had a basically bland view of sex, almost a disinterest. Maybe being a gynecologist turned sensuality into mundane mechanics. I wished I could have shown her the passion I saw in Genie through our living room window; maybe that would have stirred something new in Marilyn. I decided that night that it was up to me to make Marilyn feel what she had never known. I wrapped my arms around her and began kissing the nape of her neck, and then her ear lobes, which I knew she enjoyed. At first she didn't move. But then, when she realized that I was going to continue and wasn't just kissing her good night, she rolled over and whispered to me half-asleep in the dark.

"Michael, that feels lovely, but I have to get up in five hours."

"It'll help you get to sleep."

"I've got to rest, Michael. Debra Bruning's in labor. The hospital may call any minute for me to make the delivery."

I ignored Marilyn and kept kissing her. I ran my tongue down her back, then slipped my mouth between her lovely white thighs and used my lips to caress and suck on her powdered and perfumed sex. I could feel her brain working away, trying to decide whether to go with the pleasant feelings she was receiving, or to cut everything off and order me to sleep. But I kept at it, still trying to connect with her. After what seemed like hours of work with my mouth, her juices began to flow and I could taste the fact that she'd given in to the feelings of pleasure. Then I rolled her onto her back, spread her legs open, held down her ankles with my hands and concentrated on sensual calistenics with my tongue. Marilyn began to get aroused. I knew this because she picked up her pillow and used it to cover her face.

Something in Marilyn compelled her to bury herself in darkness when she became aroused. I always wondered why, but could never explain it. Marilyn certainly had no idea; it was simply necessary for her. Without the pillow and the darkness she simply couldn't begin to let go. Was she afraid of something that she needed to hide from me? Or was she shy about letting me see her excited? Did she need the darkness to fantasize about other men and sexual adventures? Whatever it was, I didn't like it, but had long ago learned to live with it. As disembodied as she needed to feel, I required connecting with her. The fact that I couldn't see her face, and that she didn't want me to, didn't help matters. I tried to console myself with the idea that at least I knew Marilyn's secret needs enough to excite her to some degree. I was able to arouse her and she did respond. At least that was something.

I gradually became aware that the pillow over Marilyn's face was rocking up and down at a regular rate. This meant that she was thrashing her head back and forth underneath it and was reaching a threshold of excitement. If she were lucky, if she were able to sustain whatever fantasy she was spinning for herself, and if I licked and sucked in the perfect order, I knew that although she might never actually have an orgasm this way, she could come close. I kept at it and Marilyn began to moan. Feeling her respond, I increased the speed and lessened the pressure of my tongue. This excited her further. Her hips undulated over my mouth, craving more contact. Marilyn was excited.

Then the telephone rang. I couldn't believe the timing. Marilyn tossed the pillow from her face, pulled herself away from my mouth, and picked up the receiver. It was probably the hospital ordering her down to Debby Bruning's delivery. Whatever it was, I knew that our love-making was over. The mood had been broken and would not return for her that night. I wanted to connect with my wife. I wanted to feel whole once again. I thought about tearing the phone from the wall, but I knew she'd just take the extension in the other room. All I could do was sit up and listen to the conversation.

"Hello?" Marilyn inquired. Then she turned to me and covered the receiver. "It's for you. Some black woman, I think."

I took the phone. What black woman would call me in the middle of the night, I wondered.

"Hello?" I inquired into the receiver.

"You motherfucker!" the woman at the other end of the phone shouted at me.

"Who is this?"

"You're gonna be real sorry you shot my husband, just you remember that, motherfucker!" she screamed, and then hung up the phone.

The line went dead. I set the receiver down and faced Marilyn, who had obviously heard the whole thing. Instead of being angry, she was frightened.

Saying nothing, she rolled away from me and turned out the light. The call had scared me, too. But giving in to panic would only lead to further disaster. I tried to comfort Marilyn by snuggling close to her and kissing her tenderly, but it was like embracing the bedpost.

"Let's get some sleep and talk about this tomorrow. I'll tell the police about the phone call; they'll take care of the wife, I promise you."

Marilyn nodded, then buried her head under her pillow. The conversation was over. We were in a crisis, that was for sure.

The fear and horror that I couldn't drive from my mind made the night even worse. Every time I closed my eyes, I saw the mangled and bloody head of Robert Allen lying on my drugstore floor. As certain as I was that I had done the right thing in shooting him, I was revolted and disgusted by the actual consequences of my act. Blowing a man's brains out with a .38 went against everything I felt was civilized and human. It had saved Genie, but it had also degraded me and turned me into a savage. I felt guilty and sick. I wanted to talk to Marilyn about it, but bringing it up would have grossly weakened my position on the health spa. I needed sympathy; she wanted obedience. She gave me no choice but to remain silent.

I tried again to sleep, but I was tormented by the image of the crippled junkie. For whatever reason and with whatever intention, I had shot a man at point-blank range, destroyed a part of his brain, and watched him collapse to the ground in a pool of blood. Every time I thought about him I wanted to vomit. What right had I to destroy something so sacred as another's life? The fact that he was trying to destroy me in no way tempered my remorse. My intellect was convinced I had done the right thing; it was my stomach and soul that were sickened.

I lay in bed the entire night afraid to close my eyes, afraid to see the living corpse of Robert Allen as I vividly remembered him. But near dawn I found a stronger image that successfully, if temporarily, drove the horror from my mind. I fantasized about Genie. She was in my living room, on my couch, and it was me she was straddling, not Nick. She was aroused and excited by me. Why was it that Marilyn couldn't respond to me the way Genie responded to Nick? I had read Kinsey, Masters and Johnson, and had studied biology, anatomy, and psychology. Yet I couldn't understand why was Marilyn so distant. Was it her? Was it me? Was it something between us? I could come up with no answer. I was alone, unable to talk to my wife about my innermost fears, plagued by horror, and comforted only by licentious, voyeuristic fantasies. It was a long and terrible night.

6

The next morning, as I unlocked the front door of the pharmacy, I heard the quiet rumble of a well-muffled motorcycle engine idle and stop not two feet behind me on the sidewalk. My first thought was to berate myself for being so stupid as to be out, alone, in front of my store without my gun. This was the end for me, I knew. I whipped around to face my attacker. There was Genie's father, my friend Ed Cotler, astride his BMW motorcycle. Ed was certainly one eccentric-looking lawyer sitting on his black bike, wearing a crash helmet, and dressed in a Saville Row charcoal and chalkstripe suit. I had always wondered what juries thought about the black motorcycle boots that stuck out from under his immaculately pressed trousers. Probably they didn't even notice. Ed claimed that only British woolens would hold a crease after the ten-mile freeway ride to the downtown courtroom. Who would dispute him? Ed shut off his engine, removed his helmet and gloves, extended his meaty right hand, and grinned at me.

"You son-of-a-bitch. Saving my daughter's life. How can I thank you?"

"Hey, I didn't do anything; it was a water pistol."

Ed grabbed my hand and pumped it enthusiastically.

"Like hell it was nothing. When I got home last night at one o'clock from the Bar Association meeting in San Francisco, who was waiting up for me but Genie to tell me all about it. Anne, of course, was frightened. You know how she is about physical danger. But Genie, Jesus. She described the whole thing moment-to-moment in detail. Hell, it sounded better than a Clint Eastwood movie. You should have heard the way she talked about you. If I didn't know you I'd say you were a combination of Superman and the Lone Ranger."

"I'm sure she exaggerated." If Ed had known how excited it made me to hear that Genie had been so impressed, he'd have pulled out the snubnosed pistol he carried and shot me on the spot.

"Don't be so modest, Michael. Hell, you found yourself in a situation, stood your ground, analyzed what was happening, and then acted. You did what we only talk about. You're a real credit to your friends and to the community. You're a hero. I'm telling you, you deserve recognition for this."

"Ed, I didn't even think about it; I acted out of instinct. Honestly. Don't make a big deal out of it."

"Bull-*shit*!"

Like all men who commonly swear, Ed emphasized the second syllable in that most descriptive word. But what did he mean by his disagreement with my statement? Given my impulses toward Genie, my instincts told me to quiet Ed down and keep large distances between him, myself, and his daughter.

"You know, Michael, when I was in the Marines we had something for doing what you did that's sorely missing in civilian life. You know what that is?"

I shook my head. I couldn't imagine.

"Medals."

"Medals?"

Ed nodded.

"You deserve a public award. In wartime the Marine Corps would have given you something big. Maybe even the Congressional Medal of Honor, who knows? In the face of a clear and apparent danger you selflessly risked your own life to knock out an armed enemy and save your friends and associates. And my daughter. You see?"

"If you don't mind, Ed, I'd rather just let the whole thing quietly go away. It's not something I want to repeat, if you know what I mean."

"Michael, that's what I've always liked about you—you're so damned modest." Ed grinned like a proud father and stuck out his hand again. I shook it.

"I have to run, I'm late for court, but I wanted to thank you in person. I'm proud to be your friend. I mean it."

"Thanks Ed, I appreciate it."

"Don't thank me; hell, you're the one who deserves the thanks. As soon as I get out of court, I'm calling the mayor. Mark my words: you're going to get an official commendation from the city for this. You wait and see."

Ed hit the starter button on his motorcycle and the big twin-cylinder engine roared to life.

"Ed," I yelled over the idling engine, "please, just leave it as it is. Don't make a big show out of it, okay?"

"No way, Michael. In my book you're a real-life hero. In this day and age, in this town, we not only need heroes, we've got to encourage them. And to do that we've got to treat 'em right. You leave that to me."

Ed buckled his helmet, slipped on his gloves, clicked his transmission into gear, saluted, then accelerated down the street toward the freeway.

Exactly what I didn't need was more attention. Things were bad enough as they were; with an award from the city Marilyn would go apeshit. I hoped Ed would just calm down; unfortunately I knew that wasn't his style.

I bought the morning *L.A. Times* from the newspaper dispenser outside the pharmacy, then entered my store. It was only seven forty-five, which meant I'd be alone, without any employees, for another fifteen minutes. I turned on the fluorescent lights and walked down the aisle toward my office. I don't know exactly what I expected, but I did wonder if the place would look different since I'd shot the junkie. It was just as it always was; the cleaning crew, for once, had done an impeccable job. There was no trace of blood, not a scuffle mark. Not even one can of Right Guard was out of place. The store was so immaculate that it almost made me wonder if the shooting had actually taken place. It was disgustingly modern to wipe out all traces of such history. Not that I expected a plaque to be carved in stone and erected in place to honor the event. But somehow I thought that there should have been something recognizable to indicate that an episode of such significance for so many people had taken place in the store. Even a lousy bullet hole in the wall would have been sufficient. But the place was as clean as a baby's nursery.

I wondered what would happen if a marker were placed at the site of every robbery or homicide to signal the community that it had suffered a loss and that its humanity had been compromised and diminished. Wouldn't such a landmark remind us how fragile our lives actually were and how easily we could die? I suppose some people would think that millions of death monuments commemorating victims would turn the cities of the United States into a gruesome and depressing landscape. But I think it would throw the savage state of our society into a clear and obvious picture; we couldn't pretend any longer about the downward slide our nation has taken. Those markers would remind us, everywhere, of how violence and death insulted our idea of ourselves as a civilized people.

Back in my office, I opened the paper to the front page of the "Metro" section. The robbery was headline news. Luckily, the article contained no picture of Genie or me. Instead, it was illustrated with a bloody photograph of Robert Allen, the junkie, as he was being lifted off the floor, unconscious. The article described what had happened in the most basic terms, with no drama and little detail. Nothing was even mentioned about the needle marks on Mr. Allen's arms. It simply stated that he had tried to hold up the store with a child's water pistol and was now in critical condition at County Hospital. His wife, Alice, was quoted as being enraged over the shooting of her husband; he was "harmless," she claimed. Right. A harmless drug addict who robs, holds hostages, and threatens innocent lives. The junkie was being kept alive, on life support equipment, to the tune of thousands of dollars a day, courtesy of the taxpayers of the City of Los Angeles.

The day passed just as my partner Jerry had predicted. We did land-office business, literally tripling our normal daily gross. Customers came to shake my hand, to "meet the man who took care of business," as one of them put it so politely. I was a curiosity, a man like most of them, except that I had just done something way out of the ordinary, which was to shoot a bullet through another man's head while defending my private property. The people who came into my store that day seemed to take great pleasure in my action, as if I had done something they couldn't do for themselves. I had obtained justice for them. I had announced that we didn't have to be victims. One man even told me that my action had given him the courage to go out and buy a gun to defend himself. Was this good or bad, I wondered.

That day I heard terrible stories from other store owners. Burglary stories. Mugging stories. Rape stories. One horrible personal invasion after another in which privacy, private property, individual dignity, personal safety, and the whole gamut of society's safeguards seemed to be breaking up, unprotected, on the rocks of moral chaos. These customers, unlike Marilyn, approved completely of what I'd done to the junkie. These people wanted to stop running. One woman told me that she and her husband had been robbed so many times at the little liquor store they owned that they had sold out, moved to a rural area, and opened a small grocery store. Three months later they were robbed and her husband was shot. Because they were so far from a hospital, it took two hours for the ambulance to arrive and, as a result, her husband died. Had the robbery and shooting taken place in their old liquor store, the husband would have easily survived—a hospital had been only one block away. The woman applauded what I'd done to the junkie; she only wished she could have done it herself to the robber who shot her husband.

Marilyn called me in the morning, wondering if I had made a decision. It was bizarre; everyone in the store was congratulating me on being a hero, while my wife wanted me to run from Los Angeles and hide. But before she and I could even discuss it, we were interrupted by a reporter from the CBS Evening News who came to do an interview.

I could hardly believe that what I had done was actually newsworthy enough as to warrant a piece on the seven o'clock news; but who knew what was news anymore? At seven o'clock Dan Rather gave us nothing more than illustrated headlines combined with human interest stories. Somehow, the reporter told me, I fit into the latter category. Crime and victims' rights were big issues. And the mid-mannered druggist saving the life of a young girl from a crazed drug fiend was a classic story. As the reporter asked me question after question on camera, and I answered in my modest way, I couldn't believe the footage would ever be used for anything. That is, until the mayor called.

Mary, the cashier, put the call through while the interview was underway. The reporter kept the camera rolling while Mayor Anthony Malcolm himself congratulated me on my heroism, then asked if I would accept a commendation from the City of Los Angeles for my actions. He explained how important he believed it was for the general public to see courageous and honorable behavior visibly appreciated and rewarded. Obviously he'd been talking to Ed Cotler. But what did it matter? There I was in front of the CBS news camera being asked by my mayor to accept an award. It would have been hard enough to refuse, which I tried at first to do, even if I'd been alone with the mayor. But in front of millions of viewers, how could I deny his request? So I agreed.

I knew Marilyn would go crazy, and immediately after saying yes and hanging up the phone I began to be afraid. I had spent my entire life avoiding letting myself be singled out. Now, suddenly, I was a media darling doing exactly what my father would have loved. I was making a public spectacle of myself—grandstanding. My father had always wanted to be a big shot, out in the limelight. He never made it. I had worked at remaining anonymous, and now was not only on the evening news but in every newspaper. There would be consequences to this, I reminded myself. I had a wife and daughter. A business. I was in a very vulnerable position if someone wanted to hurt me or my family.

I reminded myself that it was of primary importance for me to remain calm, not panic, lead my normal life, and not let myself get too involved with the media and all of its craziness. I ended the interview and told Mary and the other employees not to allow any other reporters back to see me. I withdrew into my office, locked the door, and tried to focus on my quarterly financial statement.

An hour later my phone buzzed with ominous news; Genie was standing by the drug counter and wanted to talk to me. I certainly couldn't say no to her. Nor did I want to be seen with her in public. I asked Mary to put her on the phone. Quietly I told Genie to meet me up the block at a little Iranian delicatessen where we could have some privacy.

7

The House of Tehran was tiny, dark, and anonymous. One could easily imagine fanatics gathering in the dim booths to discuss their terrorist plans. I entered through the back door, having sneaked out the rear exit of the pharmacy unobserved. Hidden in a booth, I sat and waited. Moments later, Genie stepped inside the front door of the restaurant. She was more gorgeous and seductive than my most vivid fantasy. Under one arm she carried a large briefcase. Under the other she held a small cassette recorder. I waved to her. She smiled, obviously pleased to see me, came to the booth, and sat down. She put the recorder on the table and her briefcase on the seat, then looked me directly in the eyes and grinned.

"Hi," she said with just a trace of shyness. "Thank you for seeing me."

Genie chose to sit in an interesting place. She didn't slide over next to me as she would have had she been my girlfriend, but neither did she sit poised on the edge of her seat as if she were ready to run. She chose a neutral middle ground where I could feel the heat radiating from her but couldn't quite touch it. I felt she was telling me that things between us could go either way, and that it was up to me to let her know which direction it would be. She was tempting. My god, how she was tempting. But I had made up my mind, I told myself; I was not going to behave like a crazy man. No sir. Genie and I would be friends, and that was it. I had made a commitment to myself on this decision and I would be firm. This was absolute.

"What can I do for you?" I said in a cool tone, hoping to dampen her enthusiasm.

"With all the confusion with the police and everything, I never got a chance to thank you properly for saving my life. So thank you, Michael. You were really terrific."

In spite of my commitment to myself, she excited me. I knew that if I followed my feelings, they'd carry me down the sewer into chaos. I had to change her perception of me.

"Genie, don't make a big deal out of it. It was just a water pistol, remember?"

"No, Michael, don't be so modest. You didn't know it was a water pistol."

"How can you be so sure?"

"Because you wouldn't have shot him if you knew his gun wasn't real; there would have been no need."

"What would you think if I told you," I tried to sound as cold and detached as possible, "the only reason I shot him was exactly because I knew his gun wasn't real and he couldn't shoot back?"

"I wouldn't believe you."

"Not even if it's true?"

"You wouldn't have shot the guy if you knew; I'm sure of that."

"How can you be so sure? You don't know me."

"I know you're not that kind of man."

"Oh you do, huh? What if I told you that you're wrong? That I am that kind of man."

She didn't answer. Her expression had lost its former quality of unlimited adoration.

"Why are you doing this, Michael?"

"Doing what?"

"You're playing with me. I'm being sincere with you. Why can't you accept that? I thought you wanted to be friends."

It made me very sad to see the pain in her face, but I knew I had to put it there to protect me from myself.

"Genie, I'm not playing with you. I just don't want to see you jumping to fantastic conclusions."

"You mean, like you might have saved my life?"

"For one."

"Michael, I was there, remember? There was real danger. You acted with courage, no matter what you say now. I know what went on. What you did yesterday was real. Part of the reason I'm here right now is because I want other people to know about it."

Genie pointed to the tape recorder on the table.

"I talked to the editor of the school paper. I'm on the staff, you know. She wants me to write an article about the experience. About a real-life hero, not the B.S. they show on TV. I thought I'd do it from my point of view, in a kind of tough, spare style, as if I were Hemingway. You did a great thing yesterday, Michael, and I want people to know about it.''

"Genie I'm just the local pharmacist," I said, weakening, "I'm not a hero."

"You are, Michael."

The look was returning to her eyes. And it was getting to me. The swelling between my thighs convinced me.

"I'd rather you didn't write such an article."

Genie stared at me for a moment, thought this over, then reached for the tape recorder, set it between us, and pushed the "record" switch. The little cassette began spinning. We were on tape.

"Okay," she said, "tell me why not."

"I'd appreciate it if you'd turn off the recorder."

"Why's that?"

"Because I can't have a conversation that's supposed to be private when that thing," I pointed to the recorder, "is going."

"Privacy is very important to you, isn't it?" she asked innocently, clearly enjoying my sudden discomfort. This was one very clever girl.

"Genie, turn it off," I insisted.

"Why is privacy so important to you? Are you afraid I'll find out something about you, something you want to keep a secret? Or are you just shy? Is that it, Michael?"

"I'm shy. Now turn it off. Please."

"Under one condition."

"Look Genie, if you don't turn it off I'm just going to get up and walk out of here."

"You don't want to hear the condition?"

"Okay, what's the condition?" I tried to sound as bored and disinterested as possible.

"Tell me why you're being so cold to me today, when yesterday you claimed to be my friend."

Genie was a very smart girl, that was for sure. Just like Marilyn, she went straight for the jugular.

"I do want to be your friend," I stalled.

"You think the way you're acting tells me that?"

"I just want you to be realistic about what happened."

"That's not the truth and you know it."

"Then what is?" I asked quietly, terrified she would tell me about my feelings toward her.

"That's what I asked you," was all she answered.

We were at a stalemate. I could feel the desire in me mounting. And mounting was exactly the right word, because that was just what I wanted to do at that moment. All I could think about was peeling off Genie's clothes and mounting her right there on the table in the Iranian delicatessen. I wanted to wrap myself around her, spread her thighs, have her down on her hands and knees, and slip into her from behind. I wanted to merge into that beautiful rear end of hers and rut like a beast in heat. I was sure the Ayatollah Khomeini would read my thoughts and kill me for them. But at that moment I didn't care. I wanted Genie. I wanted the adoration. Such a need was a terrible thing, I knew. I had to drive away the temptation.

"The truth is. . . ." I whispered.

She leaned closer to hear. I had to phrase my next thought perfectly or I would be in big trouble.

"Genie, the truth is that I wasn't a hero for the simple reason that I was never in any danger. The junkie never saw me. I was in a no-risk situation. He had no chance. It was like stepping on an insect. To be a hero one has to be at risk. There is no risk in stepping on a cockroach, is there? If there were, every exterminator in the world would be entitled to the Congressional Medal of Honor."

"I think you're underestimating the situation."

"And I think," I said in my most condescending tone of voice, "that when you get older and a little more mature, you'll realize that I'm right. You're looking at me and the situation as a child would look at Superman."

That hurt her, I could tell. She immediately shut off the tape recorder and stood up.

"You know, Mr. Marcus, I've changed my mind. You're right. You're not a hero. If you're not a hero, then there's no story for me, is there? Thank you for the time."

"Genie, even though we disagree, my name is still Michael, remember?"

"Mr. Marcus. You don't want to be friends, that's obvious. You know, yesterday I thought you were different from the other older men I know. I thought you were shy on the outside but, inside, open and generous. Unpretentious. I thought you had real heart. But I guess with all the excitement and everything, I was just imagining things. My father always accuses me of having an overactive imagination; maybe he's right. I wanted you to be a hero for me. So I made you into a hero. But you're really just like all the rest of the men, aren't you? I shouldn't have tried to make you into something you weren't. I'm sorry. And I'm sorry to have wasted your time."

She picked up the tape recorder, then reached for her briefcase. There were tears in her eyes. What she had said moved me deeply. I despised myself for being so cruel; she was an extraordinary girl. At that moment I knew that in spite of all my fears, I didn't want to lose her. I grabbed her hand before she could touch her briefcase. It was awkward; one second before I had been ice cold to her and now I was holding her hand. I had to find a way to be friends with Genie. It would be a test of myself. There was no reason, I wanted to believe, that I couldn't just bury my sexual feelings and simply grow to know her as a young friend. I rationalized that I had to face up to and conquer my temptation, in the flesh. If I drove Genie away, the temptation would reappear later, directed at some other woman. Genie was too interesting to lose simply because I couldn't quite understand a small part of myself. At least, that's what I told myself.

"Genie, please. I'm sorry. I know I haven't been very nice to you. Stay and talk to me for a couple more minutes. Please?"

"Sorry, Mr. Marcus, I've got to go."

"Genie, I do want to be your friend and I want to explain to you why I've been so distant and cold. Will you sit down and let me tell you?"

"I want you to let go of my hand so I can leave. Good-bye, Mr. Marcus."

"Michael," I reminded her.

"Mr. Marcus, please let go of my hand." Genie indicated the few other customers in the dim restaurant, some of whom were staring at us suspiciously. "If you don't let go I'm going to yell."

"Genie, please, I do care for you," I whispered, "so much it frightens me. I was the way I was because I wanted to drive you away. Please don't go. I know now I don't want that. I'll be nice to you, I promise. Just sit down and talk to me, what do you say?"

I could see her resolve softening.

"I need another chance," I pleaded. "I did you a favor;

remember you asked me not to tell your father about that Nick character. Do me a favor and sit down, okay?''

My embarrassing plea worked, and she sat back down. This time she positioned herself farther from me. She wasn't taking any chances; if I chose to be unpleasant to her, she was ready to run. Genie stared at me, waiting for me to make the next move.

''I'm thirty-four,'' I began, ''I'm married, and I have a daughter. You're seventeen. I love Marilyn. God, this is embarrassing.''

Genie said nothing.

''Can you understand that it doesn't make sense to me why I'm so drawn to you? I mean, I have everything in my life I ever thought I wanted. But I see you and you excite me. What can I say? That's the way it is. You're smart, direct, enormously appealing, so alive, so spontaneous. You're totally bad for me. Listen to me telling you this; it's crazy. I'm crazy. But I trust you. And I do want to be friends with you. Do you think that's possible?''

Genie considered my question. She seemed almost amused by my admission. I wondered if she'd pay me back by being mean to me. I hoped she was bigger than that.

''You said you wanted me to sit down so you could talk to me. What do you want to talk about?''

''Thank you,'' I told her gratefully.

''Now you're starting. Remember what you told me yesterday about saying that.''

I had to smile; it was so generous of her to give me another chance.

At that moment the fat, fiftyish Iranian waitress came over to take our orders for coffee. When she left, Genie and I looked at each other for a moment.

''So, what do you want to talk about?'' she teased me.

''I think we should start with something easy.''

''Like what?''

''Oh, I don't know,'' I hesitated. ''How about something light, like what do you do for fun?''

''Now you're interviewing me.''

''We've got to start somewhere, don't we?''

For a moment she didn't answer. The waitress brought the little cups of Turkish coffee. Genie and I both took sips of the thick, dark brew.

"You're a strange man, Michael. I'm really not sure if it's right for me to be sitting here talking to you. It's getting a little weird, isn't it?"

"Maybe that means we're both learning something new. I know I am. What do you have to lose?"

"Tell you what," she murmured with a teasing smile on her face, "I'll stay here and talk to you for a bit if you'll let me interview you for that article."

"First tell me what you do for fun," I tried to be evasive.

"Is that a yes or a no?"

I nodded.

"Okay," she told me, "I like to read. Hemingway is my favorite author. I've read everything by him. His first book, *The Sun Also Rises*, is his best, don't you think?"

I nodded again.

"I also like to go to the beach," she continued, "and surf. In the winter, I ski. But I like surfing better—it's not so cold."

"Where do you surf?"

"Rincon. County Line. North toward Santa Barbara. I used to like Redondo, by the breakwater, but it's gotten too rough lately. The homeboys drive you right off the waves."

Did those names bring back memories.

"The Redondo Breakwater," I muttered nostalgically. "You know, I once rode it at twenty feet. It was terrifying. I wish someone had taken a picture of me."

"You surfed?" Genie seemed incredulous.

"Yeah."

"In a million years I never would have guessed that."

"I look that out of shape, huh?"

"It's not that," she blushed. "You don't look, excuse me, the type."

"Suits and ties conceal a lot, don't they?"

"You really surfed Redondo?"

"When I was fourteen I even bleached my hair blonde."

"Now I don't believe you."

I grinned.

"Ask my mother, I know she's got a picture somewhere."

"That's something I'd love to see. Hey, I could use that picture for my article. 'Mild mannered druggist reaches deep into his surfing past to drag out the soul of a hero.'"

"It sounds like something from the *National Enquirer*."

"I meant it as a compliment."

"I really look that 'mild mannered'?"

Genie nodded without hesitation.

"Is it the clothes? The haircut? What?"

"Everything. You know what you look like. I would love to see that photo of you with the bleached hair." She squinted at me, as if she could see into the past. "I bet you looked real cute as a blonde."

She was so sincere she made me blush. I felt sixteen again.

"I can just picture you with a tan, long hair, baggies by Katin, surfboard by Jacobs, right?"

"Dewey Weber."

"One of those long jobs. Nine-five, right?"

I nodded.

"You must've had a lot of fun," she continued. "Those were the classic times. Empty beaches. Waves to yourself. Dick Dale and the Delltones. The Beachboys. 'Surfin' U.S.A.' Hodads. Woodies. Beach bunnies. Frankie Avalon and Annette Funicello in 'Beach Blanket Bingo.' God, that was a silly movie. I'd like to have known you then."

"You wouldn't have liked me."

"I bet I would; you sounded real cute," she teased me.

"Sounded?"

She ignored my inquiry.

"Were you any good?"

The sexual feelings stirred up and grabbed hold of me.

"As what?" I'm afraid I leered.

"As a surfer."

"I did come in second once in the fifteen and under division of the Huntington Beach Surfing Contest, in 1963."

"Really?"

"Yeah. Look it up in the records."

"I believe you." Genie seemed genuinely impressed.

This filled me with joy; we were actually on our way to becoming friends. Now if only I could feel that I was mastering my sexual attraction to her. I was working in the tradition of the puritanical fanatics; some church would eventually dub me "Saint Marcus," I tried to kid myself. Some joke. Some saint I'd make. The only church that would consider me a saint would be the Holy Church of My Mother, Temple Gloria Marcus, an institution so unorthodox that its only consideration was monogamy; no other religious, moral, or ethical questions mattered. My mother herself had carried the stone tablet bearing the one commandment, "Thou Shalt Not Commit Adultery," directly down the mountain from God to her congregation, which was her older son—me. Did anyone but my mother really care about my behavior?

"Why'd you quit?" Genie asked.

"What?"

"Surfing."

"When I was fifteen my father was hospitalized. He couldn't work for almost a year. I took a job after school to get money for college. I worked from three until eleven every day for Chicken Delight. I studied in the mornings before school. That was the end of the surfing for me."

"Wow." She seemed surprised by this information.

"That's how I felt about it. I couldn't believe what hit me."

"That's so real. So basic. So heavy. That's really something."

"I could have done without it."

"Do you realize," Genie grinned brightly, obviously trying to change the mood, "that you quit surfing the year before I was born? If you still have your surfboard, it's older than I am."

"Thank you very much. You trying to pay me back for being mean to you?" My voice had an edge to it. Anger.

"Michael, it was just an observation. I was fitting the pieces of your life against mine to see how they match up."

"Yeah, well, if you want to be friends with me, making observations about me as a geriatric case isn't going to help. You know, by most standards I'm still a young man."

"Michael," she addressed me most seriously, "you're very sensitive about your age, you know that?"

"It seems to me you're the one who's so sensitive about my age; I mean, you're always bringing it up, aren't you?"

"It was just an observation."

"You didn't seen to like my observation about *your* age, as I recall."

Genie thought this over.

"You're right," she finally admitted. "I'm sorry."

"Thank you."

"We're friends again?"

"Yes."

"Good. Now will you tell me why you're so sensitive about your age?" she grinned provocatively.

"Shall I tell you first how I'm going to kill you?" I offered back.

Before Genie could respond, Mary, the cashier from the drugstore, was standing by our table. She had come to tell me that Lieutenant Peterson of the L.A.P.D. was waiting for me in the store. Apparently he had something important to discuss. I told Mary that I'd be there in a minute and she returned to the pharmacy. When I turned back across the table, Genie was staring at me with a funny look on her face. Did I amuse her? Was she making fun of me?

"I had an idea," she began. "Do you really want to be friends with me?"

"Absolutely."

"Well then, let's do this. Saturday morning, how about you and me going surfing together?"

"The two of us?" I stalled, terrified by her directness.

"Yeah."

"With no one else?"

"That's what 'you and me' means."

It was a dream come true. And a nightmare as well.

"God, I would love to. But I can't."

"Why can't you?"

"I've got to work."

"You can't take a Saturday morning off? Isn't it your own business?"

"Yeah. But I have responsibilities."

She smiled at me, clearly enjoying my discomfort. "Yesterday you told me we weren't friends because we hadn't spent time together alone. I want to spend some time with you and now you're telling me you don't want that. Do you or do you not want to be friends?"

"Genie, think about it; it's not that simple. What am I going to tell Marilyn? What are you going to tell your dad? We can't say we're two friends who just went to the beach together. They'll never believe that.

"Michael, how old are you?"

"We're back on that subject, are we?"

"No. Sorry. I didn't meant it that way. I already know how old you are, remember?"

"So why bring it up?"

"Because you're behaving like you're twelve."

"I don't understand."

"Michael. I'm not going to tell my father I went to the beach with you. Why do you have to tell him?"

"I have to."

"But why?"

"Because, Genie, what if someone sees us?"

"We'll go somewhere where they won't, how's that?"

"L.A.'s a big city. But when it comes to this kind of stuff it's a small town. Someone always ends up seeing you."

"Oh yeah? I went out in public with Nick for the last three months and no one saw me."

"I saw you."

For a few seconds she said nothing. Obviously she was offering me something and I was rejecting it. In her eyes and maybe even in my own, I was behaving in a manner that she would probably have called "flaky."

"Michael, I'm inviting you somewhere. To have fun. To do something you haven't done since you were what, fifteen? Do you want to find a way to do it or not?"

Genie certainly knew how to tighten the screws; there was no way I could deny the issue the way she presented it.

"I don't even have a surfboard."

"I'll borrow one for you; how much do you weigh?"

"Genie, I haven't ridden a wave in twenty years. I'm out of shape. Why don't I spend a few weeks jogging, then we'll go."

She laughed.

"When you were fifteen, did you jog to get in shape for surfing?"

"When I was fifteen I was in shape for surfing; I didn't need to do anything."

"Look Michael, it's like what I said before—do you or do you not want to let yourself have some fun? We're not talking about climbing Mount Everest here; we're talking about a couple of hours at the beach. Do you want to go, yes or no?"

My whole life seemed to hinge on the moment. Making the decision about shooting the junkie had been simple compared with going or not going to the beach with Genie. I looked across the table and studied this beautiful girl who was waiting for me to answer. What was she thinking, I wondered. What did she want with me? How did she interpret what I had told her about why I had been so cold to her? Her face appeared to be so open and innocent, yet she was acting so cleverly. She claimed to be only seventeen, which in fact I knew to be true. In so few years, how had she learned to be so provocative and direct, so shy, and at the same time so self-confident? Somehow I knew that she and I hooked into each other; exactly where that was, I wasn't sure. But I knew that I had to find out.

"Okay. I'll find some way to get away Saturday. But you've got to promise not to tell anybody. Is that a deal?"

Genie put her hand to her chest as if she were saluting the U.S. flag.

"You have my word of honor," she said solemnly, mocking my anxiety.

"Thank you."

"That wasn't so hard, was it?" she teased me.

"As long as no one finds out." I stood up. "I gotta go talk to the police." I gestured down the street to the pharmacy.

"What about my article? You promised to let me interview you. My deadline's tomorrow morning."

I shrugged.

"You were there. You know what happened. Write it as you saw it. I'll see you Saturday."

Genie stood up and for a moment neither of us knew what to do. No question about it; there was electricity between us. I extended my hand. She shook it softly.

"Okay then, Saturday," she said. "I'll meet you in the Federal Building parking lot at eight o'clock."

I left money on the table for the coffee, nodded to Genie, and walked out the back door of the restaurant. It was a very bright afternoon. In fact, it was so bright, so suddenly, that it seemed to be a different day. I had gone in the House of Tehran one person and come out another. Now the police were waiting for me. I realized that I was running down the alley. Why? Where had all this energy come from? Was I running away from Genie or was I running because I was keeping the police waiting? I couldn't give myself an answer. I only knew that at that moment I felt free of all my burdens. Marilyn and the fat farm were suddenly deflated from a crisis to just a simple problem. I was more than optimistic; I was ecstatic. I could handle anything. Bring on the challenges, I told myself, and I would master them. I was Frank

Sinatra singing "New York, New York." L.A. was my town, and my life, and I was doing it my way and it felt great. Unlike Mick Jagger, I could get some satisfaction. Genie had obviously given me the energy to run. Where would it lead? I knew it was going to require real work on my part to keep things just as a friendship, but in my state of mind, anything seemed possible.

8

I bounded in the back door of the drugstore to find Lieutenant Peterson in my office talking to Jerry Herrman. Their conversation seemed beyond serious—something grim was going on.

"Why the long faces," I inquired with my surge of enthusiasm, "did someone die?"

They looked at each other. My partner deferred to the lieutenant.

"The problem is," Peterson related, "someone didn't die. Your junkie friend, Robert Allen, is apparently going to live, if you can call it that."

"How's that?" I asked stupidly.

"Your .38 did the job on his brain, but his body is fine. The man is now a human avocado, thanks to the miracle of modern neurosurgery. If the doctor who patched him up is right, and no one pulls the plug on the life support machine, Mr. Allen could live for the next fifty years. That's where the problem comes in.

"I don't understand."

The Lieutenant's grim tone, and the concerned look on Jerry's face, sent a shiver down my spine. My hands suddenly began to sweat.

"Michael," Jerry put in, "you're not going to believe it; the story from here becomes pure shit."

I looked to Peterson for an explanation.

"Mr. Allen has a wife. Her name is Alice and she's one tough-ass bitch. She's been running around telling anyone who'll listen to her that her husband had been off of junk for more than two years. . . ."

"What are you talking about?" I interrupted, "two years, bull; I saw the needle marks on the man's arms myself."

"Michael, let Lieutenant Peterson finish," Jerry said.

"This Mr. Allen was a welder. Four days ago he lost his job after a trivial argument with his boss; Allen just shot his mouth off once too often. That night he began a little binge and went back to the needle for consolation. He sure didn't get it from his wife. She'd cut off his money. That's when he hit your store. It's a real shame, too, because the wife had arranged for her husband to check in with the psychologist who'd gotten him off junk in the past. If he'd just put off the robbery one day, none of this would ever have happened."

"Lieutenant, this is all very interesting, but why come all the way out here to tell me?"

"Because," Peterson said, "this Alice woman believes you tried to kill her husband without provocation. She's trying to force us to arrest you for attempted murder. She views you as a vigilante and wants us to go after you for 'wrongful death.'"

I was shocked; this was the last thing I had expected to happen. If I hadn't seen the gravity of Lieutenant Peterson's manner, I would have thought the whole thing was a joke.

"What do you think?" I asked Peterson.

"The department wants me to investigate, to see if her accusations are justified."

"And?" I said, an edge of anger in my voice.

"As far as I'm concerned, they're not."

"Thank you."

"That's as far as I'm concerned. The ACLU is a different story."

"What does the ACLU have to do with it?"

"This gal, Alice, is political. She's an ex-legal secretary. She knows how the system works. She got in touch with someone at the ACLU and found out they were looking for a case like this; they want to test the mayor's Community Watch concept. White folks taking the law into their own hands and shooting minorities is not popular with the ACLU. They're thinking of making you their test case."

"This is outrageous. The guy was threatening us all with a gun. And he had a hostage."

"It wasn't a gun; it was a water pistol, remember?" Peterson reminded me.

Jerry shook his head in disbelief, letting me know how sympathetic he felt.

"That's the analysis after the fact," I raged, "but no one could tell that during the robbery."

"You may have to convince a jury of that," Peterson told me without humor.

"I just don't believe it. What am I supposed to do when I'm being robbed at gunpoint, ask the junkie if he minds if I examine his pistol before I shoot him? Come on, what are we really talking about here? This isn't justice, this is a perversion."

"Michael," Jerry chimed in, "at least there's one thing you don't have to worry about. I checked and we have insurance against this kind of legal action; we're protected that way."

"Oh wonderful," I said sarcastically. "If I lose the case, is the insurance company prepared to go to jail in my place?"

"Michael," Jerry tried to reassure me, "you're not going to jail, believe me."

"You're god-damn right I'm not going to jail!"

The two men stared at me. Jerry had never seen me this angry. Lieutenant Peterson didn't know me, so he didn't have any idea of what I might do. He just stood quietly, wary.

"Both of you, turn your backs for one second; I want to show you something."

The two men looked at me as if I had suddenly lost my mind.

"Just turn around," I said. "I'm not going to hurt you, I promise. You'll find this interesting."

Both men turned their backs. Quietly I opened my desk drawer and removed what I'd been examining on and off all morning—a water pistol like the one the junkie had been carrying. I had wondered myself why I hadn't recognized that it was plastic. But even at arm's length I still found it impossible to distinguish from a real gun. But then I wasn't an expert. I wondered how well the lieutenant would do.

To find out, I suddenly grabbed Jerry around the neck with one arm and, with my other hand, shoved the plastic gun barrel against the back of his head. Jerry froze.

"Okay, lieutenant," I yelled as I pulled my terrified partner a few feet back from the detective, "you tell me, is this real or is it plastic? It may be loaded, it may not be. But if you tell me it's plastic, I'm going to pull the trigger. If you think it's real I won't. So, which is it, Lieutenant? In thirty seconds I pull the trigger either way if you don't answer. That's a hell of a lot more time than I had, isn't it?"

Peterson stared at the gun, which I kept moving around like the junkie had done.

"Michael," Jerry tried to tell me calmly, "I don't think this is funny."

"Shut up Jerry," I yelled, imitating the junkie, "just pray the lieutenant makes the right choice."

"Michael," Jerry tried getting tough, "I don't know what's wrong with you or what kind of point you're trying to make, but I want you to let go of me, and I mean now."

"Make one move, Jerry—even your finger—and I pull the trigger."

Jerry froze.

"It's not so easy, is it lieutenant?"

Peterson said nothing.

"Your thirty seconds are up lieutenant. Now which is it, plastic or steel?"

"You know, Marcus, you could do time for this."

"I want an answer, lieutenant, something good to give to the ACLU."

"Okay, Marcus. I think it's a real pistol."

It was the answer that I wanted and it made me very happy. I relaxed my grip on Jerry, who instantly spun around, enraged.

"God damn it, Michael," he yelled, "you scared me to death, you son-of-a-bitch. How could you?"

I raised the pistol and pointed the barrel to his forehead.

"Shut up Jerry."

"Michael, please," Jerry wailed.

I pulled the trigger. A stream of water spurted out of the barrel and dribbled down Jerry's face.

"You see what I was up against, lieutenant? Even you can't tell the difference."

Peterson didn't say a word.

"Michael, you're a real asshole, you know that?" Jerry whined. "God damn you, you're a shitpile. I was trying to help you, you fuckface."

Jerry charged out of the office, leaving the lieutenant and me staring at each other.

9

When I got home from work Angie, our Jamaican housekeeper and day nanny for Rebecca, informed me that Marilyn had called from the hospital to say that she would be very late. This was fortunate, because moments later Ed Cotler stopped over unannounced to discuss both the award from the mayor and the outrageous position he'd heard the ACLU was taking in my case. Had Marilyn been there, any real discussion would have been impossible. "Liberal, candy-assed, hypocritical mother-fuckers" was how Ed politely referred to the ACLU. He had actually supported the organization up to the moment they defended the rights of the Nazis to march in Skokie, Illinois. But that was carrying things too far. "Obscene injustice" was how he viewed the ACLU's position on the Nazis. And that's how he viewed the ACLU in their present role against me. Ed offered to take my case, to defend me against the "swimming pool Communists" as he described the ACLU vultures. Ed's rage and enthusiasm certainly pleased me; at that moment I needed all the support I could get. But given my fantasies about Genie, I did have second thoughts about involving Ed so closely in my life. I didn't want him to find out my feelings about his little girl. The ACLU could only send me to jail; Ed would shoot me.

It's hard to argue against Ed when he's convinced of something. He believed in the justice of my cause and committed himself to defending me all the way to the Supreme Court, if necessary. The more Ed described my legal defense, the more certain I became that not only was he the best man for the job, but also that I would never be discovered with Genie. How could anyone prove that she and I had anything other than friendship? My need at the moment was for a heavyweight legal defense, and Ed was the Mohammed Ali of the courtroom. Ed dramatized his defense strategy by acting out all the roles right there in my living room. Rebecca watched from the staircase, transfixed by his performance. Of course she didn't have the slightest idea what he was talking about, but she applauded when he was finished.

"Better than 'Simon and Simon,' " was her comment.

I knew enough to hire a winner, and Ed had won for me before. I was glad Marilyn wasn't home to hear the kind of trouble I was potentially involved in; things were bad enough without her becoming even more anxious.

When Ed left, Angie brought out a plate of cold chicken for me to eat while I read to Rebecca. My daughter was in love with the books of Dr. Seuss. That night we were reading *The Cat in the Hat*. Even though I enjoy Dr. Seuss myself, I was hardly in the mood to read fantasies. But Rebecca was my daughter and she had her needs. So I read to her. In fact, for the short time she was able to stay awake, *The Cat in the Hat* was actually diverting, taking me out of myself, away from my troubles, and connecting me to the rich, vivid, imaginary life of my four-year-old sweetheart.

After another *a cappella* rendition and an encore of "California Girls," Rebecca fell asleep. I was left on my own and all of my anxieties returned. For the first time in my life, I couldn't interest myself in *The Journal of American Pharmacology*. Even an article on the latest beta blockers, which normally would have fascinated me, I found unreadable. This was a clear sign that I was in big trouble. If I couldn't concentrate on something as important as beta blockers, given the fact that so many of my customers were taking them for heart problems, obviously my mental state was seriously deteriorating. I turned to the new study of Bendectin, the most commonly prescribed medication for pregnant women with morning sickness. I knew this piece would be of great interest to Marilyn and might afford us a channel of communication. But no matter how hard I tried to focus on the damn thing, I couldn't make any sense out of it. It was as if I were reading Japanese. I opened *Newsweek,* hoping something lighter might capture my attention. This didn't work either; everything seemed irrelevant to my life. I tossed the magazine on the living room coffee table and turned on the television, which was an even worse idea; no one lived like the people on the sitcoms, although I was sure millions aspired to that fantasy. This was mass cultural pathology. I shut off the TV set.

Sitting in silence in my living room, I was immediately enveloped by the memory of Genie naked on my sectional sofa. Forbidden desires had to be driven from my mind. But how?

I tried to divert the feelings to Marilyn. However, envisioning Marilyn on the sofa abandoning herself to me with the passion

Genie had demonstrated with that surfer proved an impossible stretch of imagination. My thoughts immediately swooped back to my forbidden seventeen-year-old beauty. It frightened me that Marilyn was becoming inexorably intertwined in my mind not with pleasure, or sex, or joy, or friendship—but with the role of a demanding business partner clamoring for me to sell off everything meaningful so that she could buy her health farm. I also knew that I was seeing only a small part of Marilyn. I knew that it was my perception of her that was affected, that she was a far more complex and interesting person than I was picturing. I simply shut off when I heard her talk about that health farm project. I hated the idea of the spa, and the more she talked about it, the more I transferred that hate onto her, until she became the spa. So I was the one who was having the problem, not Marilyn, I tried unsuccessfully to convince myself. But the delusion was hard to sustain.

Marilyn was simply, unquestionably, obsessed about the spa. And ever since her compulsion had taken concrete form in the physical planning of the health resort, our relationship had taken a sterile, sexless turn for the worse. What had happened to the Marilyn I had known, loved, and married? The serious medical resident, who cared about her patients and had contempt for the patronizing, paternal, macho gynecological traditionalists? The Marilyn who had vowed to conduct a personal, woman-oriented practice? And succeeded at it. And what had happened to the woman who was the mother of Rebecca? The woman who grew up in New York, raised by guardians, thanks to the automobile accident that killed her parents when she was only four; the woman who had vowed to raise her family in the traditional way, so that her daughter wouldn't grow up in a cold, isolated environment like the one Marilyn herself had so painfully endured? Wasn't Escondido and the health resort a California version of Marilyn's childhood isolation? Were we all destined simply to repeat our pasts? Was I watching Marilyn's chickens coming home to roost without her having the power to alter her emotional destiny? It seemed that I was watching the woman I loved being swallowed whole by her childhood experiences. Her softness and vulnerability had faded from view; the obsession was turning her into an untouchable iron.

I was a man, with a man's needs. I craved affection and tenderness, appreciation and respect. I had seen enough of continuous debate while growing up with my mother and father to know that it was not my style. Marilyn had once been so tender with me. To the outside world she had always been tough and even a bit cold. But she'd opened up to me from the first moment I met her. I think she trusted something in me. Some pain or damage that I'd experienced resonated with her suffering. She felt comfortable with my own psychic injuries. She knew I wouldn't hurt her. With me she could let her hair down. She could be the little girl with the lonely childhood whom no one had loved, whom no one had tucked into bed at private school, to whom no one had responded except with the most formal of cards at birthdays and Christmas. Marilyn had reacted to all of this just as I had done to my childhood pain; she had thrown herself into the world of achievement in order to obtain some semblance of self-worth. At the least, we both obtained praise from our teachers for getting all A's in school. I think I was the first man who gave validity to her past by understanding her suffering. The number of times we told each other about the torments of our childhoods and the number of times we cried, literally, over the unnecessary cruelty of those in charge of us linked Marilyn and me together forever as loyal, affectionate friends and lovers. At least that's what I'd thought. Now something was splitting us apart. I felt terribly lonely. My fascination with Genie, I knew, was only a symbol of that loneliness. It was my connection with Marilyn that was the problem.

That's when the inspiration came to me. It was so obvious I wondered why I hadn't thought of it before. Marilyn needed a psychiatrist—it was as simple as that. She had an obsession. Obsessions were projections of neurotic disturbances. Specialists in treating neurotic disturbances were called psychiatrists. The problem was how to go about getting her to talk to a psychiatrist. Then I realized that Marilyn was probably so tormented by her obsession that something as simple as my suggesting that she talk to an expert might be just what she secretly wished. This insight lifted an enormous weight from me. I couldn't wait for Marilyn to return home. Now we had something to talk about.

The timing couldn't have been worse. Marilyn walked in the front door just as the eleven o'clock news was running a follow-up piece on the robbery, sensationalizing the story with the new ACLU angle and the organization's outrage at my "Wild West mentality." I reached to shut off the television, but Marilyn stopped me and listened carefully to the whole story. When it was over she flipped off the set. I expected a tirade; from the look on her face, she obviously had something to say. I made an effort to head off her rage by telling her about Ed and his passionate commitment to defending me all the way to the Supreme Court, if it proved necessary. For a moment Marilyn said nothing, which was strange. Then she came over to the couch and sat down next to me. She looked very sad, moved by something.

"Michael, you do know I love you, don't you?"

"Of course."

"I know I've been hard to live with lately. Don't think I'm not aware that I've been driving you crazy with my health spa plan. I am sorry it's upset you."

"Thank you for being aware of it." Her suddenly considerate tone surprised me. Where was she heading?

"I heard the business with the ACLU at the hospital. To be honest with you, my first impulse was to be angry. But then something happened that changed my whole way of thinking. It involved Mrs. McGathern. Do you remember me telling you about Mrs. McGathern?"

"Vaguely."

"She's the fanatic who wouldn't have her baby in the hospital— the home birth woman, remember? The one with the difficult pregnancy that looked to be full of complications. It took me months to talk her into having the baby at Cedars. But she still insisted it be fully natural. Well, tonight she went into labor. You know what the first thing she said to me was?"

I shook my head that I couldn't guess.

"She wanted me to knock her out with anesthetic. Not even an epidural. I couldn't believe it. Two days ago she was still arguing with me about having the baby in the hospital. You know what had happened?"

"What?"

"Yesterday her husband was killed in a motorcycle accident. Some drunk in a truck ran a red light. Boom, just like that, the baby had no father and Mrs. McGathern had no husband. She didn't care about anything when the labor started, least of all coping with natural childbirth. You know what I did?"

I listened.

"I convinced her to go through the whole Lemaze procedure. I coached her in place of her husband. And she did it. It was hard and it was painful but she gave birth to a healthy baby boy and thanked me for helping her make the birth so meaningful. She might not be able to bring her husband back, but at least she lived up to her aspirations with the birth. You know what she made me realize?''

Again I didn't know.

''That lately I've been so afraid of something happening to you or Rebecca that I've actually been destroying what we have together. You've been telling me that for months, haven't you?''

''I tried.''

''I guess it took Mrs. McGathern to help me hear you. Thank you for not giving up on me.''

This observation of Marilyn's was very moving to me. And I told her so. We sat on the couch holding each other. Then we began to kiss. For the first time in ages I not only felt close to her, but sensed she sincerely desired me. I couldn't help wondering if the couch itself had some magical properties, first with Genie and Nick, and now with us.

''Shall we go to the bedroom where it's more comfortable?'' Marilyn suggested.

So much for the couch. We headed for the bedroom.

If someone had asked me at that moment if I thought that the sex Marilyn and I were about to have would break down some of the barriers and open new connections between us, I would have answered, ''without question.'' But except for the affection on the couch, it was the same as always. There was only one way Marilyn could achieve orgasm. I had to lie flat on my back, immobile, while she sat on top off me, totally controlling the motion and pressure of her clitoris against my pelvic bone as I caressed and pinched the tips of her nipples with my fingernails. The slightest wiggle on my part would throw off her concentration and end any possibility of her eventual climax. That night I lay perfectly still with her on top of me, and as she started to get excited, I began to recite the only sexual fantasy that could arouse her.

The story began with me, as the mysterious stranger, seeing her on the street and enticing her into my taxi where I tied her hands behind her back and took her back to my house. Inside my basement dungeon, servants stripped off her clothes and commanded her to put on knee-high leather boots, a black leather miniskirt so short her ass was visible, and a white lace-up bodice that exposed her breasts. She had to wait there for me, for hours.

Then, at my pleasure, the door to her dungeon swung open and I entered wearing a black hood and cape.

At this point, Marilyn, sitting on me and thrusting against my pelvis, was actually beginning to get deeply excited. But for her to approach orgasm, the fantasy had to continue, as uninteresting as it had become to me over the years. Why she required this to get excited I never understood. She hadn't needed the fantasy when I met her; even during our first year of marriage she had orgasms without it. How had it come to be such a necessity for her? And why? The questions saddened me; but the fact was that she needed it. And if I wanted to please her, I had to participate in the monotonous obsession, her own personal interpretation of *The Story of O*.

In her fantasy, we were locked together in the dungeon. The only part of my anatomy she could see was my erection, which stuck straight out from the opening in my cape. I told Marilyn that I wanted only one thing, and that was her. "You are totally under my command," I said, demanding she get to her knees and suck me.

This part always excited Marilyn. Here she began to pick up steam, thrusting against me faster and more forcefully. When I could see she was getting close, I had to go for her big fantasy, to push her over. Without the big finale Marilyn would plateau on a high level of sexual excitement, but never get off.

In the monotone that was required for telling her fantasy, I ordered Marilyn off her knees and over to the stone wall, where I handcuffed and chained her, facing away from me. Then I commanded her to bend over, spread her thighs, and prepare herself to receive me. I told her how wet she was and how juicy and swollen she had become.

"What do you want?" I would ask at that point.

"I want you. I need you," was her answer.

With Marilyn still on top of me, thrusting hard, I described to her how, in the fantasy, I slowly approached her and took each cheek of her hot little ass in my hands, spread them apart, then rubbed myself against her inflamed and slippery flesh.

"Oh, stick it in me. Please. Stick it in me. I need you now!" Marilyn would pretend to beg while she was pounding back and forth on top of me, eyes closed, living her fantasy.

I felt so alone; I was only the storyteller, serving Marilyn's needs. She was connected to something deep in her unconscious. I was connected to nothing. I marveled that I was even able to sustain my erection in the face of such loneliness and sadness. I did it to please Marilyn, who at this point was balanced right on the edge of her orgasm. To help her over, I had to phrase things perfectly.

While my body remained immobile underneath her, I described how slowly, very slowly, I slipped my huge swollen self deep inside her. She was wet, tight, and hot, which made me as hard as an iron rod. When I was so far inside of her that it felt as if I would come out her throat, I commanded her to thrust against me with everything she knew and felt.

"Fuck me," I commanded Marilyn.

That night my timing was right and Marilyn made it over her plateau, coming with a huge groan and a lot of little thrusts of her pelvis. For a few moments she sat still, then she opened her eyes and looked down at me.

"Would you like to roll over?" she asked.

"Sure."

We turned over. I was now on top. She knew I hadn't yet come. I started to move slowly, thrusting back and forth very tenderly, trying to feel as much as I could. The problem was that once Marilyn came, she couldn't get excited again. At that point, she felt virtually nothing. It was more lonely than masturbating because I could see on Marilyn's face that she wasn't even remotely connected to me. It was all mechanical. She would just watch me slide in and out of her, but nothing could rearouse her. I felt as if I'd been transformed into a necrophiliac. In order to excite myself, I had to close my eyes and think of other women. Before Genie, my fantasies were all about lovers who actually enjoyed my touch, didn't need to be either dominant or submissive, liked me, liked my body, and were not obsessed with any all-encompassing fantasy. That night, another phantom woman sprung to mind with no effort at all: Genie. As long as I kept my eyes shut and didn't look down at my immobile wife, I could easily imagine I was intertwined with my responsive seventeen-year-old friend. I concentrated on Genie and moments later came in a quick, mildly satisfying rush of sperm. Afterward, I felt alone and cut off from Marilyn. It was very depressing.

For a moment I lay quietly. Then Marilyn wrapped her arms around me and snuggled close, which was very unusual for her. Normally after sex she just washed, then went to sleep. Did her sudden intimacy mean she was still aroused?

"Michael," she kissed me sweetly, "when I told you what I thought about in the hospital with Mrs. McGathern, I didn't mean I was through with my idea for the health resort. I just meant I loved you and didn't want to drive you away with my obsession, as you call it. I still think it's the best thing for you, for me, and for Rebecca. You understand that, don't you? Doesn't this ACLU business tell you it's the best thing for all of us?" She kissed me again.

I stared at her for the longest moment. We were back to square one. It was the same position, redecorated. Then I had a realization so profound that I almost laughed. Yes, the ACLU lawsuit was a bizarre twist. They wanted one of two things: damages for wrongful death or, if the junkie didn't die, money to pay for a lifetime of medical care. It would be an expensive, depressing, long-running court battle, no matter what the outcome. But I suddenly saw a glimmer of hope for myself and Marilyn underneath all that gloom.

"Sweetheart," I said gravely, "do you understand what this ACLU lawsuit means?"

She listened and said nothing.

"It means the store now has what's called a "clouded title." Until the lawsuit is settled, which Ed says could take years, there's an as yet unknown financial claim against the pharmacy. In other words, no one can buy the place until they know what the store owes the ACLU and the junkie."

Marilyn's lovely body stiffened. Anger fairly seethed out of that well-tended skin. She got out of bed, glared at me, then disappeared into the bathroom.

I waited for the reaction, which wasn't long in coming. The bathroom door opened, and she stuck her head out.

"I love you, Michael," she spit the words at me, "but you are a really stupid son-of-a-bitch for shooting that junkie. You've really screwed it up this time."

Marilyn went back into the bathroom and slammed the door. I could hear the water running. Angry or not, she would meticulously cleanse her face.

10

On Saturday morning at eight o'clock I was waiting in the parking lot of the Federal Building at Wilshire and Sepulveda. It was an extraordinary June morning, the first day of a heat wave, already eighty degrees and climbing. The surf report on the radio for south-facing beaches was three to four feet—perfect conditions. Any bigger and I could be in a lot of trouble. I didn't want to look like a fool; after all, it was twenty years since I'd last ridden a surfboard. I was bigger, heavier, slower, older, and even, honestly, a little balder. A humiliation in the water was definitely not what I needed.

By eight-fifteen I began to worry. Waiting was tough enough, but waiting for Genie was a killer. What if she stood me up, I tormented myself, how would I handle that? I was reminded of my anxiety the day before, when I'd driven down to the Con Surfboard Shop in Santa Monica to buy myself a board. Back when I surfed, back in the Stone Ages of wave riding, I'd had a Dewey Weber—nine foot, five inch, foam and red fiberglass hand-shaped by Dewey himself. It had a redwood stringer and a mahogany skeg. But at the Con shop, all I saw were high-tech, six-foot-long, hot dog midget boards. They were beautiful creations, no doubt about it. The glasswork was immaculate, their shapes were undoubtedly far more efficient than those in my day; they looked more aerodynamic than the space shuttle. I remember thinking that perhaps the U.S. government was missing a bet by not turning over its aircraft design contracts to some of the better surfboard shapers. The image of a cruise missile as beautiful as a board made just for the Banzai Pipeline amused me no end. I imagined the face of a Russian interceptor pilot as he tried to describe the candy-apple-red cruise missile surfboard that had just streaked over the Russian border at treetop level.

The problem was, I wanted one of the old jobs, one like I used to have. The sixteen-year-old kid behind the Con counter stared at me, incredulous, when I told him what I was after. He talked to me as if I were a living relic from the museum of natural history, a human dinosaur.

The kid sent me down to Hermosa Beach, to the old Jacobs Surfboard Shop. I couldn't believe it still existed, but there it was in the same location, a shack with a store in front and a production shop in back. But all the boards on display were the same streamlined, midget, modern rockets. They didn't look like they could float my weight, much less be stable under my stance. No, I wanted what I had known. The store was empty, so the eighteen-year-old Sean Penn look-alike behind the counter had the freedom to think about my request. Through the obviously clouded haze of his stoned brain I saw a concrete memory precipitate down into his consciousness—probably the first real thought the kid had formed in months. He disappeared into the back and returned clutching exactly what I was looking for. A nine-five Jacobs surfboard, state of the art in 1964. They'd been using it as a shelf for paint cans. I was one happy fellow. The kid sold it to me for thirty bucks and thought I was crazy. The rack that I bought to hold it to the roof of my car cost more than the surfboard. I drove back to the pharmacy, energies like a sixteen year old; I couldn't quite believe that strapped to the roof of my Oldsmobile was a real, honest-to-goodness Jacobs surfboard. Mine.

Marilyn of course thought I was crazy when I told her I was taking up surfing again. Right off she ran down the dangers, starting with shark attacks, moving on to razor-sharp underwater rocks, and culminating in riptides. I couldn't have compiled a more thorough list myself. The fact that I had surfed so much as a kid and knew how to deal with these problems cut no ice with my wife.

"Sharks don't discriminate between experienced and inexperienced surfers," she claimed authoritatively.

The fact that a person has less of a chance being attacked by a shark while surfing than he did of being hit by lightning while walking down Rodeo Drive meant nothing to her. Statistics or not, Marilyn was a city girl, from Manhattan. She could slice with confidence into a woman's body as long as it was within the confines of a hospital. But take her out into nature, like for a swim in the Pacific Ocean, and she felt as connected to the tides and rhythms of the real world as a shark would have felt shopping in Beverly Hills. I think the reason for her discomfort went beyond her limited experience of the outdoors. Marilyn basically didn't trust situations where she wasn't in total control.

And the Pacific Ocean was not something she could control. It was rough, dark, turbulent, filled with waves, weird tides, and shifting bottoms. To enjoy it, one had to adapt to it; no one could tame it. Marilyn's idea of ocean swimming was to wade waist deep into a lagoon on the western side of a Caribbean island. The proverbial bathtub. Obviously, she was not at all interested in taking up surfing with me. In fact, as I waited for Genie in the parking lot, Marilyn was at County Hospital conducting an all-day seminar on current techniques of dilation and evacuation: the latest in high-tech abortions.

Marilyn and I had fought continuously for two days, basically over her frustrations and fears about the "clouded title" consequences of the ACLU lawsuit. When I finally, very gently, suggested that she might find some relief from her worries by talking to a psychiatrist, she turned on me and yelled, "You're the one who needs the shrink, not me!" Poor Rebecca came downstairs in tears and it took an enormous effort on my part to calm and reassure my frightened daughter.

I decided the only solution was to wait Marilyn out. With treatment not a possibility I could only hope that time itself might ease her obsession to escape everything she'd worked to achieve.

My greatest fear was that, after city life the next thing she'd want to get away from was me. Then perhaps she'd jettison Rebecca. I figured I had to just sit tight, keep my own sanity, and try to pursue some kind of fulfilling life on my own. Marilyn could be the tenderest person, delighting in such miracles as the blooming of her first home-grown amarylis bulb. She could be such a joy to spend an afternoon with at the museum. She was so endearing as she taught Rebecca the rudiments of reading. But all that seemed far, far away. The subtleties were gone. I knew that if I couldn't maintain a balance for myself, a life outside of Marilyn's paranoid world, I'd be sucked in with her and our marriage would be over. No, I told myself, the Saturday with Genie was just what I needed to help me maintain my perspective on life. The problem was, where was she?

The time was eight twenty-five and the parking lot of the Federal Building had slowly shifted in my mind from an anonymous meeting place to a wasteland of humiliation. I double-checked my watch against the clock in the Oldsmobile; they were within thirty seconds of one another. I would give Genie ten more minutes. Was she trying to make a fool out of me?

At that moment, I was startled out of my thoughts of Genie by the loud roar of a new Porsche roadster downshifting crisply into first gear. I watched as the $40,000 black-on-black convertible idled across the parking lot and stopped beside the drive-up mailboxes. With the canvas top up and the chassis of the lowered sports car close to the ground, the driver had a difficult time reaching high enough to slip his legal envelope into the mail slot. He was only two inches short, but no matter how he stretched his arm he couldn't quite reach the opening. It was funny to watch the snakelike hand twist around in the air above the Porsche, unable to find the slot. I tried to get a glimpse into the car to check out the driver, but the Porsche's windows were tinted black and I could see nothing. That's when the door opened and the driver got out. It was my brother, Joe.

My first reaction was to hide, which I did. I scooted down in the Oldsmobile and peeked out through the rear window. All I needed was for that scumbag to see me with Genie and I'd be paying him off for the rest of my life. Joe would use my innocuous meeting with Genie to wrangle money and favors from me forever. I remained hidden and watched my brother as he mailed his envelope. Joe was wearing a beautifully made Italian charcoal pin-stripe suit. He had a conservative haircut, spit-shined shoes, and a perfectly straight demeanor. No one would have known he was gay. No one would have known he was a crook. He looked more legitimate than I did. A stranger would have identified him by his appearance as a financier or a lawyer. But I knew it was an act. With the Porsche and the suit, he was obviously trying to convince someone that he was substantial. I had no illusions about my brother. He had probably rented the Porsche for the day; where had he ripped off enough money to buy that suit? Then I remembered my mother mentioning Joe's new business. The money for the suit had probably come from her. She'd said something about him being involved with investments and banking. I pitied the poor investors. Knowing Joe, he was setting them up for the poorhouse. I wondered if I should retain a lawyer to begin work on his legal defense. The hell with it, I told myself. I'd helped him out too many times as it was.

Joe climbed back into his Porsche and drove out of the parking lot without seeing me. For this I was very grateful; finally, one good omen.

Genie, Genie, Genie, where the hell are you? I knew I was

nervous. That was clear to me in the morning when I spent a half-hour on the toilet dumping out what seemed like a week's worth of digestion. I had tried to convince myself that the outing with Genie was not about sex, but simply involved innocent recreation with a friend. Athletics helped keep the mind clear. A sound mind in a sound body. All the cliches. But I finally had to admit to myself that I was excited as hell about going to the beach with Genie. And scared, too.

At that moment I heard a horn honk. My first impulse was to duck out of sight, certain it was my brother Joe coming back to torment me. I was wrong. It was Genie behind the wheel of her Mustang. A surfboard was strapped to its roof. She parked beside my Oldsmobile and shut off her engine. She was forty minutes late and I was angry.

11

Through the side window of my Olds I waved, smiled coldly, and gestured for her to wait a moment. Genie nodded. I got out of my car and carefully scanned the parking lot. The place was as quiet as the adjacent Veterans Administration cemetery. I unstrapped my surfboard from the Olds and quickly buckled it next to Genie's on top of her Mustang. I locked my car, then carried my canvas bag containing my towel, a second pair of swim trunks, suntan oil, and a change of clothes to the open passenger door of Genie's car, tossed my bag into the back seat, and got in.

"You actually made it," she said with a twinkle in her eye.

"Genie, do you realize I've been waiting here for god-damn forty minutes?"

She said nothing.

"You know," I continued angrily, "it's not much fun sitting in this parking lot watching people mail letters. Ten or fifteen minutes, that I understand. But forty minutes. Genie, if you wanted to meet me at eight-forty, why not just tell me eight-forty?"

The twinkle disappeared from Genie's expression.

"Michael, would you rather not go?" she asked flatly.

"No," I answered tensely, "I'm here and I want to go. I just don't like waiting."

"It doesn't sound to me like you want to go. This was supposed to be fun, remember?"

"And you were supposed to be here at eight o'clock, remember that?"

"Michael, you're so uptight. Maybe you just think you want to go. Maybe this isn't the right thing for you to be doing."

"Genie, come on. Start the car. I've been looking forward to this all week. I even bought that surfboard."

She looked at me oddly. It was the same look the kid in the Con surfboard shop had given me.

"You bought that?"

I nodded.

"I thought you found it in your garage; that it was your old board."

I shook my head.

"Nope. I bought it yesterday."

"Jeez. I didn't think they even made boards like that anymore."

"They don't. I found it in an antique shop on Melrose."

"Now I know you're kidding. Where'd you get it?"

"An antique shop. It was expensive. I have a certificate proving that this board was first owned by Teddy Roosevelt. Before he was a Rough Rider."

"Very funny. Really, where'd you get it?"

"Jacobs Surfboards in Hermosa Beach. They were using it as a shelf for paint cans."

"Why didn't you just buy a new one?"

"Because it's what I knew. Why were you so late?"

"We're back to that, huh?"

"Uh huh."

Genie pointed to the back seat, to her canvas bag.

"I wanted to make us something nice for lunch. It took longer than I thought, okay? Or do you want to keep torturing me?"

"I think I'd like to keep torturing you," I laughed.

Genie nodded, not amused, but started the engine, and drove out of the parking lot. Other than a little smog, it seemed like a perfect day. Genie accelerated onto the San Diego Freeway and headed south. Suddenly all my anger was gone. I felt like a kid again. I was going to the beach with my surfboard and my chick. In a sixties Mustang. I flipped on the radio, hoping to hear the Beach Boys sing "Surfing U.S.A." What I got was Men at Work. I shut the music off.

"Where are you taking me?" I asked.

"You're just going to have to wait and see," she said.

Great, I thought, another mystery; just what I needed. At least no one had seen us in the parking lot. Even though my anger had dissipated I was still ridiculously tense. For the first time that morning, I took a good look at Genie. All she was wearing was a tiny ice-blue bikini covered by an oversized T-shirt with the word "Heaven" printed across her breasts. The girl was practically naked, even more arousing than I remembered. Between me and those breasts was only the flimsiest layer of cotton. Oh my god, did my erection return with a fury. I was glad I had chosen to wear jeans over my swimming trunks or my most basic impulses would have been revealed, undisguiseable. I tried to convince myself that it wasn't her body that I wanted but her friendship. I fought to forget her sensuality, diverting my eyes from those marvelous thighs, that cupcake of a tight little ass, those supple muscles, that luscious skin. I concentrated on the construction of the Mustang's dashboard, but it didn't do much good. Every time I looked over at Genie, bamm, my hard-on was back more fiercely than ever.

"If you're interested," she interrupted my fantasies.

"Yes?" I mumbled. Of course I was interested.

"That article I wrote about the robbery is in the glove compartment."

Welcoming the opportunity to behave like the mature adult I was supposed to be, I pulled out her school newspaper. There, on the front page, as the featured article, was the story. The bold type over Genie's byline read, "Ten Minutes to Die." I began to read.

The first thing I felt was the hand. It grabbed my face from behind and covered my mouth, choking me. I couldn't breathe. Then a hard, cold object pressed against the back of my head. It was his gun.

"Make one sound and I'll blow your brains all over this drugstore!" the voice commanded me.

I froze. This was a robbery. I was a hostage. Would I live or would I die?

I quickly read through the factual, but highly melodramatic, account of the robbery. Genie portrayed me as the strong, silent hero, a cross between Clint Eastwood and John Wayne. Not a word was mentioned about what she was doing in the drugstore

in the first place. Certainly nothing was said about what I had
seen take place in my living room between her and Nick. This
remained a secret between Genie and me; its absence from the
article made me feel closer to her, like a fellow conspirator. Of
course, her description of how I rescued her didn't include
anything about the attraction I had felt between us in my office,
nor did it mention the erection that had so troubled me during
our first little talk. I wondered if she knew about it.

The way Genie portrayed me throughout the robbery was more
than flattering; she idealized me, making me into a man of
passion and action, a man who behaved with courage but
wouldn't flatter himself by admitting it. She felt I was "the real
thing," and "the genuine article." I assume she didn't mean I
was simply Coca-Cola.

I had to admit that the article excited me. No one had ever
referred to me as a hero—certainly never Marilyn. Even though I
knew that Genie was young and obviously exaggerating, it was
still a wonderful feeling to read about myself in print described
in such admirable ways. As a kid I had watched all of those John
Wayne movies and had dreamed of being a man of action. That
was in my surfing days. When real life set in, John Wayne
became meaningless. For example, I never could figure out how
the noble Mr. Wayne would have dealt with my father. Would
the Duke have killed him for hurting my mother? Or would Mr.
Wayne have run away west? Perhaps he would have demanded that
my father shape up and start treating the family right—or else. Or
else, what? It seemed that the simple heroes, the men of action, had
no answers when it came to the complex world in which I lived. I
gradually gave up believing in men of action and the possibility of
becoming one. I went to work to earn money for college. I became
"old reliable"—the quiet achiever. And it had all stood me very
well until recently. Reading Genie's article jolted me back to my
teenage fantasies. In her eyes, I was a hero. She was obviously
taken with me and this was an idea I found truly exciting.

I looked over at Genie. Her forehead was perspiring. The day
was warm, but it wasn't that warm. I wondered if she was
nervous too. She was waiting for my reaction to her article.
Desire engulfed me. What I wanted to do was to lick every drop
of moisture from her lovely brow. But I restrained myself.

"I like it," I told her. "You did a very good job of describing
what happened."

"You just saying that or do you really like it?"

"Hey, I'm not in the habit of lying. I like it. You captured the danger of the situation. And what it felt like to be a hostage. The only thing I don't agree with is your description of me. Gary Cooper I'm not. I was just fed up with being the victim. Anyone could have done it."

"Michael, you do know that's not true."

"You asked me what I thought; I'm not going to lie to you."

Genie gave me a peculiar look; she didn't buy my story.

"But you did like my article."

"Very much."

"Does it seem professional to you?"

"It could have come from the *L.A. Times*."

"My father didn't think very much of it. He thought there were too many adjectives and emotions and not enough facts."

"He's a lawyer, remember."

"He's also an arrogant asshole sometimes. I think it's the best thing I've ever done. Just once, why couldn't he say something nice to me?"

Who knew why fathers did what they did?

"Well, I think it's a terrific article. I mean it."

"Thank you." Genie seemed pleased.

"Are you serious about going into journalism? You sure seem to have the talent for it."

Genie's face lit up with enthusiasm.

"I would love to do that. You can't imagine. Get out of here. Travel. Move to another country. Maybe be a war correspondent like Hemingway. You think a paper would hire me based on that article?"

"I'm not an expert on these things, but I would."

"Michael, have you read Hemingway?"

"Some. I remember liking his short stories best."

"Me too. Do you remember 'The Short Happy Life of Francis Macomber'?"

"A great story."

"How about 'The Three Day Blow'?"

"Another good one."

"And 'The Killers,' if that isn't sensational."

I nodded.

"The man really used his experiences. Really lived and wrote about life. That's what I want to do. Michael, can I ask you something?''

I nodded again.

"Will you give me an honest answer?''

"No. I'm going to lie to you if I possibly can.''

"Be serious. I need an honest opinion, okay?''

"Okay.''

She hesitated.

"I tried to write that article like Hemingway. Remember me telling you that when I came to interview you?''

I nodded.

"Did I succeed?''

"Hmm,'' I muttered, considering how to answer. I tried to recall what it was like to read Hemingway. A lot of short sentences. Very spare prose. Little use of adjectives.

"If it takes you this long, obviously you think I didn't make it work. You don't have to kid me, Michael. I'm tough. I can take it. I don't want charity. Just don't lie to me.''

Genie concentrated on the road ahead. The expression on her face was grim.

"I think you're over-reacting a little here, Genie. I haven't even answered your question and you're taking it the wrong way.''

"Look,'' she spoke sharply, "it's a question of style and it either works or it doesn't. If you have to think about it so hard, it doesn't. Tell me it sucks and I'll leave it at that, okay? I can't stand being B.S.'d.''

"So you don't really want to know what I think, is that it? You can read my mind, jump to conclusions, and I don't have to say a thing. ESP, huh? Tell me what I'm thinking about now.'' I stared at her with a blank expression on my face.

Genie continued to drive. She remained angry.

I stuck my face up near hers.

"Where's your ESP now?''

"You're blocking my view of the road, Michael.''

"That's not what I'm thinking.''

Genie looked over at me and couldn't help but be amused by the manically serious expression I had contorted onto my face. She relaxed a bit.

"Okay. I'm sorry. What do you think?''

"Look, I'm not an expert on Hemingway. The last time I read those short stories was when I was in college. But I think you captured his style. Which is terrific. What's different is the content—the personal, human revelations. You left out why you were in the drugstore, what had gone on between us in my office, your feelings about it, me, and what you thought were my feelings about you. A lot of stuff we haven't talked about. I think you know what I mean.''

Genie said nothing. I watched her carefully. She gave no indication of her reaction to my observations.

"I think Hemingway would have based his whole story on those secrets, don't you?''

After quite a long time thinking about it, she finally spoke.

"It is a school newspaper, you know. They wouldn't have published it if I'd written it that way.''

"They published Hemingway.''

"Not in my school newspaper.''

We drove on in silence for a few minutes. We were passing Long Beach, home of the Queen Mary and the Spruce Goose. I couldn't believe the time had gone by so quickly. Everything was moving very fast. Genie had deliberately avoided discussing the implications of what she had left out of the story. It had been difficult for me to even bring it up, but it had seemed very easy for her to ignore.

"So, where are we going?'' I tried once again.

Genie grinned, enjoying this little bit of power she had over me.

"Michael, you're just going to have to wait. Or can't you stand the suspense?''

"That's right, I can't stand suspense.''

"You're just going to have to bear with me,'' she answered wickedly. "And trust me.''

I longed for everything to be as simple as she wanted me to believe. Did I have a choice about trusting her? Would a reasonable person trust her? What I sensed in her at that moment was something quite different from what she wanted me to perceive. On the surface she was cheerful, energetic, and happy. But I knew in my bones, somehow, that her state of mind was quite different inside, much darker and far more troubled than she wanted me to see. Perhaps she'd wanted to talk about it with me from the beginning but my anger over her being late had caused her to withdraw and approach me with caution. Genie seemed superficially very calm. Yet I felt that all I had to do was to say the wrong thing and she'd overreact in a flash like she did with her newspaper article. Given my mother and Marilyn, I sure had known my share of crazed, difficult women; was Genie another one of them, I wondered. Give her the benefit of the doubt, I told myself.

12

I couldn't believe it when she turned off the freeway at the Camp Pendleton Marine Corps training base in San Onofre where the Marines controlled miles of beach and used it to train amphibious assault teams. When I was a teenager, the Marine Corps' beach was reputed to have the best surfing in Southern California. This was not because the waves were superior; they were no better than at Malibu. The advantage of San Onofre was that no one was ever in the water; the beach was devoid of surfers. The reason was that, unless you had a boat, there was no way to get to the beach except by sneaking across the Marine base. This involved climbing a barbed-wire fence with a surfboard, then slithering, belly-down, over five hundred yards of U.S. government property which, rumor had it, was thoroughly mined. Surfers had to avoid roving Marines in jeeps and armed patrols who supposedly shot on sight. And of course there was the occasional machine gun or mortar practice. Surfers riding waves made excellent moving targets, so the stories went.

At age sixteen, only the most heroic surfers bragged about having ridden the big ones at San Onofre. Two friends of mine claimed to have evaded the Marines, surfed, and survived. But their stories sounded too much like other stories I'd heard from big talkers at the beach, so I never believed them. I had figured the surfing at the normal beaches wasn't so terrible that I wanted to risk being blown to smithereens or doing time in jail for trespassing. I never even got close to surfing San Onofre. Now, with Genie, that's exactly where I was headed.

Was she crazy, I wondered. Then I remembered reading that the government had opened a part of the beach to the public somewhere in the area of the San Onofre nuclear power generator. The plant used ocean water to cool its reactor. Which was worse, trying to evade a bunch of trigger-happy Marines or surfing in radioactive ocean water? Surgeons could remove bullets; nuclear radiation caused cancer. I had enough problems without worrying about glowing in the dark from one lousy day in the ocean.

Genie pulled the car onto the shoulder of the road and shut off the engine. Up on a post was a very official sign that read "U.S. government property. No trespassing. Violators will be prosecuted." Genie turned to me, grinning like a fiend.

"Well, here we are."

She reached into the back seat and began collecting her things. At least we weren't near the radiation, I thought. But did she actually believe that I was going to risk my life just to spend a few hours in the salt water?

"Genie," I asked, "where are we going?"

"There." She pointed beyond the frightening government sign.

Through the fence I could see a wide, grass-covered, undulating plain leading to what I assumed was a low palisade over the beach. I pointed to the metal sign.

"What about that?" I asked her.

"What about it?"

"That's U.S. government property."

"So?"

"So? It's illegal to trespass. We could go to jail."

"Michael, you worry too much. It's okay. There isn't going to be any problem. Trust me, remember?"

"What about what the sign says?"

"Michael, it was all explained to me. Think about it. Who is the U.S. government?"

"I don't understand."

Genie looked at me as if I were a fool.

"We're the U.S. government," she explained. "We own the property, so it's okay for us to use it."

"Genie," I tried patiently, "that's a very nice idea. But you know it isn't true. B-52 bombers are U.S. government property. Does that give us the right to walk onto an Air Force base, grab a plane, and fly it away?"

"Of course not; we're not qualified to be pilots. But this is just land—dirt, sand, and water. We're fully qualified to use that. Have you ever been to Yosemite?"

I nodded.

"Isn't that U.S. government property?"

"Genie, it's not the same thing."

"I say it is."

"Genie, this is the Camp Pendleton Marine Corps base. Restricted government property. The soldiers carry guns. It used to be said that the place was mined. Do you know what mines do? They sit there under the dirt. You can't see them. But they can feel you. When you step on them, boom, they explode, blowing you up into little pieces of confetti. It's not worth the risk."

"Michael, there are no mines in there," she said flatly.

"How do you know?"

"Because I surfed here two weeks ago."

She picked up her canvas pack and swung open the door of her car.

"You coming or not?"

"Why can't we go to a nice public beach," I whined, "so I can start surfing again without having to worry about being blown up or shot at? What do you say; is it really so terrible to make it easy for me the first day?"

Genie looked at me as if I were a child.

"Michael, I'm trying to make it easy for you; that's why I brought you here. You know, when you used to surf, as I hear it, the beaches were empty. Those were the golden years. Now, everywhere you go, it's a war; surfers fight like dogs over three square feet of water. People have been knifed and shot over waves. Is that what you want on your first day in the water? That's why I brought you here. I don't see any other cars, do you? We're going to be the only ones on the beach. Isn't that what you want?"

"If we get there."

"We'll get there. Now come on."

Genie got out of the car and locked her door. I didn't move. She grabbed her surfboard from the roofrack, leaned it up against the Mustang, and bent down to talk to me through the open window of the passenger's door.

"You coming or not?"

Hanging down, staring me right in the face, were those two perfect breasts, so squeezable, suckable, nutritious, and tantalizing.

"Uh," I answered idiotically.

"Are you afraid, is that it?"

Genie's nipples had gone hard and were pressing themselves with conviction through her bikini top and T-shirt.

"Me, afraid? No. Absolutely not."

"Michael," she tried to reassure me, "compared with what you did in the drugstore, this is a piece of cake."

"I just don't understand why we should take unnecessary chances; I mean, there's got to be some beaches that aren't crowded."

Genie reached for her board.

"Michael, this'll be worthwhile, I promise you."

My erection returned with a vengeance. Did she mean what I thought she meant? What the hell, I told myself. Then I gathered my sack of clothes and got out of the car. Genie locked the door. I removed my surfboard from the roofrack.

"Follow me," she commanded.

I looked around for danger. The whole area appeared to be deserted. Was that true, I wondered, or was it all a trap? What the hell, I told myself again, and followed Genie to the chain link fence.

13

Genie led me fifty yards, then stopped and pointed to a ditch under the fence. This was to be our entry point into the Marine base. Genie slid her board under the chain link barrier, and scrambled after it; within seconds she was inside, waiting for me. Her look challenged me to follow. I quickly studied the landscape in all directions and saw no one. Genie smiled. Standing there in the sun with the surfboard under her arm, she seemed so vital, so firm and ripe that I thought of her as a human mango whom I wanted to eat right there, on the spot.

As quickly as I could, I pushed my surfboard under the fence, dropped to my belly, and dragged myself after the board, inside the perimeter of Camp Pendleton. I stood up, fully aware that I was on U.S. government property, the Marine Corps training base. I was trespassing, breaking and entering, perhaps an attempted robber in the eyes of the law; maybe even part of a Soviet espionage scheme. What I was doing could send me to

jail. I could lose my pharmaceutical license. If we were caught, I
thought, my whole life would just wash away. In one moment
my years of work would be reduced to zero, the long-suffering
professional would become a worthless, unemployable convict
housed at government expense in a federal penitentiary. All
because of my desire for my friend's seventeen-year-old daughter.

Genie turned toward the beach and strolled casually across the
bluff toward the ocean. Had I become one of those thick-headed
guys who'd follow a great ass anywhere, even over a cliff, as I
seemed to be doing? Jesus, I suddenly realized, I was like my
father; I was doing exactly what he would have done. I felt
myself beginning to sweat, terrified of myself. I was becoming
everything that I'd fought against in myself. My father had
ruined my childhood with his insanity. He had ruined my
mother's life. Certainly he had contributed to the corruption of
my brother. Crazy father, crazy son.

Standing there by the fence, watching Genie, I could just
barely hear my father laughing. He would have been so pleased
to see me involved in something as idiotic as I was doing that
day. Certainly he'd have felt vindicated from all the condemna-
tion he'd received from me. I tried to convince myself that what
I was involved in Camp Pendleton was different from what my
father had done in his day. Genie and I were on a simple
adventure, like river rafting. Innocent. Besides, I wasn't about to
get caught at it, as my father inevitably would have, and thus my
family wouldn't have to bail me out of jail. No, I was going to
pull off this day cleanly and perfectly, with no legal consequences.

I ducked low as if bullets were being fired at me and hustled
across the bluff after Genie. No one seemed to be watching;
there were no soldiers visible anywhere. It was Saturday and on
Saturday soldiers got the day off like everyone else, I tried to
convince myself. That explained the lack of patrols.

By the time I reached the edge of the palisade Genie was at
the bottom, on the beach. I took one more look around before
descending. For a mile in all directions I could see nothing alive
except for the few bits of grass blowing on top of the low bluffs.
Clutching my surfboard tightly, I scurried down the path to the
beach.

Genie met me at the bottom with another one of those silly
smiles on her face, obviously mocking my hesitation. She was
just too young, I realized, to understand what I was risking. She

was a child. She'd always been taken care of, protected. That sardonic smile of hers told me everything about how limited her life had been. Yet there were things about men and women I felt she knew much better than I did. How could that be? Where did her knowledge come from? Was it in her genes, or did it come from her environment? A classic question; unanswerable.

"Some minefield, huh, Michael?"

I shrugged, still not convinced.

"You just have to learn to trust me, that's all."

"I'm here, aren't I?"

"And is it not great?" Genie pointed out at the water. A south well formed long series of slow-rolling, perfectly shaped, three-to-four-foot breakers. It was eleven o'clock in the morning, eighty-five degrees, clear sky, no wind, and not one surfer in sight. The beach was ours alone. The conditions were perfect.

"You just going to stand there," Genie teased, "or are you going to show me what you can do?"

I gave her a sarcastic grin, stripped to my swimming trunks, grabbed my board, and strutted confidently down to the water. Once I hit the surf I had no reason to worry; below the mean high tide line the ocean was public property and the Marines couldn't touch me. The only problem would be getting back to the car. That I would worry about later.

Genie stood on the beach and watched as I waded into the cold ocean. I hadn't been in the Pacific in probably fifteen years, certainly not since I began pharmaceutical college. But as soon as I had waded out to waist deep water and that cold surge of surf foam blasted me in the balls, I was instantly shocked back to my teenage years as a surfer. No matter how ready a man thinks he is for the water, the first time a wave breaks against his nice, warm, dry crotch, the experience is always a surprise. I stood still for a moment, taking in deep breaths of air, waiting for the jolt of pain to ease.

Then I slithered onto my surfboard, prone, chest down, and began paddling into the waves. It all came back to me more quickly that I would have believed. My instincts were intact. Sure, there were the first few side-to-side wobbles as I accustomed myself to the balance of the board, but within moments I was comfortable and in control. I headed out of the shallow water toward the breakers. I felt fifteen again. Time had stopped. I was an ageless surfer. Life consisted only of the beach, the water, the sun, and the beautiful blonde waiting for me on the sand. I was organic, macrobiotic, synergistic, and linked viscerally to the entire universe. I was alive again.

Confidently, I tried a beach break roll to get past the first big wave. The move worked, just as it had twenty years before. Rotating upside down as the wave hit, I let the surf break harmlessly over the bottom of the board and pass. Then I popped up, rolled upright, and paddled out over the next roller. Within moments I was outside the surfline surveying the breakers, looking for the perfect position, just as I'd done almost every day between the ages of twelve and fifteen.

Genie stood on the shore, watching. I gestured for her to come out, but she didn't move. She probably hadn't believed my story about the Huntington Beach surfing contest, wanted to see what I could really do, and was testing me. Just as I was testing myself. Did I still have it? Would it be as wonderful as I remembered? I watched a few sets roll through and planned my move.

The key to surfing is balance, which comes from instinct and experience. The basic pattern is simple. The wave comes in. The surfer paddles, catched the rolling water at the right point, and is propelled to speed by the face of the building wave. At that point he stands, finds the center of gravity on the board, then works the wave, moving forward to the nose to speed things up and rocking backward on the board to stall, which lifts the board back up the face of the wall of water. The surfer walks the board, back and forth, in tiny, subtle, almost imperceptible movements. Watching, it looks so easy. In fact, it isn't hard, if you're good. But like everything that requires great subtlety, surfing takes a long time to learn. Some people develop the moves; some never do. I once had them. Did I still?

With Genie watching from the beach, I couldn't sit in the water forever. I saw a good wave coming and figured I might as well find out what I remembered. I accelerated into position, swung the board around toward the beach, and began paddling in the same direction as the wave. The roller caught me, lifted me, and in moments I was up to speed, synchronized with the ocean. I got to my feet, turned sideways, and cautiously stood up. Hallelujah, I was surfing again! The old Jacobs board shot down the face of the wave just as it had in the past. What a feeling, just me and a piece of fiberglass-covered foam, propelled by the whole fucking Pacific Ocean. I was a rocket, a ballet dancer.

Baryshnikov on a Polaris missile, guiding myself with Poseidon behind me. I was inspired, screaming across the face of the sea. But then, more quickly than I expected, the curl caught up with me. My old self would have immediately rushed for the nose. When I finally did, it was too late. The wave picked me up, spit me over the falls, then broke on top of me.

The enormous green mass of sea smashed me down and pounded me into the sand. I held my breath and the wave passed. Then I surfaced, swam to my board, mounted it, and paddled back out for another try.

I stayed in the water for hours, working the waves. I should have been exhausted, but the experience was so exhilarating it seemed to punch me right through my normal limits of endurance. My moved had come back to me. I wasn't as strong, but the balance and control were still there. I began to have some good rides. I pushed myself further and further. A few times I even felt inspired. Eventually reality did catch up, however, and I began to tire. One more ride, I told myself, and I would head in. I sat in the water, waiting. I wanted the last ride to be a good one.

Set after set rolled through, but no wave was good enough for me. It was all so familiar. I was in a time warp, my age irrelevant, my problems with Marilyn unimportant, my legal difficulties meaningless, even my torment over Genie seemed remote and petty—I was waiting for the perfect wave, waiting as all surfers have from time immemorial, for the right moment and the flawless wave. One set looked too small, the next sloppy. A wave approached that appeared to be perfect, but as it got close a subtle defect became obvious in its break. Then what looked to be a good one turned out to have a clumsy peak. The next possibility became an unrideable wall of water. I must have sat there for twenty minutes before I spotted it, the fourth wave in a big set. At first it was just a small rolling mound, rising out of the calm dark sea. The swell quickly began to spread into a giant wave rolling itself up out of the depths. The center of the wave rumbled toward me, growing and widening until it became a galloping hill of slippery green water. The shape was perfect. My position was dead-on. It was my wave.

I swung my board toward the shore and began to paddle. I was quickly up to speed. The wave took hold of me, lifted me, and shot me forward on a propellant of seawater. I blasted down the

face of that six-foot wave in classic sixties Micky Doyle style.
When I hit the trough I cranked a hard right, stepped back, and
let the wave come under me, lift and deposit me back up on its
face near the break. Then I ran for the nose, ducked low, and felt
the curl break over my back—I was riding the tube. The board
picked up speed, shout out of the curl, and flew down the face of
the wave. Then I stepped back and repeated the whole sequence.
I was able to go in and out of the tube five separate times. It was
extraordinary—a ballet with the entire Pacific Ocean as my
partner. I was in harmony with the world, attuned to every
natural vibration. It was as perfect and thrilling a ride as I'd ever
had. I neared the end of the wave, which was getting smaller and
faster. The curl was catching me. I ducked low, moved forward,
and drove the board for all the speed I could get out of it. The
tube caught up with me just about the time I hit full speed. The
tail of my board was in the wave, but at that point I was moving
fast enough to stay up with it. The break remained right on top
of me, but I was able to remain on my feet and continue to bomb
through the surf at a fantastic speed. I remember hearing a noise,
a humming sound. At first I couldn't figure out where it was
coming from. The faster I went, the louder the hum became.
Then I realized that it was me—my board was planing over its
hull-speed and the skeg was vibrating from the extreme force.
The hum became the music of perfection. Green water. The
breaking curl. Speed. The sun. Genie on the beach. That
moment was everything I'd always dreamed of in surfing. It was
a perfect moment, unforgettable. There I was, a man who for
twenty years had lived his life only for the future, suddenly
feeling as if the window to my dark room had opened, and I'd
been flooded with the marvellous beauty of the vivid present. I
felt in harmony with all of time, history, the gods, and nature.
All the risks I had taken that day seemed absolutely worthwhile.

The wave petered out, and so did my energy. I had ridden the
tube of water for almost a quarter of a mile and was very close to
the shore. I paddled to the shallow water, stood in the sand,
slung my surfboard under my arm, and began the long walk back
up the beach to Genie.

14

I approached Genie feeling more alive and vigorous than I can ever remember. She stood in the sand, the classic blonde surfer girl waiting for her man. A simple image, or so it seemed. But as I got close to her I could see that instead of being thrilled to see me, Genie was distant and rather quiet. Real life was very different from the Annette Funicello and Frankie Avalon beach party movies of my high school days.

"Just answer one question," I demanded, still euphoric, "did you hear the hum?"

"The hum?"

"From my skeg. On that last ride my skeg hummed like a buzz saw. You couldn't hear it?"

"No," she answered flatly. Something was wrong.

"Are you okay?"

"Yeah. Why?"

"You seem very, I don't know, different. Did something happen while I was in the water?"

"No."

Genie was answering me in monosyllables.

"You should go out there; the waves are fantastic. You saw my last ride?"

Genie nodded.

"Genie, I do have to thank you. This place is really something."

"Good," she answered. "How about some lunch?"

"I can wait. Why don't you go ride a few waves while the shape is still so good. I'd love to see how you do it on your short board."

"I'd rather eat something."

"Whatever you want."

Genie nodded distantly, then went to work unpacking her canvas lunchbag. I set my surfboard in the sand, dried off, and spread out my towel by the plaid tablecloth on which Genie was arranging the food. I couldn't believe what she had brought: Camembert and Gourmandise cheese, duck liver paté, homemade by her from birds shot by her father, raw carrots, celery, Greek olives, French bread, a bottle of Chablis, and a small homemade chocolate cake.

Looking at such a feast, I suddenly realized that I was starving. I hadn't eaten a thing that day. Normally on Saturday morning Marilyn and I made a big breakfast together, either waffles or pancakes. It was a tradition we had started when we first met, when she was still a resident. Back then, the only morning she had off was Saturday; Sunday she was on duty at the hospital. Out of romantic sentiment, we had continued the Saturday breakfast ritual after she finished her residency. Since the birth of Rebecca, it had become even more important; Saturday mornings were one of the few times we all knew that we would be together. Of course Rebecca loved the waffles and maple syrup; what kid didn't? But that Saturday Marilyn had left early for her seminar at the hospital. Rebecca had spent the night at my mother's—the two of them were going to Disneyland for the day. I had been left alone. My anxiety over Genie and the surfing had apparently gone directly to my stomach, and I'd found it impossible to finish even a single cup of Viennese drip coffee. But having passed my test out on the water, the smell of all that wonderful food suddenly overwhelmed me.

"Genie, this is incredible. Unbelievable. You really went all out."

"Thank you," she said quietly.

Everything was delicious; so good, in fact, that I suddenly realized I was wolfing it down like a starving man. Genie, however, was hardly eating a thing. She sat quietly, nibbling on a piece of French bread and staring out at the ocean.

"Genie, talk to me, will you? Something's wrong; I'm not blind, you know."

She smiled absently.

"Eat, Michael, there's nothing wrong."

It was hard to eat with much enthusiasm when she seemed so distant. I tried complimenting her again on the lunch, but nothing I said aroused any enthusiasm in her.

"Was it my surfing?" I finally asked.

"What are you talking about?"

"On the way to the beach, you had a good time making fun of me and my old board. Did I disappoint you out there?"

Genie stared at me for a moment before speaking. I had the feeling that she wanted to confess something.

"You were good; better than I'd have thought."

"Is that the problem?" I asked naively.

"What problem?"

"Why you're so, I don't know, withdrawn."

She examine me closely. There was a look in her eyes, a paranoia. For a moment I felt panic. Who was this girl? What was I doing there with her?

"You obviously don't like the way I'm acting," she spit out. "How would you like me to be?"

"However you are. I thought something was wrong. Driving down here you seemed so happy. Now you seem somewhere else. I thought something had happened."

Suddenly Genie smiled broadly and mechanically. It was as if she had put on a mask of animation and enthusiasm. The mask was patently fake.

"Well, I'm sorry Michael. Is this better?" she chirped. "Is this the Genie you want to spend the day with at the beach? Little Genie, the blonde surfer girl? Hello Michael. God you were terrific out there on your board. You were bitchin'; a real banzai, gonzo surfer. I'm real impressed. I mean it, Michael." She flashed me her biggest grin. "How'm I doing? Better now?"

"You want to tell me what's bugging you?"

"Bugging me?" she mocked. "Hey man, where are you coming from? What's 'bugging me'? How old are you, anyway?" Genie took a big bite from a celery stick and resumed staring out at the surf.

I set down my food.

"I guess if you don't want to talk to me, we should leave. I didn't come all the way down here to watch you stare out at the sea. I thought we were friends. I thought we could talk. Obviously you don't want that. I think we should go back."

I started to gather the food and repack it in Genie's canvas bag.

"Wait a minute, Michael." She grabbed my hand and stopped me. "If I tell you, will you promise not to get mad at me?"

"Why would I get mad at you?"

"You yelled at me this morning, didn't you?"

"Genie, I didn't yell at you. I don't yell at anybody. It isn't in my nature. I sometimes wish I could yell at people. I do remember being angry. But I wasn't yelling."

"Well, you did. I would have told you then, but I can't stand being yelled at."

"I really yelled at you?"

Genie nodded.

"That's something new for me. I mean, I knew I was angry. I actually yelled, huh?"

She nodded again.

"Well, I'm sorry. What were you going to tell me?"

"You promise you won't laugh at me?"

"I promise."

"It has to do with the robbery. The junkie."

"What about it?"

"I'm scared, Michael."

"Of what?" I asked quietly.

"You name it. Last week I was a normal person. Well, maybe not exactly normal, but at least I saw things that had a future. Since the robbery all I've been able to think about is that people are out to get me. A car backfires and I'm sure someone's shooting at me. I walk down the street and someone looks at me sideways; I'm sure he's going to rape and murder me. Suddenly the world's become a concentration camp and I'm the victim. At night I lie in bed, I can't sleep. I hear a noise. What is it, I ask myself. It's the junkie, come to get me. He's out of his coma, escaped from the hospital, and is coming to pay me back for screwing up his robbery. Look at my eyes."

I looked at her eyes.

"What do you see?"

"They look a little tired."

"You see these circles?" Genie pointed to dark hollows under her eyes. "I never used to have these. I haven't slept in two days."

"I haven't been sleep so well myself."

"Do you think about what I think about?"

"Yep," I answered.

"Then you know, don't you? You know what's the worst part? At night I think I hear the junkie climbing into my room through the window. I'm lying there in the dark and I'm suddenly aware of him in the room. I can hear him. I can smell him. Every nerve in my body tells me he's there, ready to kill me. I'm terrified. Sweating. And I'm paralyzed. I know that what I have to do is turn on the light. But I also know that if I turn on the light he'll see me and kill me. But if I don't turn on the light he'll kill me too. I mean, that's why he's come, isn't it? I'm like a little kid, afraid of the dark. Night monsters. My teddy bear won't help me with this one. I have to turn on the light. Which finally I do, expecting at any moment a huge stainless steel carving knife to plunge down into my heart. I flick the light on. And, of course, the room is empty. The junkie was only in my head. Michael, it feels like I'm going crazy. Day and night. Is this happening to you? Do you think I'm going nuts?''

''I have it at work. The phone buzzes and, boom, every time I think it's another robber. When I'm in my office and hear a loud voice in the drugstore, the first thing I do is reach for my gun. I think I've taken it out of the drawer twenty times since the robbery. I know what you're feeling. We went through something much scarier than either of us realize.''

''So you don't think I'm going crazy?''

''Absolutely not. I think there'd be something wrong with you if you didn't react like you are.''

''I was thinking maybe I needed to see a shrink; I mean if it continues.''

''I don't see how that would hurt you.''

''My parents don't see how it would help me.''

''What do they think you should do?''

''My dad sees the whole thing like it was a shootout in the Wild West. You know how he is. Now that it's over he tells me to forget about it, stop living in the past, move on to the future. He thinks I'm making too big a deal out of the whole thing. What does my mother know? She's just happy I wasn't killed. She'll do anything to avoid facing unpleasant problems. I think as far as she's concerned the whole robbery is as real as something from the Rockford Files. You're the only person I can talk to seriously about this thing. You're lucky. At least you have a wife to discuss it with.''

''What would you think if I told you I couldn't talk about it with Marilyn?''

''Are you kidding?'' Genie seemed genuinely shocked.

''She's a little like your dad on this subject. She has one view of things and that's it. She thinks I'm an idiot to even own a gun, much less shoot that junkie. She doesn't really want to hear my feelings.''

''You're telling me you're married to someone that you can't talk to?''

''About this, yes. We talk about other things.''

''Jeez, that's what I'm most afraid of. I see my mother and

father; I don't think they really have anything to say to each
other. I don't want to be trapped like that. I don't want to go
through my life bored. How can you stand it?''

"Have you ever heard the expression 'there are good times
and there are bad times'? Every relationship goes through that.
You have to give it time.''

"I don't think I could bear it. Look at me; three days of not
talking about it and I'm a wreck. If I were married to someone
and couldn't connect to them, I'd be out of the house in a flash.''

I nodded without committing myself. Genie studied me, aware
that she had hit a nerve.

"I didn't mean that as a criticism of you," she backtracked.
"I'm talking about myself.''

We were quiet for a minute. Genie began to eat, which
seemed like a good sign. In fact, as we sipped the wine, the
conversation became very easy. We were friends again, talking
simply about our lives. I envied Genie's honesty and her ability
to talk openly about her crazy relationship with Nick. She'd met
him while surfing in Malibu. Nick lived in Santa Barbara Harbor
on a small powerboat and earned a living, when he could, diving
for abalone, and when he couldn't, stealing cars for chop shops.
The way this business worked, Genie explained, was that when a
body shop needed a new front end, for example, for a Mercedes
that had been in an accident, the owner of the body shop would
call Nick. He would steal a car of the same year and model, strip
off the front end, and sell the parts to the body shop for a quarter
of the cost of new ones.

Genie was already half in love with Nick when she found out
about this side business. Her instinct was to help him reform.
She believed in him and in his talents as a fisherman. Thanks to
the sea otter with its protected status and taste for shellfish, Nick
claimed, the abalone stock was headed down the tubes. This was
the reason, Nick said, he needed the extra money from the chop
shops to see him through the difficult period until he could fish
successfully for something more plentiful. Genie accepted this
story until she discovered Nick's affinity for methedrine; on top
of everything else, Nick was a speed freak.

Genie was aware, even at her age, that she was frequently
attracted to difficult, exciting, and personally powerful young
men whom she felt she needed to nurture in some way. Nick was
an extreme example of that sort of relationship. A sometimes

violent example, Genie admitted, although the violence was never directed at her. Nick got high, picked fights, drove like a maniac, and crashed his car more than once while street racing. Although she enjoyed Nick's manic energy, Genie didn't want to die, which she felt was becoming a distinct possibility if she remained a part of his life.

As Genie talked about Nick I couldn't help wondering how I fit into Genie's scheme of things. Did she sense in me, I wondered, a hidden craziness on the order of Nick? Maybe Genie's sensitivity allowed her to feel and respond to my own private torments. From the way she described the similar person-alities of her various boyfriends, I seemed to be the latest and oldest in the long string of tortured men she had known. I tried to deny this insight with the observation that her interest in me came after her traumatic drama with the junkie. Horrible experi-ences had a way of changing a person, I told myself, hoping that Genie was drawn to me for better reasons than her usual ones.

The combination of sun, wine, food, and surfing did me in; I began to get sleepy and lay down in the sand. Genie finished her wine and did the same. We stretched out on our backs with our heads only a few inches apart, our bodies spread out, open like flower petals to the sun above. We continued talking with our eyes closed. I felt Genie's presence almost as a part of myself; her soft, low voice was so close and so intimate that it felt she was a part of me. The smell of salt, mixed with Genie's sweat and perfume, filled my nostrils. Sea gulls shrieked. Waves pounded the shore. Genie and I lay there on the empty beach chatting away like long-separated best friends. The world outside of the two of us seemed to disappear and I felt safe, cocooned, free from pain. I relished the sound of Genie's voice, inhaled and savored her odors; we became disembodied souls connected in the most perfect of worlds. We were languid. We were serious. We were funny. We were lovers. We were everything possible between a man and a woman, all without moving, touching, or seeing one another. A great peace came over me, as if once again I were enveloped in my childhood cradle, protected there on the sand, rocked out of danger by the bosom of the sea.

Then a different but familiar smell—at first I thought it was burning leaves—floated by my nostrils. By the time I realized that the fragrance was marijuana, I felt the cigarette slip between my lips. I opened my eyes to see Genie holding the joint to my mouth. At that moment her action seemed like the most natural gesture I could imagine. I inhaled the grass and savored the flavor. I had never been a druggie. Like everyone in college I had smoked a little marijuana, but I was never crazy about it. It left me feeling inarticulate and stupid. Other people seemed to enjoy this as a high, but I hated the sense of myself as a dumbbell. Once I began pharmacology college I avoided anything that could possibly taint my professional career. Even parking tickets worried me. By the time I had passed my boards and was licensed, I had seen enough doctors and druggists with substance abuse problems to have no doubt that even the slightest flirtation with controlled pharmaceuticals led nowhere but to self-destruction. Marijuana also had little aesthetic appeal for me; I hated smoking. I hated the feeling of heat in my lungs. And I disliked the look of the marijuana itself. As a pharmacist I was into the beauty of my product.

From the earliest I could remember, I had loved the appearance of capsules, tablets, and all the related paraphernalia—the bottles, jars, measuring devices, labels, antiseptic containers, and all the rest. I could sit for hours staring at my shelves. It seemed to me that modern art had nothing on capsules. Clear colors molded into perfect shapes. Solid gelatin capsules had the same purity of color, form, and function as did surfboards. Hold a solid gelatin capsule up to the light, and a marvellous candy apple red shimmered back with a depth and brilliance unrivaled by the most fabulous of painters. People around the world were blind as far as I could tell; every day they swallowed great works of art in capsule form without ever noticing. They were eating Rembrandts. Chewing on Gauguin's. Chugging down a Van Gogh and a couple of Renoir's. For chasers a Mondrian. Yet they never knew it. Definitely an art exhibit of pharmaceuticals was in order.

After college, it was not difficult to avoid grass; I had a business to build and was working my tail off to pay back my loans. Marilyn made avoiding marijuana even easier because she hated drugs. She believed medication necessary for sickness but condemned recreational drug use as part of the downfall of modern civilization, responsible for so much of the current violence in society. Marilyn was such a fanatic in this area that I was convinced Rebecca would someday pick up on her rigidity, rebel, and consume every controlled substance she could steal from my shelves.

However, despite all my fears and high principles, at that

moment I was lying in the sand next to an incredible knockout of a seventeen-year-old girl, smoking grass, getting high on a United States Marine Corps base and fantasizing about running my tongue over every square inch of Genie's body. I mean, it was ironic; there I was worrying about my daughter's behavior ten years down the road when, at that exact instant, I was contemplating far worse.

Genie again slipped the tightly rolled joint into my mouth. My response was to suck it in deeply, hold it as long as I could, then let it out. The world narrowed to just myself, the joint, and the beautiful girl who was getting me stoned. Genie's presence shot like a warm shadow over my face, down my chest, over my stomach, then finally curled around my balls to harden my cock. I opened my eyes to find Genie sitting over me, watching my face. I smiled. She nodded, then leaned over and kissed me. Her full lips pressed against mine, softly, with conviction. It was a kiss of exploration, of quiet passion. We held the kiss, then she withdrew, smiled like the Sphinx, lay back next to me, closed her eyes, and fell asleep.

Did she want me to continue kissing her? What was she telling me? My wish was to take her in my arms and devour her. But I didn't want to frighten her. I didn't think she was quite ready for me yet, and the last thing I wanted was for her to interpret my need for her as merely a quick anonymous hump on a deserted beach. No, I wanted her to want me just as I wanted her. I had to be slow and gentle. Perhaps I was just afraid; it may have been as simple as that. I lay back in the sand and took Genie's hand in mine. My impulse was to place her hand on my crotch, which at that moment resembled one of those nylon, space age, rip-stop tents advertised in the back-packing magazines—my swimming trunks stretched tight and held taut by my very solid tent pole, whose only ambition in life was to be petted, stroked, sucked, and enveloped by the beautiful young girl lying next to me. I closed my eyes. I was in heaven.

That perfect day at the beach was everything I had ever dreamed of as a teenage surfer. Why had it taken so long for this to happen? Where was it going to lead? My life was in her hand, so soft and reassuring. It was a moment more vivid than anything I'd felt in years; a moment to remember for the rest of my life.

15

I must have fallen asleep, because when I opened my eyes the sun was low in the sky. Something was wrong. I realized that Genie was furiously shaking my arm.

"Michael," she yelled, "wake up. We've got to get out of here—and fast!" She pointed to the sea.

The Pacific Ocean was covered with what seemed like hundreds of small landing craft moving from large stationary naval warships offshore. They were all headed our way. It looked like D Day at Normandy. No doubt about it, we were right in the middle of a Marine Corps amphibious assault. At any moment the palisade above the beach would be swarming with soldiers. It was war games, with Genie and me in no man's land. Already I could envision the headline in the morning *Times:* "Pharmacist and Teen-age Lover Arrested on Military Property." I could feel my glands surge to full throttle, cranking out adrenalin at a rate Old Faithful would have envied.

Genie and I grabbed our boards and clothes, left the food, and charged up the bluff faster than I would have believed possible. We were scared shitless. Although it seemed like hours, it took us only moments to get to the top, where I was amazed to see that no jeeps or soldiers were waiting to escort us to jail. Down at the beach, rubber rafts full of Marines in combat gear were entering the surfline. Genie and I ran like maniacs across the top of the palisade to the chain link fence, where we simply threw everything over the fence onto the roadside. In our panic, damage to possessions seemed immaterial. Genie slid under the fence, and I followed right behind her. We both stood up. I couldn't believe we had escaped. We were once again on public property, on the shoulder of the highway. Free. No jail. No public exposure. No grand humiliation. Genie and I looked at each other and began to laugh. What had been danger became comedy—an enormous relief. Then I gave her a big bear hug and we both cried out in pain. My chest, neck, and shoulders ached from sunburn. I looked down at myself and saw skin the color of cooked lobster. Even Genie, who already had some tan, was mildly burned. We had fallen asleep in the sun like two stupid kids. I'd brought ointment for this possibility, medication which I'd left in the back of her Mustang. Solarcaine to kill the pain, then a cortisone cream to help the skin heal.

I turned in the direction of Genie's Mustang. The car was gone. At first I thought I was simply disoriented and facing the wrong direction. But I wasn't. The car was definitely not there. I turned and looked in all directions. The road was flat for at least a mile both north and south. No Mustang was visible anywhere. Obviously someone had stolen it.

I looked at my watch. It was five o'clock. I should have been home already. Even if the car had been there, we were two hours from Los Angeles. I would be very late. Marilyn would find out about Genie and me. Nothing had happened, I told myself. I was innocent. Yet I knew I was screwed.

As embarrassing as it is to admit, I went crazy and began yelling at Genie that it was all her fault for putting us in that situation. At first she tried to reason with me, pointing out that it was perfectly legal to park where we had and that having the car stolen was not something she had arranged. She tried to convince me that she was the one who should be upset, not me; after all, it was her car that was gone, not mine. But I remained enraged. How would I get home? I was supposed to go out to dinner that night with Marilyn, in fact to a dinner party at Genie's parents' house. How could I explain myself? We were going to have to call the police, fill out a report about the stolen car, and there would be my name linked with Genie's on another official public document. What would I tell Ed? Or, more specifically, how would I live through the experience of telling Ed, what with his temper and his pistol? He wouldn't have any illusions about what I was doing at the beach with his daughter.

Thinking fast, I came up with a plan. The stolen car was simply a question of money. Dollars on wheels. What were a few thousand bucks compared to my life, my marriage, and my reputation? I proposed to Genie that we hitch a ride to the nearest town, rent a car, then drive back to Los Angeles, where she could fill out a form with the local police, notifying them of her stolen car and leaving me totally out of the picture. Her insurance would then buy her a new car; and for all her trouble, I promised to kick in a thousand dollars on the side. Genie could see that I was a man in panic, a crazy person. She suggested that I was being hysterical, then simply chose to avoid further argument and agreed to my plan.

Without a word she walked to the side of the road, stuck out her thumb, and stopped the first vehicle headed our way. It was a pickup truck driven by an aging hippy who introduced himself as Mel. Genie and I tossed our surfboards and bags into the bed of the truck and got into the cab. Mel accelerated south. I remember looking at him, thinking that he probably wanted to ask how the surfing had been on the Marine base. But I was so tense and so angry that my expression stopped any conversation before it could begin. I wanted to kill, and somehow Mel knew it.

We hadn't driven more than two or three miles when Genie suddenly shrieked and pointed to the other side of the highway. There, facing north, was her Mustang.

"Stop the truck!" I yelled at Mel.

The man was no fool—he could spot a madman. Mel slammed on the brakes and pulled off the road. Maybe he thought we were going to rob him. Certainly he was sorry he'd ever picked us up. When the truck stopped, Genie and I jumped out and grabbed our possessions from the bed. One second later Mel popped his clutch and took off like a drag racer. There was one hippy who'd be more careful about picking up hitchhikers.

Genie and I ran across the road to the Mustang. No one was inside. There were no dents, no tow marks, no broken windows, and no exterior damage. Even the door was locked. The interior was another story. In the dashboard where the radio and cassette player had been, there was now a big rectangular hole with wires hanging out. Genie unlocked the door. I strapped the surfboards to the roof and we got in the car. She put the key in the ignition, and miracle of miracles, started the engine. We were in business. Late but safe.

I tossed our bags into the back seat. Genie threw the car into gear and took off north. I would have some explaining to do, but at least my life would still be intact.

16

The drive back to Los Angeles was not what I would call the greatest experience of my life. Genie was silent the entire trip. Nothing seemed to cut any ice with her, not my speculations on the stereo theft, nor my effusive thanks for the terrific lunch she had concocted, nor even my apologies for my rage by the highway. I was sure I had blown it with Genie. She had to be very disappointed in me for losing my cool, as she might have put it, and behaving like a child. I had acted very badly, there was no doubt about that. As Genie drove I sat quietly in the passenger seat, mentally abusing myself. The worst part about the stereo theft was that I couldn't even turn on the radio to blot out the terrible silence between us. The hundred mile drive home seemed like a continental crossing.

For my sunburn I used Solarcaine. But what could I spray that would dampen the terrible pain I felt in my soul? Those few hours I had spent on the beach with Genie after surfing were some of the most enjoyable I had ever experienced. Now, thanks to my behavior by the roadside, I had guaranteed that they would never be repeated. I was a jerk of the highest order. Genie was right to remain silent. She had taken a risk, just as I had. Her father, if he had known she spent the day with me, would have killed her too. Yet when the crunch came by the highway, Genie behaved like a competent adult while I regressed to the state of a slobbering infant. Her silence was the appropriate response to my embarrassing behavior. She didn't tell me off. She didn't humiliate me further. She simply said nothing. What was there to say? It was over.

Genie drove her Mustang into the parking lot of the Federal Building at precisely ten minutes to seven. We were very late, but at least I had done something to cover my tracks; when we stopped in Anaheim for gas, I had phoned Marilyn and told her not to expect me until seven. Instead of being enraged, she took the delay calmly and simply told me to get home as soon as possible. Something was going on.

Genie parked and I quickly transferred my dinged-up surf-

board from her car to mine. Then I grabbed my bag from the
back seat of the Mustang, tossed it into the Olds, and faced
Genie through the open driver's window. She looked at me with
the same quiet, opaque expression she had maintained all the
way up the coast. This was not how I wanted the day to end.

I thanked her again for the wonderful day and everything that
she had done to make it so special. I apologized again for my
behavior by the highway. I tried to convince her that the panic
part of me wasn't the real me, as she knew from the drugstore. I
told her I hoped she'd give me another chance. As she put her
Mustang in reverse and prepared to back out of the lot, she
smiled and left me with the most unexpected farewell.

"Hey, Michael. The part of you that went nuts over the car is
the part of you I like best of all. You're human. And you let me
see it. You should do it more often; it'd be good for you."

And with that, she drove out of the lot. What was that
supposed to mean? Did she like me? If she did, why had she
been so quiet all the way home? Did it indicate she wanted to see
me again? I got in my Oldsmobile, started the engine, and
headed for Brentwood, more than a little confused.

17

Eight minutes later I was home. I reviewed my story for the
tenth time, and all the details of my supposed car trouble seemed
ironclad. But as I entered my front door, I couldn't help
remembering some of my father's imaginative reasons for being
late. Ironclad stories only seem ironclad until they are told to a
suspicious wife. No matter how elaborate, my father's stories
had always seemed transparent lies. Oh God, I thought, I was
doing to Rebecca what my asshole of a father had done to me.
What I feared the most, I had become.

The battle for which I had prepared myself never occurred.
Marilyn seemed simply happy to see me and urged me to shower
and dress as quickly as possible. She had already changed, was
ready to go, and sat with Rebecca at the living room coffee table
assembling a jigsaw puzzle. Strangely enough, Marilyn was
bubbling with energy and seemed happy and content for the first

time in months. Rebecca wanted to know how I had enjoyed the surfing. I told her it was fun. Then she scared the piss out of me by saying, "Mommy and I saw you on TV." I panicked. My first thought was that the local news station had covered the war games at Camp Pendleton and had filmed Genie and me in the midst of all the action; a wonderful human interest angle. Genie and I were fucked, after all. But before I could reveal myself, Marilyn explained that she and Rebecca had watched the six o'clock news, which featured a story on surfing. Marilyn had explained to our daughter that surfing was what her father was doing that day. I headed upstairs for a shower, home free.

The reason for Marilyn's mood became clear as we drove to the Cotler's. Over lunch at County Hospital, Marilyn had pitched the concept for the health resort to a couple of surgeons who were old classmates of hers. Not only did they love the idea, they immediately committed themsleves to half of the million-dollar investment Marilyn was seeking. Furthermore, they assured Marilyn that they knew plenty of other doctors who'd stand in line to finance the other $500,000. The surgeons were convinced her idea was a gold mine, and encouraged her to get to work immediately finding a site for the spa.

I pointed out to Marilyn that enthusiastic discussions were very different from money-in-hand. But she claimed that she had known both men for almost ten years and that their word was as good as gold. It wasn't worth arguing about, I decided. If the money actually came through, we could decide later what it meant for the two of us. I had to laugh at the idea of surgeons owning a health resort. If Marilyn couldn't make people look and feel better with carrot juice, jogging, steam baths, and massages, the surgeons could always take corrective action with the knife. We were on the threshold of a new age. The future was now: the sick could be healed, the ugly made beautiful, and the beautiful turned into gods. All they needed was the time, the money, and Marilyn's resort. She even had a name for her spa: The Good Life Clinic. I wanted to vomit.

Marilyn was so excited by her success that I don't think she noticed my lack of response. Why couldn't she see that there was no place for me at the health clinic? What I wanted was my marriage back. I wanted passion. I wanted love. I wanted friendship, companionship, respect, affection, and loyalty. I wanted to feel joined to Marilyn as man to woman, not as limited partner to general partner. What had gone on at the beach between Genie and me that day reminded me of what had once been there between Marilyn and me. I wanted Marilyn to see me, to recognize me, to care about my feelings, my needs, my deeper urges and aspirations.

Marilyn and I walked up the steps to the Cotler's front door. In the driveway was Genie's Mustang, looking just as it had on the drive home. The surfboard was still attached to the roof. Genie was home. I wondered if she would be eating dinner with us. Could I handle that without giving myself away? I saw Marilyn glance at the surfboard, but she obviously hadn't made the connection. I had such an impulse to tell her all about my day, to shake her with the truth, to do anything that might wake her up to the fact that our marriage was in terrible trouble.

But at that instant the front door opened and Anne Cotler, as formal, pleasant, and collected as ever, ushered us inside.

18

The dinner was not the simple little get-together to which Ed had invited us, supposedly to meet a few of his old friends. Some old friends. Anne directed us to the living room, where Ed greeted me with a wide grin and a big pat on the back, thrust a drink into my hand, kissed Marilyn, then led us around the room and introduced us to the six other guests. First on the list was the well-known judge Howard Shumway and his regal, somewhat younger wife Anita. Shumway was a big man in both the Republican party and the National Rifle Association. He congratulated me in the most formal way on my "heroic" performance in the drugstore while, at the same time, I had the distinct feeling he was also checking me out for some inscrutable purpose. Marilyn held her tongue; the man's fame and reputation were facts she couldn't ignore.

After a mysterious wink and a nod exchanged with the judge, Ed led us to the next couple, Republican State Senator Hart Walker and his wife Jane. The man was speaker of the house, a tremendously political position in California. I felt from him the same thing I had sensed from the judge; I was being scrutinized for some purpose I didn't understand. The senator was effusive in his praise of how I had handled myself with the media after the shooting. "You're a natural," he said.

The last couple we met was the financier and land magnate Edgar Wilkens and his wife Angelica, a former movie star. She was in her fifties, used too much makeup, and appeared a little the worse for wear. Wilkens was the same short, balding, Germanic hunk of Black Forest ham I'd seen in television interviews. The self-made California powerhouse. A kingmaker. Ed had asked me to dinner with three Republican superheavyweights. Why?

As we sat down to dinner, Ed raised his wine glass in my direction and proposed a toast.

"To my old and dear friend, Michael Marcus, a man of character, maturity, and courage; a true modern hero. A man I know all of you have admired. A man whose personal and political future we all believe to be so promising. To your first victory over the ACLU. And to your many future victories in the political arena."

Everyone at the table, including the shocked and suddenly worried Marilyn, clinked their wine glasses enthusiastically against mine. I was the man of the moment and the kingmakers wanted to make use of me. My action in the pharmacy had, in their minds, propelled me from an anonymous, back-alley spear carrier to a leading man in the play of local political life. As the food was served, the Republicans began their pitch in earnest.

Wilkens believed the court case could be a great springboard for a career in Republican politics. If I played my cards right, he said, Robert Allen and the ACLU could do for me what Joe McCarthy and the House Un-American Activities Committee had done for Richard Nixon. I couldn't very well tell him I didn't want to end up like Richard Nixon. Wilkens, the judge, and the senator made it clear that they were willing to back me in a shot at the state assembly seat from my district. The election was one year away and they needed a new face to go up against the liberal Democratic incumbent. I was already a hero in the district, they believed. All I had to do was to follow through, stay visible, and I'd be a shoo-in. With their assistance, of course.

Now, this would have been a heady moment in any man's life. Here we had the leaders of the local Republican community offering to draft me into a statewide position of leadership. I'd be a man of real power and influence, deciding the fate of men, influencing the times. Who knew where it might lead, they prodded me, perhaps to a national political role in the House of Representatives or even the Senate. They were confident that I was the right kind of man, made of the right kind of material, destined for the right kind of success. There were no lefties in the room, that was clear. They hinted that if the breaks came my way I might even be the first Jewish president. Times were changing, they claimed. It didn't take a genius to know that it wasn't Bob Dylan who had told them that.

I wanted to believe their sales pitch. I had worked my way from nothing into my present success with the pharmacy. Who knew what was possible? Why limit myself; why not see how far I could go? Dream. If a peanut farmer and then an actor could become president, why not a druggist? An accident had happened at the pharmacy that had changed my life. I had become a celebrity. Now these men wanted to help me use my visibility to extend my success. Obviously they wanted something from me in return. It wasn't exactly as if the they would own me, but it certainly would be to their advantage to have handpicked the man in power. I listened carefully to their proposal. After all, I was hardly in a position to offend them; I was the one under indictment, the one with the legal battle. I needed all the support I could get.

I sat quietly nodding, sipping the best Montrachet I'd ever tasted and nibbling at the delicious roast duck with orange sauce. For more than an hour the power brokers assaulted me with their schemes. I ate and drank as if I had no limits. Everything went to my head, and by dessert I was nearly floating out of my chair. That night I was all things and could do anything. Even my sunburn didn't hurt. No one had ever before gone to such lengths to flatter me.

If I took the Republicans up on their offer, Marilyn's plans for our life would be totally obliterated. I heard her trying to explain to the judge and Wilkens, who sat on either side of her, the plan for her health clinic. Their disinterest confused Marilyn. She didn't understand that these men were not Republicans by chance. They held firmly and sincerely to the conservative ideology that the first priority in life was to make oneself wealthy, thereby benefiting the world with the byproducts of their entrepreneurial accomplishments. They had succeeded, they were rich, they could freely choose any lifestyle they wanted. In terms of their bodies, they believed in the idea of buying health. This was opposed to Marilyn's idea of sweating one's way to health.

These men had already sweated as much as they were going to sweat and that was long ago, over money; certainly they didn't want to sweat over anything as mundane as exercise. No, these men wanted to enjoy their wealth; they never wanted to sweat, ever again. They liked rich food and comfortable couches. Nautilus machines and jogging suits were for the loonies. As far as these Republicans were concerned, sweating one's way to health was for the lower classes, the workers of the world. The chief executive officers, the owners of the world, were men who funded medical research projects, hospitals, universities, and even governments. If a part of their own body, like the heart, went bad they wanted to be able to buy a brand new one. The use of exercise to stay in shape was as ridiculous a concept as recapping the worn tires on their limousines. Marilyn couldn't fathom this, and therefore she couldn't understand why she wasn't getting through to the men. That fact and the direction in which these powerful guests were trying to steer her life, punctured any pleasure she might have taken in suddenly being asked to join establishment's inner circle.

I, on the other hand, was having a wonderful time. The food and compliments kept rolling in and the Montrachet kept flowing. If Marilyn had been able to recover her sense of humor, she might have had as satisfying and enjoyable an evening as I was having—up to the moment the doorbell rang at ten o'clock.

Ed left the table and opened the front door, which I could just see from my end of the dining room. The young man standing in the doorway was obviously Genie's date. He was about eighteen years old, blonde, with a short, almost punk haircut, dark sport coat, black slacks, white socks, black pointed shoes, and wraparound sunglasses—the living image of the drug-crazed hipster. It was ten o'clock on a Saturday night and he was just now picking Genie up. Where could they be going at ten o'clock? Moreover, how could Ed allow his seventeen-year-old daughter to go out with something who looked like that? What time did this creature expect to bring Genie home? What would they be doing? Ed led the date out of sight into the den, then quickly returned to the dinner table.

My first impulse was to condemn Ed for allowing his daughter to go out with such trash. But I was hardly in a position to say anything. I realized that I had suddenly lost all interest in the proposals regarding my political future. The Republicans were still selling, but I had quit buying. I felt only one desire, which

was to grab Genie and convince her to dump the scumbag in the
den and spend the rest of the evening with me.

As Judge Shumway thundered on about the need for men of
vision and courage in the political arena, I saw Genie descend
the staircase and pass by the dining room. Before she disappeared
into the den she hesitated for a moment and fluffed up her freshly
washed mane of blonde hair. She was making herself look
attractive for the jerkball in the next room. I couldn't stand it. I
wanted her to be preening just for me. But she never even looked
into the dining room. I felt that to be a deliberate challenge, a
provocation. It would have been so easy for her to come in and
say hello. It was her house, after all. But she never acknowl-
edged my presence. She simply turned away from the dining
room and let me watch her lovely rear end (covered by turquoise
linen trousers) vanish into the den.

If felt myself to be a fool. There I was, after that incredible
afternoon at the beach, sitting listening to Judge Shumway when
I could have been out somewhere in the night, alone with Genie,
enjoying passion. As the judge rambled on all I could think
about was Genie in the den with that sleazeface. Finally I
excused myself. As I left the table I felt many eyes watching me.
I pretended to head straight for the bathroom; but after crossing
the foyer, out of sight of the dining room, I went straight for the
den.

Genie's back was to me and she was laughing. The young
idiot was sitting on the couch, playing stubborn while Genie
tried to pull him to his feet; she obviously wanted to go. He was
enjoying stalling her. Probably he liked all the physical attention
he was getting as she tried to yank him up. When he saw me, he
suddenly became solemn, let go of her hand, and stood—a born
hypocrite. Genie swung around. I think she thought I would be
her father.

" 'Scuze me,'' I muttered, ''I'm looking for the powder room.''

Genie nodded knowingly.

"Mr. Marcus,'' she teased, ''you mean to say you've been
coming to this house for what, five or six years, and you don't
know where we hide the bathroom?''

"I thought it was through here.'' I gestured lamely to the far
side of the den.

"Try that way.'' Genie gestured back across the foyer beyond
the dining room. ''Oh, I'm sorry. Terry, this is Mr. Marcus. He's

the man from the pharmacy who saved my life.'' Then she
addressed herself to me. ''Terry writes the jazz column for the
school paper.''

Terry and I shook hands.

''I could have sworn the bathroom was through that door,'' I
stalled, again pointing across the den.

''You know, you may be right.'' Genie grinned at me
mysteriously. ''Let's try it.''

Genie led me through the den to the door at which I'd pointed.
She twisted the brass handle and I stared into a small paneled
closet. Every shelf and wall was covered with plaques, metal
trophies, diplomas, and citations from every charity group, legal
foundation, and politician imaginable. All bore the name Edward
Cotler. Genie grabbed an oversized silver mug and handed it to
me.

''This is big enough to pee in, don't you think?'' Genie
offered, loud enough for Terry to hear.

''Thank you very much,'' I said, handing her back the mug,
which was engraved ''Winner, Mixed Doubles, L.A. Country
Club, 1983 Club Championship.''

Genie put the mug back where it belonged, closed the door,
and turned to me.

''Mr. Marcus, you look so tan—did you go to the beach
today?''

''As a matter of fact I did; you're very observant. You look
like you were in the sun yourself. Don't tell me, I bet you went
surfing. I remember your father telling me what a good surfer
you are.'

''You think he knows?''

''He told me.'

''Ask him if he's ever seen me surf.''

We stared at each other for a moment. I wasn't sure where to
take the conversation.

''It's funny we both went to the beach today. I saw people
surfing. Maybe it was even you. Where did you go?''

''Camp Pendleton.''

''Camp Pendleton? That's a Marine Corps base. You can't surf
on military property.''

''Oh you can't, can't you? How would you know?''

''You can?''

"They have to sneak in," Terry volunteered. "I think it's crazy."

"Sounds crazy to me."

"Well I had a pretty good day. A perfect day in fact. Except for my stereo getting stolen."

"You should go back there; perfect days are hard to come by," I suggested, testing her.

"I thought about it. But repeating yourself never works, does it, Terry?"

The slimebag shook his head, agreeing with her.

"You have to move on to new things. Like Nietzsche said, people who repeat the past are condemned to live in the past," Genie misquoted.

"Nietzsche never said that, I said that. It just sounds like Nietzsche," Terry corrected her.

"You're telling me," I teased her, "that Nietzsche wouldn't surf twice at Camp Pendleton, even if he had a great time?"

"Hey man," Terry corrected me, "Mr. Nietzsche wouldn't have surfed once; the Germans, you know, they weren't into surfing."

"Well, I think Nietzsche would have been an idiot if he'd had a good time doing something and not tried it again; maybe it would be even better. Good things aren't necessarily worse the second time, are they?"

Before Genie could answer, Terry interrupted with the suggestion that they had to leave immediately if they intended to make the last jazz set at the Lighthouse.

"Across the hall, Mr. Marcus. Good night." Genie pointed to the powder room.

"Thank you, Genie. 'Night." I hadn't gotten an answer, and realized that my despair must have been evident in my expression.

"Nice meeting you, Mr. Marcus." Terry led Genie toward the front door.

As Terry rotated the brass doorknob, Genie turned and gave me a secret wink. My heart fluttered. The front door opened. They were gone.

I went across the hall into the bathroom and stared at myself in the mirror. I was drunk, sunburned, and very tired. I wanted to be with Genie. I also wanted to be with Marilyn. Nothing made sense and now I had to go back into that dining room and listen to more political bullshit from the power brokers. The men at the table wanted to run the world, as, in a very different sense, did Marilyn. I just wanted harmony. I dreaded sitting back down at the table. And I dreaded the speech I would get from Marilyn on the way home. The fact that I was even listening to what the Republicans were offering would anger her.

In the mirror, I saw one lonely and confused druggist. The problems confronting me didn't remotely resemble those discussed in pharmaceutical college. I was on my own. The face in the silvered glass reminded me of someone familiar, a face I couldn't place at first. Suddenly I recognized the face: it was my father—I had become him. My life had turned into his. What horror. I wanted to smash the mirror and obliterate the face. Instead I controlled myself and went back to the dining room, resumed my seat at the table and drank glass after glass of cool Montrachet. The power brokers kept selling. I tried to seem interested. But no matter how much I drank, the face of my father remained in my mind.

19

Marilyn insisted on driving home. She made it very clear that while the other people at Ed's might not have been aware of how much I'd had to drink, she had certainly noticed and was not impressed. To Marilyn, a glass or two of wine with dinner was okay. But to put down a bottle or more, as I had done—she considered that suicidal. Nothing was worse for the body than alcohol. She was fond of repeating that it was the single most difficult chemical for the liver to metabolize. All the way home, she criticized me for jeopardizing my health and for endangering our lives through my seeming interest in the power brokers' schemes.

As she drove, Marilyn methodically listed all the shortcomings of politics and was even more thorough than she had been about my surfing. If awards were given for knowledge about the specific dangers of common everyday activities, my wife would undoubtedly be the world champion. I once teased her that the only reason they didn't have a TV game show called ''Disaster'' was that someone, somewhere, knew she would always win. She would be the undefeated champion of gloom. "Roller skates," I imagined the unctuous host announcing. Bang, Marilyn would hit the buzzer faster than Shirley Muldowny accelerating her dragster off the starting line. While the other contestants were still thinking, Marilyn would be reciting all the hazards of roller skating. On the subject of my being in politics, she pulled out all stops, starting with "A" for assassination, and moving on down through phony life-style, lies, hypocrisy, humiliations, lack of personal privacy, corruption, lousy pay, on and on until she finally called it quits in our driveway with the letter "Z" for Zionism—as a Jewish politician she was sure some Arab fanatic would kidnap or kill me.

At home, Marilyn seemed to enjoy the fact that I had trouble fitting my key into the front door lock. It reinforced her point about how much wine I'd consumed. As she reached to help me, I made a supreme effort and opened the door unassisted. We entered the living room and she resumed her harangue about political life.

"Marilyn," I interrupted her, "do you want to know what I think about going into politics, or do you want to just keep telling me what you think?"

Before she could answer, Debby, the fat sixteen-year-old baby-sitter entered the living room from, where else, the kitchen. Cookie crumbs clung to Debby's upper lip. It was always a wonder we had any food left in the house after Debby spent a few hours taking care of Rebecca. "The doughnut eater" was how I referred to Debby, whose name I had trouble remembering. While Marilyn settled the tab with Debby, I went upstairs to check on Rebecca, who was sound asleep. She looked as calm and connected to life as I had felt lying next to Genie on the beach. I wished I could sleep with as much peace and serenity as my daughter. As I kissed Rebecca good night, I heard the front door slam and the doughnut eater's car start. Our larder was now stable until Debby's next visit.

Marilyn entered Rebecca's room, kissed her good night, rearranged her blankets, and led me out. I headed straight for the bathroom, compelled by a gigantic urge to pee. Marilyn followed and talked to me over the stream of highly diluted vintage Montrachet.

"So," she demanded, "tell me what you think about going into politics."

Politics I knew wasn't the issue; our whole relationship was at stake.

"Marilyn, we need to have a serious talk; are you up to that?"

"Are you up to it?" she said, mocking my boozing.

I ignored her sarcasm.

"You want to change all of our lives with this health clinic, right?"

She nodded.

"This is your wish and ambition, right?"

"What are you getting at?"

For someone with as much alcohol under my belt as I had, I thought I was doing pretty well. Although my body was a little wobbly, my head seemed surprisingly clear. I felt inspired and had an idea about how to get through to her.

"Marilyn, suppose I had a wish or ambition that was different from yours. Suppose, for example, that it involved my entering political life. Just suppose. It would mean that my aspirations would be in conflict with yours, in a major way. If I did what I wanted, you couldn't do what you wanted. And vice versa. I could hardly run a juice bar in Escondido and campaign for state assemblyman at the same time, right?"

Marilyn stared impassively, waiting to see where I was headed. I was impressed; she actually was listening. There was hope after all.

"We'd be in conflict," I continued. "A major conflict. How would we resolve such a conflict? I mean, this isn't the kind of thing you can solve just by flipping a coin."

"You're telling me you're serious about going into politics?" She spoke without emotion.

"I'm not saying whether I am or I'm not; I'm trying to discuss something between us. Us, as a couple, as husband and wife, as parents, as friends, as lovers, with a life and a future together. We have a problem to solve together. A decision to work out together. I love you, Marilyn, and I want to know how we get through such a conflict."

"If you think about what you just said," she told me after considering my statement carefully, "you'll realize you already answered your own question."

"I don't get you."

"Basically you're questioning what's in the long-term interest of the family, meaning you, Rebecca, and me. The answer is obvious.''

"Maybe to you; but I don't see it.''

Marilyn let out a deep sigh; this meant a lecture was on the way.

"Michael,'' she spoke patiently and affectionately, "ask yourself what you want out of life. What's important? Is it money? Health? Love? Power? Obviously you want to be a success, but what kind of success? I know you'll answer 'yes' to family, but what use is a family if it's a hollow symbol, a fake touchstone, like we both had growing up? We've been over this a million times. I thought we wanted a real life, with friends, with a community, with children, traditional values, something optimistic and healthy, not cynical and corrupt like power politics. Do you want to raise Rebecca in smoke-filled back rooms with men like Edgar Wilkens and Judge Shumway? That isn't the life we wanted.''

"What if I changed my mind? You changed your mind about your practice. Now you want to run this health clinic.''

"Michael, there are changes, and then there are changes that make sense. The health clinic is an evolution of my practice. Preventive medicine. Something positive. What is politics? It's regression. Life in the sewer. How is that an extension of anything you've been living for? I sat across from that judge and I really listened to what he had to say to you. Such B.S. I was disappointed in you. I heard the man I love, to whom I am married, with whom I have a child, seriously considering the ideas of corrupt, ugly, greedy power mongers. You used to have such ambitions. Is this the man I married, I asked myself. Who are you, Michael? You know what I thought tonight?''

"What?''

"You're going to get angry with me.''

"What do you think?''

"I don't know why, but something's happened to you. I don't know what to call it. Exhaustion. Tension. Stress. An outsider might even label it a nervous breakdown. I don't know if this kind of thing is inherited, but your mother was right—you are behaving like your father. Michael, for me, for Rebecca, will you go and talk to a shrink? Please, Michael; I love you and don't want you ending up like your father.''

"My father?''

"Yes, your father."

"Marilyn, god damn it, you and my mother. Leave my father out of this. My father was a certified schizophrenic; is that what you think I am?" I was furious.

Marilyn just stared at me. This pushed me over the edge and I began to yell.

"You want to be nasty? You want to play dirty? That's your privilege. Just don't be a bitch. Here I am trying to talk to you about a problem we face as a couple and what do you do? You turn the whole conversation into a farce. Only a cunt would dismiss everything I said by accusing me of being crazy. Thanks a whole lot. You're terrific."

She answered me very quietly in that tone a rational mother adopts when scolding a naughty child.

"Michael, you called me a cunt. You know what I think of that word. I want you to apologize."

"How about apologizing for telling me I was going crazy like my father? I mean, what the hell is that about? Don't you see that once you decided I'm crazy, then nothing I say makes any difference?" I glared at her.

"I want an apology Michael."

"Well, you're not going to get one until you give me one."

We both stood our ground in the bathroom.

"Marilyn," I tried being rational, "this is exactly what I was talking about. Here we have a conflict. Our views of a situation are in opposition. How do we resolve this problem?"

"Apologize."

"No. You know you behaved badly first. I simply was describing to you in one word how you were treating me."

"You won't apologize?"

"No."

"Okay, fine. Have it your way."

Marilyn charged out of the bathroom and slammed the door. The woman I loved had just dismissed me as a lunatic.

I brushed my teeth, then ventured out into the bedroom. It was empty.

"Marilyn," I called.

There was no answer. I walked into the hall.

"Marilyn," I hissed quietly to avoid disturbing Rebecca.

Again no answer. I looked into my daughter's room, where I saw Marilyn curled up on the single bed across from Rebecca.

My wife was going to spend the night away from me, in another bed—the classic, infantile punishment.

I kneeled down and whispered into her ear.

"Sweetheart, this is ridiculous," I said in my most patient tone of voice. "Will you come into the bedroom, please?"

Marilyn pretended to be asleep.

"Marilyn, I know you're not sleeping; you haven't been in here more than two minutes."

"Shhh," she whispered almost inaudibly, "you'll wake Rebecca."

"Marilyn, I need to talk to you."

"In the morning, Michael, I'm too tired now."

"Please, Marilyn," I pleaded, "it's important."

"Good night, Michael."

She rolled over, turning her back to me, which made me even angrier.

"Is this what you want, separate bedrooms? Is that how you think we're going to solve the problem?"

"Ma, ma," Rebecca awakened and whimpered.

"There, you see," Marilyn chided me, "you woke her up."

"Marilyn, dear, you know, a person doesn't have to be gynecologist to recognize a cunt. Enjoy your separate bedroom."

I stormed out of Rebecca's room, returned to the master bedroom, slammed the door, and crawled under the covers. I was alone. My brain was on fire. The room seemed to be rocking with rage. I glared at the pink bedcovers, the drapes, the big pillows, everything that Marilyn had brought to the bedroom to make it her home; my first impulse was to tear it all up and throw the phony, homey decorations right out the window. Some home. Some marriage. As far as I could tell Marilyn had just removed herself from the relationship and was obliterating me from her life.

I couldn't sleep. The clock told me it was two-oh-four in the morning. I was alone, like a prisoner in solitary confinement. I lay there in bed surrounded by Marilyn's possessions, by so many memories of her, by so many things that reminded me of my love for her; I had everything in the bedroom except the most essential ingredient, which was Marilyn herself. My anger and loneliness were suffocating me. I got up, dressed, went downstairs, and walked outside. The June air was still warm. Night-blooming jasmine wafted through the garden. It was a smell that brought back memories of my surfing days when I would stay out late with friends, looking for girls, on the prowl. Night-blooming jasmine offered the possibility of hope. I had an urge to roam. I went to my car, started the engine, and backed out of the driveway. I needed more air, more freedom; the highway seemed to promise help.

20

Driving made me feel better. I don't know if it was the motion, the change of scenery, or just the need to deal with the simple and manageable task of operating an automobile; but I had found something I could control.

I headed west on San Vicente. Like every romantic in Los Angeles, I instinctively felt that the sea air would help to clear my head. I rumbled toward the beach listening to oldies but goodies on the FM. That night they were playing only the oldies but baddies. I needed hope in my life and I wanted some of it to come from my radio. But Dion and the Belmonts didn't offer hope. I tried another frequency. The preacher on the Baptist station offered his own brand of hope, but it was not the kind that could do me any good. The Spanish broadcasters, I couldn't understand. Punk rock, jazz, and the news were the only other stations operating, and all of them sold hopelessness on a grand scale. I cut off the radio.

Then I became aware of something odd. I looked in the rear view mirror and saw headlights bearing down on me from behind. It was a maniac, speeding and weaving—probably a drunk. I whipped the wheel of the Olds to the right just in time to avoid the Datsun 260Z, which shot past me at what seemed like a hundred miles an hour. If I hadn't pulled over, the guy would have obliterated me. I watched him race down San Vicente and disappear around a curve. Someone was going to die that night as a result of that Datsun.

When I reached the end of San Vicente, I parked the Olds and locked the door. A walk through the park on the cliffs overlooking the Pacific seemed in order. It was something I hadn't done since I was a teenager. However, I had forgotten that the world of the early sixties was different from the beach life of the eighties. In addition to the palm trees, manicured walkways, salt air, and well-trimmed lawns, the park now had winos and misfits sleeping off their grief on the concrete benches. I told myself to be brave; drunks, after all, were harmless. So I strolled through the park pretending to be oblivious to the boozers. In spite of my bravado, the walk terrified me. It seemed as if I were taking a stroll through a Beirut minefield. Violence, and the potential for it, lay all around me. It was a park full of desperadoes. I avoided their glances. Then came the shock, my deepest fear in the flesh: the one man who wanted to kill me.

A bloodshot eye stared out from behind the trunk of a thick palm tree. It was a chillingly familiar eye, set in a terrifying familiar face. Could it be the twin of the junkie I had shot in the pharmacy? No. Obviously it was Robert Allen himself, recovered from the bullet I put in his head. Why hadn't someone told me? That's when I realized that he must have been following me, waiting for me to make myself vulnerable so he could kill me in revenge. Instinctively I knew that Allen was the one driving that Datsun sports car, only pretending to be drunk so that I wouldn't notice he was following me.

I knew immediately that I had to get back to my car and get out of there as quickly and as calmly as possible. If I showed any fear, I'd be finished. Walking smoothly but briskly off the path onto the grass, I kept a tree between the junkie and myself. If he planned to use a pistol, it would be more difficult to hit me if I never quit moving, so I didn't stop.

I walked faster, but he stayed up with me. It was amazing; how could anyone make such a fast recovery from a bullet wound in the head? Such a medical miracle was impossible; they couldn't have released him from the hospital; he must have come out of his coma and escaped. The man was mentally disturbed; probably back on junk again, already. That's what gave him the strength to follow me at that hour of the night. And since he was on junk I knew he would have absolutely no compunction about pulling the trigger and blowing me away. I couldn't believe I'd left my warm, safe house and driven all the way to the beach only to confront this horror in my search for peace. At that moment the most likely peace seemed like it was going to be the peace of the grave.

I ducked down and began to run. The junkie sped after me. I

charged into the street, expecting to be felled by a gunshot at any moment. I was a difficult target, moving fast, but I feared he might get off a lucky shot. Finally I reached my car, unlocked the door, shoved the key into the ignition, and cranked the starter motor. The engine turned over but didn't catch. I looked up to see the junkie running toward my window.

"Come on, you son-of-a-bitch," I yelled at the engine.

But the junkie was on top of me. My life was over. I saw the man take his hand from his jacket pocket. At that instant the engine caught. It was too late, I remember thinking, expecting at any second to be shot. I threw the transmission into drive and cranked the wheel just as the junkie's hand came up by my window. In his palm was a pint bottle of Jim Beam.

"Please mister," he yelled, "I just need a dollar. You gotta dollar for a man down on his luck?"

I looked closely at the man. As much as he resembled Robert Allen, it wasn't the junkie. What I had seen in the dark was not the person himself, but a reflection of my own fears. I was reliving the robbery, drowning in suppressed guilt and remorse. I had shot a man and blown his head open like a watermelon. In my mind, blood was everywhere. Voices were screaming. Life had become a concentration camp where people either murdered and tortured or were victims. Which was I? In the store, saving Genie, I took control and prevailed. But in the dark I was a victim of the shooting, in the grip of an emotional trauma as real as the junkie's physical trauma. Without answering the boozer in the street, I floored the accelerator and roared off into the night. In the rearview mirror, I could see the wino flip me the bone as his parting gesture.

For a second time that day, adrenaline rocketed through my veins. All I could think about was Genie. I needed to talk. I needed a friend. I needed to be held and comforted. I could hardly drive home and tell Marilyn I was scared; she would laugh at me. "I told you so," would be her reaction. She'd use my fear against me until she had me happily behind the counter of her juice bar, squeezing carrots.

I made a decision. It was a crazy decision, but I had my needs too. I slowed the Olds, made a left turn, and headed east. Even with a ten o'clock date, I knew Genie had to be home by now. I had to talk to her.

21

The Cotler home was dark, as were all the houses in this respectable Brentwood neighborhood. What reasonable person would be awake at three-thirty in the morning? Genie's Mustang was in the driveway, parked in a different spot from where it had been when I arrived for dinner. That was a good sign; it meant she had moved the car and was home, probably asleep.

After cruising past the Cotler house a second time, I drove around the corner and parked. What I was planning to do was definitely risky, but I didn't want to take any more chances than necessary. Minimum exposure was my plan.

From the Olds I surveyed the situation. The street was as quiet as Forest Lawn. No one was outside. No police drove by. It was now or never.

I opened the door no more than a foot, slipped out, crouched low, locked the door quietly, then sprinted around the corner to the yard of the Cotler property. The house was dark and quiet. In the dim light, its California Gothic Tudor architecture seemed to add a particularly grim and depressing tone to my already considerable anxiety. But I slowly worked my way around the base of the structure, studying the second story, trying to remember the floorplan so that I could determine which of the windows was Genie's. Suddenly headlights rounded the street corner and headed in my direction.

Without hesitation I dove into one of the huge oleander bushes shielding Ed's ground floor windows. The headlights moved slowly down the street and stopped in front of the house, not twenty feet from me. It was a police car. Had they seen me? Had some neighbor with insomnia spotted me and called them? How could I ever explain myself if they caught me? I was a friend of Ed's, the local celebrity of the moment, a potential political candidate (even possibly a future U.S. president, according to the power brokers), and here I was, hiding in a bush outside the Cotler house in the middle of the night. The papers would have a field day. I turned myself into Michael Marcus, the human gopher, and dug myself down into the oleander bush.

The police car shone a spotlight over the house, briefly illuminating my bush. The cops obviously didn't see me because they turned off their light and drove slowly away, down the block. My lucky night. For a few more minutes I lay in the dirt without moving. The police car disappeared and didn't return.

After pulling myself out of the bush, I slipped around to the side of the house and stood facing what I was sure had to be Genie's window. What if I were wrong? Believe in yourself, I commanded my fears.

I grabbed a few pebbles from the flower bed, then moved back from the house to get a better shot at Genie's window. The first stone I lobbed bounced off the window with a noise that sounded like a gunshot. I ran for the nearest bush and hid, expecting all hell to break loose in the form of Ed's double-barreled twelve-gauge. Surprisingly, nothing happened. It took a couple of minutes to get up the courage, then I threw another rock at the window. Again I got no reaction. By rock number five I was discouraged. Either I had picked the wrong room, or the girl was a very heavy sleeper. In either case, I couldn't keep standing there throwing rocks; someone was bound to see me. Rock number six was going to be the last one. It hit the window, hard. I ducked once again in the nearest bush. The window slid open. Someone had heard me. I buried myself in the bush waiting for the shotgun blast. Instead, all I heard was the window opening. I looked up. Peeking out of her room was Genie.

My ploy had worked. I stepped out from behind the bush and waved. Genie stared down at me. Lit only by the faint glow of a distant streetlight, Genie was exquisite. Her blonde hair contrasted dramatically with her tanned face and the night, combined with the drama of the situation, made her even more attractive than I had remembered. Genie recognized me, smiled mysteriously, held up her index finger and gestured for me to walk around to the front of the house. I nodded. The window closed and she disappeared from sight.

This was a turning point in my life. Once I entered that house I knew that there was no way I could ever go back to my old, anonymous life. If Ed caught me inside, no story I could invent would ever begin to explain what I was doing with his daughter. But at that moment, instead of feeling drained by the danger, I felt vigorous and energetic, fully alive, as I had that morning at San Onofre. This was an adventure and it excited me. I had spontaneously engineered a crazy scheme and it seemed to be succeeding. I was like a spy dropped behind enemy lines. Although I was terrified, my head felt so clear that no problem appeared too difficult to solve; I could accomplish anything.

I scurried around the house, hid behind a large planter, and watched the front door. Moments later, the little red light of the alarm system flicked off. Then the door opened and Genie beckoned to me. After looking in every direction and seeing no one, I bolted across the entry way and slipped inside the Cotler house.

In the dark foyer, I watched Genie close the front door without a sound and reactivate the burglar alarm. When she turned to me, the mischievous smirk on her face comforted me. She was amused by my presence. Genie put her finger to her lips, needlessly reminding me to say nothing, then gestured for me to follow. I obeyed.

As we tiptoed up the carpeted staircase, I felt my heart beating like a bass drum. All Ed had to do was wake up and I was a dead men. Halfway up the landing, I realized that the Mexican cotton shirt Genie was wearing as a nightdress was the only clothing she had on. Shorter than a miniskirt, it concealed nothing. Climbing the stairs with Genie a few steps above me, I saw that gorgeous ass I'd been admiring all day at the beach, now without bikini or underwear. I wanted to bite into it. Rub my tongue over it. Suck on it. Fondle it. Stroke it. Rub myself against it and then slip myself between those honey-colored thighs. I would follow her anywhere. In fact, for all I knew she could have been leading me straight into the business end of Ed's sawed-off twelve gauge.

Genie turned left at the second floor landing, away from her parents' bedroom, and led me down the wooden floor to her own room. The old oak creaked with every step; the twenty feet to her room seemed to take hours. I was sure the noise would awaken Ed, but we made it to the bedroom without a hitch and Genie shut the door behind us.

She went to her bed, sat down, and looked me over, still seemingly amused by my presence. I started to explain why I was there, something about going down to San Vicente in the middle of the night and finding myself being chased, terrified by the junkie, who I was sure was going to kill me. But before I could finish Genie cut me off by standing up, pulling her Mexican blouse up over her head, and throwing it on the floor. She was completely naked. It was everything I had hoped for.

And more. Genie sat down on the bed, pulled back the covers, and waited for me to make a decision.

I had dreamed of this moment for a week. Now that it had come, I was terrified. I checked the bedroom door, certain that Ed was about to come charging in. But the house was soundless. I examined Genie, who sat crosslegged, yoga style, on the bed. The window behind her was still open and there was just enough illumination from the streetlights to show me a beauty, a softness, and an open sensuality in Genie that even I hadn't seen before. Genie had become once again the girl that I had seen through my living room window, the Empress of Passion. She was my fantasy come true, changing my life once and for ever. My right knee started to shake uncontrollably; I was frightened, yet I wanted her so much. To cover my embarrassment, I pretended I had an itch and began to scratch wildly at my knee. This amused Genie even more. She was suddenly up from the bed and standing in front of me, smiling. She unbuttoned my shirt, then began to run her hand lightly over my tender, still sunburned chest. I had made the decision when I threw the first rock at her window; the die was cast. What the hell, I told myself, I've gone this far; what the hell.

I wrapped my arms around Genie and kissed her for what seemed like hours. I couldn't believe her tongue; it seemed to shoot in and out of my mouth like a trained serpent. How could a seventeen year old learn about such things? Genie didn't give me time to worry about it. She unzipped my trousers and reached down into my boxer shorts to stroke my now very swollen erection. Decision time was long past; now was the time to savor the moment.

Genie slid down my shorts and trousers and began to suck on my erection, at the same time fondling my balls. I couldn't believe the level of excitement she aroused in me, or the exquisite delicacy with which she drew me back and forth between her lips. She seemed to get a real kick out of seeing how far she could take me down her throat; it took every ounce of self-control I could muster to keep from losing everything. Never had I experienced a woman like this. In order to reduce my level of excitement, I diverted my attention to the mundane; I took off my coat, which I realized was covered with dirt from the oleander bush. Then I unbuttoned my cuffs and slid off my shirt. I looked down and again almost lost it. With her right hand

Genie softly stroked my balls, while at the same time, with her left hand she played with herself. It was too much. Only thoughts of Ed and his shotgun kept me from shooting myself down her throat.

Suddenly I felt her right hand creep under my balls, work its way between the cheeks of my ass, and then, wham, a slippery wet finger shot up my rectum and pressed firmly against my swollen prostate. Holy God, I moaned, paralyzed by pleasure. I was still standing in my shoes and socks with my bare ass pointing to the bedroom door. I couldn't allow myself to get the whole treatment and still have my shoes on. I had to cool things down. I pulled back for a moment. Genie looked up, surprised. I slipped off my Johnson and Murphy's, removed my socks, stepped out of my trousers and shorts, and stood for a moment facing Genie as naked and as erect as I have ever been.

All my sense of danger, even of time and space, had vanished. Where I was, who I was, where I came from—nothing any longer mattered except passion. I slipped into bed beside Genie and resumed kissing those pulsing, blood-filled lips. In bed Genie transformed from the delicate, slightly shy creature of the day into the aggressive sexual animal I had seen on my couch with Nick. I was used to women who were just the opposite, women like Marilyn who were personally aggressive but sexually inhibited. There, in her bedroom, Genie pulled out all the stops. She was all over me, stroking me, thrusting her hard little breasts in my mouth, sucking on my cock, then squatting over my face, allowing me to eat her swollen pussy. Faster and harder she thrust against my mouth. She knew what she liked and she made it very clear when she needed it. Her breathing became more rapid. She began to pant.

Suddenly Genie jumped off my face, slid down my chest, spread her legs, planted her feet flat on either side of my body, and took me with the same fierceness I had seen her take Nick in my living room. It was more than I had imagined. I was swept into the jungle and became an animal, sweating, thrusting, twisting, plunging back and forth into Genie's passion. It was the lovemaking of the barbarians, fucking as I'd never known and never could have imagined, sex at its most primitive. Genie grunted and groaned through gritted teeth; she was approaching climax. Her eyes closed, her breathing became heavy and rapid. The grip of her vagina around my erection felt wetter, hotter, and her hips moved harder and faster. She began to moan quietly. Then she grabbed my shoulders with an amazing viselike grip, a grimace spread over her face as if she were being tortured, and she began to pound her pelvis against my crotch. After a minute of this wild ride, she came with a long, quiet, feline cry. This excited me, obliterating my ability to control myself. I thrust hard into her and came in a rush that seemed to draw from every cell and capillary in my body. Throughout my orgasm Genie gripped me, minutely thrusting with every last spasm from my erection.

At that moment, I suddenly became aware of a light shooting into Genie's room from under her door; someone was outside in the hallway. Genie stiffened. A look of panic crossed her face.

"Get in there, fast," she whispered, pointing across the room to her closet.

I didn't have to be told twice. I tiptoed quickly to the closet and slipped inside behind a heavy wool dress. Genie shoved my clothes under her bed. The bedroom door slowly opened before I even had time to slide the closet shut. The dresses would hide me, I hoped. Genie lay in bed, pretending to be asleep. I couldn't help but notice that she had pulled the covers up primly around her neck.

Ed Cotler entered the room wearing a handsome embroidered Chinese silk robe. My time has come, I thought; death in Brentwood was only moments away. Without making a sound I slid down to the floor of the closet and prayed to God, if there was a God and if He was listening, to hide me. In the face of death, one's childhood religion suddenly comes back vividly.

As Ed approached Genie's bed I noticed two odd things. First, Ed's hair was freshly combed. Why would he do that in the middle of the night? The second strange thing was the noise Ed was making through his nose. He was inhaling as if he had a head cold or an allergy. I realized that he must be smelling something. And the something that he smelled was obviously sex. I felt like an animal in the jungle with Genie; our nest had just been invaded by a rival beast looking for a mate. The new male was sniffing out the territory. There, in the closet, I was living out a nightmare that would have been popular in ancient Greece. Euripides could have been writing about my closet. I was acting out a Greek tragedy. It frightened me to remember that Greek tragedies all had the same ending: death.

Ed knelt beside Genie's bed, took another deep breath through his nose, and touched his hand to Genie's sweaty forehead. He then smelled his fingers in a strangely intimate and sensual way that sent a chill through my body. This was his daughter. A father doesn't smell his own flesh and blood like that.

"Genie," Ed gently touched his daughter's shoulder, "are you okay?"

She rolled over, pretending to be still half-asleep.

"What? What time is it?"

"I heard noises. Moaning. I thought something was wrong. You cried out; I was worried you were having a nightmare."

I was the one with the nightmare, I thought from my perch in the closet, sure that at any moment Ed would turn and discover me. But then I noticed a weird reaction from Genie. She watched her father with a certain wariness. As they talked she kept the blankets pulled high around her neck, as if she were more worried about her father seeing her shoulders than she was about being caught with me.

"Dad, it's okay. I just had a bad dream. That robber again. I'm sorry I woke you. I'm okay now. You can go back to sleep, thank you."

"Genie," Ed said quietly, "you know I love you very much and want to comfort you, if I can. You used to let me comfort you; why don't you let me help you now?" Ed began to stroke Genie's shoulder with a quite unfatherlike caress.

Genie pulled her shoulder away from him. I couldn't believe what I was seeing. This was a very sick scene.

"Dad, it was just a dream. Please. Let me just go back to sleep. I'm fine now, okay?"

For a few moments Ed said nothing. What if he attacked her? What would I do? If Ed tried to assault Genie and I saved her, how could I possibly explain what I was doing naked in her closet? But I would have to help Genie; I couldn't stand by and watch her father molest his daughter. I listened carefully. Genie was a clever girl who I hoped could get herself out of this one without me.

"We used to be such a comfort to one another," Ed continued. "Why do you deny that comfort to yourself now? I could be very helpful to you, Genie."

"Dad, thank you. But I just want to go to sleep. Please." Her tone was friendly but firm, giving Ed no room to maneuver.

"If that's what you want. Remember, I'm only down the hall if you need me. Just yell and I'll be here, do you know that, Genie?"

"Yes, dad. Good night."

"Good night, sweetheart."

Ed held a kiss on Genie's forehead for far too long.

"You know I want the best for you, sweetheart."

"Thank you, dad. Good night," she told him coldly.

Ed stood and turned toward the door. I buried myself deeper in the closet. Ed reluctantly left his daughter and headed for the hall. As he passed me, unaware of my presence, I was horrified to see that my friend Ed had an erection under his silk robe. I had an urge to murder him on the spot. I was suddenly nauseated; a lump of vomit rose in my throat. I took a deep breath. The lump held, rising no further. Finally Ed made it out of the room and closed the door. I heard his every footstep as he walked down the hall and vanished into his own bedroom. The hall went black as the light cut off. Ed's bedroom door closed. I looked up at Genie, who gestured for me to wait.

Ed's bedroom door opened again and footsteps padded back down the hall to her door. Genie lay down and pretended to be asleep. Ed opened her door and looked in. He shone his flashlight on Genie. Apparently she looked unreachable because he closed the door and returned once again to his own bedroom. Finally I heard his door close.

Genie rolled over, sat up, and listened. The house was dead quiet. I didn't move. She got out of bed, crossed the room, and crawled into the closet beside me, where she gave me a quick kiss.

"You handled that very well," I whispered.

"You didn't do so bad yourself, old man," she teased me back. "I think it's time you finally come out of the closet, don't you?" She grinned at her little joke.

"Listen," I said seriously, "I have to ask you this. I heard what your father said; did he do to you what I think he did?"

Genie pulled away from me and went cold.

"Michael, if you don't mind," she whispered, "I'd rather not talk about it."

"I can understand that. But Jesus, Genie, it'd be hard for me to believe if I hadn't been here and heard it myself. I feel horrible for you. I mean, you've been living with this for how many years?''

"Michael, just drop the subject, okay?''

"I couldn't help what I heard, Genie. It was awful.''

"Forget what you heard. You didn't hear it right.''

"Then what did I hear?''

"You heard me ask you to forget it.''

"But why?''

"Because I'm asking you to.''

"You think that's going to do you any good?''

"Michael, my problem with my father is long over with.''

"From the way you pulled the covers up over your shoulders it didn't look that way to me.''

Genie's look was suddenly very cold and very hard.

"Do you see him in the room with me?''

"No.''

"Do you see him in bed with me?''

"No.''

"Then let's just drop it, okay?''

"Genie, if you ever want to talk about it, I'm here.''

"Thank you, Michael.''

"I say this as your friend. I mean it. I don't think you should hide what's gone on. You're the one who suffers, not him.''

"Is this what you call not talking about it?''

"I just wanted you to know my opinion.''

"Thank you.'' She remained distant.

"I'm not afraid of your father, you know.''

Genie said nothing.

"I mean,'' I continued, ''unless he comes in here with his twelve gauge; that I'm scared of.''

"He's never done that.'' She grinned mischievously. "Yet.''

"Thanks a lot,'' I pretended to worry. "What *does* he do when he finds friends of yours hidden naked in your closet?''

"It's never happened.''

"Which has never happened; friends hiding in the closet or him finding them?''

"As I said,'' she teased, "it's never happened.''

"For a smart girl, you're suddenly not very articulate. That's all you're going to tell me, huh?''

"Michael, I didn't take my clothes off because I wanted to come into the closet and talk with you, you know what I mean?''

Genie began to caress the inside of my thigh. Within moments she was stroking my blossoming erection. Yes, I did know what she meant.

Sex with Genie was so good that for the first time in my life I understood in my bones how I had the makings of an addict; a part of me wasn't that far from the junkie who had tried to rob me. If I hadn't seen the sky outside begin to get light I think I would have stayed in bed with Genie forever. I had forgotten Marilyn, forgotten my business, even forgotten Rebecca. But with day coming, I'd be a dead man if I were discovered in the Cotler house.

Genie retrieved my crushed clothes from under the bed and watched me dress. She was terribly amused by my appearance, which I realized, when I looked in her mirror, resembled something of a tramp—my clothes were crumpled and still covered with dirt from the oleander plant. I actually thought this was a good thing because it would make me harder to recognize outside. How I would explain it to Marilyn was another story.

The sky brightened so quickly that, once I was dressed, Genie and I didn't have time to talk. I wanted to make a date to see her again, but she only pointed in the direction of her father's room and whispered that she'd call me at the pharmacy on Monday. We kissed for the final time.

Genie threw on that tantalizing Mexican blouse of hers, carefully opened the bedroom door, and signaled for me to wait. She crept silently across the hall, pressed her ear against her parents' bedroom door and listened. Then she turned and gestured that the coast was clear.

I tiptoed down the creaky hallway, terrorized by the thought of Ed, and descended the stairs in record time. Genie shut off the burglar alarm and swung open the front door. Both of us knew that it was not the time or place for sentiment. I stuck my head outside, took a quick survey of the still sleeping neighborhood, nodded good-bye, and slipped out the front door, which I heard close immediately behind me.

I scurried around the front of the house without glancing back, expecting at any moment to hear that fatal blast from my lawyer's well-oiled twelve gauge. I kept my head low and pumped away at my legs, sprinting down the block like an Olympic hopeful, until I suddenly realized that I had made it. I was safe. I had enjoyed one hell of an adventure, and I had lived through it.

The door of my Olds opened without a struggle. The engine started on the first crank. Everything was working. I put the car in gear and headed home. I had entered a new world. I felt exhilarated, freed from the bonds that seemed to have been strangling me. But what had I actually done? Who was I? Had I gone crazy like my father, as Marilyn had said? Was the euphoria I felt a sign of schizophrenia? If I were going crazy, it felt so good that I wondered if maybe going crazy wasn't so bad after all.

By the time I pulled into my driveway, the sun was beginning to peek up over the horizon. It was Sunday morning and everyone in my neighborhood was still asleep. Then I remembered my appearance. How would I explain myself, a married man with a daughter, coming home at five forty-five on a Sunday morning looking like a bum? What would Marilyn think? I hoped that she was still asleep so that I wouldn't have to say anything, consoling myself with the knowledge that I had just enjoyed the most extraordinarily vivid twenty-four hours I could remember. I had done the forbidden and I felt fully alive; no matter what happened now, I told myself, I always had an adventure to remember.

As I got out of the Oldsmobile I felt the presence of my father, watching me, amused. I could hear the crazy old guy chuckle as he called to me, "What are you going to do now, big boy?" Yes, he was enjoying my problem. He had been in my situation many times himself. That's when the feelings boomeranged back onto me. I became horrified by my behavior. Guilty. How could I be so proud of my adventure when I had behaved in a way that, when my father did it years before, had been so painful to me? A long-hidden part of my character had just leaked out of its tightly sealed bottle. I was making a mess. My mind began to race, trying to figure out a way to stuff the leakage back into the bottle. Even then I knew it wasn't possible.

22

I smelled of sweat, sperm, and pussy. To go into the house carrying such an aroma would destroy everything that remained between myself and Marilyn. As I contemplated my next move I was aware of the early morning heat—at six in the morning the sun was already cooking the city. That gave me an idea. I walked down my driveway to the back yard and pretended to be interested in the temperature of the swimming pool. I bent down and splashed the surface of the water with my fingers. In doing so, I leaned forward in a way that would make it seem, if Marilyn were watching, that I was still drunk. I leaned farther, and tried to make it appear that I had suddenly lost my balance. I fell into the pool with a big splash, clothes and all. My hope was that the chlorine would kill all the stains and smells of my betrayal. The pool had cost me $15,000 at a time when $15,000 was a gigantic sum of money. I had built it for Marilyn, so she could swim laps for exercise. I had never particularly enjoyed it myself. That morning, however, I thought it was the best investment I had ever made.

I paddled around on the surface of the water as if I were amused to find myself swimming with my clothes on. Just as I had hoped, Marilyn had been watching. By the time I pulled myself out of the water, she had run out the back door, dressed only in her robe, in a panic, ready to dive in and rescue me. But before she could get to me I was up and out of the pool.

Marilyn threw her arms around me and began to cry, squeezing me with all her might and sobbing uncontrollably. I held her tight.

"What is it?" I asked softly.

She tried to answer but was too upset to talk. I simply stood there, dripping wet, hugging her, moved by what she was feeling. I sensed that she had been up all night, unable to sleep, frightened, not just for me but for us and our marriage. Her tears told me that she loved me and wanted nothing bad to happen to me. The hard, driven, obsessive Marilyn was suddenly vulnerable again.

"Hey, I'm here; I love you; you don't have to worry," I tried to comfort her, which only made her cry more ferociously. The more she wept and the tighter she held me, the harder it became for me to breathe.

"Marilyn, it's okay. Honestly. I'm fine. I just slipped on a wet spot here and fell in. You see I'm fine, don't you, sweetheart?"

She finally relaxed her grip.

"Michael, I was so frightened. I didn't know where you had gone. Anything could have happened to you last night. Promise me you won't ever run out like that again, please Michael."

Marilyn was sincere. She was my friend again and she loved me.

"You have my word, if you'll promise me something, too."

"Anything."

"Don't try to win arguments by kicking me out of bed.'

"Oh Michael, I promise. That was so stupid. As soon as you left I knew it was wrong. All night, all I could think about was that if something happened to you, I was the one who had driven you out; I was responsible. I won't do it again, I promise. And you won't run out of here either, do you promise?"

I promised. Marilyn began kissing my face and neck, showering me with affection, gushing over me in a way I hadn't seen in years. I have to admit that I liked it. I had wanted her to want me for a long time. Now it seemed that she did. I wished it had happened hours earlier, before I had left the house. But passion works in strange ways, and I figured I should just accept it. Exhausted or not, I enjoyed her touch and began to respond as she unbuttoned my shirt.

"Michael, let's get you out of these wet clothes."

Marilyn removed my shirt and began to kiss my chest. Moments later she opened my belt, unzipped my trousers, then slid everything, underwear included, off onto the concrete deck. Without even checking to see if the neighbors were peering over the fence, she squatted over me and proceeded to hump me with an uncharacteristic urgency. It took her no more than two minutes to come in a blaze of passion. Ten seconds later she was off me. I was astounded. What had happened?

"Michael, we've got to get you inside and dry before you get sick."

I nodded, nowhere near orgasm. Marilyn didn't seem to notice my need. Should I say something? Should I just be happy that

something had obviously changed, and that at least I hadn't had
to recite the fantasy?

"Come on, get up." She extended her hand.

I nodded again.

Marilyn took my hand and led me into the kitchen, where she
grabbed a towel from the linen closet, and began to dry me. By
then my erection had gone and all I could think about was sleep.

"I want you to go upstairs and get into bed," she said. "I'm not
on call today and I'm going to disconnect the phone. I'll take care
of Rebecca. These are doctor's orders, Michael; you need rest."

"You're right, sweetheart. Thanks for understanding." I kissed
her gently on the forehead and headed up the stairs. I was overjoyed.
For whatever reasons, something in Marilyn's awareness of me had
changed dramatically. Our old connection was back, if only for the
moment. My fears lifted; I had, somehow, for some reason, been
given a second chance. I was determined not to blow it.

23

In spite of the early morning light in the bedroom, I was so
exhausted I fell asleep almost as soon as I laid my head down on
my pillow. It was as if I were in a coma. I don't remember
tossing, I didn't get up to pee. I don't even remember dreaming.

What finally woke me was a hand, shaking my shoulder. I
opened my eyes to find Ed Cotler and Marilyn standing over me,
staring down with grave expressions on their faces. My first
impulse was flight; I thought, "Oh shit, Genie told her father
about us and he told Marilyn." Ed had come to get me; in five
minutes I'd be a corpse. Instantly I was fully awake, one hundred
percent paranoid. I leapt to the other side of the bed and scouted
the room for an escape route as I simultaneously watched Ed's
right hand, expecting at any moment for him to pull the pistol
from his tennis jacket pocket and blast me away. Marilyn, I
assumed, would probably fire one last shot herself, for good
riddance—the coup de grace. Naked, poised on the edge of the
bed ready to spring, I tried to evolve a plan.

"Michael, hey, relax," Ed told me. "I'm sorry; I didn't mean
to scare you. Take it easy."

Warily, I studied him and Marilyn, certain at first that it was a trick. But they seemed sincere. I had misjudged the situation. My floating guilt, so obvious now, had almost given me away. It was like when I was a kid and could never figure out how my parents always found out when I did something that they had forbidden. At first I believed they hired private detectives to follow me and report on my activities. Later I developed the idea that adults had the power to read their childrens' minds. As I crouched by the side of my bed, it seemed that the events of the last twenty-four hours had triggered some sort of infantile regression and reactivated my childhood fantasies—I was attributing to Marilyn and Ed the powers I had once assigned to my parents.

"Jesus, you scared me," I admitted to Ed. "I must have been having some sort of bad dream. I'm sorry."

"Hey, I'm the one who's sorry. You okay?"

"Yeah. What time is it?"

"Three o'clock," Marilyn answered.

"In the afternoon?" I asked.

Marilyn and Ed nodded. I couldn't believe I had slept for so long. I could see they didn't care much about that; they obviously had something else on their minds.

"So what's going on?" I asked Ed. "Why are you here?"

"We got a bad break today; I wanted to be the one you heard it from."

I waited for the latest revelation.

"A friend of mine in the D.A.'s office called me. . . ."

"Don't tell me," I interrupted, "they're going to indict me."

Ed nodded.

"If the junkie dies, it's going to be manslaughter. In the meantime they're going to charge you with assault with a deadly weapon as well as attempted murder. And the ACLU is pushing them to pursue the wrongful death angle."

"The bastards," I muttered.

Marilyn said nothing, I could see that she was upset. Despite our truce that morning by the pool, I feared that the latest news had reactivated her long-standing obsessions.

"So what do we do?" I asked Ed.

"We fight on all fronts."

As I expected, Ed had already worked up a game plan. His was a multipronged approach, part legal, part political, and part media hype. The basic idea was for me to remain in the public eye as a highly visible local hero. Ed believed in popular sentiment and its power over the opinions of juries. He wanted me to speak in public, give interviews to the press on citizens' rights, appear at benefits on behalf of politicians like Mayor Malcolm, and speak out on the individual's right not only to bear arms, but to defend family, home, and property. Ed also mentioned that Edgar Wilkens, the financier with whom I'd had dinner the night before, had called to say how impressed he had been with me. Wilkens had apparently likened me to a "Jewish Jimmy Stewart," a man who listened thoughtfully, spoke softly, but "carried a big stick." I suppressed my desire to laugh at that one. Had Genie told Ed about my "big stick," his reaction would no doubt have been far less enthusiastic.

What could I do but agree to follow Ed's advice? He was the expert and I was the one in trouble. Anything to keep myself out of jail. Ed was pleased by my immediate approval of his plan, and bubbled with optimism as Marilyn walked him downstairs to the door.

As soon as they were out of the room, I jumped into the shower. I wanted to be dressed before Marilyn returned. If she wanted to fight with me after hearing Ed's news, being naked would put me at a disadvantage. Why did I feel that way, I wondered, as I hurried to the shower. I could come up with no answer.

Marilyn and Ed must have talked downstairs for quite awhile because by the time she returned to my room, I was fully dressed with only my tennis shoes left to slip on. I felt ready for anything, although I really had no interest in fighting. I wanted to continue where we had left off by the pool, when she and I both knew that she loved me, needed me, and could see that I so cared for her. I was afraid that everything that had transpired between us that morning had already vanished in reaction to the latest news. While in the shower I had concocted a plan based on tenderness. I wasn't going to let her provoke me, I told myself. I would keep things on a higher, more personal, more intimate plane and reach out to the part of her that had responded to me by the pool. I wanted to remind her of what was possible between us and start connecting as a couple, as lovers, as husband and wife, as friends, and as parents. We had to reopen the doors that our disagreements had been closing between us, not through debate, but through affection and understanding. What we needed, I proposed to tell her, were not arguments about morality and politics, but to tell one another our most basic fears, to expose our real selves. Only that would enable us to regain our once unshakable sense of mutual trust.

Marilyn stood in the door watching me tie my tennis shoes. It reminded me of when we had first become lovers and she had enjoyed helping me not only dress, but clean myself as well. Whenever we took showers together she had insisted on soaping and scrubbing every square inch of my body. At first it was a little embarrassing and made me feel as if I were an infant being washed and inspected by my mother. But then I came to enjoy it as an intimacy only possible between adults who not only truly loved one another but were inspired by that love to be tender and physically sensitive to one another. As she watched me tie my tennis shoes I realized that Marilyn and I hadn't washed each other in years.

As I smiled at her, I could feel her mind racing all over the planet. I was afraid she was about to jump into her attack mode; she seemed to be on full alert. I pretended not to notice and made a casual show out of tying and retying my right tennis shoe.

"Can you believe this?" I offered. "Fifty dollar all-American sneakers and after one month I've gotta tie double knots to keep the laces from coming undone. It's a disgrace. Next time I'm going to buy the twenty dollar shoes made in Japan; I bet they last forever."

"Take 'em back."

"Right. And I'll spend half an hour arguing with some kid over a fifty cent shoelace I can get for free in the pharmacy. There ought to be a law against this nickel and dime bullshit." I laughed at a sudden inspiration. "You know, if I were elected to the Assembly, I could get the State Department of Transportation to issue a recall notice on these shoes. I mean, this is a mode of public transportation, isn't it? What are the consequences to the health of the residents of California? Our state has to have the largest number of joggers in the country. Think of the number of broken bones, concussions, abrasions, and deaths these laces must be causing. I bet it's worse than the injuries caused by the defects in the '73 Pinto. I'm on to a potentially hot campaign topic, don't you think?"

"We've got to talk about this, Michael," she said with great gravity.

"I knew you'd think it was a good issue."

"Be serious, Michael; I'm talking about what Ed said. You're in big trouble, you realize."

"I do."

"You're facing jail, Michael. Like in the state penitentiary. San Quentin. The big time."

"It's not going to happen, Marilyn. Everyone says that."

"Everyone said that about Haldeman, Erlichman, and Colson. Did Nixon's political connections keep them out of jail?"

"Marilyn, believe me, I don't want to go to jail any more than you want me to."

"That's not going to stop them from sending you."

"You're right; that's why I need Ed to defend me."

Marilyn frowned.

"You don't trust Ed to defend me?"

"Michael, in this kind of craziness, you never know how things are going to end up. You know I hate situations like this. It's like with books—the first thing I read is the ending. I have to know how things turn out. Michael, this frightens me. I don't know the ending here. No one knows. It scares me."

"Look, it scares me too, I'll be honest. But so did that asshole that put the gun to Genie's head. What if the pistol had been real? What if I'd done nothing and he'd shot her? How do you think I would have felt then?"

Marilyn's answer astounded me.

"Michael, believe it or not, last night while you were gone I thought about that too. I asked myself, what if it had been Rebecca in the store who had been held hostage. If the robber had shot her because I had made you give up your gun, I'd never have been able to forgive myself."

"You really think that?"

"I'm entitled to change my mind, aren't I?"

"Of course you are, sweetheart."

I stood and gave her a tender kiss to which she responded with surprising warmth.

"It doesn't change the way I feel about getting out of this city, Michael. You're a living target working in that store. It's only a matter of time until the gun some robber carries is a real one. Or the hostage is Rebecca. The fact that I know you do need the gun is all the more reason to leave, don't you see?"

I reminded myself of my resolution not to get angry and not to debate with her.

"Reason or not, I can't go anywhere or even think of selling the pharmacy until after all the legal problems are resolved. You understand that?"

"No."

"You don't remember the 'clouded title' business?"

"Of course I do. It's just that there's been some good news since yesterday."

I waited. In my stomach I felt the old sinking feeling.

"My surgeon friends called this morning. They met again last night, talked, and liked the idea of the spa even more. They don't want other investors. They want to put up all the money themselves. They've committed a million dollars to us, Michael. We don't need to sell the pharmacy to build the spa. We can get out of here in spite of the legal problems."

"Congratulations," I offered without enthusiasm.

"That's all you have to say?"

"It's enough isn't it? I mean, it is what you want; I'm happy for you. Honestly."

"You're not happy for both of us?"

"Marilyn, as wonderful as the health clinic sounds to you, my basic problem with the place hasn't been answered yet; I don't see anything for me to do there."

"What's so wonderful about your life here, other than your impressive reputation as a living target? I'm trying to get at what stops you from growing and changing. Don't you want to live in a better place, Michael?"

"Believe it or not, I actually enjoy what I've accomplished with the store. When I took over the place it was nothing. Now it's a going business. *My* business. I built it. That's very satisfying to me; I guess you don't understand that."

"You can build the health clinic and make that go, too. If you give it a chance, I'll bet that a year from now you'll feel the same about the clinic as you do about the pharmacy."

"Marilyn, what do I do about the fact that I couldn't care less about juice bars, Nautilus machines, jock straps, and the knee problems of overweight, over-fed, middle-aged matrons? All my life I've loved the pharmaceutical business. God knows why, but I do. Now when it's finally successful, you want me to sell it to do something I'm not even interested in. Don't you see? I'll go crazy living in some health clinic."

"And you're not going crazy here?" she asked in a sweet voice.

The woman certainly knew how to push my buttons. I restrained my impulse to hit her.

"Marilyn. Just this once, please, let's not start up; try to consider my side of the situation."

"You want me to look at the whole picture," she smiled innocently.

"Exactly."

"To start with, you're facing jail. And, of course, who knows how many more robberies; the junkie was the third this year, right? And we're not yet into July. Then we have Mr. Forty-Nine Percent, Jerry Herrman, who for the rest of your life is going to collect half of what you built, for doing zip. Correct?"

"Sweetheart," I tried to be nice, "I'm trying to get you to see how this feels from my point of view. I do not want to argue with you."

"Who's arguing?" she said as if I'd wounded her innocence. "I'm simply trying to consider all the factors."

"Well let's just leave Jerry out of the factoring, if you don't mind."

Marilyn looked at me as if I was crazy.

"You're defending Jerry? Since when? The guy's a goddamn parasite and a greedy one at that; how many times have you told me that yourself?"

"He did come through when I needed the money and no one else would lend it to me."

"Yes. And now, thanks to you busting your ass, he earns a fifty percent annual return on his investment."

"Marilyn," I explained patiently, "I'm not going to argue about this. The fact is, as you remember, my father had cancer, no insurance, and the hospital wanted a cash deposit before they would admit him for surgery. What was I going to do, send my father to the charity ward at County Hospital? I don't care who you are, you don't let your father die in the charity ward if there's any way you can avoid it. No matter what I think about Jerry, no matter how much I hate him, no matter how disgusting he is, and no matter how much I hate paying him those dividends, the asshole believed in me enough to buy into the business when no one I knew would touch me with a ten foot pole. Remember?"

"Michael, please," she said after a moment of quiet, "give the spa a chance?"

"Marilyn, stop for a second and think: Escondido Last Weekend. Didn't I sit in those hot tubs with you? Didn't I eat that bean sprout salad? Didn't I jog with you? We inspected the weight rooms, toured the kitchens, studied the architectural layouts, and questioned every god-damn aspect of their operations. Isn't that giving it a chance?"

I couldn't believe it was only one week since we'd been to Escondido, one week since I'd seen Genie fucking Nick, less than a week since the robbery, and only a few hours since I'd spent the night with Genie in her bedroom. More had happened to me in these few days than I'd experienced in the past five years.

"Michael, I'm asking you as my friend and my husband for help. I want you to give it a chance. Please. One step at a time. Help with the proposal for the investors. And help me with the plans. See if it grows on you. See if being part of it doesn't interest you more. Will you do that for me? If not for me, then for Rebecca. And by the way, you promised Rebecca you'd take her to the ponies today, remember?"

I looked at the clock. It was almost four. If I drove like a maniac, I could just make it to the valley in time for Rebecca to get the last few laps around the track before the pony ride closed.

"Where is she?" I asked Marilyn.

"Downstairs watching TV."

"TV?" I couldn't believe Marilyn was allowing our daughter to watch TV in the afternoon.

"What else could I do? We had to talk. Did you want her to hear us?"

"You're right. I just don't believe it." I kissed her on the cheek. "Listen, I gotta go or we won't make it. See you back here in two hours, okay?"

"Can't I come with you?"

"You want to come with us?"

"There's a new antihistamine I want to try."

Marilyn normally stayed away from pony rides. As cute as Rebecca looked on the backs of those animals, horses made Marilyn ill; she was allergic to their hair.

"Okay, then, let's go."

I turned toward the door.

"Michael, will you help me plan the clinic?"

I blanched.

"Marilyn, we're late."

"I need your help. Do you hear me, Michael?"

"Okay, you've got it. With the plans. But no commitment after that. In the meantime, I need your support with my legal problems, okay?"

Marilyn extended her hand.

"I think we've got a deal."

It was depressing to have to make such a formal arrangement but, I rationalized, the deal was a start; at least we were moving forward on something. It was a risk I had to take.

24

At the pony ride, I hired the inevitable photographer to take a picture of Marilyn and myself standing proudly beside Rebecca, who was sitting on the back of a Shetland. My wife thought I had lost my mind; normally I hated sentimental photos and the screaming families that posed for them. But at that moment and on that day, I wanted to remember that we were the perfect picture of the happy family. Everybody was getting everything they wanted from everyone. At that moment, on that afternoon, we all believed we shared the same dream. In the morning, driving home from Genie's, everything had seemed so complicated. At Pony Land, life was once again simple and clear. Mother and father watched their beautiful daughter ride the horsie, perfect parents with a perfect daughter, all of them leading the picture-perfect life, with perfect plans for the future. The fact that such plans were abstractions, removed from the guts and marrow of life, was not something that would appear in the final photograph. In my confused state I looked forward to seeing the simple picture. I very much wanted to believe that it was the real one.

25

Monday at the pharmacy I was more tired than I'd been after my eventful night with Genie. Marilyn's antihistamine hadn't worked, and by the time we got home from Pony Land her sinuses were so clogged her breathing sounded like an out-of-tune saw. The result was no sleep for either of us.

All day I had a real problem with the clock. I felt like a kid in high school waiting for the bell. Except that I was an adult pharmacist waiting for his seventeen-year-old lover to call. Eleven o'clock in the morning seemed to arrive at four in the afternoon, even with the heavy morning workload.

Business was simply extraordinary and we were buried by an avalanche of prescriptions; it was almost as if everyone in West Los Angeles had gotten sick over the weekend. Call after call poured in from doctors and patients. The druggists worked frantically, filling orders. Normally I would have been delighted. But Milt was out with what I supposed was a terrible hangover (he called it the ''flu'' on the phone) and for some reason everyone else was in one of those foul, black, Monday morning moods. The work went without pleasure. Adam accused Al of screwing up a customer's order of Tagamet. Al blamed the problem on our numerical referencing system and tried to put it all on my shoulders because I had not updated our inventory procedures with the $30,000 computer he kept urging me to buy. But all I cared about was Genie. Why didn't she call?

I tried to remember back to high school and when it was we had breaks between classes long enough to make a telephone call. Lunch. Nutrition, for sure. As I thought about other possibilities it horrified me to realize how desperate I was to hear from her. One part of me yearned for the sound of her voice, while another part of me was truly alarmed by my need. Every time the phone rang, which was almost continuously, I jumped, trembling with both excitement and terror, hoping it was Genie and praying that it wasn't.

By lunchtime I was a nervous wreck. Many of our customers

wanted to deal only with me personally. Women called, wouldn't give their names but demanded to speak to "Mr. Marcus." Each time I thought it was Genie. I was wrong; by one o'clock she still hadn't phoned. I tried hard to remain calm and function on auto-pilot with the doctors and patients. But my emotions were fibrillating up and down like an out of control yo-yo. One of the druggists would yell, "Michael, telephone!" and my pulse rate would jump from seventy-two to a hundred and ten. I would pick up the phone, but it was never Genie.

The capper to the day was my partner Jerry, who paid me his usual late afternoon visit. He sashayed into my office, closed the door, stared at me, then flashed his arrogant grin.

"What is this," he leered, "my partner, Michael, has a suntan. I don't believe it. Are you sick? Have you gone crazy? What have you been doing this weekend? You've actually been outside, enjoying yourself? Don't you know druggists are supposed to look pale, sick and overworked? Who do you think will trust a pharmacist with a suntan?"

"Jerry," I pointed to the door. "I've got a lot of work to do, so just get out of here and leave me alone, if you don't mind. Unless you have something specific to discuss."

"Hey," Jerry said, throwing his hands up in the air, "who am I to get in the way of profits. See you tomorrow."

Jerry left. I didn't even look up.

"Michael, line two!" Harry yelled from the counter.

I jumped. School was out by then and it had to be Genie. I yanked the receiver to my ear.

"Hello?'

It was Mrs. Vincent wanting a refill of Motrin. Of course we could deliver it in two hours.

Genie not only didn't stop by after school, she never called. I even stayed late on the pretext of finishing up the last of the orders, but she never showed up. One part of me plunged into despair. Another part was overjoyed—temptation had been taken out of my hands and I could remain the happily married man I wanted to be.

26

That night I resolved to be the good husband, extend my peace with Marilyn, and drive Genie completely from my mind. The last item on my agenda was made easier by the pain and humiliation I had endured all day as a result of her silence.

After playing with Rebecca and putting her to sleep, Marilyn and I worked together on the financial projections for the health clinic. She had a meeting with her potential backers the following night and wanted to make sure all her figures were in order. We stayed up until one in the morning plugging up all the holes in her prospectus. On paper, the spa certainly looked like a winner. If Marilyn could hold her costs to the numbers she estimated and get the kind of occupancy rate she anticipated, not only would the investors earn thirty percent per year, plus depreciation, but we ourselves would quickly become rather wealthy. The deal was structured so that the surgeons had forty-nine percent of the operation with no decision-making capabilities. Marilyn and I, as the general partners, had fifty-one percent ownership as well as total control. If one wanted to live on a diet of whole wheat, avocados, and celery juice, her spa was certainly a profitable way to do it.

All evening I successfully suppressed my urge to telephone Genie by forcing myself to concentrate on the financial plans at hand. Willing myself to the task became a kind of test of my sanity. Apparently I succeeded, because at the end of the marathon work night, Marilyn happily confided that she was moved by the intensity of my commitment to her project. She admitted that she'd harbored doubts about the promise I had made to her on Sunday. But she'd been wrong about me, she confessed, and she apologized for doubting my word. I smiled modestly, as if to tell her that she should not underestimate me in the future.

As I washed and undressed for bed I knew my burning concentration had done me no good; I still wanted Genie. I shut off the bedroom light and crawled under the covers, only to get the surprise of my life when Marilyn suddenly grabbed me and began to kiss me with a fury. It was one-thirty in the morning and she was aroused. Who knew what had excited her? But this was what I wanted, I told myself: Marilyn passionate. It was ironic that the passion came so soon after my night with Genie. I wondered if, in some way, Marilyn sensed what had happened. She and I never did discuss where I had been on Saturday night. She didn't ask; I volunteered nothing. I hadn't lied to her, yet there was clearly a secret between us.

Responding to Marilyn's caresses was easy at first. I could feel her opening up a little, relaxing, and I was hopeful. Definitely, it was an improvement. But as she became more highly aroused, her old sexual obsessions quickly took over. She asked me to tell her "the story," and we were back to Marilyn the slave and me the master, while in reality she was the master, sitting on me, her passive, subservient husband. She became excited and I grew bored. But I did my duty, kept my erection, squeezed her nipples on cue, and recited the story as she liked hearing it. As if to thank me, Marilyn came more quickly than usual, climaxing in a sudden rush. I felt like a dildo, a human vibrator connected to a speaker phone. I wondered if I couldn't just record the fantasy on tape and play it when required; I was sure it would work just as well.

Immediately afterward she was, as usual, dreadfully embarrassed by her need for the fantasy and wanted me to forget everything that I'd said. Knowing that I hadn't yet come, she rolled over on her back and urged me inside of her. As I began to get hard again she reached between my legs and lightly stroked my balls, which she knew aroused me.

"Oh, fuck me Michael," she moaned, "fuck me with that big fat cock of yours."

Marilyn continued on in this vein because she thought it excited me. In theory she was right. The idea of Marilyn being aroused by me was exciting; the problem was that if I opened my eyes and looked at my wife I could see immediately that she was not, in fact, passionate at all. I needed uninhibited frenzy but, instead, got by-the-book mechanics. So, with one of Marilyn's hands on my balls and me in her spent vagina, I fantasized back to Genie squatting on the bed as we thrust against one another, covered with sweat, straining, smashing, caressing, fucking like all get-out. This memory got to me and within moments, I came inside of Marilyn.

I flopped down on the bed beside my wife and kissed her.
"How was it?" she asked.
"Wonderful," I lied.

27

Tuesday's work dragged even more slowly than Monday. My
only thoughts were of Genie, Genie, and more Genie. I answered
the phone, filled prescriptions, and tried to be the model druggist. But my mood was foul and I found myself over-reacting
and yelling at every petty problem.

By four o'clock I was going crazy; Genie still hadn't called.
What had happened? Did she hate me as a result of Saturday
night? Did our night together bore her? Did I perform badly in
bed? I mean, every man wonders how he stacks up as a lover,
particularly compared with eighteen year olds. At least she could
have the decency to tell me, I raged in my mind.

At four-ten Ed Cotler called, momentarily scaring me. But all
he wanted was to arrange for us to get together and plan how to
deal with my upcoming indictment. He would have come over
that night, but he had to go to San Francisco on another case. We
agreed on a date and I quickly got off the phone before I was
tempted to ask about Genie.

At five Marilyn called to confirm her eight o'clock dinner
meeting with the surgeons to discuss the financial proposal we
had prepared. She didn't know what time she would be home,
but assumed that it would be late. Marilyn was so considerate
she had even arranged a baby-sitter for Rebecca, in case I
wanted to go out. Had she booked Genie, I asked, incredulous.
No, the sitter was Debby the doughnut eater, Miss Deep Fry of
1986. I wished Marilyn luck with the surgeons. She blew me a
kiss over the phone, then hung up.

At that moment I heard a quiet knock on my door.
"Yeah?" I yelled angrily.
The door opened. It was Genie.

28

All of my fears and reservations vanished as I studied the knockout who stood in my doorway grinning at me. She had me completely in the palm of her clever little hand. I wondered if she knew it.

"Hey mister," she teased, "what are ya doing tonight?"

I cringed and glanced through the open door into the drugstore, hoping none of the employees had heard her teenage temptress tone of voice. Fortunately no one was near my office. I shut the door. Genie obviously enjoyed my discomfort.

"So what about it," she continued, "you going to make me ask twice?"

"You're serious?"

"Of course."

Genie seemed very pleased with herself. She looked different that day, more sophisticated and stylish, although still in the punk rocker vein. Was it for my benefit? Her white blouse ballooned down into the same skin-tight turquoise cotton trousers she had worn Saturday night. Red high heels. Red sash around the waist. Lipstick and makeup. Impossible to resist.

"I thought you were going to call me yesterday."

"I got hung up."

"You couldn't get to a phone for one minute?"

Her eyes narrowed. She obviously didn't like the tone of my voice.

"That's right."

"No one's that busy, Genie."

"Michael, you sound like my father."

"You said you would call; I was worried about you."

"Sorry. Listen, next time figure it this way; if you don't hear from me, I'm fine, okay? Now what about tonight?"

"What do you have in mind?"

"You free?" Genie asked with a leer in her eye.

"You're asking me out?"

"Why not?"

"What will you tell your parents you're doing?"

"Leave that to me."

"I'd like to. But I want to make sure we avoid certain problems. Like them finding out, you know what I mean?"

"We did okay Saturday, didn't we? Trust me, Michael."

"That business with your father Saturday night was too close for me; I can't take a repeat of that."

Genie flashed that fantastic smile of hers, innocent on the surface, yet hinting at so many lascivious possibilities. It was enough to drive anyone crazy.

"Does that mean you won't come visit me again?" she pouted theatrically.

"Not like that, in your room."

"Not even if no one were home?"

"Genie, that was crazy, doing that Saturday night."

"But it was good fun, wasn't it, Michael?"

There was that salacious grin again.

"Yes," I answered simply.

"Don't be too enthused. I mean, you didn't seem to have such a bad time. Or am I wrong?"

"You know you're not wrong."

"So, you going to see me tonight or what?"

Before I could answer, the office door swung open. It was my partner, Jerry. The man had impeccable timing.

"Michael . . ." he started to say, then saw Genie and stopped himself. "Excuse me; I thought you were alone. I'll come back later. Sorry."

Jerry started to leave when he suddenly stopped and turned to Genie.

"Aren't you the Cotler girl?"

Genie nodded.

Jerry stuck his jaw out proudly in my direction; an obnoxious remark was in the making.

"I see why you saved her from the junkie," he leered at me as he left the office.

"Who was that asshole?"

"My partner, Jerry Herrman."

"Great guy," she offered sarcastically.

"I like your first description better."

"How'd you come to get involved with him?"

"It's too long a story."

"Will you tell it to me tonight?"

"You know," I told her, "you're very pushy for a seventeen year old; anyone ever tell you that?"

"You don't seem to mind too much."

"I don't know," I stalled.

Genie stepped around my desk, kneeled in front of me, then leaned forward and kissed me passionately on the lips.

"That wasn't much of an 'hello' you gave me when I came in, Michael."

"Genie, please, someone could walk in."

She stood up."

"I shouldn't kiss you?" she said, pretending to be hurt.

"Just not here."

"How about tonight?"

"You don't quit, do you?"

"And you don't know how to say yes, do you?"

She waited for my answer.

"Okay," I gave in without a struggle. "Where do we meet?"

Genie seemed to enjoy my anxiety as we worked out the details of our rendezvous. The plan seemed foolproof. Then she gave me another of her quick kisses and flew out of the office. My mood, I noticed, was immeasurably improved.

I carefully wiped my face, cleaning every remnant of Genie's lipstick from my skin. All I needed was for one of the druggists to associate Genie with lipstick stains on my face and I'd be paying salary increases, profit sharing, and presidential-style health and pension plans. I had just done what I had sworn to myself all day I would never do again, which was get together alone with Genie. I hated weakness. The realization that I was clearly my father's son, both in blood and now in behavior, did nothing to alleviate my disgust with myself.

The office door swung open. It was Jerry, closing in for the kill.

"You didn't tell me how pretty she is."

"Jerry, she's just a kid."

"Some kid—she's gorgeous, Michael. You didn't tell me because you're keeping her for yourself, aren't you? Hey, you have a tan. She has a tan. You can't fool me. I know you 'holier than thou' types; you're made of flesh and blood just like the rest of us. I envy you Michael. She's really something. I mean it. You're right to keep her from me."

I was sorely tempted to grab my .38 from the drawer and blast the bastard. But I controlled myself. I had to admit that Jerry was perceptive; I wondered if it were as obvious to everyone else.

"Jerry, you may not realize this, but it's actually a lot of work running this drugstore. What I suggest is, if you want to jerk yourself off, go do it out by the magazine rack with the other kids; at least that way I can get something done in here, okay?"

Jerry laughed. I envied his poise.

"Michael, don't be so serious. Relax. I meant it as a compliment. She's a great looking gal."

"She's also Ed Cotler's daughter, if you remember. I've known her since she was eleven. How would you like me to talk the way you're doing about one of your daughters?"

"I only wish my daughters were half as pretty as Miss Cotler."

"For a grown man, you can be pretty disgusting sometimes, you know that?"

"So I've been told."

"Jerry, what do you want?" I asked after staring at him for a thoughtful moment.

"I just went over the day's sales. Do you realize that since the robbery, business is up forty-two percent?"

"That's revolting."

"I think it's fantastic."

"I suppose you think that if I were to shoot another couple of people I could double our volume?"

"I'd never say that. But we're living in strange times, Michael. With this wave of publicity, your upcoming award from the mayor, the articles in the papers, the stories on TV, what I've been thinking is that we should take advantage of it. Strike while the iron is hot. We should open another store. Franchise. I've got the cash. We could move fast and make some big bucks out of this. What do you say?"

"I'll think about it," I responded without enthusiasm.

"That's it? This is a big idea. I expect a big reaction. How do you feel about it? Don't you want to make big money?"

"What I want to do is think about it."

"You mean you don't know what you think about it so you want to think about it?"

I nodded.

"Well, how does it hit you on a gut level?"

"I don't have an immediate reaction."

"You want to think about that, too?" Jerry said with some sarcasm.

"That sounds like a good idea.'

"You're a hard man, Michael. I've just come up with a million dollar idea and all you can do is think about it. Well think hard, okay?"

"I will. Thank you, Jerry."

I pretended to return to my work. Jerry took the hint and left. He was angry. This was the one bit of leverage I had on him and I had to figure out how to take advantage of it. Jerry had made one minor error when he bought into my business. He had forgotten to build into our agreement his right to own anything other than the existing store; he had no legal interest in franchising or expansions. I could open ten other stores across the country and he would have no claim to any ownership. Somehow, there had to be a way to use his desire to franchise to extricate myself from my partnership with him. Maybe I could get him to give up his share of the present store in exchange for some part of the future. I wondered how much potential he thought we actually had. This was a situation I would have to play very cool.

29

I had arranged to meet Genie at eight-thirty at a Mexican restaurant called La Cabaña, down by the Marina. This not only gave me time to play with Rebecca for an hour, but allowed a little last-minute strategy planning with Marilyn before her dinner with the surgeons.

La Cabaña had endeared itself to me years ago when it had been just a simple tin quonset hut left over from World War II. The best feature of the restaurant was not its green plastic booths, nor its cheap prices, nor even its excellent food; its secret lay in the skill of the old Mexican woman who stood in front of a steel griddle making corn tortillas by hand. I used to watch for hours as she patted the ground corn mixture into salad-plate sized cakes that, when cooked, swelled into the most delicious concoctions—different animals entirely from the cardboardlike, machine-made items packaged in the supermarkets. I hadn't been to La Cabaña in five years. Marilyn, being from New York, hadn't grown up on Mexican food and didn't particularly care for it. It also didn't go with her diet; "too fatty," she claimed. Which it was. But it was also delicious. Would the tortilla lady still be there?

I parked my car on Rose Avenue and walked down the dark block to La Cabaña. It was always a thrill to walk in this neighborhood because of its location right on the fringe of the local ghetto. Ethnic food eaten in an actual ghetto always tasted better, I felt, not because it was more authentic, but as a result of the spiciness of a potentially dangerous situation. It did occur to me that letting Genie drive herself alone through this neighborhood was perhaps a mistake. On the other hand, I reminded myself, she was a very clever girl and could certainly take care of herself.

I approached the restaurant just as an ambulance, its siren wailing, pulled away from the curb and roared off toward some hospital, Marina Mercy most likely. There was considerable commotion by the front door, where two policemen were questioning bystanders. The ambulance apparently carried a patron of the restaurant. Had there been a fight?

As the cashier directed me to a table, I couldn't quite believe how La Cabaña had changed, thanks to the magic of two-by-fours and plaster. The quonset hut had been expanded and was now a large restaurant. But the green plastic booths were the same; there were just more of them. The big change was in the center of the place, where a huge bar was now located—obviously the profit center. I was watching the bartender mix a batch of margaritas when I spotted her. Or more accurately, when I first heard her. From behind the bar came a rhythmic slapping which I instantly recognized as the sound of human hands patting out tortillas. I got up from the table, walked around the bar, and there she was—the same ageless Mexican woman, standing by her griddle making one tortilla after another. How old was she? She could have been sixty. She could have been ninety. It was impossible to determine her age.

I watched her work, fascinated. Never had I seen anyone so content. Her skill consisted of grabbing a small ball of dough from a wooden bucket, flattening it with her fingers, working it with her palms, then finally slapping it back and forth into its traditional shape. This was history I was watching. She could have been an Aztec mother preparing food for her family. She did work that was necessary and knew with certainty her place in society. I tried to read her face. Did she resent what she did? Did she hate her boss? Did she feel exploited? Did she feel she lived in the middle of a culture in chaos? Did she have a tormented and crazy love life with her husband? "No" appeared to be the answer to all of my questions. On the tortilla lady's face was serenity. She felt appreciated, a part of the center of her community. She wasn't running after men, or lusting after power. She had no hunger for possessions. The woman lived in harmony. The restaurant needed her far more than she needed it. She was the restaurant; without her it was nothing.

As I watched the tortilla lady, the thought ran through my mind that perhaps if I could learn to do what she did I, too, would be content. I considered approaching the woman. An apprenticeship was probably the way to do it; certainly there was no Tortilla College in Mexico. Would she accept an apprentice? If she would, would it be me? I spoke no Spanish and she didn't look like she knew English. Culturally, I didn't appear to be the ideal candidate. How could I explain to her why I wanted to be a tortilla maker? Would she understand? She would, I knew that after one look at her face. It was a crazy idea. I could imagine the conversation in which I told Marilyn that I had given up the pharmacy for a career making tortillas. She'd have me committed. The truth was that the woman making tortillas appeared to have a much richer and more meaningful life than anything Marilyn and I could conceive of. But Marilyn would only be interested if I could prove how the tortilla diet reduced serum cholesterol levels. Or that making tortillas by hand was aerobic— better than jogging for the cardiovascular system. She would even understand if it succeeded as a meditation, as long as I did something practical like write a book about it: *Zen and the Art of Tortilla Making*.

"What is the secret of life?" I would ask the tortilla lady. Her answer would be simple: "Pat the dough flat, cook it evenly, not too long and not too little, eat it slowly, then wash out your bowl."

"Michael, what are you watching?"

I jumped and spun around. It was Genie.

"Hey, I didn't see you. You look great."

"Michael, I've been standing behind you for almost five minutes watching you stare at that lady; she's a little old for you, isn't she?"

"Just shows what you know. Come on, let's sit down."

But Genie didn't budge. She wasn't going to let me off the hook that easily.

"You're not going to tell me why you were watching her?"

"Yeah okay." I decided to take the chance. "Look at her face."

Genie examined the woman's face.

"Now you tell me, have you ever seen a happier, more peaceful person?"

Genie watched the woman for a minute, then turned to me.

"You're crazy, you know that?"

"You don't think she's happy?"

"Who knows, Michael. I'm sure she is at moments. Just like everyone else."

"You don't think she's happy all the time? I mean, like content with her life. You don't see an extraordinary person in there?"

"I see a poor old Mexican woman who knows her place and is content to stay in it. I'm a romantic, Michael, but not that romantic."

I looked at the tortilla lady and thought about what Genie said. Maybe she was right. Then again, maybe she wasn't. How would I ever know?

"Do I get a kiss hello?" Genie teased me. "Or are you afraid your girlfriend over there," she pointed to the tortilla lady, "will be jealous?"

I scanned the restaurant, saw no one even remotely familiar, took the chance, quickly kissed Genie on the lips, then led her to the table.

The dinner conversation ended up being very different from what I had expected. My fantasies about the tortilla lady led Genie and me into a discussion of the nature of happiness, during which I heard all kinds of interesting observations from her about politics, ideals, and the way she hoped to live. Genie reminded me of girls I had known in college. I would have described them as Bohemian: girls claiming to be dissatisfied living as their mothers had, girls looking for adventure and excitement, not for a night but for their entire lives. I could picture Genie in the 1930's running off to Paris to become a novelist. In the fifties she would have bummed around the country, on the road with Jack Kerouac or Lenny Bruce. Had she gone to college in the sixties, it definitely would have been Berkeley. Perhaps she would have ended up with Ken Kesey or Tim Leary. Her great regret was not having lived in the early sixties so she could have gone to Mississippi and been part of the Freedom Rides.

It all seemed rather strange and incongruous. Here was this classically gorgeous California surfer girl. Yet most of her questions to me had to do with what I had done in the late sixties and early seventies. Had I known Eldridge Cleaver and Bobby Seal? Had I dropped acid with Baba Ram Dass? Had I been to Esalen or Sandstone? Had I fought in Vietnam? The list went on and on and covered all the big activities of the era.

What I found remarkable about Genie was that she seemed to understand and even approve of my explanation for not having done any of the things she asked about. The facts about my family and my obsession with work were clearly acceptable to her. What seemed important to Genie was my spirit, that I wished circumstances had allowed me to experiment a bit more with my life. She felt we were two of a kind. Both of us admired the freedom of the sixties, yet neither of us had known it. Genie, in fact, had just read *The Electric Kool-Aid Acid Test* and she longed to be part of such an adventure. She tried to liken my experiences with my schizophrenic father to life with the Merry Pranksters, as if living with my father was akin to living in the middle of the Haight-Ashbury in 1967. I explained to Genie that madness was not something to romanticize; that it was actually terrifying, destructive, and horribly painful, particularly when, as a child, you couldn't figure out what was going on. But I don't think she really believed me. She trusted her own ideas. However, although she disagreed with me, she didn't put me down for my opinions. In fact, she was very tolerant and I found myself able to really relax with her. The margaritas helped bring on a little levity. Soon we became very playful. I even joked with the waiter about the ambulance I had seen drive away from the restaurant.

"Had the person they hauled away eaten here?" I asked the man.

The waiter nodded and pointed to a booth against the wall on the other side of the room.

"A woman over there had bad chest pains," he told us. "Then her heart stopped. But the paramedics shocked it and it started again."

"What had the lady eaten?" I asked joking, implying that was the cause of the coronary.

"The number four, just like you had." The waiter grinned, pleased with his comeback, and walked away.

That night all of my grief, rage, and torment miraculously vanished and were replaced by a sensual, cheerful optimism. Genie and I laughed over the most incredibly painful details of our lives. Everything that would have hurt me to think about that morning now seemed terribly funny. It was a remarkable transformation that I couldn't begin to explain to myself.

The conversation led to Nick, Genie's ex-boyfriend. She confessed that she hadn't told the full story about him, and she wanted me to know everything. Obviously he still had some hold over her. What she had seen in Nick was the wild, exciting, romantic, young man right out of the sixties, the counter-culture personified, the surfer-fisherman who lived off the land—handsome, self-sufficient, and sensual. But what really impressed her was the way he earned his living.

One weekend in the spring, when her parents were out of town, Genie managed to get away with Nick on an overnight fishing trip. It was just the two of them on his twenty-six-foot fiberglass powerboat. They left Santa Barbara Harbor at dawn on a Saturday morning and blasted across the channel toward Santa Rosa Island. Their goal was Beecher's Bay, a half-mile-wide anchorage protected from the prevailing forty-knot winds by fifty-foot cliffs jutting almost straight out of the Pacific. The ninety minute crossing was a wild and wet ride, far rougher than anything Genie had imagined. Nick handled the seven foot seas like an expert, piloting his fast craft through the dark and turbulent water which Genie knew, in less skilled hands, would have been very dangerous. Out at Beecher's Bay, winds howled down from Point Conception with a fierceness she hadn't known possible. Nick referred to the area as the "Cape Horn of the

Pacific.'' Genie had no reason to doubt him. They anchored in the lee of the cliffs and Nick began to dive for abalone.

Nick taught Genie how to run the ''hookah,'' the air compressor that allowed him to breathe while he was under water. Commercial abalone divers don't use scuba gear because it's uneconomical and allows for much less diving time than the hookah, which simply pumps surface air via hoses down to the diver. Genie had a tremendous responsibility while Nick was below; in fact, she realized that he was trusting her with his life. If something happened to his air supply while he was very deep, Nick could be a dead man. No one had ever given her such a critical task. She was moved by his belief in her abilities.

However, fishing for abalone had distinct drawbacks, as she saw that day. Throughout the seven hours that Nick dove, she had to sit outside by the hookah, exposed to the howling wind and chilling temperature. As wild and beautiful as the channel appeared between Santa Rosa and Santa Cruz island, it was extremely cold and uncomfortable. Despite all of Nick's time underwater, he was able to land only four saleable pink abalone worth, maybe, $40 wholesale. To Genie, it seemed a scary and unprofitable business.

That night they anchored as close to the cliffs as possible. Although Nick claimed to have anchored there hundreds of times, Genie was up all night, frightened by the continuous weaving and bobbing motion of the hull, as well as the sound of the wind screaming off the bluffs. Spending the night in that plastic, four- by-seven-foot cuddy cabin, eating Hamburger Helper with Rice-A-Roni, was not what she had anticipated. It was a rough, cold, hard, and dangerous way to make a living.

The second day out they made the rounds of Nick's lobster traps. Here they had good luck and hauled in a respectable load, enough to pay for the gas, oil, and food and even have fifty bucks left over as profit. But the work here also was back-breaking. Full-throttle runs from one trap to the next. Retrieve the float from the water, connect the line to the hydraulic pot hauler, then crank up the trap from the depths as fast as possible. As soon as the trap broke the surface, it was swung aboard and dropped to the deck of the pitching boat. Only one trap out of twenty came up with a lobster inside, and half of those were undersized and were legally required to be thrown back. The rest of the traps had to be opened and rebaited with the horribly

smelly fish heads Nick had saved for this purpose. Then it was
back into the water for the trap and on to the next float. That
Sunday certainly wasn't a day of leisure. By the afternoon Genie
had begun to wonder where Nick really got the money to buy his
boat, his new pickup truck and the snazzy clothes he favored.

On the long ride home Nick confessed to his sideline of
stealing cars for chop shops. But within a couple of weeks, even
that didn't make sense to Genie. There just wasn't enough
money in car theft, as Nick was doing it, to support his
expensive habits. Finally he admitted that he was also dealing
drugs. Coke, amphetamines, and PCP were his specialties, all of
which Genie had already experimented with on numerous occa-
sions. She had no prejudice against drug dealers, and saw the
occupation as both romantic and hazardous. She was smart
enough to realize, however, that unlike the dangers of commercial fishing, drug dealing happened to be highly illegal and
frequently led to nasty vendettas involving serious injury, murder, or at the very least, long-term vacations in federal peniten-
tiaries. As exciting as it might be to have a boyfriend in jail, the
reality of the situation was more than she felt she could handle.
Once she realized the scope of Nick's activities, she became too
frightened to enjoy him. As unique as he was, life with Nick
dramatically increased her own chances of dying. Although
death was an interesting concept to Genie, it was not something
that she wanted any part of in reality.

In my optimistic mood, as Genie told me about Nick, I
couldn't help but make the comparison between him and myself.

In a bizarre way, Nick and I were both in the same business.
We both sold drugs. The difference was that I did it legally and
he didn't. Genie had been attracted to Nick. Now she was
attracted to me. I suspected that he and I had to have more in
common than anyone would have thought at first glance.

It was such a strange sensation to sit at that table with Genie,
so passionately drawn to her, so sexually excited by her, yet
knowing that everything I felt about her was considered grossly
immoral and illegal under the laws of both the state and the
federal government. I had crossed a line I had thought I would
never even approach; I had become a criminal. At the moment I
was strangely unafraid; I had no idea where it was all going to
lead. Could it end anywhere but in disaster? Every criminal, I
suppose, asks himself questions as he steps over that forbidden

border between the legal and the illegal. Everyone who traverses that line finds a way to rationalize his own particular situation. Each person wants to believe that the path they follow is an exception to the law and is not only necessary but makes reasonable sense. That's the moment outlaws define themselves, celebrating their courage to step outside the conventional boundaries of society. For me, at the restaurant, realizing I had become an outlaw was an exciting moment. Life was suddenly dramatic, like in wartime. Real enemies were after me. The police and the courts wanted to jail me. I had a mission to accomplish with Genie. I wanted to survive and succeed in that mission. I had to make it through.

Over coffee, Genie and I talked about what to do next; we could hardly sit in the restaurant all night. Genie had an idea that caused her to giggle. Driving to La Cabaña, she had passed a complex that billed itself as an "Adult Motel." She had never been in an adult motel and had never seen a porno film. Genie wanted to know if we could rent a room in the motel and watch a film together.

Out of that restaurant in record time, we drove in her car to the Sea View motel. Genie waited in the Mustang while I went to take care of a room. The office was really just a cage, something like the cashier's window in a drive-through fast food restaurant. The man behind the glass barrier appeared to be in his early twenties, a college student, tired, overworked, probably barely earning enough money to see himself through the semester. He asked me how long I wanted the room. I reserved it for two hours. Fifty dollars was the charge. I paid in cash without looking him in the eye. As he gave me change from the three twenties, I noticed the book he was reading: *Basic Pharmacology*. He was studying to be a druggist. Someday I might even run into him at a Pharmaceutical Association meeting where, horror of horrors, he might recognize me. It was too late to ask for my money back and run; the damage, if there ever were to be any damage, had been done.

"Room sixteen if just across the motorcourt," he told me, returning to his book.

I scanned the half-empty parking lot for familiar faces and, of course, saw none. Then I walked to the Mustang and held the door open for Genie.

"All set," I told her.

Genie was hard-pressed to keep up with my fast walk to number sixteen. I quickly unlocked the cheap particle board door and gestured for her to enter. I followed and immediately double-locked the door from the inside. Then I turned to inspect the room. It was decorated in cheap motel sleaze, all purple, with a king-sized water bed. My first thought was bacteria. I was paying to rent a room that appeared more fertile than a laboratory petrie dish culturing disease. I saw herpes, syphilis, gonorrhea, and who knows what else lurking in the fibers of the well-used linens and blankets. By the foot of the bed stood an old color TV, chained and cabled to the wall. Stay or go, I asked myself. The place had obviously been vacuumed and dusted since the last guests. But no amount of scrubbing could ever make it feel clean; burning it was the only solution I could see. The room held a sense of lives lived in despair, of drunken couples copulating in desperation, hoping to momentarily block out both the future and the certainty of death. The atmosphere was that of a sinking lifeboat in an ocean of hopelessness.

Genie flashed me that smile of hers.

"God, this is great; better than I ever imagined."

"Really?" I inquired innocently.

She nodded.

"You going to write a piece on this for your school newspaper, too?"

"You never know," she smiled, holding open her arms.

I embraced Genie with a passion. She clung to me, wrapping her long legs around my thigh and squeezing herself up against me. I forgot about the room, forgot about death, forgot about everything, and just let the feelings of sex sweep over me. It was amazing how quickly the animal in both of us took over and blotted out the world from which we had just come. Within moments we were undoing buttons, sliding open zippers, unfastening hooks, stripping off pants, and slipping out of underwear.

Then came that wonderful thrill, possibly the most exciting moment of the night, when our bodies were both finally naked and first touched together, breast to breast, hip to hip, toe to toe. Pressing up against Genie and embracing her was like the shock one gets jumping into the ocean on a cold winter day—every nerve ending in my body came alive and screamed with feeling. Genie and I stood in the center of the room, kissing, for what seemed like hours. Occasionally, I would look up at the gold-flecked mirror on the ceiling and admire our reflection. Genie was so extraordinarily beautiful; I felt young again, as if I were blossoming for the first time.

Suddenly a loud metallic click, like a door latch unlocking, shattered the silence of the room. It was followed by voices and music. Terrified, I jumped away from Genie. Someone had entered the room, I was sure. I calmed down and traced the sound to the television, which apparently had been turned on by the distant manager. On the screen, *Behind the Green Door* was beginning. It was porno show time. Genie and I looked at each other and laughed. It had frightened her, too. I shrugged as if it were nothing. Then I remembered Debby the doughnut eater and my daughter.

"Genie, turn the volume down and watch the movie for a minute; I have to make a call."

She nodded, pulled down the bedcovers, and sat yoga-style at the foot of the bed watching the now silent porno film

With my back to Genie, I went to the phone and dialed my home. Debby answered. Of course, she was chewing on something. Rebecca was asleep. Marilyn had called to say that an emergency cesarean would keep her very late at the hospital. I told Debby that my Pharmaceutical Association conference would also be late and that I might not be home for a couple of hours. That was fine with her; she simply reminded me that after twelve she got time and a half. As well as all she could eat, I almost added.

After hanging up the phone, I turned around and got a new shock. Genie was sitting on the bed in the same yoga position, but as she watched the copulating images on the TV, she was masturbating herself with her right hand while simultaneously caressing her nipples and breasts with her left hand. I was instantly aroused, fully erect. Unselfconsciously, Genie shifted her gaze from the TV set to my cock, then slid herself back away from the television onto the middle part of the bed, all the while continuing to masturbate. She lay still for a moment, watching the couple in the porno film. Then she beckoned to me.

I climbed onto the bed, where I could see what she was watching. A man was lying on his back, naked, on a bed with two women. The man had an enormous cock; in the film it looked to be over a foot long. One of the women squatted over the man's erection and drew herself up and down in slow motion. The other woman squatted over the man's face and thrust herself against his hyperactive tongue.

"Hold my legs," Genie commanded.

I did as she requested and pinned her legs down. She continued to play with herself, obviously very excited. On the television the woman being eaten was approaching an orgasm, as was the woman riding the man's cock. So, apparently, was Genie. The woman being eaten suddenly started screaming with pleasure and pressed hard against the man's mouth. This excited the other woman, who started to thrust with great vigor against the man's cock, arousing him further. He spread his legs apart and began to arch himself upward, as if he could push himself further into the woman above him. Everyone on the screen was moaning. As was Genie. At that moment the woman riding the man's cock screamed with pleasure as she had a tremendous orgasm. The man, however, was not there yet and kept pumping away. The woman who'd come, momentarily spent, lifted herself off of the man, who for a few moments kept thrusting his huge penis up into the air as if he were fucking the sky. The man couldn't stand it, grabbed himself, and began masturbating wildly while the second woman still sat on his face, letting herself be eaten. The first woman became aroused again at the sight of the man masturbating, pulled his hands from his huge dick, and began sucking on him. This clearly excited her and she furthered her own pleasure by openly playing with herself with one hand as she squeezed the man's balls with the other. Everyone on the screen was panting and moaning, as was Genie, whose legs I was still holding down.

The woman sitting on the man's face began to scream in an extended howl of pleasure. As she came in a long series of spasmodic movements, the man's face turned red, his eyes closed, and he, too, began to scream. At that moment the woman sucking on him pulled her mouth away, the camera moved in for a closeup, and a huge stream of pure white sperm shot across the screen like Old Faithful.

Genie gritted her teeth and shifted her gaze to me.

"Michael," she urged me, "I need your big cock now. Fuck me, Michael."

I climbed onto Genie and slid inside of her. She was so wet and warm, yet so tight. Almost as soon as I was deep into her, she began to writhe and moan, shoving herself hard against me.

It took every ounce of self-control I possessed to keep from shooting myself off into her. Genie hovered on the edge and then came with a shriek. An instant later she lay back limp on the sheet. I remained inside of her, still hard. I licked the sweat from her forehead and tenderly kissed her face.

"Michael, that was amazing," she moaned softly.

Genie opened her eyes and stared past me to the television set. The trio were at it again. This time, one of the women lay on her back while the man sat between her legs, holding them open, and slowly slid in and out of her. The second woman sat on the first woman's face and was being eaten as well as being sodomized by the first woman's index finger. Genie became excited again and began thrusting against me. For a few minutes it felt as if Genie and I had melted into the scene on the television. Five bodies in a room and all doing nothing but fucking. Genie began to moan, then came with another one of her shrieks, causing me to finally lose control and blast an incredible orgasm into her. We lay in one another's arms, soaking wet and momentarily sapped of all strength.

I became young again that night. Strong. Connected to passion. It was too wonderful for words. As physically exhausted as I was when we slunk out of the seedy motel, spiritually I was flying high, feeling powerful, energetic, and most of all, euphorically optimistic. Life again had a million possibilities; all I had to do was choose and they would be mine. It was the way I had felt as a kid, surfing, before my father's illness had pushed me into the adult world and forced me to discipline myself so harshly.

I couldn't help thinking of my old man as Genie drove me back to my car outside of La Cabaña. How many times, I wondered, had my father found himself in a situation similar to mine? If my dad's problems with my mother resembled at all my difficulties with Marilyn, I certainly could understand the motivations for his seemingly crazy activities. It astounded me how wrong I might have been in thinking of my mother as simply the innocent, injured party to my father's insanity. That night it occurred to me for the first time that my mother might have always been demanding, unforgiving and embittered and that maybe she, in fact, had been the one who had driven my father crazy. Such an insight fascinated me. Would I ever know for sure?

Genie parked her car behind mine, shut off the engine and lights, and smiled at me.

"So, you have a good time?" she teased.

"I've had worse."

"Think you want to see me again?"

"I'd consider it," I teased back.

"Michael, we're pretty good together, aren't we?"

"Too good."

"How can we be too good?'

"I didn't expect this; it scares me."

"That means you like me."

"That's exactly what it means."

"Well, I like you too. But you know that."

"I like hearing it."

"So do I."

For a moment neither of us said anything. I didn't know where to go from there.

"Something's wrong; what is it, Michael?"

"Nothing."

"Michael, come on. I feel it off you; tell me what it is."

"Promise you won't laugh."

"You didn't laugh at me; why should I laugh at you?"

"Uhh. The truth is, I don't want to go home. I have to but I don't see how I can. It seems crazy but I don't know what else to do."

"You think it's easy for me to go back to being Ed's cute little girl? The other night you saw how he is."

"What are we going to do, Genie?" I spoke seriously and deliberately. "This could get out of hand very easily."

"You don't think it's out of hand already?" Genie was amused.

"That's what I'm trying to avoid."

"You know what we should do?" she asked me.

I didn't, but I also was not crazy about the way she said it. Something was coming, I knew, that I didn't want to hear.

"You and I should do what we weren't able to do in the sixties. What you wanted to do. What I want to do. We should be spontaneous. Buy an old bus and just take off. Cross the United States together, put the bus on a boat, and head through Europe. See the world. Have that adventure. Think about it, Michael. If we're good together now, we'll be great together after a year on the road. Let's change our lives and do it, what do you say? It's crazy. But the whole world is crazy today. I mean, why the hell not?''

Jesus, I thought, another woman who wants to change my life. ''Genie, it's a lovely idea. But I have my daughter, my wife, and my drugstore to think about, remember? I can't just run away from everything.''

''Says who?''

''Says me.''

''I thought you wanted to feel something, to change your life.''

''I do.''

''Then do it.''

''Genie, it's not that easy to just throw away everything you've worked your whole life to build.''

''Remember what Lenin said: 'One step backward for every two steps forward.' To make progress you've got to give some things up.''

''That's easy to say, but doing it is a whole different story.''

''That's what you said about going surfing with me; did that turn out so bad?''

''You're serious about running off with me? You'd actually do it?''

''Michael,'' she leveled her gaze at me, ''I don't say things I don't mean.''

''What about finishing high school? And college? How are you going to be a journalist without going to college?''

''You don't think a year travelling around the world with you would teach me more than a couple of semesters at school?''

''Genie, listen. I have a problem with the law—the junkie's wife is suing me, remember? I can't go anywhere until we resolve the case or they'll put me in jail. Changing my life is one thing. Changing it to live in the penitentiary is something else.''

''Michael, you're not going to jail.''

''That's what I hope, too. But you never know, do you?''

''My dad says there's no chance of your doing time.''

''Yeah, well, you ask if he wants to do the time for me in case he's wrong.''

''He's not wrong, Michael. That's what's so terrible about living at home. That's why I want to get out of there. He's always right about everything. There's no room in his world for anyone else to even breathe, much less really live.''

"Genie," I spoke quietly and patiently. "You're an incredibly smart girl. What's going on here between us is wonderful, totally unexpected—magical. And I want it to continue but it scares me. Who knows where it's going to lead? The trip you're talking about sounds great. But I can't do it now. And you can't. Running away from your father, running away from your dreams of journalism, that's wrong. That's like a modern version of the girls who got married at eighteen just to get out of the house. You don't want that, do you?''

That last remark infuriated Genie.

"All I wanted, Michael," she yelled, "all I suggested, was that if you want to change your life you do it now so that in twenty years you're not still behind the counter of the drugstore regretting what you didn't do. I was trying to help you, Michael. I thought it'd be good for both of us. But I can see that you don't understand.''

Genie leaned forward and gave me a cool peck of a kiss on my cheek.

"Goodnight Michael. Thanks for dinner and the movie; it's been fun.''

She leaned over me and opened the passenger door. I didn't move. Instead I swung the door closed.

"Genie, come on; let's not end the night like this. If I disappointed you, I'm sorry. I care about you, you know that. It scares me so much. I don't know yet what to do with my feelings toward you. Everything's happening so fast, be a little patient, will you?''

"Does that mean you'll at least think about what I said? You'll think about the trip?''

"Yes.''

"Promise?''

"I promise.''

"If you really think about it, you'll realize it's not such a bad idea.''

"Genie, I told you I'd think about it.''

I was telling everyone lately that I would "think about" their proposals. I said it to Marilyn about the health spa, to Jerry about franchising, to Ed about my legal defense, to the Republican power brokers about politics, and now I was saying the same thing to Genie. If I actually thought about everything that I said I would consider, I'd have no time for anything else. There was nothing to think about; I was simply stalling. Why did no one see that?

Genie and I lingered over a last long kiss. I couldn't seem to get enough of her. In fact, my erection began to reassert itself and I wondered if we shouldn't try it one more time there in her car outside of La Cabaña. Finally I decided it was too late and too risky; and there'd be no place for us to clean up. So I got out of the Mustang. Genie promised to call me the next day at the pharmacy. I unlocked the door of my Oldsmobile, got in, started the engine, and waved goodbye to Genie, who drove off. It was one-fourteen in the morning. What the hell was I going to tell Marilyn this time?

30

For the second night in a row, I was blessed. After racing home across the city, I discovered that Marilyn was still at the hospital. There was nothing to worry about. I paid off the doughnut eater, then checked on Rebecca. My daughter was peacefully asleep, safe and healthy. I pulled the blanket up over her chest and sat with her for half an hour, listening to her breathe. The fact that she was alive, a product of mine, and that every day she grew and changed never ceased to amaze me. I could watch her for hours. The one thing I knew I could never do was give her up.

Shortly after two I went to sleep. At three-thirty Marilyn awakened me. She was wired, excited as hell, and she wanted to share her good news with me. The surgeons had loved her proposal and confirmed their promise to back her to the tune of a million dollars. Marilyn showered me with kisses. She attributed her success to my help with the prospectus. Her dream, "our dream," she kept telling me, was now going to be a reality thanks to my coaching. Without me, she repeated, it couldn't have happened.

I had to admit that this energetic, optimistic, loving side of Marilyn was very appealing. For the moment, all of her tension, her obsessive drive, was gone, she was vibrant and affectionate.

We were victorious and she wanted to share her elation with me. In fact, she had even brought a bottle of champagne up to the bedroom with her. She toasted "our partnership, our friendship, and our future."

Marilyn and I drank together. This in itself was something extraordinary because in the last year I had seldom seen her indulge in anything stronger than Perrier. Something was definitely changing.

After the first glass, she poured each of us a second, then surprised me again. Just as she had done on Sunday morning by the pool, she stripped off her clothes and crawled into bed. She wanted me. Having had only one hour of sleep since my romp with Genie, I was exhausted and more than a little anxious about contending with a horny wife. But the possibility of intimacy with the Marilyn of old—the warm, loving woman I had courted and married—miraculously got me going.

Within moments she was on top of me, pumping away furiously. Whether it was the champagne that propelled her or the news about the health spa didn't matter. I felt a real difference. She had changed. Not only was she looking at me, she was responding to *me* sexually, not to a fantasy.

But my pleasure was short-lived. Her excitement reached a plateau and went no further. As hard as she tired, she was unable to climax. So she shifted gears and urged me to recite "the story." I hid my discouragement and narrated an abbreviated version that propelled her straight through to orgasm. Moments later she rolled off me, exhausted. My dashed expectations made the moment particularly depressing. The vivid memory of Genie made it even worse. I was a lonely man condemned by fate to the unsatisfying service of his beautiful wife's needs.

"Did you come, Michael?" she inquired.

"At the same time you did, sweetheart," I lied. "It was wonderful."

"I'm so glad," she purred. "I do love you, Michael."

"I know that, sweetheart."

Marilyn closed her eyes and almost instantly was asleep. I wish it had been so easy for me. I lay in bed, totally conscious, until my alarm finally went off at six-thirty.

31

Wednesday at work I was too tired to do anything other than mechanically answer the phone and delegate as many prescription orders as possible. Such tasks as metering out the correct dosage of belladonna for Mr. Jacobs took double or triple the time they would have ordinarily. Knowing I was exhausted made me extra cautious; on top of everything else I didn't want to make a mistake and kill a customer.

Oddly enough, the tired fog I was floating in somehow comforted me. I realized that for the first time in my life, I felt loved by women. Marilyn, Rebecca, and Genie, each in her own way, adored me. Being loved simply for myself was not something I had ever really known in the past. But that morning I felt it, and it gave me strength as I stood at the counter, filling prescriptions and making small talk with the stream of curious customers who continued to come in simply to congratulate me on my handling of the robbery.

By lunchtime, as I waited for a call from Genie, I became acutely conscious of time and how incredibly slowly it was moving. In an attempt to compensate for my lack of sleep, I drank cup after cup of coffee. This resulted in me feeling even more spaced out than I had in the morning. I was beyond the simple reach of caffeine; what I needed was sleep. By two o'clock I was so tired I could hardly read the keys of the typewriter. That was when I took my first chance of the day and did something for which I would have fired any employee: I went back into the storeroom and surreptitiously swallowed two capsules of Dexedrine. Ten minutes later I was wide awake. Fifteen minutes later I was wired. Five minutes after that I received the shock of my life.

Standing behind the drug counter filling an order, I became aware of an odd sensation: someone was watching me. But when I looked around the store, I saw nothing unusual, just my employees plus ten or twelve customers. I tried to go back to work, but the feeling persisted; I was sure someone was staring at me. I wondered if I should attribute the feeling to the

Dexedrine; paranoia is one of the drug's most common side effects. The more I tried to shrug off the sensation, the more it persisted. Someone in the store was studying me, I was sure. But who? And where? With my eyes I slowly made a sweep of the pharmacy. But again the place seemed normal. Could it be what Marilyn had feared: another robbery? My thoughts turned to my pistol and where it was hidden.

Suddenly a familiar face popped up across the counter from me. It was Genie's ex-boyfriend, Nick.

"Could I talk to you for a minute?" he asked with an ostensible politeness that failed to conceal something ominous.

I pretended not to recognize him; after all, we had never actually met.

"Yes?"

He checked out the other druggists to make sure no one was listening.

"I think you'd be happier if we could talk alone," Nick said quietly.

"Pardon me, young man, but who are you?"

"You don't know me?"

"Should I?"

Nick spoke in a low, threatening voice.

"Don't bullshit me, Marcus, you know very well who I am."

"Young man," I tried to sound indignant, "unless you want the police to introduce us, I suggest you turn yourself around and walk your ass out of my store. And fast, before I get angry."

Nick leaned across the counter to make sure I was the only person who heard him.

"I don't think you want to do that, Marcus. I think you'd rather go someplace where we can be alone and I can show you some pictures I took of you and a young girl we both know. I think they'll interest you."

The horror of the situation became clear when I examined the snapshots behind the locked door of my office. My fears had taken shape in the form of black and white, eight by ten nightmares. Not only had the scumbag photographed Genie and me surfing at San Onofre, he had picture after picture of us lying on the beach kissing, smoking dope, and hitchhiking after her car (it was obvious now who had stolen the stereo). He even had photos of us leaving La Cabaña arm in arm, parking in the lot of the porno motel, and entering room number sixteen. Nick claimed to have other pictures of us inside the motel room that he'd taken with infrared film through a gap in the curtains. Those "hadn't been processed yet," but would be in another twenty-four hours, if I happened to be interested in seeing them, too.

My first impulse was to grab my .38 from the drawer and blast the kid right between the eyes. I could explain it as another robbery. The only problem was that he was unarmed. Without an obvious weapon, I could hardly plead self-defense. I wondered whether more problems with the ACLU and the law would actually be worse than the blackmail I was now facing. I managed to restrain my rage; the least I could do was to find out what Nick wanted. I could always shoot him later.

"So what's the point of this?" I asked.

"Photography's a hobby of mine. You two seemed like a good subject for a photo essay. 'May-December Love,' I'm going to call it."

It took every ounce of self-control I could muster not to shoot Nick on the spot.

"Why show these to me?"

"I figured you might like to buy them. I don't know if Genie told you about me. I've been in the fishing business. The last year has been real bad, thanks to El Niño. I've decided fishing is too unreliable and I want to go into a line of work that's more steady, like photography. It's something I've always been good at; I mean these are pretty high-quality photos, given the conditions they were taken in, don't you think?"

I said nothing.

"What I figured was, you might like to help me out in my career move by buying a few portraits of you and your girlfriend. What do you think?"

Nick was so god-damned cocky; I wished I had his little blackmail pitch on tape because I knew no jury in the world would convict me for shooting him after they had heard his revolting line of reasoning.

"Does Genie know about this?" I asked.

"I don't see any reason to bring her into it, do you?"

"You really think you can get away with this?"

"I'm here, aren't I?"

"You expect me to pay you for these?"

"I have no doubt about it at all."

"I suppose you want me to buy the prints while you keep the negatives."

"Hey, I'm simply a photographer; you can buy as little or as much as you want."

"Right. If you were me, what would you buy?"

"I don't know. You're a married man. You've got a prosperous business. You don't look like the kind of guy who does things half-way. No, you're definitely a first class sort of person. I think you'd want to buy everything, negatives and all."

"I suppose you have a price in mind for everything—some kind of package deal."

As Nick stared at me I could feel the wheels in his brain spin like crazy as he reviewed the figures he was carrying in his head. He was asking himself if he was being too greedy. Or perhaps he wondered if he should demand more for his artwork. What he was evaluating was my fear and how much he thought my marriage and reputation were worth to me.

To be honest, I was terrified almost to the point of paralysis. I tried to sit calmly and appear as if the pictures meant very little to me. All the little bastard had to do was to show the photos to Marilyn, or, God forbid, to the police, or even to Alice Allen, the wife of the junkie, and my life would be over. The police would arrest me for statutory rape, contributing to the delinquency of a minor, oral copulation, so on and so forth. And the ACLU would crucify whatever defense I formulated against their wrongful death charges by attacking my character as morally defective. I would be a rapist as well as a murderer. Marilyn would, of course, ditch me on the spot and I'd lose all rights as a father to Rebecca. What divorce court would give custody of a young daughter to a convicted child molester? The Pharmaceutical Association would instantly withdraw my license, leaving me without any means of support. And Jerry would take over the drugstore for peanuts.

As I sat waiting for Nick's answer, I knew that, in fact, the endless list of my fears was meaningless in light of what Genie's father's reaction would be. His rage and jealousy over my betrayal would compel Ed to blow my brains all over the street. Nick definitely had me with his blackmail; the question was, for how much?

"Why don't you tell me what you think they're worth to you?" Nick finally proposed.

"What do you want for them?"

"I asked you what you thought they were worth."

"Look, when you come into my store and want to buy something, I tell you how much I'll sell it to you for; that's what I'm asking you."

"Let's start with this." Nick grinned arrogantly. "While I figure out what they're worth to me, why don't you demonstrate that you're serious about buying by giving me some sort of deposit?"

"That's not the way I do business."

"That's the way you're going to do it with me."

"You want a deposit, name me a price first."

Nick's eyes narrowed. He wanted me to know he was a tough guy.

"Listen, Marcus, these are my pictures and we'll do business my way. Unless you'd rather have me send a few copies to, say, Genie's dad. Or to the police."

"Nick, I don't really think that's going to help anything."

"Oh, congratulations, you finally remembered my name. You are a smart man. Now why don't you be reasonable and think about that deposit."

"As long as I've been in business, I've never believed in buying things on time. I'm not about to start now with you. Give me a price on the whole shebang and I'll give you a yes or no."

After thinking it over for a moment, Nick made me his offer.

"What I could use right now is $250, a hundred tabs of Methedrine, and a quarter ounce of dental-purity cocaine. That's the deposit. I'll figure the total price tomorrow when I see how the infrared film turns out."

Controlling my panic was very difficult. If I gave Nick drugs I would be jeopardizing my career. But no matter how I looked at it, I was screwed; Nick had me. There appeared to be no way out of the problem. Nick had nothing to lose.

"Cash I can give you. But the pharmaceuticals will take a couple of days. What you're asking for can't just disappear; it's got to be accounted for to the federal government."

"However you want to play it, Marcus. You only give me part of what I ask, I'll only send part of the photos to Genie's dad. That sound fair enough?"

"Nick, listen. I'm trying to be straight with you. I'm trying to work with you. Give me a break, will you?"

My mind was reeling. I saw disaster at every turn. No options seemed viable. I needed time. How could I get time? My only choice was to buy it.

"I've given you my terms, Marcus. The choice is yours."

The son-of-a-bitch was not budging. That's when I should have shot him.

"Okay, let me see what I can do. Wait here."

Nick nodded impassively.

I left my office and went back to the store room where the Methedrine and cocaine were kept in the safe. I guess I could say I was lucky in the sense that no one saw me open the combination lock. How would I deal with the triplicate forms? How would I cover the loss? Drugs don't just disappear. It looked like this was another one of the questions that I needed time to think about, time that I hoped I was purchasing with what Nick called "the deposit." I had to get those negatives.

I brought the drugs as well as the $250 back to my office, closed the door, and set them all on the desk. Nick seemed very pleased with himself as he slipped his "deposit" into the blue nylon backpack he carried on his shoulder.

"I'll be in touch tomorrow," were his parting words.

As soon as I was alone, I gathered up the incriminating photos Nick had left behind. Should I destroy them, I wondered, or should I save them as evidence against him? I knew Genie had to see them; maybe she could figure out a way to deal with the asshole.

For the rest of the afternoon I was a madman. All I could envision for myself was the public exposure and humiliation I would undergo as a result of Nick's photographs. My name, my reputation, my family, and my friends—everything that I stood for and that was important to me would be stripped from my life and shredded. Those few wonderful hours with Genie were now costing me everything I had ever earned. I should have shot Nick. I couldn't think of anything else to stop him, other than giving in to the blackmail. The only solution that even hinted at a possibility rested with Genie. Perhaps, I thought, she would have a clue about how to deal with Nick. I sat in my office waiting for the call she had promised to make. By four o'clock I still hadn't heard from her. She had already proven herself to be erratic about phoning. But as I waited, I began to wonder if she weren't in on the blackmail. Could it be that Genie was actually in love with Nick and that he had forced her to go with me to the porno motel just so he could take the pictures and blackmail me? Suddenly this scheme seemed all too real. Blackmail would give Genie the money to get away from her father, with or without me.

I began to see myself as a real sap, a naive fool. I had believed Genie and believed my feelings toward her. She had seemed so sincere, so honest, so forthcoming, and I had fallen for it. How different was I from those men I saw every day in Beverly Hills, the sixty-year-old guys with shirts unbuttoned to their navels, wearing heavy gold chains around their necks, who walked down the street arm in arm with their twenty-two-year-old fashion model girl friends? These men wanted to believe that the girls loved them. It was obvious to everyone that the men grossly deceived themselves; the girls loved what the men bought for them. When the buying stopped, so would the love. With Genie, I had gotten myself into the same sort of relationship.

The Dexedrine continued to blast through my system, increasing my paranoia at an exponential rate. The later the day became, the more Genie's silence confirmed my worst fears of her involvement in the blackmail. I began to hate her. I had jeopardized my life to save Genie, only to find that she was robbing me in a way so complete that, compared to her, the junkie was a penny candy shoplifter. I remember telling myself that if I could figure a way out of this one, I'd be content to sit quietly behind the counter of Marilyn's juice bar for the rest of my life, serving fresh carrot drinks to fat ladies in jogging suits.

By five-thirty I still hadn't heard from Genie. That's when I began to call her house. But every time I called, either her mother or the Mexican maid answered and I set down the receiver without saying a word. After hanging up for the tenth time, I quit calling. I was so paranoid I almost expected a cop to come bursting into the store and arrest me for placing crank calls to the Cotler household.

What I experienced that afternoon had to be the condition known as "going crazy." I was not acting like my father, as I had been so afraid of doing; I had *become* my father. My thinking was irrational, my grip on reality had gone, and my judgment was nonexistent. In all the hours since Nick had left, I had gotten nothing done except to truly terrify myself. What I needed was a plan, a way to deal with the blackmail. But nothing convincing came to mind. In spite of my suspicions I knew I still had to talk to Genie; she was the only one with the potential to help. But where was she? That night I did something my employees couldn't believe—for the first time ever I left work early and delegated the task of closing the store to Al.

My first destination was University High School. Normally I would have found it embarrassing to cruise the parking lot and surrounding streets looking for Genie's Mustang. I wasn't some horny teenager looking for a pick-up. Or was I? Anyway, she wasn't there. Then I drove past her house. No Mustang there, either. Where the hell could she be? My paranoia told me that she was ensconced in some motel with Nick, splitting the loot, snorting the cocaine, and fucking him on a water bed, courtesy of my $250 deposit.

32

At home that evening I did my best to behave calmly, pretending to listen carefully as Marilyn detailed blow-by-blow, the surgeons' reaction to all aspects of her health clinic proposal. Complicating the whole business was the presence of my mother, who was over for her weekly dinner. Considering my inner turmoil, I put on a remarkable performance.

My mother was her usual font of enthusiasm regarding our future life in Escondido. Marilyn had cleverly promised Gloria not only a place to live at the health clinic, but guaranteed her the gift shop concession as well. The fat farm now offered my mother not only a safe, comfortable home for life, in intimate proximity to her son and granddaughter, but allowed her to be independent with her own lucrative little business. She had been guaranteed paradise by Marilyn—golden years of true twenty-four carat happiness. As Marilyn described the surgeons' reaction to her proposal, my mother giggled with excitement like a teenager. All her dreams were coming true; it was Christmas in June that year for Gloria Marcus.

I did my best to behave as if I shared their fantasy. But thanks to Nick's new career as a blackmailer, utopia seemed far off and unattainable. If Nick were to pursue the exposure route, Marilyn would be left with no choice but to jettison me. And my mother's pretty picture of the happy family and perpetual peace would flush down the toilet faster than a bag of joints during a police raid at a fraternity party.

Rebecca's reaction to Marilyn's report was particularly unnerving. As my wife had explained it to her, life at the health spa would be every Tom Sawyer, Becky Thatcher, country girl, and animal lover's fantasy—a Disneyland of the rural life. No child could resist such a pitch. Every fiber of Rebecca's little body seemed to vibrate with enthusiasm for the cute baby animals and the vegetable patches. Marilyn's dream had become our daughter's. How could I ever explain to Rebecca that, thanks to my indiscretion with Genie, I had destroyed everything she had been promised?

As the dinner continued (and it was a particularly delicious concoction of bay scallops in court bouillon sauce to celebrate the occasion—the first dinner Marilyn had cooked in weeks) I drank more and more wine in the hope of reducing my anxiety. Finally, the Dexedrine wore off, lessening my paranoia but permitting my despair to return full-blown. Rather than relieving the strain, the wine did nothing. I felt like the man with the hollow leg. The more I drank, the more I peed, but that was it. The alcohol had absolutely no other effect. Marilyn and my mother sat at the table enchanting Rebecca with country life fantasies while I sat in my chair, drinking and nodding, inert as the Buddha.

As crazy as I knew I was becoming, I couldn't help being fascinated by Marilyn. In her exuberance over the health spa, the light, delightful side of her personality had clearly re-emerged, reminding me of the Marilyn I had first known and loved when she was still a resident in med school. In those days nothing seemed to destroy her vitality; even exhausted, after having been up and working for seventy-two hours straight, she never lost the ability to poke fun at herself. Now, with her escape from the imagined grimness of her life suddenly possible, the old Marilyn felt free to reappear—just when I had trapped myself in a scandal that guaranteed I'd never be able to enjoy her.

Like all sinners, I considered confession. What would happen, I asked myself, if I just leveled with her? Marilyn would then either have to accept what I'd done or abandon me. What worried me was that if I told her about Genie and the blackmail,

Marilyn would see only how it affected her, and would ditch me on the spot. No, I realized, I was going to have to get out of the blackmail trap entirely on my own if I wanted any possibility of preserving my marriage.

During dessert my mother began one of her pleas for me to appreciate the latest crock of business bullshit my brother Joe had been feeding her regarding his "exciting new career." My mother had the lunatic notion that I might talk to Joe about using some of his investors to finance the health spa, rather than funding the mortgage through a bank as we planned to do. For God knows what reason, my mother still believed Joe to be a misunderstood genius. "His star will rise one day and blind us all," she had told me once. Joe had already cost me plenty, both emotionally and financially, and I had not the interest, patience, or desire to even think of having anything to do with him least of all in a financial scheme.

But my mother had to promote the idea of family unity. And since there was only her, myself, and Joe in the family, the only thing she could promote was her golden baby. As I listened to her pitch, I said nothing of seeing Joe outside the post office the morning I sent surfing. I could only imagine my mother's horror at the fact that I had avoided greeting my brother. Had I even mentioned my suspicions about the buyer of that fancy suit he was wearing, my mother would have gone apeshit. What did my brother know about money except how to spend it? Where was my brother his whole life except on the take from my mother? And where was he with all of his big deals when dad got sick and had to have cash for the hospital? Joe was broke and I had to sell off forty-nine percent of my god-damn store to that asshole Jerry Herrman. Fuck Joe. And fuck my mother for taking him so seriously. If he was doing something crooked he deserved to go to jail. His arrogance and irresponsibility had hurt me enough as it was; I was going to have nothing more to do with him, in spite of my mother and her fantasies. Families that stick together with members like Joe spend their days wallowing in the sewer. I got up from the table.

"I have a little problem at work I have to go over; we can discuss Joe another time, okay mom?"

"I told him about the spa, Mikey. He thought it was a wonderful idea; he's the one who suggested the idea of his investors. You should talk to him."

"You told Joe about the spa?" I was enraged.

"He is your brother," she said self-righteously, as if that made the betrayal acceptable.

"I vaguely recollect that, mom. But we asked you not to say anything to him, didn't we?"

"It doesn't matter now; you've got your surgeons for the down payment. You don't have to keep things a secret. Mikey, he's your brother; you can trust him."

"I asked you not to tell him, mom, and you told him. You're the one I can't trust. Excuse me."

I started out of the room.

"Mikey!" my mother called to me.

I ignored her.

"Mikey," she called again, "it just came out in conversation; it was nothing."

By this time, fortunately, I was in the den, almost out of range.

"Mikey, please talk to me."

I closed the door and locked it. Alone at last, I unlocked my briefcase and once again glanced through the pictures Nick had left with me. There were only twelve hours left to work out a response to the blackmail. I sat and stared at my legal pad, unable to come up with anything. Why hadn't Genie called?

Through the door I could just barely hear the mumbling of my mother and Marilyn. I couldn't understand what they were saying, but I assumed that Marilyn was doing her best to soothe and pacify my mother. Marilyn enjoyed my mother, a fact that I had at first, years ago, found hard to believe. I'd always seen my mother as a demanding woman who few people had the patience to endure. But she and Marilyn had liked each other on sight. Marilyn became the appreciative daughter my mother never had. And my mother comforted Marilyn, who'd never known her own mother. I wondered how much they really did have in common. If they were as similar as I feared, I could be in big trouble. Should Nick choose to expose my behavior with Genie, Marilyn, just as my mother did, would bitterly blame me, the man, for causing her so much grief. Unlike my mother, however, Marilyn would simply leave me, as she believed my mother should have done with my father.

Rebecca interrupted my musings to kiss me good night. An hour later my mother left. Two hours after that, with no solution in sight, I gave up and joined Marilyn in the bedroom. Both of us were exhausted. The difference between us was that when she closed her eyes, she fell asleep. I lay awake, tormented.

At one-forty I got out of bed and went into the bathroom. I had made a decision and knew what had to be done. I dressed, tiptoed silently down the dark stairs, and left the house. The Oldsmobile's engine started right up and within moments I was driving west, very fast.

33

Minutes later I was standing in the bushes outside the Cotler house, once again tossing pebbles against Genie's bedroom window. After only two throws the casement opened and that beautiful grin of hers flashed down at me. Genie appeared so pure and innocent that for a second I almost forgot my suspicions about her involvement in Nick's blackmail scheme. After gesturing for me to meet her at the front door, she disappeared inside.

I worked my way through the shadows to the front of the house. The strange thing was that, unlike Saturday night, I was completely unafraid of Ed Cotler and the possibility of being discovered; what obsessed me now was uncovering the truth about Genie. The alarm light flicked off, the front door opened, and Genie beckoned for me to enter. I obeyed and again followed that lovely creature up the stairs. Moments later we were in her bedroom. Genie closed the door securely. In the darkness she couldn't read the grim expression on my face.

"I thought you weren't going to come here any more," she teased.

Without a word I opened the envelope and spread out on her bed all the photographs Nick had left with me. My action confused Genie until she turned on the desk lamp and examined the evidence. As she looked at the pictures I carefully studied her expression for any hint of complicity. To her credit, Genie seemed stunned. But people were so complex and mysterious; I wondered if she were a good enough actress to make me believe she was innocent when she wasn't. After examining the last photograph, Genie turned to face me.

"Where did these come from?" she whispered.

"Don't you know?"

"How would I know?"

"Think Nick."

"Nick?"

Genie seemed incredulous.

"Yeah. Good old Nick. He brought these into the store today. He's blackmailing me."

"Blackmailing you? I don't believe it."

"I didn't either. But the pictures are kind of convincing, aren't they?"

"It's just bizarre. Nick is really doing this?"

"I figured you might know something about it."

"Oh you did, huh?" Genie eyed me angrily.

"Well, he was your boyfriend. You told me some of the things he's already done; maybe you knew about this, too."

"You think I'm part of this?"

"Genie, I don't know what to think. Do you know what these pictures could do to my life? I'm a dead man six ways to Sunday if these ever go public."

"After last night you honestly think I want to ruin your life?"

"That's why I'm here, Genie. I mean, what the hell is going on? You and I have a little fun together and the next thing I know I'm being asked to pay for it with everything I've ever earned. What should I think about it? I want to know. What the fuck is this all about? I'm waiting to hear, so tell me."

Genie slipped from the bed, went to her closet, removed a shoebox, and extracted a joint from a hidden compartment. She opened the bedroom window, lit a match, and took a deep drag of marijuana. She offered some to me, but I wasn't interested. Genie then approached the bed, knelt in front of me, looked straight into my eyes, and spoke quietly.

"Michael, it really hurts me that you think I'm part of this." She pointed to the photographs. "When I told you last night I wanted to leave everything and run off with you in a bus and travel around the world, did you think I was kidding? You think that's something I just tell every guy I go out with? What I feel toward you is real; it's not something I've ever felt before. It scares me. Don't you understand I'm telling the truth? Listen, I'll tell you how I'll prove it to you. Right now, this instant, let's split, just the two of us, with the clothes on our backs. If you'll do it, I'll go with you. This instant. What do you say? Do you believe me now? I mean, you can't blackmail someone you can't find, can you?''

She certainly did seem to be sincere, I had to give her that.

''Genie, I can't get out of this by running away; there's too much at stake here.''

She shrugged. ''I still can't believe Nick is doing this.''

''Well, take another look at the pictures then; they're just as real as the fact that he's coming back to the store tomorrow for more money and drugs. And you've got to help me figure out how to stop him.''

Genie looked at me with an odd expression, as if I had confused her.

''You've already paid him something?''

''I didn't have any choice.''

''Oh boy,'' was all she said.

''What does that mean?''

''You shouldn't have paid him anything.''

''Yeah, well, what else was I supposed to do?''

''One thing I know about Nick; if he thinks he's got you once, he believes he has you forever. You have to stop him from the beginning.''

''Genie, if I didn't give him anything he was going to mail copies of those pictures to your father. I had to stall until I could figure out how to handle him.''

She shook her head. She didn't agree with me.

''You should have told him to go screw himself; that's the only language he understands. He likes to scare people. That's what he did with me. When I finally told him to drop dead, that's when he left me alone.''

''You call those pictures leaving you alone?''

''He's not here, is he?''

''I don't know; maybe I should look in the closet.''

Genie glared at me angrily.

''I'm sorry,'' I apologized ''that was a low blow. But I've got to figure out what to do, Genie. I've got to get those negatives.''

She was quiet for some time.

''There's only one thing you *can* do.'

''Which is?''

''Tell him you'll kill him if he doesn't give you the negatives. Tell him you'll shoot him just like you shot the junkie. He knows that if he's dead those pictures aren't going to do him any good.''

"What if he doesn't believe me?"

"Tell him to go to L.A. County Hospital and take a good look at the human vegetable that tried to hold up your store.''

I remember thinking that it's easy to talk tough when the tough talker isn't really the person in the jam.

"Genie, if Nick sends out those pictures, do you know what's going to happen to us? I mean, your father, Marilyn, the police, the courts; we're going to be screwed.''

I had hoped to inspire a little panic in her and get her thinking. But instead she just stared at me as if she were seriously contemplating something more profound than I could imagine. Genie remained calm. Was it because she was stoned? I wondered if it was doing me any good even to talk to her. Obviously, I had already thought of threatening Nick. But I had rejected the idea because I knew empty gestures never worked and real threats had a way of compelling one to carry them out. Murder was not my idea of the best way to handle the situation. It had certainly occurred to me as a solution, but I didn't think I could carry it out.

"You would still have me," Genie stated quietly, answering a question I didn't, at that moment, remember asking.

"What?"

"If Nick sends out those pictures, you'd still have me. Michael, believe me, I won't desert you. We could take off together. Start a new life, like we talked about. Who knows, it might be the best thing that ever happened to you.''

Now the paranoia really washed over me. Just when I'd come to believe that Genie had nothing to do with the blackmail, I suddenly realized that exposing me would benefit both her and Nick, even if, as she said, she had lost all romantic interest in the scumbag; he would get his payoff and she would get me. I controlled myself and said nothing—such a Byzantine idea was almost too crazy to take seriously.

"Genie," I tried patiently, "other than threatening Nick, what else can I do?"

"That's all you can do," she said simply.

"What if you talked to him?" I asked her.

"It wouldn't do any good. He's committed himself and you've

gone along with him. I can't imagine he would change because of anything I said.''

''So I have no choice but to threaten him?''

''That's right.''

''And if he doesn't believe my threat, it's fine with you if I kill him?''

Genie blanched.

''If you tell him about the junkie in the hospital, he'll believe you.''

''But if he doesn't, I have your permission to kill him?''

''Michael, of course I don't want you to kill him. I don't want anybody killed. Nick just needs to think that you'll kill him; that'll stop him, I guarantee you.''

''Genie, people do funny things when their lives are threatened. They don't always make reasonable decisions. I mean, look at me. Your friendly neighborhood druggist is being blackmailed and what do I do? I threaten the blackmailer with death. A week ago I couldn't even have imagined this situation. And Nick, he's starting where I'm finishing. What if my threat, instead of cooling him off, makes him angrier?''

''What's your alternative?''

She had me there.

''Michael, I don't understand you; in the drugstore, when someone threatened you with a gun, you acted without hesitation. Now you're scared. What's happened to the 'People's Avenger'?''

Genie was mocking me with the *Herald-Examiner's* lurid headline describing my actions in the hold-up.

''He's not convinced he'll be lucky twice.''

''You don't have a choice, Michael.''

The worst part of the whole thing was that Genie was right; I didn't have a choice. Probably I should have shot Nick in the drugstore as my first impulse had directed me. At least it wouldn't have been premeditated. To the police it certainly would have been highly suspicious, but it would have come down to the word of a dead man against mine.

I got up from the bed.

''Genie, thanks, you've been a big help.''

''You're going?'' She seemed surprised.

I nodded.

Genie smiled seductively.

"Stay just a little longer?"

"I wish I could. But I haven't slept in two days; I'm exhausted."

Genie nodded that she understood.

"If Nick contacts you, will you call me immediately?"

She nodded.

"Listen, where does the asshole live, anyway?'

Genie wrote down his address in the Santa Barbara Harbor.

"Can I come talk to you at the store tomorrow?"

"You were going to talk to me today, remember?"

"Michael, I couldn't. I'm sorry. Can I come tomorrow?"

"Of course," I weakened. "But listen, think of something to use against Nick. Is there some crime of his you can prove, something he would be afraid of having known? It would make things a lot easier for me."

Genie nodded again.

"At least will you kiss me good-bye?"

That I couldn't resist. But a quick embrace led to a long embrace, and I made myself release her before it became too serious and brought on more trouble. Reluctantly Genie scouted the hallway, then led me downstairs and out the front door. I scurried down the block to my Oldsmobile, terrified.

34

Marilyn was awake and waiting for me. Where had I been? What had I been doing? Why had I run out of the house at that hour? I actually considered telling her the truth. Instead, I told her that I hadn't been able to sleep and had gone for a drive, hoping that the night air would relax me, as it had on Saturday night.

"Did it?" Marilyn demanded.

"How will I know," I asked her, "until I put my head down on the pillow?" Clearly unconvinced, she gave me the benefit of the doubt and accepted my story, which amazed me. One week before she would never have been so generous. What had changed?

I craved sleep, but I couldn't even get close to dozing. Around and around thoughts of blackmail raced through my terrified and

exhausted mind until finally, very late, I evolved an approach
that seemed foolproof. The big question was, would it work in
the daylight? `

35

The next morning I dragged my tired ass to work, ready to put
my scheme into motion. To brighten my outlook I again took
refuge in my professional inventory and swallowed two capsules
of Ritalin, which quickly softened the grating edge of exhaustion. Let Nick come in now, I thought. I'm ready for the
son-of-a-bitch.

The first scare of the morning was a phone call from Ed
Cotler. His intent was innocent enough, but my reaction to him
almost created a problem. Ed simply wanted to remind me of the
four o'clock ceremony I had promised to attend at city hall with
the mayor, who would present me with an award from the
chamber of commerce. But when Ed's voice first came on the
line, I was sure he was calling about the photographs he must
have just received from Nick. A death call. My death.

Ed, who's very shrewd, heard the anxiety in my voice and
repeatedly questioned it source. I blamed overwork and a recent
bout of insomnia. Ed accepted my explanation and hoped my
condition wouldn't interfere with my ability to make a short but
gracious speech when I accepted the mayor's award. Apparently
I was going to be the centerpiece of a big media event kicking
off the mayor's reelection campaign. Ed reminded me that the
more support I gave the mayor, the greater the possibility that I'd
receive assistance with both my legal problem and my future
political career.

"Tit for tat," as he so delicately put it.

"How can I run for office if I'm in jail?"

"Michael you worry too much. You're not going to jail; trust
me."

Did I have a choice? I wondered how far trust would get me
with Ed, the mayor, the district attorney, or the Republican party
if Nick's photographs should arrive in their morning mail.

After hanging up the phone I tried to compose something

reasonable to say about citizen's rights and the mayor. But I was lacking in inspiration. All I could think about was the plan I had evolved do deal with Nick and the possibility that it might free me from his blackmail.

My fear was that Nick wouldn't believe my bluff. If I threatened to kill him and then didn't, he'd be collecting money from me until the day I died. I asked myself which was worse, killing the blackmailer and possibly going to jail, or letting Nick expose me and thereby destroying everything worthwhile in my life? On a purely rational basis, my life was worth much more to me than Nick's. He was a psychopath, without any sense of remorse or guilt, who clearly intended to murder me in one form or another. I wondered if I killed him and then was later tried for the murder, whether I couldn't argue that my action had been simple self-defense. Nick wanted to obliterate me; I stopped him by putting a piece of lead in his heart. Would a jury believe me? Certainly the story was true. However, it was also true that if I pulled the trigger on the scumbag, it would be a premeditated action. I would be up for first-degree murder and the electric chair.

In my thirty-four years I had never seriously contemplated killing anything, much less anyone. But now, in less than two weeks' time, I had shot one man and was seriously planning the murder of another. Compared with me, my father had been a model of sanity. In fact, I found myself wishing my father were still alive; I needed his advice. Who else but my father could have understood the predicament I was in? Where was he now that I needed him? I knew exactly where he was: the same place I would be if my plan for Nick didn't succeed—six feet under.

I didn't have long to wait. The phone buzzed and Mary announced that a kid named Nick was waiting to see me. "Should I send him back to your office?" she asked.

Blow his fucking head off with a shotgun, I wanted to tell her. Send him back to the office in a pine box. But I simply told her "yes."

As soon as I saw the blackmailer all my hyped-up confidence vanished and terror returned. Nick swaggered in, full of himself, coked to the gills, I was sure. It was a few minutes after one in the afternoon and there we were: the pale, conservative druggist facing a tanned surfer in jeans and Hawaiian shirt. Nick appeared to be the model of health; in reality, I knew him to be a packaged cesspool of sickness. Nick closed the door behind himself and appraised me.

"What can I do for you?" I offered coldly.

For a moment he studied me.

"What can you do for me?" He mocked me with a sneer. "You know god-damned well what you can do for me and you're gonna do it fast."

Nick tossed an envelope of photographs onto my desk—infrareds taken in the porno motel. "What you're going to do is, you're gonna buy these from me."

"Do you have any idea what's in this drawer here?" I asked calmly, pointing to my desk.

"For your sake I hope it's money."

"Not quite."

I slid open the drawer, pulled out the .38 revolver, and pointed it directly at Nick's forehead.

"This is a Smith and Wesson .38 caliber revolver. If I pull the trigger, within one-hundredth of a second a piece of lead will cut a half-inch diameter hole right through your scheming little brain. What I suggest you do, if you value your life, is to drop this whole blackmail idea, give me the negatives, forget you ever met me, and don't ever come around here again. And if you don't think I'm serious, go down to the County Hospital and take a look at a Mr. Robert Allen, who was the last guy that tried to fuck me. You might have read about that one in the papers."

Nick didn't say anything. He just sat staring into the barrel of my pistol. The gun didn't seem to faze him; it was my attitude he was trying to fathom.

"You should know, Marcus, if I don't call a certain friend of mine in Santa Barbara by four o'clock this afternoon, copies of these photos will automatically be mailed to Genie's dad, your wife, and the police. So go ahead and pull that trigger; it doesn't matter to me."

I should have shot him right then. But if he was telling the truth and the police received copies of the photographs, my case for killing Nick in self-defense wouldn't look very good. It would be murder one, good-bye Michael Marcus.

"Nick, you're getting in way over your head here and I think you know it. Now what I'm going to do is to be real nice and give you a break. I'm going to give you twenty-four hours to think over what you're doing and then I'm going to get serious. I hope by that time you'll change your mind and bring me those negatives." I set the pistol down on the desk in front of me, with the barrel pointed directly at the blackmailer.

"I did't come here to be given a deadline," he answered arrogantly. "I want twenty thousand bucks cash, four ounces of coke, and this."

Nick pulled a typed sheet of paper from his pocket—a neat list, itemizing quantities of virtually every controlled substance and abused drug a pharmacist was likely to stock, from amphetamines to morphine and on down through Tuinal. If the FDA ever caught me giving those drugs to Nick, I'd be locked up forever. I had to admit that Nick's inventory was thorough; he didn't seem to have missed a single potentially profitable, street-saleable drug.

"Sure you don't want some Extra-Strength Tylenol too, in case you get a headache from all this?" I offered lamely, attempting to appear tough.

Nick just glared at me.

"If you think," I continued, "that just because you know how to read a light meter I'm going to give you this stuff, you're crazy. I'm a patient man. I believe in giving a guy a second chance. You should reconsider this, Nick, before you regret what you've got yourself into. I don't want an answer from you now. Just go home, think about what I said, and tomorrow bring me those negatives."

"If I were you, I'd have a look at those pictures." He pointed to the envelope on my desk.

"I have no doubt Ansel Adams would have envied your abilities. But that isn't the point and you know it. I want you to think about the consequences of what you're doing."

Nick angrily curled his lip.

"I'm through playing around with you, pal. I want the money and I want the drugs. And now, or you're in deep shit, understand?"

We stared at each other. It was as I feared. I had played my hand and he had called my bluff. The only alternative now was to shoot the bastard and take the consequences.

At that moment the phone rang. Both of us jumped.

"It's my cashier; I have to answer it."

"Make it quick."

What Mary had to say was simultaneously terrifying and a relief. I told her I would be out in a minute, then hung up.

"You ain't going nowhere until you give me a deposit on your bill," Nick articulated eloquently.

"You know who's outside that door?"

Nick said nothing.

"Lieutenant Fred Peterson of the LAPD, plus three cops and my attorney. They're here to take me downtown to book me for attempted murder. If you like you can go with us."

Nick didn't know whether to believe me or not. From the expression on his face, it was obvious he wanted nothing to do with the police. By accident I had found a crack in his iron wall.

"You're bullshitting me."

"Hey, I wish I were; you think I want to go to jail?"

"If you called the cops, Marcus, those picture are as good as in the mail."

I couldn't take his arrogance anymore. I raged at him quietly through gritted teeth.

"God damn it you stupid shithead; they're here to arrest *me*, not you. And I didn't do a fucking thing except to save Genie's life. I'm going to jail no matter what happens, so I have absolutely nothing to lose by shooting you. Now get your ass out of my store and tomorrow bring me those goddamn negatives."

Before Nick could answer, someone knocked on the office door. Nick froze.

"Yes?" I called.

"Michael it's Ed. What can I say? This is a surprise for me, too. I didn't expect such a fast indictment. I'm sorry."

"Ed, I need one more minute, okay?"

"The sooner you get out here," he answered, "the quicker it'll be over with."

"I hear you."

I waited a moment, listening to Ed's footsteps clomp back toward the front of the drugstore.

"Believe me now?" I asked Nick. "That was Genie's father."

"He's your lawyer?"

I nodded.

"Now if you don't want me to introduce you to everyone, here's what you're going to do. Walk out that door and immediately turn left. You'll find a toilet. Wait in there until you hear me go. Then get your ass out of the store. And tomorrow, bring me those negatives. Is that clear?"

"It's not going to be that simple, pal," Nick glared.

"Listen, asshole, I don't know how to make it any plainer; you've gotten everything you're going to get out of me."

I stood up and opened the door for him. The coast was clear.

"If I were you," Nick warned me, "I'd hide that envelope so no one accidentally opens it."

I nodded. Nick vanished behind the door of the men's room. I locked the envelope in my desk, put on my sport jacket, left my office, locked the door, and headed out into the pharmacy where I could see the lieutenant waiting to meet me, along with a horde of photographers, newsmen, and video crews. I later found out that Ed had tipped off the media as part of his effort to stimulate further public support for my situation.

36

The booking was even more humiliating than I'd imagined. It wasn't simply the fingerprinting, or the mugshots, or the endless questions (birth date, single or married, mother's maiden name) the forms demanded. It wasn't even the charges that made it so bad, although "attempted murder and assault with a deadly weapon" certainly did nothing to improve my state of mind. The absolute horrible thing was the sense I had of losing my identity. They stripped me down to a nameless lump of flesh, a criminal, just like all the others behind bars—an animal, under the lock and key of the police and judicial system. I entered the jail as Michael Marcus, pharmacist and substantial member of the community, father, husband, provider, property owner, taxpayer, and local hero; one minute later I was reduced to a number, 3410986, the latest on a long list, indicted for murder.

The downtown Los Angeles jail reminded me of nothing so much as a gigantic public toilet on whose sleazy seat I'd never even have considered sitting. During the booking they not only sat me on it, they shoved me right down into its revolting bowl. I became an organic part of the institution of pain, vomit, and fungus. The dregs of the city had pissed on the floors, bled, fought, killed one another, jerked themselves off, and fucked all the weak ones up the ass. I was just one more rib roast on the butcher's shelf. My soul was instantly separated from my flesh;

the spirit was screaming for freedom, but the meat was secured in the cooler. I was in jail. Many men, I had heard, claimed the experience to be ennobling. But I was no Eldridge Cleaver or Marquis de Sade. I was Michael Marcus, the druggist. I was a little man, trying to live as best as I knew how. My crime was wanting to feel something, to be alive, to protect my own. I had no business in jail; not only would it not make a man out of me, I knew it would destroy me.

Throughout the booking I had trouble breathing, as if I were drowning. But no one came to my rescue. Some of the police actually seemed sympathetic to my problem. One confided that he thought the charges against me were "a load of shit." Nevertheless, it was me they were putting in jail, not the cop. I was being martyred as a result of political and ethical conflicts in the community. I was simply a symbol for the debate, a Ping-Pong ball for the entertainment of the god-damned lawyers. No one cared about me; my value was as a flag, to salute or to step on, depending upon political allegiances. Conservative supporters of the mayor loved me. The liberals wanted to put me to death. In neither case was I a man with a heart, lungs, guts, and a head. They had turned me into a public figure with no right to feelings.

After bail was made, Ed Cotler whisked me out of the jail, claiming that the booking had been completed in record time because of pressure from the mayor. Of course the mayor had a selfish motive; he needed me out fast so that I could receive my award from the chamber of commerce.

As we descended the broad concrete steps from the jail to Ed's waiting car, reporters and news crews swarmed around us like vultures over a dead cow. Ed fielded the questions, claiming, as all lawyers do, to be outraged by the gross miscarriage of justice against his client. Ed described me as a hero, exaggerating my actions to the point where officially being declared by the pope to be a saint would have seemed barely sufficient. I had to admit that Ed handled the situation very well; I was truly grateful to him because, in fact, I was sill in a state of shock from the booking. I felt myself to be on the edge of insanity; no matter which direction I turned, someone seemed to be trying to dominate and control my life and there didn't appear to be any way out.

Ed rushed me the few blocks downtown into the back entrance of the Biltmore Hotel. Before getting out of the car, he straightened my tie and lent me his comb to organize my hair. Moments later we were inside the banquet hall listening to Mayor Malcolm thank the members of the chamber of commerce, five hundred men and women seated beneath the dais at tables, for their past support and present commitment to his reelection. They applauded.

Once the room was quiet again, the mayor kicked into his campaign theme of bringing down the inflated costs of city government through further community participation on the part of its citizens. Eventually this led him to the chamber of commerce award for "Citizen's Action," of which I was to be the first recipient. The mayor introduced me. The reaction of the audience was bizarre: they gave me a standing ovation, and a sincere one.

Half an hour earlier, at the jail, I'd been treated as a piece of dogshit. Now respectable citizens were giving me enthusiastic support. I stood at the podium marvelling at the waves of applause. What I couldn't understand was how two such upstanding civic and political groups as the ACLU and the chamber of commerce could have such different viewpoints on my behavior toward the junkie. One wanted me dead, the other was giving me the local version of the ticker-tape parade. The contrast was almost too much for me to handle. The mayor shook my hand and handed me an inscribed plaque.

"We need more men like you," he told me, as he actually addressed the audience and the television cameras. "Your actions have made the people of Los Angeles proud. Let's only pray that your heroism can provide hope, the hope to inspire others to act with the selflessness and courage that you so ably demonstrated."

The mayor stepped back from the microphones, leaving me all alone to speak on nationwide television. It was my big moment. Given what had just gone on in jail, my first impulse was to tell them all to go fuck themselves. But my situation was obviously too precarious for such childishness.

"You have no idea how much I appreciate this award," I told the audience. "It's real encouragement to be honored for saving the life of a young girl. At the time I didn't think about it; I just did what I thought was the right thing. It was what I was taught as a child and what I still believe today. I'm glad you share that belief with me. People who rob, kidnap, and threaten our children with violence don't deserve to walk the streets of our community.''

I was interrupted by massive applause from the audience. I must have looked rather surprised; I certainly hadn't expected another ovation. Fortunately the clapping continued long enough for me to regain my bearings and continue.

"Thank you. But you know, a lot of people out there don't seem to agree with this idea. They'd rather see our city turned into a war zone than have its citizens protect themselves. In fact, just today, one of those groups convinced the district attorney to arrest me for attempting to murder the man who took the hostage in my store. If you can believe it, I came directly here from being booked at the jail.''

I held up the award for the audience to see.

"I'll tell you, I'm glad to have you all on my side. As I said, your support today is particularly encouraging. But if this award is going to mean anything for your sons and daughters, for safe neighborhoods, we're going to have to realize that the struggle has only just begun. By coming here today, by giving me this award, by supporting Mayor Malcolm and his Community Watch program, you're saying that you're in it for the long haul, that you're committed to straightening up the mess in our society and once again making it possible for decent people to live decent lives in this city, without fear. For that I thank you.''

Again I received a spontaneous standing ovation. Strobe lights and flashbulbs went off like fireworks. I saw reporters commenting into their minicam units. Ed looked very pleased, and the mayor gave me the "A-okay" handsign. Obviously they all thought I had done well. If they had only known how close I was to cracking up. A month before, I never would have believed I could live a life that was so different on the surface from the sense of myself that I carried inside. Perhaps everyone felt that they were living lives in public that had no resemblance to their true inner feelings.

37

That night the eleven o'clock news treated my simultaneous indictment and chamber of commerce citation as a bizarre human interest conflict of coast to coast importance. Kelly Lange shook her head on camera in disbelief at the end of my story. Then my telephone began ringing; Ed, my mother, State Senator Hart Walker, Marilyn's surgeon investors, reporters, you name it and they called. The final straw came at twelve-thirty when someone from *People* magazine phoned to do a profile on me. At that point I unplugged the phone. I had heard from everyone but "Sixty Minutes," and I had never really wanted to talk to Mike Wallace anyway.

What I needed was sleep. I suggested to Marilyn that we go to bed. Things had been so hectic that she and I hadn't yet had a chance to talk about the events of the day. I expected her to be enraged, but she was strangely subdued. I'd have expected all the publicity to horrify her. However, instead of blowing her top, she was not only sympathetic, but supportive of the legal strategy Ed had devised and implemented. Marilyn's generosity so moved me that I almost told her about Genie and the blackmail, in order to clear the air. But it was one thing for her to accept me as a public figure on television; it was quite something else to understand and forgive me for the business with Genie. If I was having so much trouble handling it, I asked myself, how could I expect Marilyn to tolerate it? No, what I had to do before telling my wife about it was to definitely end the affair with Genie as well as untangle myself from the blackmail.

We went to bed exhausted. Within moments Marilyn was snoring. For me, however, it was another long night without sleep. I had set my alarm for five in the morning. My story was that I had to get up early to make up work lost because of my legal problems. The real reason had to do with my plans concerning Nick, which were about to be seen through to their conclusion.

38

By five-fifteen I was out of the house and by five-thirty, inside the pharmacy. Ten minutes later I was on the Ventura Freeway, heading north with the .38 Smith and Wesson weighting down my jacket pocket. Michael the pharmacist was now Michael the assassin. I swallowed a Ritalin. Within minutes I felt as alert as I could ever remember. I tried to keep in mind, as I drove to Santa Barbara, all the good things that I had in my life with Marilyn and Rebecca, those specific emotional connections that the blackmailer was trying to blow away with his photographs. I needed to be angry when I saw Nick, and I wanted that anger to be real.

I approached Santa Barbara Harbor a few minutes before seven. I parked, leaving my car as far as possible from my destination; I didn't want my license plates to be seen near the public dock.

I found Nick's pier about seven-fifteen. His fishing boat was tied up near the concrete launch ramp adjacent to the Santa Barbara Sailing Association. A narrow wooden gangway led down from the cement seawall to floating piers against which row after row of small boats were secured. I was surprised at how busy the harbor was at that hour. Twenty boats were backed up on the launch ramp waiting their turn to be put into the water. It looked as if every two-man commercial fishing boat in Santa Barbara was being readied for the day's work. I had always thought fishermen started out much earlier. Then I remembered the heavy fog overlying Santa Barbara; obviously the weather had forced a delay. No sane person heads out into heavy fog in a small boat, if he can avoid it.

As I stood on the seawall and studied the situation, I realized the whole setup was very different from what I had anticipated. When I thought of fishermen I thought of old Winslow Homer paintings, of New England dories, or skip-jacks, dragging for oysters under sailpower. The boats down in the water bore no resemblance to my fantasies. The locals used fiberglass power boats called "Radons." These were twenty-five feet long, almost skiffs, with largely open decks and tiny, angular, spaceshiplike cuddy cabins in the bows. Bolted to the sterns of these craft were two outboards so huge they appeared to unbalance the hulls. This was high-tech fishing, California style.

I descended the gangway and worked my way past the other young fishermen on the dock, finally stopping beside Nick's Radon. I had not expected such a public situation and tried to appear inconspicuous, keeping my back to the men working on the dock and making no eye contact. No one seemed to pay any particular attention to me.

I verified Nick's slip number against the one Genie had written on the paper, and tried to peek through the round porthole. But it was tinted black and nothing inside was visible. I listened intently but could hear no noise. I almost hoped Nick wasn't there.

Warily, I stepped aboard the strange craft, being particularly careful about causing the Radon to rock; I wanted the element of surprise on my side. As I worked my way around the plastic milk crates of fishing gear, I suddenly felt a tug on my jacket from behind. Instinctively I reached into my pocket, grabbed my pistol, and swung around, prepared to fire. But it was nothing, a false alarm. The fabric of my jacket had caught on the cotter pin of the hydraulic pot hauler. I let go of the pistol, freed my jacket, then quietly approached the main hatch.

Before trying the hatchcover, I glanced around the area to see if anyone was watching. Although the dock was swarming with fishermen preparing their own boats, no one seemed to notice me. So I tried the hatchcover, which turned out to be unlocked. Very quietly, I slid the wooden door open. Below was the one-room cabin. Nick was asleep, alone on the vee-berth. I had feared finding him with some woman, which would terribly compromise my anonymity. This was a lucky break.

As I tiptoed down the companionway steps, Nick began to stir. I closed the door behind me just as he awakened. With my hand on the gun in my pocket, I sat on the companionway steps and waited for him to recognize me. Nick sat up and appraised me as he struggled to rouse himself from his slumber. He appeared hung over and looked terrible; I assumed it was from the drugs he must have been taking. We sat for probably five minutes looking at each other without saying a word. I kept the pistol pointed at him as I checked out his living quarters. The cuddy cabin was as spartan as a tent. There was a foam pad for a mattress, a sleeping bag, a two-burner cooktop, a Porta-potty, a battery-powered five-inch television, and a net hammock to hold his clothes. This was a man with nothing to lose.

"Good morning," I offered.

Nick said nothing.

"I thought I'd save you a trip and come for the negatives myself."

Again he remained silent. The boat tied in front of Nick's started its engines, making conversation difficult.

"I assume you've got the negatives here somewhere," I spoke louder. "If you'll just hand them to me now, you can save us a lot of time."

Nick waited until the neighboring boat shut off its engines. Then he spoke quietly, with menace.

"First I want the money and the goods we talked about."

"Nick, we've already been through this," I said calmly. "I told you yesterday, you've gotten as much as you're going to get. So just give me the negatives and the prints, I'll leave, and you won't have any trouble."

Nick grinned sadistically.

"Marcus, you may think you're some kind of Jedi warrior with mind control, but I've got some news for you; this isn't Star Wars here, this is real life. Either you're going to give me the money and the pharmaceuticals or I'm going to send copies of those photos to CBS, NBC, ABC, and *The National Enquirer,* who'll pay me real well for my efforts. Don't think I didn't see you on the news last night; that was a real fine speech you made, yessir."

Before I could answer, we heard voices nearby; Nick's neighbors were working in the stern of their boat, not ten feet from the cuddy cabin. The last thing either of us wanted was for someone to overhear the conversation.

"Do the engines on this thing actually run?" I asked.

Nick nodded.

"How about giving me a little tour of the harbor so we can talk without interruption?"

"Okay. But you gotta take your hand out of your pocket. I don't want to hit a swell and have that thing go off accidentally and shoot a hole through the boat. This is how I earn my living, you know."

What bullshit. If he earned such a good living with the boat, why was he trying to shake me down? At that moment it didn't really matter—his point about the gun was right. I took my hand out of my pocket.

This was the signal for Nick to get moving. Naked, he crawled out of his sleeping bag, pulled a pair of old swimming trunks up over his ankles, then gestured for me to move my feet; I was blocking the lid of the Porta-potty on the floor.

"I gotta take a crap first," Nick stated.

What could I say? I moved my feet. Without the slightest inhibition, Nick dropped his swimming trunks and squatted on the toilet. As he sat staring at me, I tried not to pay attention. But I had to hand it to him. I could never have taken a shit in public like that, sitting three feet from a man holding a gun on me. But Nick did it. Within less than a minute the scumbag was able to relax enough to relieve himself with considerable, and I might add, smelly, freedom. It completely confirmed my earlier evaluation of Nick as a psychopath. Only someone that sick could shit in public so readily. Nick had no sense of anyone's feelings other than his own; I existed only as part of the decor—a meal ticket standing next to the toilet. It was intimidating. I knew I would have to correct his attitude, and fast, if I hoped to achieve my aim.

As soon as Nick finished with the Porta-potty, he went up on deck, and started the engines. I stood on the companionway steps, virtually beside him, while he uncleated the docklines and eased the boat away from the pier. Within moments we were idling across the harbor, headed for the ocean.

Had the circumstances of the morning been other than they were, I would have enjoyed the boat ride. The harbor was lovely. The fog had lifted and the water was covered with slow-moving boats heading out for their favorite fishing grounds. Brown pelicans and seagulls flew everywhere, hoping for a free breakfast courtesy of the live bait operators. There were even seals swimming and barking through the harbor. With the exception of Nick, it was a beautiful sight.

The blackmailer steered his boat into the main channel and gave the sandbar near the harbor entrance a wide berth. Within moments we were out on the ocean which, fortunately, was as smooth as a billiard table.

"So here we are; what do you want to talk about?"

"Nick, I don't think you really carefully considered what I told you yesterday. I'm pretty generous to give you a second chance. Why not be smart and take advantage of it?"

"That's all you have to say?" He asked with obvious contempt. "You made me come all the way out here for that?"

"I'm not going to spell out what's going to happen to you if you don't accept my offer."

"You asshole. Nothing's going to happen to me and you know

it. It's you who's up to your neck in shit if you don't come through. I ain't wasting any more time, Marcus. Either you produce the goods by ten o'clock tomorrow, or those pictures are going out to everyone who'll do business with me.''

"Nick, you're making a big mistake not accepting my offer. You better think about it.''

"No, you better think about it, Marcus. And take another look at those photos while you're at it; they might make things a little clearer for you.''

Nick rammed both throttles forward and the Radon shot up onto plane like a drag boat. If I hadn't been standing in the companionway braced against the cabin, I would have been thrown into the water. I wondered if that wouldn't have been better. At least then Marilyn and Rebecca would have been spared the horror of the blackmail. And except for the minute it took to drown, I would have been saved from all future pain.

Nick steered the boat in a big circle and sped back to the harbor at forty knots. By the breakwater he cut back on the throttles and slowed down to the eight-knot speed limit. Without saying another word he motored back to his dock space, tied up, and shut down the engines.

"Twenty-four hours, Marcus. I'm not kidding.''

Nick gestured for me to get off his boat.

"You think about what I told you,'' I reminded him.

"No,'' was all he answered as he descended into his cabin. I stepped back onto the dock and headed for my car.

39

The drive home felt like a suicide run. As I sped through Carpinteria at eighty miles an hour, I reviewed the meeting with Nick in an attempt to convince myself that what I had told him might yet cause him to back down. But I didn't believe it. I had made an empty threat and Nick knew it. The battle had been lost at the moment Nick took that shit right in front of me. My arguments had been directed to someone with a soul. But no one with a soul could have shit in front of a stranger without at least some attempt at privacy. Nick, I realized, was an animal.

Animals cannot be trained with rational arguments. Animals, as an old Rottweiler trainer once told me, are like Germans; they only understand the stick.

I tried to think of a stick that would work on Nick. He was correct to think I wouldn't kill him. But there had to be something that would get to him. His fear of the police? Some trouble with a woman, perhaps?

My options had reduced themselves to either paying him off or suicide; I saw no other way out. I had failed in my efforts to be John Wayne. I was failing in my attempts to come up with a new plan. I just couldn't seem to enter into the thought processes of the bastard on a low enough level where I could understand and then outmaneuver him. I needed someone to advise me. Who did I know well enough to trust with my problem? Who would be able to come up with a solution? I could think of no one.

As I sped south, all I could see were narrowing options, death, humiliation, loneliness, and the destruction of everything I had worked so long and hard to build. All because of two nights with Genie. It was now undeniable; I was screwed.

40

My intention, when I got back to the pharmacy, was to lock myself in my office and try to figure out my next move with Nick. Instead I found myself in the middle of a three-ring circus. It was only nine-forty in the morning and the place was packed with reporters, television news crews, curious customers—even the writer who had called in the middle of the night from *People* magazine. Some Hollywood producer wandered in and tried to buy the rights to my story for a television movie. It was unbelievable. The happiest man in the store was my partner Jerry, who was selling the crowd everything and anything that wasn't bolted down. It was just my luck that nothing of interest was happening in the world. That week the PLO hadn't blown up any busloads of children; no Armenians had assassinated any Turks; there wasn't even a good plane crash. The news media were hungry for stories, and they chose to land on me.

To get away from the chaos inside the store, I slipped outside and tried to make an unobserved end run in through the back. But some kid, who turned out to be a stringer for the *New York Times*, spotted me in the alley, shoved his tape recorder in my face, and started asking questions. Within seconds it became a feeding frenzy for the media as all the other reporters stampeded out, pleading for exclusive interviews, demanding answers to questions, and recording every move I made on film and tape. At that moment I was too depressed about Nick to even consider talking to the press. I simply answered "no comment" to everything while I unlocked the back door of the pharmacy. Then I straight-armed my way through the reporters blocking my path, charged inside, slammed the door behind me, locked it, sprinted past my startled druggists, and barricaded myself in my office.

Through the door I could hear the reporters shouting, insisting I come out and talk. When I didn't respond, they quickly took another tack and began creating a story out of interviews with the other employees and druggists, who weren't at all unhappy with the idea of being on television.

I resumed work with my legal pad, once again reviewing my options with Nick. But the noise from the store was driving me crazy and I couldn't get anything done. Even if I chose the route of paying the blackmail, I realized that the close scrutiny of the reporters would make it impossible for me to siphon off the drugs from the storeroom shelves. And the $20,000? How long would it take those media sharks to discover that I had gone to the bank for an emergency loan? Even if I could somehow get the money and the drugs without anyone seeing me, with all the craziness going on I'd never have the time to invent the quantity of fictitious documents necessary to fool the Drug Enforcement Agency and the FDA. The god damn reporters were making everything impossible. I fantasized shooting them as well as Nick. At the height of my rage, I heard a banging on my office door.

"Michael, let me in. I have to talk to you." It was the sweet voice of Mr. Charm, my partner Jerry.

"One second."

I opened the door just wide enough to let Jerry slip inside, alone. The reporters outside began yelling questions. I ignored them and locked the door.

"Are you crazy?" demanded Jerry, wild-eyed with greed. "Get out there and talk to them. This is our big chance. Let 'em interview you in front of our sign; we'll get millions of dollars of nationwide free advertising. Tell them anything. By the time the evening news is over, we can franchise across the country. Owl-Rexall will be a name from the past; after tonight, 'Marcus' Drugstore' will be a household word.''

I didn't move.

"Michael, come on. Get going. Just a few words in front of the sign. It can't hurt you. Don't be stubborn. Think of Rebecca's future.''

"Get out of here, Jerry.''

"Michael, for once in your life, be reasonable. Don't blow the opportunity. Come on, get out there and talk to them. They're nice fellows. They think you're a hero. So do I. You've got the public on your side. Keep them there.''

"Jerry,'' I told him venomously, "you don't understand what's going on here. I'm asking you nicely to leave. That means to open the door and go. Alone. I stay here. Good-bye, Jerry.''

"Michael, god damn it, I'm your partner. I'm on your side. I'm trying to help you. How can it hurt to talk to those reporters? Five minutes of your time, Michael.''

I got up from my desk, walked the two steps to Jerry, grabbed him by his shirt collar, and lifted him off the ground. I was a man possessed and it frightened him. I didn't care.

"Jerry, I don't give a fuck whose partner you are. In fact, I don't give a fuck what you think. I asked you to get out of here; now get. Is that clear?''

I reached for the door knob and without even waiting for my partner to answer. I unlocked the door, opened it, pushed him outside, and slammed the door behind him.

"You're making a terrible mistake, Michael.''

I ignored Jerry and returned to my desk.

"Why is he making a big mistake, Mr. Herrman?'' one of the reporters yelled to Jerry. To drown out his answer I turned on the portable radio I kept in my office. Out of the speaker came the rock group Police, singing something in impressive harmony. That was what my life needed, I thought, harmony. I turned the radio up louder.

The rest of my day was spent contemplating my options. There seemed to be only two: suicide or blackmail. I combed my Rolodex in an attempt to discover some forgotten name from the past that might help. But I only drew the same blanks I'd been drawing for days. I just couldn't think of anyone ruthless enough for me to count on. Then I got lucky. About four o'clock my mother called on my private line. I answered, thinking it must be Marilyn. Had I known it was dear old mom I never would have picked up the receiver.

"Michael," she began, "I just want you to know that I talked to your brother this morning; he saw you on TV last night and is very proud of you."

Knowing her, the explanation for the call could hardly be so simple. I said nothing and waited for her to get to the point.

"Michael, your brother told me he thinks you're in far more trouble than you know. He asked me if you really have the best lawyers. A friend of his who's in the ACLU told him that they're going after you with everything they have. They're no dummies, the ACLU. Joe's friend told him they want to send you to jail as a test case. I can't understand it; the junkie's wife gets free lawyers and you have to pay through the nose to keep yourself out of jail. Anyway, Joe asked me to ask you if he can help in any way. You see, in time of trouble your brother is right there fighting for you; he cares about you."

As he certainly should, I thought, given the number of times I kept him out of prison.

"I told your brother you'd call and talk to him about it. He can help you. He wants to help you. You will call him, won't you, Michael?"

I couldn't believe she still thought my brother could help me. What a joke. My brother couldn't pay for a traffic ticket if I gave him the cash and told him which window to take it to at City Hall.

"Thanks, mom, I appreciate the advice. I'll call him. Thank you." Any lie was fine if it would get her off the phone.

"Michael," she yelled before I could hang up, "you don't have his number."

Old Gloria Marcus was wrong again. I'd had Joe's number for years.

"Okay, mom, what's the new number?"

She gave it to me, and I wrote it down.

"Thanks mom; I'll let you know what happens."

"Call him, Michael. He wants to help."

"Good-bye, mom."

I hung up, unable to imagine the circumstances that would compel me to go to Joe for advice. Maybe if I wanted to get caught doing something crooked my brother might be able to suggest something worthwhile; for what I was involved in, he'd be useless. The only people he knew were low-lifes, scumbags, and small-time hustlers.

That's when the inspiration hit me. It was an indisputable fact: the bulk of my brother's friends were people exactly like Nick. Nick was Joe's sort of guy. Nick and Joe would probably get along famously; they would understand one another. I could easily imagine my brother having done what Nick was attempting to do with me. I knew it was a crazy idea. But then I was crazed. I would call my brother. I mean, at that point, what did I have to lose? Joe would love hearing about my problem with Genie. It would give him real pleasure to have such a juicy tidbit of knowledge to use against me for all the self-righteousness he thought I had displayed against him over the years. Joe would chuckle with amusement for the rest of his life over the secret he held about Genie and me. And I knew he would use it against me in an uncountable number of ways. But, I asked myself, so what? When it came down to it, I was better off all the way around if my brother could get me out of my problem with Nick; at least I knew how to handle Joe.

I assumed that Joe, being a crook himself, knew a lot of other crooks, and one of those crooks had to know a few real thugs. Crooks and thugs needed one another. I wasn't able to intimidate Nick, but maybe Joe would find someone who could. Other then suicide, this plan seemed my only alternative.

Making the call was difficult. I sat and stared at the number for what felt like forever. Finally I dialed. I couldn't believe I was asking my brother for something. It was humiliating. I'd always thought of myself as a much better person than Joe, not so much as a result of his troubles with the law, but because of the pain he caused to everyone close to him. He was corrupt; I was honest. He took the easy route. I worked my ass off. He was charming and everyone liked him on sight. With me, people were cautious; I was too serious. Joe always seemed to be having a good time in life while I was tense, struggling to keep everything together, up to my standards. And of course, Joe was gay, while I was straight.

"Federal Bank of Montserrat," a receptionist answered.

I checked the number I had dialed and repeated it to the receptionist. She confirmed that I had dialed the correct number.

"Do you have a Joseph Marcus there?"

"One minute, please."

I held the phone. What was my brother doing with an office in a bank? What the hell was the Bank of Montserrat? I vaguely remembered that Montserrat was an island in the West Indies about the size of Catalina. How could a bank like that afford an office in Los Angeles? What the hell would they hire Joe to do for them? It didn't make sense. As I waited, I grew even more depressed. It was crazy enough that I was calling my brother; even worse was my suspicion that I was getting myself involved in some ridiculous scheme he was trying to foist on someone.

"Mr. Marcus's office," a secretary with a French accent announced.

"Joseph Marcus please. This is Joe's brother, Michael, calling."

"One moment please."

An instant later I heard that familiar hyped-up voice of my brother.

"Hello Michael!"

"Hi Joe."

"It's so nice to hear from you. It's been a long time, hasn't it? What can I do for you, Michael?"

Joe oozed charm. It always amazed me how he could sound so smooth and be so sick. He'd been diagnosed more than once as a sociopath, a nice new name for the old fashioned, psychopath con artist.

"Mom tells me you're involved in a new business. How's it going?"

"Michael," he said with the utmost sincerity, "you just wouldn't believe it, it's so wonderful. I've finally found work I love. You know, I actually can't wait for the alarm to wake me up in the morning, I'm so excited about getting down to the office. You should come down here and see the operation. You'd be impressed. I mean it."

"I'd like that; where are you?"

"Century City. Nineteen-oh-one, Avenue of the Stars. Suite ten-oh-five."

"You're kidding." I pretended to be surprised. "I'm driving right by you in half an hour. You got time for a visitor?"

"Michael, I've always got time for you, you know that."

"Great. I'll see you in thirty minutes, okay?"

"You'll be impressed, wait and see."

"See you then, Joe. 'Bye."

"Bye bye, Michael."

I hung up the phone. Push had come to shove and I was doing something crazy. But with no choice available, crazy it would have to be. No new inspiration occurred to me; I was stuck with the humiliating necessity of asking my brother for a favor.

I unlocked my office door and peeked out into the store. The reporters and news crews had finally gone and the place was quiet again. Thank God for afternoon press deadlines, I thought as I slipped out the back door into the alley. But my joy was shortlived. Double-parked by my Oldsmobile was the young stringer from the *New York Times*.

"Mr. Marcus, I'd like to ask you a few questions," he yelled, as he jumped from his car and shoved a microphone in my face.

"No comment," I told him as I started the Oldsmobile.

The reporter ran back to his own car, got in, and fired up his engine.

"Marcus, I'm going to follow you," he hollered, "until you give me an interview. I'm a persistent son-of-a-bitch. Your life will be a lot easier if you'll just let me ask you a couple of questions now."

We both sat there with our engines idling. I was enraged; the nerve of the guy astounded me. The last thing I needed was for this asshole to follow me to my brother's office and involve him in the story. The reporter had to be stopped. Compared to my problem with Nick, this seemed simple. I got out of the Olds and walked to the window of the reporter's car.

"I don't want you to follow me," I told him nicely.

"Then just answer a few questions."

"I don't think you understand," I said with some aggression, "I don't want to be interviewed and I don't want you to follow me. Is that clear enough?"

"It's a free country, Marcus, and I can drive anywhere I want. Why don't you just answer my questions? It'll only take a couple of minutes."

"Because I don't have the time."

"Make the time," he ordered.

If he wouldn't be reasonable, then I couldn't be. From my pocket I withdrew the Swiss Army knife I use for cleaning my fingernails. As soon as I pulled open the blade, which was all of two inches long, the tough-talking reporter rolled up his window and locked his door; suddenly he was terrified.

"What the hell do you think you're doing? Are you threatening me?" he yelled as he turned on his tape recorder and pointed the microphone at me.

I said nothing. What I did was to bend down by his left front tire and slash the rubber inflating valve. A sudden satisfying hiss of escaping air told me my knife had done its job. The front tire of his car collapsed.

I got back in my Oldsmobile, waved good-bye to the reporter, and roared away from the store.

41

The Federal Bank of Montserrat was situated on the tenth floor of a new steel and glass Century City building. As Joe had told me on the phone, the office itself was very impressive. The message trumpeted by the reception room was of a company long in tradition, solidly managed, and extremely prosperous. How else could one interpret the French antiques, Persian carpets, indirect lighting, and hand-rubbed parquet floors? The Bank of Montserrat looked as if it had been in the building since the French Revolution.

Joe's secretary, a formally dressed and very beautiful French woman, led me down the corridor. The woman knocked softly on a door whose bronze lettering identified it as the office of Joseph Marcus, President. I couldn't believe it; my brother was the head of this operation! Who the hell would put Joe in charge of an international bank? Someone had lost their mind. My brother couldn't even balance his own checkbook, much less help other people with their finances. I had a sudden horrible feeling in my stomach; everything around me seemed twisted, backwards, distorted, and upside down.

"Come in," Joe's voice called.

The French secretary opened the door and I entered the beautifully paneled room. It was the most lavish office I'd ever seen; the president of France would have been comfortable working here. Joe stood up from his Louis XIV desk and shook my hand. He was wearing another custom made suit and his patented million-dollar smile.

"It's so good to see you, Michael. How are you?"

"What the hell is going on here, Joe?" My astonishment was obvious.

Joe wasn't offended; he grinned like a happy kid and nodded to his secretary, who departed and closed the door behind herself, leaving my brother and me alone.

"I told you you'd be impressed."

Joe dragged me across the room to admire the view. It was a corner office, two walls of which were floor-to-ceiling windows. To the north, Joe looked out over the Wilshire Country Club golf course. To the west lay Santa Monica and the Pacific Ocean. It was late afternoon, and the skyline was spectacular against the sunset.

"Your little brother's not doing too bad, is he?"

"You seem very prosperous, Joe. If you're happy, then I'm happy for you. I mean it."

"Thank you. I am very happy."

Joe flopped down on his couch, picked up the phone, and buzzed his secretary as he gestured for me to sit. I sat.

"Ardette, hold all my calls, please."

Joe hung up the phone, lay back on the couch, and flopped his feet up onto the glass coffee table.

"You know, Michael, I'm glad you called. Really. We've had our differences in the past, but we're still brothers. We're older now. More tolerant. More mature, I hope. I'd like to think we can forget some of our differences and be a little closer. Is that possible?"

The whole speech sounded like my mother's line of reasoning. *Was* it possible? Who knew? At that moment what I needed was a favor from Joe. If he wanted to be closer, who was I to say no to the possibility?

"Definitely," I told him. "I'm glad you feel that way, because I'd like to be closer, too."

This seemed to please him, and a big, broad grin spread across his face.

"That's great, Michael, really great. I'm so happy you called. Honestly."

Joe got up, pushed a button in the wall, and a hidden bar

swung open. It was the kind of mechanical pretentiousness Joe had always loved.

"How about something to drink?"

"Just some soda, thank you."

Joe nodded, poured me a Perrier, and for himself filled a glass with twelve-year-old Chivas Regal. He was giving me the full treatment.

"Joe, what exactly is it that you do here?"

"I'm the president; I run the place."

He handed me the drink and sat down.

"The Federal Bank of Montserrat?"

"The Los Angeles branch."

"What does the Federal Bank of Montserrat do?"

"Like any bank, we make loans," he answered casually. "And we accept deposits, just like any bank. It's really a very simple business."

"But why Montserrat? Why not the United States?"

"You do go right to the heart of things, don't you, Michael? That's what I always like about you; you don't waste time. To answer your question, a lot of people don't think of themselves as citizens of tiny little countries; they view themselves in a global context and do business all over the world. Like a lot of high-powered people in business, they have to move money fast. And everywhere in the world the banking laws are different, currency restrictions vary, tax policies fluctuate wildly, and national bureaucracies confuse everything. All of this slows down the international businessman's ability to move his funds and thus to make money. But if he deals with us, he doesn't have these problems. Montserrat places no restrictions on how we handle money. We make life easier for the international businessman who needs to move his money. We're the expediters of the banking world."

"Joe, I hope you're not going to be offended, but is all of this on the up-and-up?"

"How can I be offended? It's a good question. Offshore banking has gotten a bad reputation in the last few years. The Bank of Montserrat is one hundred percent legitimate."

"How'd you get involved?"

"That's an interesting story. The people who started the bank are old friends of mine from my stock broker days. I know you didn't believe it then, but I made some people a great deal of money. And they remembered me. I'd impressed them. So when they started their Los Angeles branch they came to me to run it. This is the god's honest truth, Michael.''

"I'm happy for you, Joe. I hope it works out.''

"You don't have to hope; it's working out already.''

"Great.''

Joe flashed me that grin of his again. The Sphinx itself couldn't have been more mysterious. Was Joe amused? Was he being mischievous? Was he angry? Joe hid everything behind that million dollar smile.

"So, Michael, I keep seeing you in the news. As private as you like to live, how are you holding up with all the publicity? I never would have thought you'd get involved in this kind of thing. You actually shot that guy?''

I nodded.

"I'm impressed. That's not the Michael I knew.''

"Maybe there's a lot to the Michael you don't know.''

"Maybe.''

"For example.'' I paused for effect. "I didn't come here just to see this office.''

"I didn't figure you did.''

"I did want to see you and your setup. But I had other reasons, too.''

At this point Joe turned solemn.

"So why did you come here?''

"Don't take it the wrong way, Joe; you're going to get a kick out of it.''

"Why is that?''

"I need a favor from you.''

"What sort of favor?''

"First, I need you to promise me that what I say will remain just between us. Is that possible?''

"Michael, I'm surprised at you. If you can't trust your own brother, who can you trust?''

He had a good point there. The fact was that I couldn't trust my brother, or anyone else for that matter. But I had no one else to turn to.

"Someone's trying to blackmail me. He's got pictures of me doing something I'd rather not have made public. The guy is crazy. I need someone to get him off my back. Someone who can

scare the shit out of him. Someone really terrifying. You know
someone like that I can hire?''

Joe's grin returned, this time as a wicked little smile. His
pleasure over my problem was obvious.

''Michael, what have you been doing?'' he asked in a voice
dripping with sexual innuendo.

''Does it really matter?''

''That bad, huh?'' he gloated. ''You're surprising your little
brother today. It's my turn to be impressed. Does Marilyn know
about this blackmail?''

''No.''

''I see.''

And Joe did; the problem obviously delighted him.

''Supposing I did know someone, as you say, 'terrifying'
—what would you want him to do?''

''Get the pictures and negatives.''

''Do you care what he has to do to get them?''

''Whatever works.''

''Must be some pretty interesting photos.''

''Joe, I've got enough problems without them. I think you can
understand that.''

''Michael, you know I'd do anything to help you. You've
gone to bat for me so many times. Tell me, can you go to the
police?''

''Not in this case.''

''I understand.''

Joe sat back on the couch, stroking his chin. I was sure he was
just pretending to think so that he could enjoy watching me
sweat it out. Joe knew he had me at that moment and was
milking all the pleasure he could from the situation.

''You think the guy who went to this blackmailer would find it
very dangerous?'' Joe asked.

''Doubtful. The guy's only twenty or so. But you never know,
do you?''

''Is he tough, I mean physically?''

''He's strong. But I think he's into drugs.''

''Michael,'' Joe squealed with delight, ''is that what this is
about?''

''No.''

''Oh, then it must be a matter of the heart. Man or woman,
Michael?''

"Joe, can you help me or not?"

"Sorry."

Sorry, my ass. He loved asking me that question. I sat quietly while Joe went back into his thinking mode. The situation was the reverse of everything that had ever gone on between us. Joe was having a great time.

"There's someone I know," Joe finally announced, "who might possibly be able to help. But you've got to give me more information. I mean, who's the guy? Where does he live? What does he want? How many pictures does he have? The details."

"There's one other thing," I added, nodding, "it's got to be done tonight. Do you think that's possible?"

"Jesus, you make it easy, don't you? You couldn't have come to me yesterday?"

"Joe, I'm here now and it's got to be done now. What do you think?"

"Let me make a call and see if my friend is available."

"Whatever he wants, I'll pay him."

"No, Michael, he owes me a favor. It'll be on me."

"The blackmailer says that if I don't pay him by tomorrow, the pictures are going out in the mail. He might just do it, too."

"Then we've got to get moving, don't we?"

I nodded. Joe picked up his phone and buzzed his secretary.

"Ardette, see if you can get Arnie O'Toole on the phone for me. Wherever he is, find him. I need him now. Thanks."

Joe hung up the phone.

"So, while we're waiting, tell me about this guy. Where does he hang out?"

I had already written all the information on a piece of paper, which I handed to my brother along with a detailed map of how to find Nick's boat. Joe studied the information carefully.

"This is clear enough," he finally stated. "Think he'll be there tonight?"

"I hope so."

"Are the negatives on the boat?"

"I wish I knew."

Joe thought this over for a moment.

"Well," he concluded, "if we can find him, I have no doubt we can persuade him to give them to us. Can I call you late tonight at home if I find anything out?"

"Absolutely. Do you know my number?"

Joe flashed me another of his grins and recited my home phone number.

My brother hadn't phoned me in two years. I could only assume he kept the number in his memory in case he were busted and only allowed that one call from jail.

"You've got a good memory," I flattered him.

The phone on the coffee table buzzed. I almost jumped out of my seat. Joe answered it.

"Yes?"

Joe winked at me and waited.

"Hey, Arnie, how ya doing? Great. Listen I got a job for you. Something mucho important to me. Personal. You free tonight? Terrific. How long will it take you to get over here? Perfect. See you then. Yeah."

Joe hung up the phone.

"Lady Luck seems to smiling our way."

"It's about time," I said weakly.

"Okay." Joe stood up and extended his hand. "Let me finish up around here so I can get going on your problem. Don't worry, Michael, you can trust me. I mean it. And don't look so scared; it'll all work out all right. You came to the right guy; this is the kind of situation I understand."

"I appreciate it, Joe. I mean it." A little humility on my part couldn't hurt anything, I figured. "And congratulations again on your new position."

"Thank you," he said, walking me to the door. "I'll speak to you tonight."

My life was now in Joe's hands. Would he be able to pull it off? As I headed for the reception room, all I was aware of was the mattresslike padding underneath the thick wool carpet. I had never walked on anything so soft. This was Joe's, as was the office. He was the president here, apparently a great success. Who knew how he'd done it? But who cared? It was there, it was real, and it gave me hope. Maybe, just maybe, Joe could get those negatives. Of course if he did, he'd see for himself what I'd been up to with Genie. I wondered what he'd do with that information. There was no way to know. I just hoped that, when the time came, I'd be lucky enough to be dealing with my brother, rather than Nick.

42

That night was horrible. All I could do was wait. I hated waiting, especially for my god damn brother, on whom I was suddenly so dependent and who I knew to be so undependable.

I pretended, for Marilyn and Rebecca's sake, to be the calm, reasonable, easy-going husband and father, chatting away as if I were not only undisturbed, but even amused by my simultaneous felony indictment and chamber of commerce award. I appeared to have no problems, no worries, and no clouds darkening my future. All the while, I tried to figure out which drug would end my life in the most painless way possible. Anything requiring injection was out; I hated needles. Barbiturates seemed to be the answer. Finally I decided that Phenobarbital was the one to count on. Old reliable. It wasn't as fashionable as some of the more modern ways to OD, but it was proven, pain-free, and would do the trick neatly and predictably.

The seven o'clock news was a big surprise. Dan Rather dubbed me the "shy hero" and, in his human interest piece on my plight, portrayed my story as a national curiosity item. I was part hero and part villain, part Jimmy Stewart and part Clint Eastwood. The fact that I wouldn't give interviews piqued Rather's curiosity and apparently enhanced my moral credibility. The way the reporter circumvented my lack of cooperation was to put together a series of interviews with everyone else who had been involved. The story started with my speech at the award ceremony, then went to an interview with Mayor Malcolm, who lauded my actions, and then cut to Alice Allen, standing next to the hospital bed on which her husband lay connected to an array of life support tubes, wires, and machines. Alice and her ACLU attorney raged on about my vigilante mentality and the human consequences to society, in the form of Robert Allen—junkie husband, and now human vegetable.

To offset this horror, they had interviewed Genie. Right in front of her high school. She, of course, described me as a true hero, a man who had saved her life without thinking of the consequences to himself. Not only did she seem sincere, she was articulate and incredibly attractive. Clearly she enjoyed standing in front of a crowd of curious students, reading from her article in the school newspaper while being filmed by CBS. I could not deny that she looked terrific; I just wished she had worn something other than a sheer silk camisole top, without bra, for the interview. As she talked seriously about the robbery, all I could think about was the shape of her breasts and how much I'd enjoy fondling them again, in spite of what it had already cost me. My erection returned with a vengeance. On TV Genie appeared so beautiful that I was sure my motive in saving her was no mystery to anyone watching.

Jerry was interviewed, as I would have guessed, in front of the store's main sign. And, of course, he gave me and the business a big plug in the name of integrity. Ed Cotler was cast in the role of the outraged attorney, fighting the system to obtain justice for his client. But it was the final interview that was the shocker. There, on the television screen, was Marilyn.

Dan Rather made a big point (and I thought a typical cheap reporter's insight) of contrasting how, while I was in my pharmacy defending as well as taking a life, Marilyn had been working at Cedars-Sinai bringing a new life into the world. I couldn't believe that Marilyn had allowed them to film her at the hospital. Not only did she hate doctors who flaunted themselves in the public eye, she had argued repeatedly with me about how such publicity makes a person more vulnerable to criminal attacks. Marilyn told me later that she had hoped to avoid the latter problem by consenting to be interviewed only if she were wearing her surgical gown and mask, making her unrecognizable to anyone who didn't already know her. As far as the first point went—her hatred of glory-seeking doctors—she felt that the issues at stake compelled her to speak out in spite of the risks.

Marilyn used the news piece to advance her views on the violence our society has grown accustomed to accepting as tolerable. To Marilyn the state of society had become obscene. She even used the occasion to plug her dream of life in a rural setting. She urged everyone in America to seriously consider the dangers that they accepted every day. She urged them to take action.

"The consequences of passivity" she feared, "were hospitals full of victims and cities of violence, life lived in a war zone, Los Angeles becoming an American Beirut." Marilyn pleaded with the public to think seriously about the state of the American community, its values, and where it was heading. Dan Rather signed off. That's when our phone began ringing.

It was worse than the night of the robbery; not only did everyone I knew call, but every acquaintance of Marilyn's also phoned. My mother, Ed, the mayor, Jerry, the head of Cedars, the list went on and on. As soon as we hung up on one person, the phone rang with another. There was not a minute of peace between callers. The worst part was that every time the phone rang, I hoped it was Joe. As far as I knew, my brother had already met with Nick and dealt with him. But how could I find this out if Joe couldn't get through because the line was busy? The calls were driving me crazy.

My mood that night went up and down from despair to elation, pessimism to euphoria. But even in my whacked-out state, I was forced to admit that there was something tremendously impressive about the way Marilyn had handled herself during the interview. In contrast to Mayor Malcolm, Ed, Dan Rather, and even Genie, Marilyn spoke with a calm, reasonable, unhyped, even profound view of the world. My wife was a very rare sort of woman. To use an old word, in its true sense, Marilyn was a genuinely noble woman—high-minded, not just in words but in deeds. She was no hypocrite. She lived what she thought. What I had seen of her on television reminded me once again of what I had admired in her when we had first met. However, the problem, I knew, was not admiring her, but living with her. At the same time, I somehow wanted her to be both high-minded and down to earth. The high-minded part was obviously there. It was the flesh and blood aspects that caused my trouble. That night I was so desperate that I strained to convince myself to simply accept life with Marilyn, enjoy her as the high-minded wife on the pedestal, and forget about the passion that had already caused me so much trouble. But even in my unbalanced state, I knew that life with a passionless, high-minded Marilyn would be bearable only for a very short time.

For what seemed like hours, my mood bounced around all over the place. One moment I admired Marilyn. Then the phone rang and I became terrified. The next moment I thought of Genie in the silk camisole and my erection reasserted itself. I hated both Marilyn's utopia and my passion for Genie; all I wanted was for my life to be simple again. My life hung by a thread, dependent for salvation on an erratic con artist. The more terrified I became of being dependent on Joe, the more obvious it became to me that in some bizarre way I still cared for the son-of-a-bitch. And he, I hoped, still cared for me. I knew that if Joe pulled off the save with Nick, I would forgive my brother anything, forever.

This was an astonishing revelation to me. Forgiveness was not one of my strong suits. I had never been able to forgive my father for all the suffering he'd inflicted on our family. Nor had I been able to forgive Marilyn for the rigidness of her obsessions. Yet at that moment, in the middle of the eleven o'clock news, I was considering forgiving everyone for everything, if only Joe were able to free me from my blackmail. Something was changing in me. Was it real? Would it last? Or was it only a temporary conversion in the face of death?

After the eleven o'clock news, which featured another piece on my plight, the flood of calls increased once again. I was too crazy to talk reasonably so I asked Marilyn to answer the phone. All I wanted was for Joe to call, and everyone but Joe seemed interested in talking to me. Where the hell was my brother? Why didn't he call me? By one o'clock the phone had stopped ringing and we prepared for bed.

"You know," I told Marilyn as she wiped the cold cream from her face in the bathroom, "you really impressed me with the way you talked on the news; you're the one who should go into politics, not me."

At this point, not having heard from Joe, I was virtually hysterical. But I still kept my outward cool and appeared to be reasonable. Anxiety wouldn't help. Hyperactivity certainly wouldn't. I needed peace. What I hoped for was a little chit-chat with Marilyn, then if I were lucky, some sleep.

"Thank you, Michael, but I have to tell you I'm afraid," Marilyn confided. "Really afraid. Something's happening, Michael, something that wasn't happening before. I don't know what it is, but I feel it. I'm afraid for us. Afraid for Rebecca. Afraid for you. You're changing, withdrawing. I feel so far from you, suddenly. What is it, Michael? Do you feel it too?"

Marilyn appeared to be so vulnerable. As usual she was being totally honest. She was telling me that she cared for me, that she loved me, and that she needed me. Not by saying the words, which I would have liked to have heard, but by acknowledging the fear that she felt. At least it was a start. She was changing, too. I had a strong impulse to tell her about Genie; but I was weak, and afraid that she couldn't take it. An honest man of passion would have told his wife what he was made of and demanded that she accept his nature for what it was. Obviously I couldn't yet accept and live with my own character. Unlike Marilyn, who expressed her needs and desires regardless of my reaction, I was unable to expose the truth about myself to her. Even my father had admitted his own true needs. The truth horrified me as I realized for the first time in my life that my father was a much better man than I was.

"You're afraid, too, aren't you Michael?"

I nodded. Marilyn set down her face cream, glided across the bathroom, and wrapped her naked arms around me.

"It's been a long, terrible day for both of us. I need to be close to you. Come to bed with me, Michael. I'm scared and I need you."

I couldn't believe what I was hearing. At any other time in the last year, such an invitation would have excited me. But at that moment, with all my anxiety over Nick and Joe, her needing me wasn't enough to distract me from my fears.

"Marilyn, it's a little late, don't you think?"

She wrapped both of her legs around my left thigh and squeezed herself against my hip.

"I haven't felt this close to you in a long time, Michael."

"I know. But aren't you tired? Don't you have to be up early tomorrow?"

Marilyn ignored me and began to kiss and bite my neck. Because of my fears about the blackmail, I felt Marilyn's caresses as irritation rather than as pleasure. She dropped to her knees and unsuccessfully tried to arouse me with her lips and tongue.

"I told you I was tired."

"I can see," she murmured. "Why don't you come to bed and let me help you relax. I've never seen you so tense."

"Give me one minute, okay?" I gestured to the toilet.

Marilyn nodded, picked herself up off the floor, and left the bathroom.

My anxiety threshold had peaked off the chart. I needed to relax; to do so I had to take my mind away from Joe. I opened the medicine cabinet and searched through our store of pharma-

ceuticals. I needed help. Escape. I started with Valium. Twenty
milligrams. But then I realized that when a person is as wired up
with worry as I was, Valium frequently has no effect whatsoever,
so I took another ten for good measure. I waited, hoping the
medication would work. I washed my face, brushed my teeth,
and used the toilet. Minutes passed. I was as anxious as ever. I
needed something stronger.

"Michael," Marilyn called from the bedroom, "what's keeping you?"

I quickly looked through the remaining pharmaceuticals in the
cabinet. The only potentially useful drug was an old prescription
of Quaaludes that Marilyn had once tried during a short bout
with insomnia. Marilyn hadn't liked the Quaaludes; that groggy,
out of control feeling had scared her. But what did I have to
lose? What the hell, I told myself, as I swallowed two Quaaludes.

What I saw in the bedroom jolted me. Marilyn lay on her
back, naked, on the bed. Her hand fluttered between her legs;
she was masturbating. As I crossed the room to her, Marilyn's
eyes followed me, probing my reaction. She had never exposed
herself like this in front of me. As far as I knew, she never
masturbated, period. What she was doing was obviously for my
benefit, in the hope that it would excite me. It probably would
have, too, if I had thought it was real. But from the detached
expression on her face, I could see that she felt disconnected
from the erotic part of herself she was rubbing. I couldn't help
remembering Genie in the porno motel, masturbating in front of
the TV. Genie played with herself because it felt good to her.
Marilyn diddled with herself as a theatrical manipulation. I
suspected that a patient had told Marilyn such a thing excited
men. But Marilyn had missed the point; for her approach to
work, she couldn't be so transparent about her play acting. On
the other hand, who was I to discourage her from becoming a
little more adventurous in her sex life? That was what I wanted,
wasn't it? Timing was the problem. That night, concentrating on
Marilyn was a growing impossibility.

Attempting to be a good sport and play along, I sat bedside
Marilyn on the bed and watched. Her pubic hair, as usual, was
immaculately trimmed and powdered. It always amused me that
a gynecologist should be embarrassed by her own pubic hair, but
in Marilyn's case it was the truth. Pubic hair that crept out under
the edge of a bikini bottom revolted her. She kept herself as

perfectly clipped as a Barbie Doll. The fact that pubic hair excited me had no effect on Marilyn. Pubic hair was something to be hidden; it was a subject not open for debate. I remembered reading stories of women who trimmed their pubic hair, not to be neat, but to excite their men. In the twenties, in Chicago, women trimmed their muffs in the shape of bowler hats. Then there was a fad of heart shaped pubics. I wondered what Marilyn would think if I asked her to trim hers into a cowboy hat or a football. She'd probably ask me for a divorce. How could she face her own gynecologist, she would have asked?

But I couldn't stop thinking about the damn phone. Where was Joe? What had happened with Nick? What was my future going to be? I would have liked nothing more than to forget about the blackmail, give myself in to an erection, and spend an hour pleasing Marilyn. Not only couldn't I manage to get aroused, but my paranoia mounted as the minutes rolled by. Was it the Quaaludes? As I watched Marilyn's finger caress herself, my mind roamed up to Santa Barbara, to Nick's abalone boat. I had the horrible fantasy that perhaps after seeing the pictures, Joe had joined Nick in the blackmail, forcing his way in as a silent partner. It didn't take much to imagine Joe suddenly shifting his alliances and coaching Nick on how to get the most out of me. If anyone hated me and would like to see me destroyed, it was Joe. Why had I involved him in this? God, was I stupid. The two of them would fuck me over and split the proceeds.

As I watched Marilyn exhibit herself I became angry. It was precisely because of her sexual detachment that I had gotten myself in all the trouble with Genie. If only Marilyn had been able to be open with me, to truly get excited in bed with me, rather than arouse herself with that endlessly repetitive "Story of O" fantasy, I wouldn't be in my present dilemma with Genie, Nick, and Joe. Marilyn lay on the bed pretending to be wanton. It was bullshit. Thanks to Genie, I knew what it meant to be truly wanton—and Marilyn's behavior certainly didn't fit that definition.

My wife turned over and once again used her mouth in an attempt to get me going. It was, as they say, to no avail. My paranoia grew exponentially and my thoughts became crazy. I began to wonder if Marilyn wasn't in on the scheme with Nick and Joe. Maybe the whole affair with Genie had been a plot

concocted by Marilyn to get me to make a public fool of myself.
That way I'd be forced to sell the pharmacy and run off to the
health spa in Escondido with my tail between my legs, in her
debt forever. Even at the time, I knew this fantasy was nuts. Yet
somehow I came to believe it was true. Such a plot put me in the
middle of a whole group of monsters, all of whom wanted to
feed off me.

At that point I knew the drugs in my system were beginning to
affect me strangely. I remember being certain, not only that the
plot existed, but that Joe and Nick were hiding in my house.
Their purpose was to listen and assess how anxious I was
regarding the blackmail. The more frightened I felt over being
publicly exposed, the more money they could get out of me. The
fact that my wife was naked, sucking on my cock while masturbating, and I still couldn't get excited, obviously gave away my
emotional state. If Joe and Nick were listening, they would know
that they had me for big dollars. My first reaction to this
observation was to consider running out of the bedroom and
surprising the blackmailers in their hiding place, wherever that
was. Then I came up with a better idea. If only I could make
myself cool down and relax, I could generate an erection, which
would convince those bastards that they couldn't get to me. I
would love to see their faces, I recall thinking, as they listened to
me screwing my wife. As the minutes passed, their blackmail
price, like their spirits would drop faster than a stone down an
empty well. The only problem was my erection—more specifically, my lack of one.

I conjured up that first image of Genie in my living room,
when I saw her squatting over Nick as she later squatted over
me, drenched in sweat and possessed by passion. The memory of
Genie caused no small amount of stirring in my loins. However,
the presence of Nick in the picture quickly squashed whatever
progress I was making. So I went back, in my mind, to the
porno motel and the memory of Genie with her compelling need
for me, her heat, the smell of her juices, and the feeling I had
inside of her. Further help came from the image of Genie on her
knees, dog-style, with her lovely ass thrust up into the air, her
cheeks spread, and life itself transformed into the frenzy of
animals in heat, humping, screaming, and snorting.

This image led to the erection I had been seeking. My next
move was entering Marilyn. Again, thanks to my memories of

Genie, I succeeded, in spite of Marilyn's true state of only partial arousal. As I began to move inside of her, I congratulated myself on achieving the beginning, at least, of my victory fuck over paranoia. I ignored Marilyn's predictable request for her perpetual "Story of O" fantasy and committed myself to a sexual marathon commensurate with my own appetites. We began in the missionary position and flopped through every configuration our bodies were capable of attaining. The longer it went on, the happier I became; if those bastards were listening, I gloated to myself, I was defeating their plans with every thrust of my hips.

"Stop, Michael, please, stop," Marilyn suddenly demanded.

But I couldn't let up. I was a man possessed, a man fucking away his devils. Those assholes listening from the other room weren't going to make a fool out of me. No sir. I would fuck from now until doomsday, if that was what it took to regain my power over Joe and Nick.

"Please, Michael, stop. You're hurting me."

"Relax Marilyn. Enjoy it. Give yourself up to it."

"Michael, I can't. Stop. Please."

We had been going at it for at least an hour. Genie, I knew, would have loved it. So would slews of other women. But not Marilyn, to whom I had become an irritation. In my drug-crazed state, I figured that the reason for this was Marilyn's connection to the blackmail plot and her realization that my virility had gained the upper hand. My paranoia was boundless.

"Michael, god damn it, what's wrong with you? Stop!"

Marilyn tried to pull away from me, but I wouldn't let her. She struggled while I continued to thrust into her; her fighting felt to me like passion, and spurred me on. She began to pound on my back with her fists.

"Michael, you're hurting me. Stop, please, Michael!"

But I couldn't; I was out of control.

"Michael, what's wrong with you? Please. God damn it, you bastard, stop, you're hurting me!"

As I neared my orgasm, my heart started beating like a tom-tom. All I could suddenly hear was a bass drum pounding out "lub-dub" in my chest. It was Sting, singing "Every Breath You Take" to the rhythms reverberating through my body. It was terrifying, a cardiovascular nightmare. I was only thirty-four; I was too young for a heart attack, I cried out in vain. I stopped moving but the explosions in my chest wouldn't quit. I remem-

bered the Toshiro Mifune movie *Sanjuro*, where the Samurai
warrior slashes his opponent through the heart with one stroke of
his sword and the bad Samurai's heart explodes, shooting blood
across the screen like a Roman fountain. I had been hoping for a
great orgasm; I had no idea I'd get it in the form of an explosion
from my chest. The last thing I remember was Marilyn grabbing
my wrist and timing my pulse. Then everything turned brilliantly
white. Where were my sunglasses when I needed them? My head
felt like it had split open. All color drained from the room. The
walls became brighter and brighter. Marilyn turned platinum,
then the color of burning magnesium. That was the last thing I
recall until I woke up in the hospital.

43

Marilyn stood over me wearing her medical coat, studying me
closely. Next to her was Irv Wittcop, our internist.

"Hello, Michael," Irv chirped in his most professionally
cheerful manner.

The hospital room was bright. It was daytime. My first
thought concerned Joe. Had he called?

"What time is it?"

"Four-fifteen."

"In the afternoon?" I asked Irv.

He nodded.

"Jesus, what the hell happened to me?"

"That's what we want to know," Marilyn said. "What did
you take before you came to bed last night?"

"Tell me first, did Joe call?"

"Joe?" asked Marilyn, incredulous.

"Yeah, did he call?"

"You haven't talked to him in two years. Why would he
call?" Marilyn gave Irv a look which implied that I was going
nuts. Irv nodded without replying.

"Marilyn," I said angrily, "don't treat me like I'm a fruit-
cake; I saw Joe yesterday at his new job and he was going to call
me today about something we discussed. Did he call?"

"No," she answered.

Shit, I thought, what the hell has happened to that son-of-a-bitch?''

"Michael what did you take last night?" Irv injected into my despair.

"What's the difference?"

"Don't be difficult, we're trying to help you. Now what did you take?"

"Valium and Quaaludes," I told them nonchalantly as if I did it all the time. "I was having trouble sleeping."

"That was on top of a bottle of wine after dinner," Marilyn told Irv.

"Michael," Irv lectured me, "I don't have to tell you; you're a registered, licensed pharmacist. I know you understand these things. What's wrong with you? Are you crazy? Were you trying to kill yourself?"

"I was trying to relax."

"Well, you relaxed real good," Marilyn told me quietly, obviously worried. "You've been unconscious for twelve god-damn hours and scared the holy hell out of us. Do you feel better now?"

"Actually, I have a little headache," I joked.

"That's just too bad, isn't it?" said Marilyn just a little sarcastically. "Last night I thought you had a coronary."

"So did I," I told her.

Marilyn and Irv exchanged another one of those "what do you do with a stupid husband" glances.

"So can I go home now?" I asked.

"I think it'd be better for you to stay in overnight, you know, just for observation."

"Irv. This is Cedars-Sinai. It's a hospital filled with sick people. Am I a sick person? No. If you want to observe me, observe me at home, okay?"

Irv and Marilyn exchanged another of their glances and I knew I was down for the count—their count.

44

Despite my objections, Marilyn and Irv made me stay in the hospital for twenty-four more hours. And with no phone calls, yet. It drove me crazy trying to appear calm, stable, and healthy, while all the time my maniacal inner life was wired up with enough anxiety to light up a city of ten thousand average Americans. Where the hell was Joe?

Finally on Sunday afternoon they released me. By the time I got home, over forty-eight hours had passed since I'd had my little conversation with my brother, and I'd yet to hear a word from him. I tried calling his office but the answering service only knew he was out of town. "Out of town"—the words burned through my brain. On his business or mine? It drove me so crazy that I even called my mother. But Gloria knew nothing about Joe's whereabouts.

Marilyn, meanwhile, treated me as if I were truly a sick patient. I had to get into bed. She brought me tea, and we distracted one another by reading to Rebecca from *The Cat in the Hat*. To an outsider, it would have looked like a lovely family scene, something out of a Norman Rockwell painting, perhaps entitled "The Sick Husband." Had the outsider been able to peer inside my head, it would have looked more like something from the canvas of Francis Bacon, filled with rotting bits of tormented meat.

But I remained cool and successfully passed myself off as normal to both my daughter and my wife. The most difficult moments were when the phone rang. I couldn't figure out why Joe didn't call. The only hopeful note in the day came when I telephoned Mary, the cashier, at home. She couldn't recall anyone named Nick coming into the pharmacy. What did that mean? Had Joe stopped the son of a bitch? If Joe had actually talked to Nick and ended the blackmail, I was sure that Joe would have told me about it, and fast. Nothing made any sense. There were too many unknowns; too much for me to worry about. The photos could already be in the mail.

Marilyn was nice enough not to bring up my behavior in bed Friday night. I assumed she blamed it on the drugs, which was fine with me. Or maybe she just didn't want to know. Whatever the reason, I apparently seemed normal enough to convince her not only that I was sane, but that Rebecca could be trusted to my supervision. Marilyn had an eight o'clock appointment with her surgeons, whom she expected to sign the preliminary contract, setting in motion the formal beginnings of the health spa. It was a meeting she had no intention of missing. As soon as she left I put Rebecca to sleep, ran for the telephone, and dialed Genie.

Unfortunately, Ed answered.

I took a chance, pitched my voice high, held my noise, and whispered in an attempt to disguise my identity.

"I'd like to speak with Genie, please, sir."

"Who's calling?"

Ed sounded suspicious. But then he always sounded suspicious; that was his nature.

"Roger," I lied in my squeaky voice.

"Roger who?" demanded Ed.

"She'll know who I am, sir."

"I'm sure she will, Roger. But I want to know who you are," Ed boomed out over the phone with authority. "You must have a last name."

What an asshole.

"Birnbaum, sir. Roger Birnbaum."

"Very good, Birnbaum. Hang on one minute."

"Thank you sir."

Jesus Christ, no wonder Genie was so frantic to get out of that house and run away. Living with that sort of behavior day in and day out, even forgetting the sexual abuse, had to be horrible. I looked down at my chest and saw that my robe was soaked through with sweat, all from my conversation with a man who was supposed to be my friend.

"Hello?" It was Genie on the phone.

"Genie?" I asked in my falsetto whine.

"Who is this?" she asked.

"Are we alone on the line?"

"I think so."

"You're not sure?"

"I'm sure," she answered.

"I have to talk to you," I told her in my normal voice.

"Oh."

"That's all you have to say?"

"I'm very glad you called, Roger. I could sure use some help on this trig homework."

"Your dad's still in the room with you, huh?"

"That's very perceptive of you, Roger."

"I need to talk to you tonight. Is that possible?"

"Maybe. Could you come over here and show me how

it's solved? It'd really help me for that test tomorrow."

"I can't. Marilyn's out and I have to stay with Rebecca. Can you get over here?"

"Maybe. God, I wish the test weren't so soon. Are you sure you have the time to help me?"

"Does that mean you can get over here?"

"I'll have to ask my dad. How long do you think it'll take?"

"Not long."

"Hold on a second."

I held. She was talking to her father, but I couldn't quite make out the words.

"Roger," Genie came back on the line, "my father says fine. I'll be over in ten minutes. But we've got to do it fast; I have a lot of other studying to do, okay? I don't have time for socializing."

"That's fine; I'll be waiting for you. Just knock on the front door."

"'Bye, Roger."

"'Bye."

I hung up the phone. I had made it over the first hurdle, getting to see Genie tonight. It was just possible that she knew something about Nick.

At that moment the phone rang I grabbed the receiver.

"Hello," I yelled.

"Michael, Ed here. How are you?"

"Ed. Hey," I said cautiously, "how are you?" I was terrified. Why was he calling? Did he know that he had just talked to me on the phone?

"Michael, is something wrong?"

"No, no, why?"

"You don't sound all there."

"Oh no, I'm fine. Just a little tired, you know."

"I called earlier. Marilyn said you were under the weather."

Good old Marilyn, covering for me.

"Oh, yes; that. I had an allergic reaction to some medication. But I'm fine now, thanks."

"I'm glad to hear that. I was worried about you."

"Thanks Ed, I appreciate it."

"I've got some good news for you."

"Yeah?"

"You know who watched that piece Dan Rather did on you?"

''Who?''

''The president himself. And I've got to tell you, Michael, he was very impressed. In fact, I heard it first hand that he told the Republican National Committee to keep their eye on you. If you play your cards right, you can ride this whole thing right into public office. You've got the president of the United States behind you now, Michael. I want you to think out your next move very seriously.''

If only Ed knew how seriously. I was thinking about it. Christ, I realized, with the president as well as the Republican National Committee watching me, what would happen if those pictures of Genie and me at the porno motel ever became public? For all I knew, they were already in the mail. The Republicans wouldn't enjoy the scandal I'd provide. I had no doubt they'd make me seriously suffer for the embarrassment I caused them.

''Ed, thanks. I appreciate it. But what do you think will happen if I do time in jail? I haven't seen too many senators elected after attempted murder convictions, have you?''

Ed castigated me for being so negative, swearing that I'd never see the inside of a penitentiary unless it was in the capacity of an elected official on a fact-finding tour. I wanted to believe him, but I was so vividly familiar with how much he didn't know about my life that there was no way I could trust his argument. I was committing the basic error in the client-attorney relationship; I was withholding information from my counsel, thereby grossly weakening his defense strategy.

As I was about to hang up, Ed told me the real reason for his call. Apparently the mayor had also been impressed by my speech at the chamber of commerce luncheon and had called Ed. The mayor asked if I would appear with him on a local cable TV news show to discuss the crime issue and to debate the merits of the Community Watch program with Hal Westheimer, the opposition's Democratic mayoral candidate.

''Does that mean the mayor will press the D.A. to drop the charges against me?'' I asked Ed.

''If you help the mayor, I don't see why he won't help you; he does believe in what you did.''

''That's all very nice, but I want this case over with. Will he go to bat for me or not?''

''Michael, don't be naive. Just help the mayor out with his election and I guarantee you he'll back you when it counts. I know the man, I've done business with him for years. This is the way these things work."

I had to do it—I needed all the help I could get.

"So give me the time and place of the debate. And thank the mayor for inviting me."

Ed gave me the details, then hung up, very pleased with himself.

At that moment, the doorbell rang; it was Genie. As soon as I let her in she threw her arms around me and planted a wet, passionate kiss on my mouth without even looking to see if anyone else was in the house. I was horrified; Rebecca could have been watching. Was Genie stoned? I wondered if this was another part of Nick's blackmail plot; maybe he wanted a good picture of Genie and me kissing in my living room to complete his nasty little "photo essay." In my desperate frame of mind it didn't take much imagination to construct a case for Genie and Nick still being involved with one another. After all, the more they could get out of me, the more the two of them would have to run off together. Kissing me by the door within easy camera range made a great deal of sense.

"Hey, go easy," I told Genie, separating myself from her and gesturing upstairs in Rebecca's direction. "More witnesses I don't need."

Genie flashed me that fabulously joyful smile of hers.

"Michael, I'm so happy to see you; I have so much to tell you. How are you? You don't look so good."

"I've been having a little trouble in the sleeping department. I've got a few things on my mind, as I think you know."

Genie nodded understandingly.

"Michael, I've been doing a lot of thinking about you. And about us. I was real impressed by that piece about you on TV, you know why?"

I shook my head; I had no idea.

"You were right about not talking to those network guys. You're different from them. Different from everyone around here. You saw through them, and I think they knew that. You know, you look like the most normal, nice, average sort of a man...."

"Thanks a lot," I offered with some sarcasm.

"Can I finish, if you don't mind?"

"Sorry."

"What I saw on that news show was something I think no one else knows. I saw a man, you, Michael, who wants everyone to think he's a normal, average sort of guy, just like everyone else. Except you're not. Not only are you a little odd, but you're actually a rebel, a closet eccentric, even something of a weirdo. The part of you that I know and the part of you I like, is the part you hide from everyone, the part no one saw on the news. But you know what? If you don't let those demons of yours out, go public with your whole self, you're going to be one unhappy man for the rest of your life."

"Am I?" I stalled. She was right in her own way, I knew. But I wasn't interested in philosophy; the blackmail was my immediate problem.

"Absolutely."

"And how do you suggest I unleash my demons?"

"I've already told you."

"By doing what?"

"Michael, you couldn't have forgotten."

"Remind me."

"You've got to give up your conventional life. Throw off your chains. Have a fling. Run off with me to New York. Life in the Village. Take that trip to Europe. Let the real Michael out of his cage. It's the only way you'll find out who you are."

"Genie, you're crazy." She had to be stoned.

"You can't do it, can you?" She challenged me with contempt. "You'd rather spend your life feeding fat old ladies carrot juice at your wife's health farm. Is that what you want?"

"Actually, at the moment, given my legal problems, that sounds pretty damn good."

"And pretty damn boring, doesn't it? I know you, Michael. How long do you think you can last behind the juice bar before you go nuts? You're like me. We don't belong here. We should be somewhere where people take chances, where life has real possibilities, where we can achieve our potentials. You're a hero, Michael, not a papaya squeezer."

"Genie, think back. I'm facing jail. I can't go anywhere. Remember?"

"B.S. You're getting off. You know it and I know it."

"I'm glad you know so much; are you in a position to drop the charges against me?"

"Michael, I heard what my dad said. I know about the mayor. Gimme a break will you?"

"You give me a break," I told her angrily. "Those pictures Nick took; if they come out, how far do you think your father and the mayor are going to go to help me?"

"You're so negative—compared to you, Nick's a lightweight. I don't know why you're having so much trouble handling him."

Finally she had given me an opening to test her allegiance.

"That's why I wanted to talk to you; I figured out a way to deal with him. If it works, the problem's going to be dead and buried."

My choice of words seemed to cause Genie some concern.

"What are you going to do?" she asked.

"It's what I've already done."

"And what is that?"

"You'll find out soon enough."

"Tell me what you've done, Michael." She seemed a little too concerned for my taste.

"I took your advice—I threatened him."

"And how did he respond?"

"He didn't believe me."

"You reminded him about the junkie in the hospital?"

"I'm not stupid, Genie."

"And he still didn't give you the negatives?"

"No ma'am."

"Jesus, he's dumb."

"That's what I told him."

"So what are you going to do?"

"It's already done."

"Which is?" Genie didn't like the direction the conversation was taking.

I phrased my answer very, very carefully. I wanted the full meaning of my actions to sink deeply into her.

"I have to follow through on my threat."

"You wouldn't."

"That's all I can do; I told you that when we talked about it."

"Michael, come on," she tried joking with me, "you wouldn't kill Nick; I know you."

"You're absolutely right. But I might hire someone who would."

"I don't believe you."

"Can you think of any other way to stop the blackmail?"

Genie thought for some time before speaking.

"Why are you telling me this?" she asked.

"I thought you should know. I mean, you are part of this, too, aren't you?"

"Not murdering Nick."

"That would bother you? You'd miss him?"

"Michael, I don't understand why you're doing this to me. Can't you see that I care about you and want to be with you? I may be young and I may have lived all my life at home with my parents, but that doesn't mean I don't feel things deeply. Death isn't a joke. We both know that. Nick was my boyfriend. Yes, Nick is also a little crazy. But I don't want him dead. Can you understand that? I mean, he's a bad person, but he's not that bad."

"But if it means he destroys my life if I don't kill him first, what do you suggest I do?"

"Nick doesn't understand what he's doing."

"I think he understands very well; that's why he asked for so much money."

"Michael," she said after some reflection, "think about this: if you left with me and started a new life, it wouldn't matter if those pictures came out. People would know about us anyhow. The pictures would be worthless, don't you see?"

"You're actually serious about just taking off with me and driving to New York? You'd really do it?"

Genie grinned mischievously.

"Give me the word and I'll leave with you right now. My car's in the driveway. I'll go with just the clothes on my back. And this."

She pulled a small roll of bills from her wallet and flourished them in front of my face.

"This is $600 cash that I've been saving for the last year in case I had to suddenly get away from my father. It should be enough to get us to New York, don't you think? Shall we do it?"

Genie gestured outside to her Mustang.

"You're crazy."

"Michael, this is a real opportunity. For both of us. We can get out of this boredom we're living in. Don't you want to do something with your life? Don't you remember those dreams you once had, Michael? I know you do. You've read Kerouac. We'll be 'on the road.' Don't you want that?''

"Genie, I was indicted for attempted murder yesterday. Whether or not they convict me and I go to jail is one thing. But if I leave the state before the trial, they'll declare me a fugitive from justice. I'm out on bail now, remember? Two minutes after we got to New York they'd arrest me, extradite me, and throw me back here in the can. Until my legal problems are over, I can't go anywhere.''

"Okay,'' she said after considering my case, "but if you could go, if you didn't have this legal thing hanging over you, would you give this all up,'' she gestured around the living room "and go with me, now? Tonight?''

Her idea was crazy. Loony. Yet, running off with her did have a definite romantic pull, a little like surfing had when I was a teenager. What could be more exciting than simply discarding the past and shooting forward into the unknown future, with only the clothes on one's back? I felt the possibility inside of me; I actually could just do it, I realized. Then I thought about what would happen if I just took off with Genie. Eventually, of course, they would find us and toss me in jail. But in the meantime I would be speeding across the United States with an underage blonde bombshell. I'd be a middle-aged outlaw. I asked myself if a short but free and exciting life of romance wasn't better than a long, conventional, middle-class struggle for existence. "Live fast, die young, and make a good-looking corpse,'' they used to say out on the water in Malibu.

"If I didn't have the legal problems,'' I lied to Genie, "I'd leave with you in a second.'' As much as I would have liked to run off with her, I knew at that moment, without equivocation, that my soul remained with Marilyn and Rebecca. Why, exactly, I couldn't articulate. But my wife and daughter seemed vividly real to me while New York and the Village with Genie were fantasy. What would Genie and I do in the Big Apple, even if we could stay out of the way of the police? How long would the romance last in a cold-water flat with her working as a waitress and me as a shoe salesman? Genie was too young and too idealistic to live such a life. After six months, we'd be behaving like an old married couple with nothing between us but disappointed dreams and some dim, distant memories of romance.

No, there was no future for me with Genie, in spite of her tremendous appeal.

"I'm so happy you feel that, Michael." Genie threw her arms around me and embraced me feverishly.

I responded politely and kept an eye on the staircase, terrified Rebecca would suddenly appear and see us.

Whether or not she knew any more, Genie was obviously not going to tell me anything else about Nick. Worried that Marilyn could walk in the front door at any time, I asked Genie to cut her visit short. She left me with the gift she had brought—a paper-back copy of Kerouac's *On the Road*. Subtle, she was not.

I kissed her good-bye and she departed. I opened the first page of the book and read, as I had expected, a highly incriminating inscription: "Think of the book we could write one day if only you gave us the chance. Love, G."

I tore out the title page, on which the inscription was written, and flushed it down the toilet. Then I went to the liquor cabinet and poured myself a tall glass of scotch. Genie, I felt, had been sufficiently reassured by my lie to wait a couple of days before seeing me again; I had gained some breathing room in that department. The next step, assuming I could resolve the problem with Nick, would be to gently wean Genie from her fantasies involving me. That completed, I could resume my life with Marilyn and Rebecca. As I sipped my J & B and fantasized about everything being neat and tidy once again, the old Norman Rockwell image of my family returned to comfort my troubled soul. But after only a moment of peace, the phone rang and every bit of my anxiety returned full blown.

Like a maniac I ran across the room, knocking over an end table. I grabbed the receiver, praying it was Joe.

"Hello," I screamed into the phone.

"Is Carol in?" an old lady asked.

"Carol?"

"Carol Schoenfeld. Is Carol in?"

"There's no Carol Schoenfeld here, you have the wrong number." I hung up, enraged. I was alone again and crazed. Where was my brother? Where was my salvation? What was going to happen to me, I cried out to the gods.

Marilyn returned home an hour later with the signed preliminary partnership agreement and two checks totaling $100,000. The surgeons had come through with their investment promises and Marilyn was flying high. Now that she had the first payment, all that was left was to find a site and build the damn clinic. I made an effort to be enthusiastic with Marilyn, but I couldn't help remembering Genie's comments about my career behind the juice bar.

Marilyn and I stayed up late talking about the meeting. Certainly I was proud of her, and I enjoyed the vitality she was once again displaying. But we never did talk about the drug reaction and my sexual behavior of two nights before, which I found strange. Marilyn had been frightened. She had felt I was changing. She was right. Didn't she want to know why? Or had her fears been assuaged by the power of the investment?

45

After another night of little sleep and no word from Joe, I arrived at work to find the pharmacy already open. Jerry, it seems, had taken over for me when I hadn't shown up on Saturday.

"You look terrible," my partner commented cheerfully as I entered the front door, "truly awful; what are you doing to yourself?" Jerry grinned laciviously. "Or should I say, what is that seventeen year old doing to you? Genie's her name, right?"

"Crawl back under your rock, Jerry; I don't start my day talking to maggots." I breezed past and locked myself in the office. A moment later a knock sounded on the door.

"Michael, I was just kidding," Jerry called. "Can I talk to you for a minute?"

I ignored him.

"Hey, Michael, don't be an asshole. Open the door. This is about business."

Everything with Jerry was about business. I opened the door and eyed him sternly. Jerry shut the door behind him and sat down.

"So . . ." he began.

I waited.

"How are you feeling? Marilyn said you were sick yesterday."

"I'm better now, thank you. Is that it?"

"Michael, I'm your partner but, you know, I also think of

myself as your friend. It's clear to me you don't approve of the way I live or have much patience with the way I do things. But when it comes down to it, I know you're my friend and would go to bat for me if I needed it.''

I said nothing. He had no idea about my real feelings.

''Something's going on with you, sometimes besides all this business with the shooting and the lawsuits. You obviously don't want to talk about it. That's okay. I just want you to know that I'm here to help if you need me. Day or night, you want someone to talk to, call me. And don't get angry because I offer; sometimes these things just have to be said, okay? You heard me. I'm done.''

''Thanks, Jerry.''

I could just picture myself telling him about the blackmail. Jail would be preferable.

Jerry got up to leave. Then he suddenly turned, as if he'd forgotten he had something else to tell me.

''Hey, I'm taking the kids water skiing this afternoon outside the Marina breakwater. Why don't you come with us? You could use some fun. Take half a day off, what do you say? I won't dock your pay, I promise.''

''I appreciate the offer, Jerry, but I should make up for what I missed here Saturday. Thanks anyway.''

''Think about it. You can always change your mind. It's going to be a beautiful day out there on the ocean.''

I nodded. Jerry nodded. Then he left. I locked the door behind him and swallowed twenty milligrams of Valium in the hope of settling myself down. The drug did nothing. Valium, I reflected, certainly wasn't as effective as it was cracked up to be. But then again, maybe it was me that was cracked up and the Valium that was fine.

A few minutes before nine I heard a bizarre tune rapped out by hard knuckles on my door. My first impulse was to kill the person who was annoying me. I unlocked the bolt and yanked open the door, ready to spill blood. Standing in front of me, all smiles, was my brother Joe. He was tired and unshaven, clutching a large manila envelope.

''Good morning,'' he chirped.

My heart began pounding with such ferocity that the pulse roaring through my ears sounded like the start of the Indy Five Hundred. I was about to find out if I'd won or lost.

"Joe. Jesus, I've been trying to call you for days. What happened?" I tried to appear nonchalant, as if nothing mattered. But I doubt that anyone, much less my brother, would have believed my bluff.

He smiled that self-satisfied broad grin of his. Joe was enjoying the moment, I could tell. I wanted to ask what was in the envelope; but knowing my brother, I had to let him tell his story at his own pace. To rush him when he was in that kind of mood would accomplish nothing.

"It's been an exciting adventure, Michael."

"And. . . ."

"Why do you think I'm here?" he leered.

"I hope you've got some good news for me."

"You think I'd be here if I didn't?"

"You got the negatives?" I asked, jubilant.

"Michael, hey, calm down. It's not as simple as that; that kid you were dealing with is one tough character."

"You couldn't get 'em?" I uttered in despair.

"I didn't say that either. Let me tell you what happened."

As I had feared, Joe couldn't just quickly let me off the hook; he had to put me through the wringer. And I was forced to take it. I nodded for him to get on with it.

"You're not even going to offer me a chair?"

"Joe, for god's sake, sit down and tell me what happened."

I had never seen my brother so pleased with himself. Slowly he lowered himself into the canvas director's chair, pretending to collect his thoughts.

"Michael, you know, you really should relax. I've never seen you like this. If you don't mind me saying so, I think you should take some Valium; it's bad for you to let yourself get so worked up."

"What happened, Joe?"

"You're sure you don't want some Valium first?"

"No," I said firmly, "I just want to know what happened."

I was having difficulty controlling my anxiety and Joe was loving it; finally he had something over me.

"First I want you to sit back and relax; it worries me to see you so upset. I don't want you to have a heart attack now. You know, by our age, this sort of stress is very dangerous to the cardiovascular system. A month ago I even took a CPR class just in case. But why am I telling you? You're a pharmacist, you know these things.''

"Joe, did you or did you not get the pictures?''

"Hey, it was a big challenge. Turned out to be very complicated. I think it's important you know everything that happened. So just settle back and relax. This is going to take a few minutes, okay?''

I nodded, barely able to control myself. I needed Joe. I also wanted to strangle the bastard for tormenting me.

"My friend Arnie and I drove up to Santa Barbara Friday night. We got there maybe two in the morning. It took a while to find the asshole's dock. You didn't tell me about the fog, Michael. Jesus, you wouldn't have believed it—it was like one of those Sherlock Holmes movies with Basil Rathbone. I felt like I should have a pipe and a bloodhound with me. Anyway, it was maybe three o'clock by the time we found Nick's slip. And you know what?''

I shook my head, indicating that I didn't know. How would I know? That was why I was so crazed.

"The son-of-a-bitch was gone. No Nick. And no boat. He was out fishing. Can you believe it? We drove all the way up there, knocked around in the fog for an hour, and he wasn't even there. Arnie felt Nick deserved to die just for wasting our time. Arnie has a very short temper. He's a good man to have with you in a tricky situation. Like, for instance, you go to the Sports Arena to hear James Brown. You bring six-foot-eight, three-hundred pound Arnie and you don't feel quite so uncomfortable, you know what I mean?''

I nodded.

"You do stick out a little more, that I admit, but at the same time, people give you a wide berth. Arnie's that kind of guy. You'd like him.''

"What happened with Nick, Joe?''

"I'm getting there. Hang on. Like I said, it's going to take a few minutes to get it all out. Okay?''

What could I do, but nod.

"Anyhow, it being three in the morning, Arnie and I were a little tired. We figured that since Nick had gone fishing he wouldn't be back until it was light—most probably later. You know, I've done a little fishing in my life, and so has Arnie. And the fish definitely bite better first thing after dawn. We guessed that Nick probably wouldn't be back before noon, so we figured we might as well get some sleep. I called the San Ysidro Ranch, booked us a nice bungalow, and we got a great night's snooze. Boy, were we tired. You ever been to the San Ysidro Ranch, Michael?''

I just stared at my brother. The bastard seemed determined to drag out the story until it did give me a coronary.

"It's a beautiful place; I'd really recommend it to you and Marilyn for a weekend. The place is real romantic, an authentic rustic retreat. Like a three star hotel in the woods, but without bugs. Very relaxing. A couple of days up there would probably do the two of you a world of good."

I tried to figure out if this was a subtle tease, implying that he had seen Nick's pictures. With Joe, who knew what it meant?

"Anyhow, morning comes around and Arnie and I have a terrific breakfast. They have this huge buffet, you know, fresh fruit, pancakes, eggs, all kinds of croissants. You should have seen Arnie shovel it down. It was really kind of embarrassing. He's not big for nothing. Anyhow, I can see you want to know how this turned out, but don't worry, I'm getting there. So Arnie and I finish eating, then drive back to the harbor, where lo and behold, there's still no Nick. Which is why I didn't call you back. What could I have told you? 'Hello, Michael, here I am in Santa Barbara and I haven't found the guy yet.' That's not a phone call. You wouldn't have been happy. I wouldn't have been happy. And it's a waste of a dime. That's why you didn't hear from me."

He paused here, pretending to collect his thoughts. Then he continued.

"So Arnie and I drove around. We checked out Montecito, where the bank is thinking of opening a new branch, did some sightseeing, you know. I even met with a couple of customers and took care of a little business. Of course, all this time we kept stopping by the harbor. But still no Nick. Finally, I asked some neighboring boat if they'd seen our boy. I told 'em I owed Nick some money and wanted to pay him back. The prospect of money always seems to inspire people to talk, you ever notice that?''

I said nothing.

"Well what do you know, finally we get some, as we say in the banking business, hard data on Nick. The neighbors didn't expect him back until Sunday night, late. He'd gone out to Santa Rosa Island. So Arnie and I kicked back for another day, went windsurfing, had a few good meals, and stayed another night at the San Ysidro Ranch. It was a real nice vacation. And I needed a rest. Anyhow, Sunday night we went back to Nick's slip and waited. Sure enough, around eleven o'clock or so, who comes puttering back but your old friend Nick. Can you believe what he had with him?''

"The pictures?"

Joe shook his head no.

"A boatload of sea urchins. Purple, spiny sea urchins. He sells them to the Japanese for sushi. You know, for sea urchins with quail eggs, all wrapped in seaweed. God, they're delicious.''

"Joe, please. I want to know what happened with Nick.''

"You've never had sea urchins, have you? Michael, you and I, we've gotta go out to a sushi bar together. You'll die over sea urchins, I promise you.''

I promised myself that if Joe didn't get to the point soon, he was the one who was going to die.

"We watched Nick tie up the boat and shut off his engine. Then we waited until the guy who was with him gathered up his gear and left. At that point Arnie and I stepped aboard, went down into the tiny little cabin, and introduced ourselves. I think we made a very good first impression, particularly Arnie. The three of us in that cabin were pretty ridiculous. I mean it's like living in a shoebox. The guy's got a two-burner stove and an ice chest, and that's it.''

I nodded that I knew.

"Michael, you would have been proud of me. We didn't beat around the bush with the guy, we told him why were were there and what we wanted. At first, he wasn't too interested in cooperating. But Arnie, you know, he has a way of persuading punks like Nick to change their minds. Arnie looks like a killer. But he's a funny guy. When he was a kid, he was very confused. The other kids made fun of him for being weird. He grew up a real loner. It was only when he got older and realized it was okay for him to be gay that he came into his own. Arnie got into athletics, weight-lifting, and really developed self-confidence. Now he's so sure of himself that he marches every year on Hollywood Boulevard in the gay parade. The guy has made a complete turnaround—he's afraid of nothing.''

I waited for Joe to continue.

"Anyhow, Arnie started talking to Nick about gay pride and how cute a lot of Arnie's friends would find Nick. Arnie questioned Nick about his own feelings about 'queers.' This wasn't a subject Nick wanted to discuss, but Arnie wouldn't let it go. Arnie acted insulted that Nick wasn't interested in gay pride. He told Nick he didn't think Nick liked gays. Of course Nick denied this. Arnie told Nick that anyone who denied disliking gays with as much fervor as Nick probably was afraid he was gay himself, which Nick claimed not to be. At this point, Arnie started quoting statistics on how many men have had homosexual experiences, which, of course, is most men. I mean, excluding you, Michael."

Again, I said nothing.

"Nick claimed to have had no homosexual experiences. Arnie pretended to be very surprised at this news. In fact, he acted as if Nick's statement was an outright lie. Then Arnie smiled and told Nick again how handsome he found Nick and how much he admired his athletic build. He was sure they could have a good time together. I could see that at this point, Nick was becoming very uncomfortable. He began to get the idea that Arnie was leading him in a very frightening direction. It was kind of funny. There Arnie was, talking to Nick so nice and sweetly, when behind all that sugar was the possibility of real menace. I could see that Nick was getting scared of the idea of himself as the focus of a homosexual gang bang. No sir, Nick didn't like this at all. I had to hand it to Arnie for zeroing in so quickly on Nick's weak point. You would have gotten a kick out of Arnie's performance. I mean, it was really convincing, his supposed attraction to Nick; I almost could envision them as a couple, even though I knew that Arnie hates trash like Nick. But Arnie was so good even I was believing his line of bullshit."

Joe thought this moment over and laughed about it once again to himself. Oh, he was having a good time with me.

"At that point, I interrupted Arnie and asked Nick if it was Arnie that was making him uncomfortable, or was it something else? Nick gave me the macho routine and claimed that nothing made him nervous. That being the case, I told Nick, I would leave the two of them alone to work things out between them. Arnie reacted as if this were a terrific idea and I opened the hatch to leave. Fear flowed from Nick like morning piss from a dog.

As I was about to leave the boat, I told Nick that if, by chance, he preferred not to be alone with Arnie, I might just be able to convince my friend to drive back to L.A. with me, if he, Nick, produced for me every negative and print of those pictures he was blackmailing you with. It took Nick a while to decide, but Arnie's supposed eagerness to be alone with him finally carried the day. Nick told me he'd give me everything. And he did. It was as easy as that. Here.''

Joe tossed the manila envelope onto my desk.

"And Michael, you may not believe this, but I didn't look at them. I just asked Nick if they were all there. He said they were. I reminded him what would happen if they weren't. He knew we weren't kidding. You're the only one who can tell if they're all there. But I bet they are.''

Truly, it was hard to believe. Not only did I supposedly have the prints as well as the negatives, but my brother hadn't looked at them. I was astonished, incredulous. Could I be free of everything, just like that? It was too good to be true; there had to be a catch. Nothing in my life had ever been that easy. Maybe that day was a first for me, I thought. Maybe I was turning lucky.

I opened the envelope and flipped through the photographs. Every picture that Nick had shown me was inside, as well as the ones he had alluded to—the photos through the curtains at the adult motel of Genie and me naked, in bed, fucking. There was something frightening about looking at those photographs. They were such a violation of my privacy, they made me feel like the victim of a rape.

Along with the photos, in separate glassine envelopes, were strips of negatives. For every print, there was a corresponding numbered negative, all on rolls of twenty-exposure, thirty-five millimeter film. It was hard to believe, but everything seemed to be there.

"Well," Joe asked when I set the envelope down, "is that what you wanted?"

"You're amazing."

"Hey," he grinned, "I told you I'd get them for you."

"You can't imagine how grateful I am to you."

"Michael. It's a pleasure to finally be able to help you after all you've done for me. I mean it."

"Still, you're incredible. My only question is, do you think he made copies of the negatives to use against me in the future?"

"It's possible, but I don't think so. Nick was one scared punk, I can assure you. The idea of old Arnie's big cock up his rectum turned out to be a real motivator; I'd be very surprised if he didn't give us everything."

Joe looked very pleased with himself. And for once it was for a good reason. Maybe he had changed. Could it be that he was finally growing up? Was Joe at long last becoming a responsible adult, complete with an honest job and genuine capabilities in the real world? It was a revelation to me that I was even thinking such thoughts; long ago I had written off the possibility of such a transformation. Now Joe had forced me to see him in a completely different light as a man, an equal, a good brother, and a loyal human being. No matter what I had once thought of him, Joe had changed. This went against everything I believed in. In my experience, people never changed. They grew older, and their behavior took on new forms, but I had never before observed what I saw in my brother at that moment. Joe had pulled off something much larger than getting me back those photographs; he had fundamentally altered my perceptions about life. Sure, he'd put me through the wringer in telling me this story. But that was petty; he had obviously wanted me to appreciate the full extent of his actions.

The fact was that before the junkie had robbed my store, my view of the world hadn't changed in twenty years. I had my niches and cubby holes into which I had fit all my experience, from my father and mother, to Joe, to women, to money, to my place in the community, who was good, what was bad, and where everything stood in relationship to everything else. But at that moment, suddenly, thanks to Joe, every one of my preconceptions seemed crazy and irrelevant. The good became the bad and the bad the good. What had been simple became infinitely complex. I felt like a man watching a game who knew the name of the players but had lost all idea of how to keep score.

"You didn't even glance at the pictures?" I asked Joe.

He shook his head no.

"You're not even curious?"

"Of course I am. But I figured it was your business; if you'd wanted me to know what was in there, you would have told me. As far as I'm concerned, it's actually better not to know. This way I don't have any responsibility. You're an adult; I assume you'll learn from this so there won't be a next time. I'm just happy I could help you out. It's been a long time since I felt like I could act as a brother. I've had a lot to think about in the last couple of years. I've missed talking to you. I've missed having a friendship with you. I think we've both missed out on a lot and I'm hoping maybe this can start us off again in the right direction. Honestly Michael, as corny as it sounds, it's a real pleasure for this old scoundrel brother of yours to finally be able to give something to you."

Joe stood and extended his hand.

"If you don't mind, I'm going to go clean up now and get to work; I've got a lot of catching up to do."

I jumped to my feet and grabbed my brother's hand. I still could hardly believe what I had heard.

"I don't know what to say, honestly."

"Just 'thank you' would be fine," he said.

"Thank you," I told my brother.

"You're welcome."

Joe suddenly threw his arms around me and gave me a big bear hug. My first impulse was to resist stiffly, but then I gave in and hugged him back.

"I need you as my brother, Michael; I don't want to lose you again. Promise me you won't let that happen."

A long-dormant part of myself welled up in my throat, momentarily preventing me from answering. I wanted to cry. What I felt for Joe was a sudden wave of pure affection—love; something I never would have guessed I'd feel again for my brother. But it was there, undeniably. And Joe saw it in my face.

"Thank you, Joe. I promise."

My brother clapped me on the back, released me, and smiled sincerely.

"Gotta go," he told me. "I have one bit of advice for you. Whatever those pictures are, I'd destroy them, fast. Like burn them, hmmm?"

Joe gave me a last smile and left my office. I was alone with the pictures and the negatives, and free. I had surfed the perfect wave and a great bubble of peace had descended over me. My life was back in order. I could move forward. I was Michael the pharmacist with a lovely wife, a perfect daughter, a reborn brother, and once again a man with the possibility of a future. I could not believe my good fortune.

"Ya-hoo," I yelled at the top of my lungs, as silly as it may sound. "Shee-it!"

My office door flew open and Milt stuck his head in.

"What's wrong?" he demanded.

"Milt, you son-of-a-bitch, absolutely nothing."

He seemed confused by my high spirits, but saw nothing obviously haywire, and so backed out of my office, closing the door behind him.

46

For the first time that I could remember, I felt the need to celebrate in a big way. I wanted to have fun, to play like a kid, to enjoy my sudden freedom. And I wanted to do it with Marilyn. But when I called her office, I was told that she was at Cedars-Sinai delivering a baby.

I threw on my sport coat, grabbed Joe's envelope of photographs, as well as the first set of prints Nick had left to blackmail me, charged out of the back door of the pharmacy, jumped into my Olds, and raced out of the alley just in time to spot my old friend Lieutenant Peterson parking his police car in the bus stop in front of the pharmacy. Fortunately the lieutenant didn't see me. I had no interest in talking to him. It was just possible he was bringing good news, but I doubted it. Whatever he had to say, I wanted some time alone to enjoy myself; I didn't need to hear any more about paralyzed junkies, attempted murder, or the ACLU. As Peterson disappeared into the drugstore, I floored the gas pedal and tore off down Wilshire to Cedars-Sinai.

I parked my car in the doctor's lot and reviewed my plan for destroying the photographs. As a consultant affiliated with the pharmaceutical department of the hospital, I had access to the medical labs—not that anyone ever expected me to use them. But in theory, the facilities were at my disposal, should I have a need for them. I had that need.

When I showed my identification to the receptionist at Bio-Science she immediately gestured me through into the inner sanctum of the laboratory. I had been there before and knew where I was going, but I still couldn't get used to the almost medieval sight of the lab in action. Six technicians sat on chairs in open cubicles drawing blood from outpatients. No matter who many times I witnessed it, I could never accept the idea of such public bloodletting. To me, there was something horrible and frightening about a stainless steel needle slipping through the skin into a vein. I was a great pharmacist, but I would have made a lousy doctor.

Moments later I had passed through into the lab itself, which consisted of a central hallway linking a complex series of interconnected, yet separate, sterile technical facilities. Computer terminals, electrical connections, plumbing lines, and all varieties of modern, automated medical laboratory equipment hung from every wall and ceiling. I went from room to room until I found my goal—the incinerator, gas-fired and brutally powerful.

Luckily the lab was empty; it was just me and the machine. I opened the access port, tossed in my envelope, shut the door, set the temperature, and hit the ignition switch. Moments later the machine boiled into action with the tremendous whoosh of pressurized gas on the move. After five minutes of burning, the cycle was completed and the incinerator shut itself off. I reopened the stainless steel door. Inside, no trace of the photographs remained—all the blackmail evidence had been vaporized. I was now truly a free man.

"Hey, what are you doing here?" a voice called from behind me.

Frightened, I jumped and whirled around.

A black man, wearing a sterile surgical gown, held a rack of test tubes obviously destined for the incinerator.

"It's okay," I told him, waving my identification, "I have permission."

Glaring angrily, the man scrutinized my pharmaceutical ID.

"You may have permission, but you don't have *my* permission. This is *my* machine. Next time you come fooling around in here you talk to me first, understand?"

"You're right, I'm sorry. I will."

The man continued to stare at me. I turned and left the room before he could question me further. Within moments I was out of the lab and on my way to the maternity ward. As little sleep as I'd had in the last week, at that moment I felt energetic and enthused. I had control of myself and my life. I had beaten the odds, gotten through the dark tunnel, and once again was on a roll.

With the confidence of John Wayne, I strode into the maternity ward and approached the nurses at the desk.

"Where would I find Doctor Marcus?" I asked.

A thirty-year-old black nurse looked up, then grinned with pleasure.

"Hey," she asked me, "aren't you Doctor Marcus's husband, the dude who shot the junkie?"

I nodded. The nurse was black. Robert Allen was black. Watch out, I told myself, this woman is going to try to get you.

"Edna," the nurse called to the fiftyish black woman working the other side of the nursing station, "this here is Doctor Marcus's husband, who shot that junkie in his store, remember?"

Edna dropped what she was doing and came over to examine me. I prepared myself for attack.

"You were on the news?" Edna asked me.

"That's right."

"CBS."

"I think so."

"The po-lice is sure sticking it to you."

"Tell me about it," I answered without committing myself.

Suddenly she thrust her hand and grinned broadly.

"I just want you to know I'm real proud of what you did. You got guts. Not like that scum that tried to stick you up and hurt that little girl."

We shook hands.

"I told Doctor Marcus," Edna continued, "that she should be real happy to have a husband like you. Yessir." Edna smiled lasciviously. "I wish I could meet a man like you; the only kind I seem to get are the kind like you shot. I've had two husbands done time for robbery, and I say you were right to do what you did."

"Thank you," I told her. "I appreciate it."

"Yeah, your wife's a lucky woman. And don't think I didn't tell her so." Edna dropped her voice to a whisper, looked around, then gestured for me to come closer. "Your wife's a funny woman, Mr. Marcus, and I hope you don't mind me saying this. She acts like she's ashamed of what you did, but I think she's real proud of you. She just has trouble admitting it, you know what I mean?''

"I hope I do. Thank you."

A light on the switchboard flashed on.

"Edna, thirty-nine is calling," the first nurse pointed out.

"Coming," Edna called to no one, then turned to me. "Doctor Marcus is in twenty-two. She just finished a delivery." ·

"Thank you."

As Edna reached for her phone I headed for room twenty-two, passing through a corridor filled with people in all stages of the birth process: pregnant women walked their way into labor, anxious fathers raced to the nursing station for reassurance about their wives' dilation, grandparents and relatives giggled and pointed through the soundproof nursery window at that newborn addition to the family on display. One exhausted man at the payphone was clutching rolls of dimes and gesticulating wildly, as if the person on the other end of the line could see his description of his new son. I knocked on the door of room twenty-two.

"Yes?" Marilyn answered from inside.

"Doctor Marcus, there's someone out here who'd like to talk to you if you have a minute," I called through the door.

I heard murmuring and waited. On the wall by the door was a Miro lithograph whose blobs and squiggles of color made as much sense to me as the chaos of my life in the last week. I couldn't see the pattern in the painting and I couldn't see it in myself; I only knew that I was free, euphoric, and wanted to share my mood with Marilyn.

My wife emerged from the room, closing the door behind her. She was wearing a white hospital coat over her street clothes. She was in her element, a model of efficiency, unquestionably competent. That day she looked more than beautiful; she was radiant. She was obviously surprised to see me.

"Michael, I thought that was your voice. What are you doing here?" Her face dropped as she answered, in her mind, her own question. She suspected disaster. "What's wrong?"

"Nothing. Absolutely nothing. In fact, everything's wonderful. I was just thinking this morning, I wanted to talk to you about last night. I feel bad about it."

Marilyn scrutinized me.

"What are you talking about?"

"After your meeting with the surgeons, you came home with some really terrific news. You had something to celebrate, something you'd worked very hard to accomplish. I was tired and sort of depressed and I wasn't very nice. I was happy for you, but I don't think I let you know that. All morning it's been bothering me. That's why I'm here, to apologize. I am proud of you, you know? Will you forgive me?"

"That's really why you came over here?" she asked, incredulous.

I could hardly tell her about my meeting with Joe, so I just nodded.

"Michael, I'm very touched. Thank you."

Marilyn looked down the hall, saw no one who could compromise her, then leaned forward and kissed me tenderly.

"Hey, what's-a-matter," I teased her, "it's so bad being caught kissing your husband?"

Marilyn laughed.

"Michael, I'm a tough guy here; I've got a reputation to preserve."

"You mean tough guys aren't allowed to kiss their husbands?"

"Not in public."

"Says who?"

"Michael, come on. You know the way things work."

"Show me where it is written."

"Michael, don't be a pain. When's the last time you saw the president of the United States kiss his wife on the lips in public? Or Caspar Weinberger, huh?"

"Who would want to kiss Caspar Weinberger?"

"Give me a break, will you?"

I pointed down the hall to a nurse who was preparing a syringe.

"You're trying to tell me that if I grabbed you and kissed you, she wouldn't respect you as a doctor?"

"I think you're exaggerating what I said."

"I'm your husband. I don't like being hidden in the closet. Why can't I kiss you if I feel like it?"

"You're making a big deal out of nothing, do you realize that?"

"Yeah," I grinned, "but I'm having a good time doing it."

"You're a bastard," she told me affectionately.

"So, are you going to let me make up for last night by doing something special with me today to celebrate?"

"What do you have in mind?"

"How about taking the afternoon off and going to the beach?"

"Oh Michael, that sounds like a wonderful idea, but I have appointments this afternoon. Patients. I can't."

"Cancel them."

"You know I can't do that."

"If you had an emergency you'd cancel them."

"If I had an emergency I'd have reason to cancel them."

"Well, then you have an emergency."

"I do?"

"Yeah."

"What?"

"If you don't cancel your afternoon appointments I'm going to spend all day here with you, kissing you. I'm going to undermine every bit of authority you ever had in this hospital."

"You're crazy."

"Oh yeah?" I yelled down the hall. "Hey, nurse!"

The nurse filling the syringe turned toward Marilyn and me. As she tried to figure out who I was, I grabbed Marilyn, planted a giant kiss on my wife's lips, and wouldn't let her go. Marilyn went rigid, like a pine board, pushed herself away from me, and straightened out her clothes. The nurse turned from us.

"One nurse down, twenty-five to go. By five-thirty even the janitor's going to be laughing at you."

Marilyn studied me closely.

"Michael, have you been taking some kind of medication again?"

"I just want to spend the afternoon with you."

"You're sure you haven't been taking something?"

"Scout's honor," I told her.

Marilyn thought it over, then heaved a big sigh.

"Sometimes you're an impossible man. But okay, you've got your afternoon; I'll declare an emergency."

"That's wonderful. Thank you, sweetheart. Just think, we might even have fun."

Marilyn momentarily flashed me a mechanical grin, to let me know she didn't appreciate my sarcasm.

"Let me just check Mrs. Candless. Give me five minutes."

"It would be my pleasure."

Marilyn disappeared back inside room twenty-two. I stood in the hallway, feeling pleased with myself. Some of the chemistry between my wife and me was returning. Never in the past could I have gotten her to cancel even one patient, much less take the entire afternoon off. Whatever was changing in her was something very good indeed.

47

We drove up Pacific Coast Highway to a place called Neptune's Net, a shack of a restaurant across the highway from the Pacific Ocean near the Ventura county line. I hadn't eaten there in almost twenty years, since my surfer days when I'd gone north to ride Rincon. The building hadn't changed; it was the same greasy spoon cafeteria on one side and fish store on the other. Marilyn and I walked through the fish area examining the contents of the saltwater-filled fiberglass tanks. Everything was alive, fresh, and cheap, like California had been in the 1950's. Neptune's Net sold shellfish and plenty of it, the bounty of the sea, cooked any way you wanted it as long as it was steamed. No novelle cuisine here, thank you very much. We had a tough time deciding among the giant Pismo clams, the Pacific spiny lobster, local crabs, Ventura County mussels, Santa Barbara shrimp, and the East Coast king, *homarus Americanus,* Maine lobster. Finally we settled on steamed clams and crab, ordered French fries and beer from the adjacent greasy spoon, and sat down at a redwood picnic table outside on the patio to wait for our feast.

Because it was a weekday afternoon, Marilyn and I had the place pretty much to ourselves. We relaxed in the sun, sipping our Heinekens, talking happily about our future life at the health clinic in Escondido. At that moment, on that day, sitting in the sun, in love with my wife, all things once again seemed possible—even being happy in Escondido. It was such an incredible relief to be free of the blackmail that the pleasure of sitting out on that concrete patio with Marilyn, enveloped in my old secure identity as Michael Marcus, pharmacist, husband, father, and soon to be health spa manager comforted me in a way that was almost unexplainable—I was a child, secure in the arms of his mother, a combat soldier, home for Christmas, honorably discharged, never to fight again.

By the time the food was served I had talked myself into an idyllic future in Escondido—I would proselytize for the Good Life clinic, and we'd all live happily ever after. But as we ate our piles of shellfish, I noticed that Marilyn was not quite as excited by my enthusiasm as I would have expected. Something was going on. When I questioned her, she whispered that she'd tell me about it after we left Neptune's Net; apparently she was inhibited by the idea that the other people on the patio—carpenters from Malibu drinking beer—might overhear her. What could she have to say that could be so embarrassing?

"Humor me," said Marilyn as she squeezed my hand, attempting to overcome my impatience. Did she know about the blackmail?

After lunch we crossed the highway and took a walk down the beach in the hope of working off the seafood in our stomachs. Marilyn held my hand as we strolled through the sand. She was a strange mixture of shyness, embarrassment, and anger at herself; I had never seen her in such a mood. Something was brewing in her. We strolled quietly and I waited.

Finally after we had walked for about a mile, we came to a dune covered deserted area of the beach where no one else was visible. Marilyn sat down in the sand and gestured for me to take the spot beside her. We were surrounded by weedlike beach grass, but she double-checked to make sure no one could see us.

"I have a confession to make." Marilyn blushed, avoiding my glance. "It's something I don't understand about myself."

Now this got my attention. For a woman with her determined, rational mind to admit to having doubts about herself, to being confused about something, was amazing.

"Will you promise you won't make fun of me?" Marilyn asked as she held my hand.

"Why would I make fun of you?"

"Sorry. It's just that what I have to say is so hard for me."

I waited.

"All morning I was at the hospital, right?"

I nodded.

"What was I doing there?"

"Delivering a baby."

Marilyn nodded.

"Do you know what I was thinking about during the delivery?"

"I assume you were thinking about what you were doing."

"Wrong. I was functioning on automatic. The delivery took care of itself. I was in a whole other world."

"The health clinic, right?"

"No."

"Escondido?"

"I was thinking about you."

"What about me?"

Without saying another word, Marilyn kissed me tenderly on the lips, then took my hand and placed it up under her skirt, which she hiked up to her hips. I felt the crotch of her French lace underwear. The panties weren't just moist; they were soaked. Marilyn groaned at my touch. I curled my fingers underneath the elastic band of her underwear and began to slide the tip of my right index finger in soft circles around the wet and swollen flesh. Marilyn lay back in the sand, spread her legs, and moaned with pleasure.

"Oh Michael," she told me, "that feels so good. Why do you excite me so much today?"

"I don't know; why?"

"When I saw you at the hospital it was a like a dream come true. All morning I wanted you and there you were. It was so strange."

"I must have read your mind," I told her.

"Oh Michael, that feels so good. Oh Michael, Michael, Michael, yes, yes, yes, don't stop. Please. Faster, Michael. Yes, that's it. A little higher. Yes. That's the spot. Oh Michael. Yes. Ohh. Ohh. Michael. Mich-ael!"

Marilyn thrust her hips in little spasms against my hand, then suddenly moaned, jerked twice more, and squeezed her legs tightly around my palm, stopping all further motion of my fingers. For a moment after her orgasm she lay quietly. Then she gazed directly, courageously, into my eyes. The sea breeze brushed over us as we stretched out in the sun.

"You know what was so strange about my thoughts this morning?" she asked.

"No."

"It was you I was fantasizing about, not that caped stranger. Michael, I'm a gynecologist. Women come to me every day and ask for my advice about their sex lives. Yesterday I thought I understood everything about sex. Today I'm so confused, I feel like I know nothing.''

For a long moment she was quiet.

''I think it's part of the same thing that I felt Saturday night. It's about fear—my fears. I'm afraid, Michael, but I haven't admitted, even to myself, what my real fears are. I've tried to put them outside of myself and blame them on the world around me. I say I'm afraid of a violent society, the urban jungle, but I'm really scared about whether I'm doing the right thing with the health clinic. What if it fails? Or what if it succeeds financially but destroys us? I've decided that nothing, no matter how beautiful or lucrative, is worth anything if it ruins what we've got together.''

I couldn't believe what I was hearing. All my hopes for Marilyn were coming true. She saw herself; she saw me and my needs. My identity had come out of the fog for her and taken form. I wanted to embrace her, and at the same time embrace Joe for saving me and giving me another chance. Marilyn was open to me. I was overjoyed. Except for one small thing: I felt guilty about my liaison with Genie and still had the need to be forgiven.

If there was ever a time to come clean to Marilyn, it was at that moment. Marilyn had changed and I felt she would understand. For myself, I had to tell her so that we could move forward together in good conscience and seek out a new understanding. I wrapped my arm around her, kissed her, gave her shoulders a big squeeze, then looked her in the eyes.

''I have a confession to make too,'' I said.

She shook her head. ''In a minute; I owe you.'' Marilyn rolled away from me, knelt on the sand, and unzipped my fly.

This surprised me. Not the act. But the fact that it was coming from Marilyn. Indeed, it was a change.

''Out here? In public?''

''Why not?''

''What if someone sees us?''

''Keep a lookout.''

Marilyn reached into my trousers and slipped my suddenly prominent erection down into her mouth. It was all rather strange; I really, sincerely, did want to confess to her but, under the circumstances it was quite difficult to get started with my story. As hard as I tried, her manipulations made concentration difficult. What difference would a couple of minutes make, I finally told myself. After all, if I started to confess while she had me in her mouth, it might be a little dangerous; no man wants to risk being bitten, no matter how deserving the cause. I chose to wait and enjoy the sunshine. There was nothing like a hot day, a stomach filled with steamed crab, and a loving wife's wet mouth sucking on one's erection to make a day at the beach relaxing. It was all so strange and exciting that within moments I lost control and came with a wonderful, surprisingly intense orgasm. Marilyn swallowed my semen, folded me back into my trousers, zipped up my fly, then looked up at me and grinned impishly.

"So what did you have to confess?"

I didn't begin to talk until we started the drive back to L.A. It took me some time to work up to it. In fact, Marilyn interrupted my hemming and hawing with a joke.

"Michael, from all the trouble you're having talking, I'm beginning to think this confession of yours is really going to be something. Should I tighten my seat belt?"

"It might not be a bad idea."

She did, in fact, tighten her belt just to tease me. Then she waited for my story. I stressed to her that it was only because of the love I felt for her, and the love that I wanted to *keep* feeling for her, that I was compelled to tell her what had happened in the last two weeks. The whole situation had suddenly become remarkably clear, just a few minutes before, on the beach. The lunch, the walk, the sex, but most of all the spontaneity of the day had made it plain to me why I had been so unwilling even to consider moving to Escondido with Marilyn. And I told her. It was her rigidity and obsession which had ground me down to the point where I had hated my life with her. I could no more have considered going to Escondido than I could have seen myself moving with her to a South Pacific island paradise. The thought of being alone with her, trapped anywhere, was a nightmare, just the opposite of the way I had felt when I met her and we fell in love. Then even an unheated, rat-infested, one-room apartment in the heart of Watts could have been made to resemble heaven.

Quality of life was largely a state of mind, I said. The point I was trying to make was that my view of Escondido had changed when I'd once again felt happy to be in her company. Suddenly, life in the country didn't seem so bad. I was very proud of what I had accomplished with my drugstore but, hell, I told her, I could build another business in Escondido—one, lousy West L.A. pharmacy wasn't the absolute greatest place on earth. The fact that I could surf again near Escondido had a definite appeal. The benefits for Rebecca seemed enormous. And there was the excitement of a change, to say nothing of the financial attraction. Just believing that I could enjoy myself moment-to-moment and day-to-day with Marilyn made all the difference in my attitude toward the health spa. In fact, I admitted, I was convinced that we would not only enjoy working together, but that we held the potential of being a truly great team.

"That makes me happy, Michael. I like this confession."

I nodded and told her the rest of it—to clear the air, I explained. I wanted her to know what her fanaticism and obsession had done to me: how much I'd been hurt and how lonely I'd become. I began with the night we returned from Escondido, the night I saw Genie and Nick screwing on the living room couch. Once I had gotten through that and my reaction to it, the rest became easier. Almost mechanically, I itemized the chain of circumstances leading from the robbery, to my own growing sense of loneliness, my alienation from Marilyn and despair over life on a fat farm, to the final blackmail plot and my unexpected and successful reconciliation that morning with my brother. Of course I skipped some of the details of my sexual passion with Genie, but the overall picture of the relationship was spelled out fairly clearly.

It took the whole drive home to tell her the complete story. Throughout the entire confession, Marilyn said nothing. She sat quietly with a blank, professional expression—the experienced, impassive, observing doctor listening to another case. I half expected her to pull out a folder and write up my history for her files.

Finally, when I had parked in the driveway of our house and she still hadn't reacted to my story, I turned to her.

"Aren't you going to say anything?"

Marilyn shook her head, then opened the car door, got out, and strode into the house as if I no longer existed. I sat in the Oldsmobile, stunned, and considered the disaster I had just created. What kind of grandiose insanity had made me think she would accept what I had done? Had my mother ever accepted my father? Had I ever accepted my brother? Everything I had worked to preserve, I had just destroyed with my stupidity. My wanting to clear the air was a delusion, like the schizophrenic fantasies of my father. I had opened my heart to my wife in the hope of obtaining forgiveness. Instead, what I received was the knife, driven in quietly but deeply, with the swift precision of a surgeon.

The door to the house opened and Marilyn emerged carrying her medical bag. She hurried to my window and spoke quickly.

"While we were playing on the beach the hospital called; I've got a delivery. I don't know when I'll be back. Angie said she can stay with Rebecca if you have to go out. Should I warn her about you, or is she too old for your tastes?"

Marilyn was really twisting the scalpel now. As much as it angered me, I ignored the sarcasm.

"We need to continue this conversation, Marilyn. Can't you give me a few more minutes?"

"I wish I had the power to stop Ruth Burkheart from giving birth, but I'm only mortal, Michael. I'm late as it is."

"Then we'll talk when you get back. I'll wait up for you."

"Don't. I have no idea when I'll be back."

"Marilyn, honestly, I love you. Remember that."

"You make me want to vomit, Michael."

Marilyn got in her BMW, started the engine, and drove off toward the hospital.

48

Paralyzed by despair, I sat in my Oldsmobile without moving. My life was over, as far as I could see. I was about to become a lost soul, without wife, child, or identity. What I had worked so hard to achieve would be stripped from me and I'd be banished. One minute I had been the pillar of the community and the next minute I had become a human cesspool. The psychic punishment I was giving myself was the same punishment I had always wanted to dump on my old man for his transgressions: torture, burning at the stake, tar and feathers. How could I have believed that Marilyn would accept my confession and forgive me? No one forgives that easily. Sins must either be atoned for or punished. I had done neither.

I studied the dashboard of the Oldsmobile as if that could give me some clue how to deal with Marilyn and what I knew was her rage, exiling me to emotional Siberia. I was about to become a man without a country when all I wanted was my home.

"Mr. Marcus," called a voice, jolting me out of my stupor. I turned to see Angie standing by the front door.

"Rebecca would like to say good-night. Are you coming in?"

"One minute," I yelled.

It was already eight-thirty. I had been sitting in my car for more than an hour. I was losing my mind. And I realized that after tonight, given Marilyn's anger, I might also lose my daughter. I dragged myself out of the car and into the house. As soon as I entered the living room Rebecca charged at me.

"Daddy," she screamed with joy, "let's play horsie."

She ran at full speed with her arms open and, of course, did not watch where she was going. As she passed the wing chair she caught her foot, lost her balance, crashed down on the floor, and skidded to a stop on the carpet by my feet. She began to wail. I picked her up and held her tight against my chest.

"Oh Rebecca. Becka. It's okay. Daddy's here. Hey, it'll be all right. Daddy'll make it better."

She continued to cry. Had she broken anything?

"Rebecca, tell Daddy where it hurts."

But she only kept crying. I gave her a squeeze and lifted her away from my chest to get a look at her. There was no blood and no abrasions. Her arms and legs were moving like windmills; nothing appeared to be broken. I pulled her back to my chest and hugged her tight. She wrapped her arms around my neck and squeezed me back.

"I'm so glad you're such a brave little girl. You did that really well, you know that? You looked just like a baseball player on TV, stealing a base. Ever think about becoming a professional baseball player, huh?"

Her sobs died out.

"There's no girls in baseball, daddy."

"There isn't?" I pretended to be shocked.

She shook her head to emphasize her certainty. Just like Marilyn, Rebecca had absolute convictions about everything.

"Well then, you'll be the first. What do you think of that?"

"I'd rather play horsie."

"Hey, I'm offering you a career in the major leagues. You'll be on TV and in the newspapers. They might even name a candy bar after you."

By now Rebecca had forgotten about her fall and had stopped crying.

"Daddy, I want to play horsie."

"You're sure you don't want to think it over. I mean, imagine a Rebecca Marcus bar. Chocolate. Caramel. Nougat. You're going to give all that up just to sit on your daddy's back?"

Rebecca nodded. Angie smiled, amused by my ploy.

"I want to play horsie," Rebecca squealed.

"So much for fame and fortune."

I got down on my hands and knees and Rebecca climbed onto my back. It was one of the oldest father and daughter games known to civilization. Rebecca grabbed my shirt collar, shrieking with delight as I scrambled around on the carpet pretending to be a bucking bronco. It always astounded me how easy it was to please her. I was envious. For Rebecca, everything was either black or white, good or evil. I used to think like that. But everything had become so confusing and complicated; there were no answers, no solutions, and even the questions were no longer very clear. Yet there I was, trotting around the living room playing horsie with my daughter. To Angie, watching us play, my life must have looked as uncomplicated and straightforward as any suburban professional's.

"Mr. Marcus?"

I stopped galloping and looked up at Angie, who was holding her purse and light summer jacket.

"If you don't need me any more, I can go home."

"Giddyap daddy." Rebecca kicked me in the flanks.

"One second sweetheart," I told my daughter. "Say bye-bye to Angie, okay? Then I'll take you for another ride."

Rebecca slid off of my back and gave Angie a quick hug.

"Oh, Mr. Marcus," Angie pointed to the kitchen, "there's a list of calls for you on the pad by the refrigerator."

"Thank you, Angie."

Angie left. I resumed my stance on the floor with Rebecca on my back. We galloped around the room until I was exhausted. Then I took her upstairs to bed, told her a brief story, and moments later she was asleep, at peace with the world. I loved Rebecca very much. It frightened me to think of losing her. As I watched my daughter sleep, I suddenly began to cry. Everything important to me was slipping away.

I tiptoed out of the room and hurried downstairs to the kitchen, where I poured myself a scotch and took a couple of large swallows. The alcoholic warmth coating my throat and stomach gave me the courage to glance through the phone pad. The first few messages were for Marilyn, from the hospital. Then came a shocker. Genie had called. Beside Genie's name, Marilyn had written "Give her my love, too." I took another long swallow of scotch. Ed Cotler was the next call on the pad. I wondered if there was a connection—first daughter, then father. I hoped not. My mother had called. The mayor's office phoned. A reporter from *Newsweek* wanted an interview. On and on. It was a big afternoon for phone calls. I couldn't believe Genie had left her name; something had to be wrong. I dialed the Cotler number and prayed Genie would answer.

"Hello." It was Ed.

I went into my nasal adolescent voice again.

"Is Genie there?"

"Who's calling?"

"Roger Birnbaum, sir."

"Is this the same Roger Birnbaum who helped Genie with her math test the other night?"

"Yes sir."

"Do you know how she did on that test, Roger?"

"No sir. That's why I'm calling," I lied.

"You helped her get an A. You did one hell of a job; you're my kind of boy, Roger."

"That's good news. Thank you, sir."

"Roger, I don't recall ever meeting you. Am I correct?"

"Yes sir."

"Well I'd like to get to know you. Any boy that can help Genie get an A in math is someone I'd like to meet. Do you play Ping-Pong, Roger?"

"No, sir."

"That's a shame. I thought we might play Ping-Pong together if you came by."

"Thank you, sir."

"How about tennis? Do you play tennis?"

"No sir."

"Golf?"

"Sorry, sir."

"Roger," Ed was obviously frustrated, "tell me, what do you do for fun?"

I thought fast. I had to get the man off the phone before he found me out.

"Equations."

"Equations?"

"Yes sir. Differential equations. I like computer problems, too."

"I see." Ed hated both math and computers. "Well that's great, Roger, really great. Come by some day so I can meet you."

"Yes sir."

There was a long silence which I presumed to mean that Ed was getting Genie. My presumption was correct.

"Hello?" Genie said coldly.

"You called me?" I asked in my normal voice.

"You're a real son-of-a-bitch," she told me in an angry whisper. "I don't believe you."

"What are you talking about?"

"You know exactly what I'm talking about."

"I do?"

"You do."

"Well it's news to me. You want to be a little more specific?"

"I'd like to but I can't talk long. I called because I have a message for you."

"From who?"

"A mutual friend of ours in Santa Barbara said that he wants you to know that what happened with the cops wasn't his fault; they were onto him before he saw your friends. But he didn't know that at the time. He said to tell you that what he told your friends was the truth. He gave them everything he had. He wants you to believe him."

"And?"

"That's the message."

"That's it?"

"That's it."

"I don't understand it." But the fact that the cops were in the message terrified me.

"That's all he told me to tell you. He tried to call you himself, but you weren't at the drugstore or at home."

"What does it mean?"

"I don't know." Genie's tone changed from detached chill to contemptuous rage. "Michael, he told me how you stopped his little scheme. How could you? I mean, hiring thugs to practically rape him. Do you know what they would have done if he hadn't given them the pictures, Michael? What kind of animal are you?"

"He brought it on himself."

"Bullshit."

"Genie, it was my life or his, remember."

"Michael, you were going to handle Nick man to man, like we talked about. Instead you hired gorillas like you were some Mafioso."

"He was blackmailing us, Genie."

"So? That doesn't give you the right to have the guy gangbanged; that's cruel and unusual punishment—torture, in fact. What kind of man are you, anyway?"

"Genie, please, keep your voice down. You don't want your dad to hear you, do you?"

"I almost don't care, Michael. You really disappoint me. Nick is a screwed-up kid, I'll admit. What he did with those pictures was wrong. But Jesus. You should have heard his voice when he told me to give you that message. He's traumatized. Terrorized. Whatever the message means, he's afraid you'll take what happens the wrong way and send those thugs out after him. You know what I told him, Michael? I told him to get out of town, to go somewhere they can't find him. Nick may be fucked up, Michael, but he's not as bad as he seems. He does have potential. But not if those animals you sent after him get to him; that'll ruin him forever. How could you?"

"You really believe that Nick is good and I'm bad? Who started this? Did I blackmail Nick?"

"Stop the bullshit. You're older and smarter than Nick. Just because he made a mistake doesn't mean you have to destroy him for it. Michael, you really frighten me. I thought you were a good man. I had such hopes for you. But you're worse than my father. You went after Nick like the Gestapo. I thought you were different, but even my father wouldn't have done what you did. It's a pity you didn't live in the 1930's; you would have made a damn good Nazi. You missed your calling, Michael."

"Genie," I told her calmly, "come over here and let's talk

about this. I don't think you're seeing this correctly. Can you do that now?''

"No."

"Please."

"No."

"I would like to talk to you."

"Well you know what I'd like?"

"What?"

"I'd like you never to call me or see me again."

"Will you come over here, please, so I can talk to you first before I agree to that?''

"No."

"You won't even say good-bye to me in person?"

"I don't want to come anywhere near someone who behaves like you."

"I think you're exaggerating the situation, Genie."

"Yeah, well I don't agree with you, Adolph."

Genie slammed her phone down, ending the conversation.

Adolf? I asked myself; did she mean Eichmann or Hitler? But the distinction didn't matter; I understood the meaning. For more than a minute I held onto the receiver like an idiot. Then, when I realized that she was really gone, I hung up too.

I had wanted to end the affair with Genie. I had promised myself to do it. I loved Marilyn and Rebecca. So I should have been overjoyed to have Genie conveniently cut me out of her life with such absolute conviction. But now I was being eliminated from *everyone*'s lives, and not gradually. Just a few hours earlier I had felt free of all my troubles, thanks to Joe. Now, I had lost Marilyn, Genie, maybe Rebecca, too—and there was a fearsome new connection between Nick and the police. I would miss Genie terribly, I knew. For a moment I wondered if I shouldn't have run off to New York with her after all, but that was ridiculous. I mean, if Genie switched her point of view on me so quickly based simply on Joe and his threat to Nick, what kind of consistent relationship could I possibly have ever achieved with her? As exciting as she was, as erotically thrilling as she had been, it simply never would have worked. Nick was actually the right person for her. The fact that I couldn't make sense out of his message was driving me crazy. Genie obviously knew more than she was telling me. Once again I dialed the Cotler household.

"Hello?" It was Genie.

"Listen, I have to talk to you for one more minute."

"Roger, I told you, I don't want you calling me any more, isn't that clear enough for you?"

Ed was obviously in the room, listening.

"Will you at least answer one question?"

"What?" she asked impatiently.

"Do you know what Nick meant when he was talking about the cops?"

"No."

"You really don't?"

"I don't know anything else."

"Genie, if I'm involved in some sort of problem with Nick and the police, you're involved too. So if you know anything, you might as well tell me now. It'll make things easier for both of us.

"Roger, honestly, I know nothing else. I appreciate all the help you've given me with the math, but I'm not the kind of girl you think I am. If you keep talking to me this way I'm going to put my father on the phone and let him deal with you, is that clear? I don't want you to call me again, Roger. Good-bye."

Genie hung up on me again. I had my answer, or my nonanswer.

I dialed Cedars but couldn't get through to Marilyn. "In surgery," was the explanation. My impulse was to run over there and plead my case in person. But I had sent Angie away and trapped myself at home.

The phone rang.

"Hello," I spoke into the receiver, hoping it was Marilyn.

"Michael, you bastard, don't you return your calls any more?" It was Ed Cotler.

"Ed, how are you? I just got home," I stalled, afraid he had finally figured out the truth about Genie and me.

"Well it's about time. You've got a big day tomorrow; are you prepared for it?"

"What are you talking about?"

"What am I talking about?! Michael, don't you look in your appointment book any more either?"

"What's tomorrow?"

"Remember your TV appearance with the mayor? That's at six o'clock tomorrow evening."

"Shit," was all I could say.

"Shit is what you're going to be in if you don't show for it. Very deep shit. What do you say I pick you up at four-thirty and drive you down there, just to make sure you don't forget?"

"You're sure it's tomorrow?" I pleaded weakly. How could I possibly deal with the television debate when my mind was on Marilyn and our collapsing marriage? I had about as much interest in performing in public as I did in being a guinea pig for chemotherapy experiments. I finished the last of my scotch, stretched the phone cord to the bar, and poured myself another.

"Of course I'm sure; look at your calendar."

"Listen, Ed, I don't belong in that debate. I mean, I'm facing criminal charges. I should stay out of the public eye to avoid prejudicing the jury, shouldn't I?"

"Michael, this is no time for stage fright. Your political career is at stake here. Let me handle the legal end. You just state your case on TV tomorrow for your right as a private citizen to defend your family, home, and property against junkies and criminals. It'll all work out, I promise you."

"But won't whatever I say be quoted back to the jury when my case goes to trial? They'll make me sound like some kind of Dodge City vigilante. I really don't think I should be part of that debate tomorrow, Ed."

"Michael, I'm your lawyer, right?"

"Yes."

"Do you think I know what I'm doing?"

"Yes, but. . . ."

"No buts," he interrupted me, "either I have your total confidence or I don't. Now which is it?"

"Ed, you know I trust you, but. . . ."

"No buts, I told you. If you trust me, then trust me. Go on that show tomorrow, say what you believe, and leave the rest up to me. Will you do that?"

"I want to believe you."

"So then believe me. What's stopping you? Is there something you're not telling me?"

"Of course not."

"You're sure?"

"Of course I'm sure. You're my lawyer aren't you? I'd be stupid not to tell you everything."

"I hear something in your voice. What is it? What's wrong?"

"I'm just tired."

"You're sure that's all it is?"

"Why would I lie to you?"

"I don't know. But it wouldn't be the first time it's happened to me."

"Oh, you think I've lied to you in the past?"

"No. That's not what I meant. But other clients have and it never works out in their favor, believe me."

Ed waited for me to say something, to come clean. I said nothing.

"Okay, can I give you some advice?" Ed finally said.

"What?"

"Take two Valiums and get some sleep."

"Thank you Doctor Cotler," I said sarcastically.

Ed hung up the phone. So did I. Then I took another long swallow of my J & B. That idiotic debate. Before I could begin thinking about what I would say, the front doorbell rang.

I scurried to the window and peeked outside. In the driveway was an unmarked police car, and standing at the front door was my old friend Lieutenant Peterson. With him was another detective who wore a grey polyester suit and a mean but boyish expression on his forty-five-year-old face. My heart began to pound, they were probably here to tell me something new and horrible about my relationship to Nick. For the first time that night, I was pleased that Marilyn had gone to the hospital.

"Lieutenant Peterson, how nice to see you," I managed with considerable charm, as I opened the door.

We shook hands.

"Michael Marcus, this is Ron Matlow from the FBI. Can we come in for a minute?"

"You have a search warrant?" I tried to be lighthearted.

The two men exchanged glances. They obviously weren't in the mood for kidding.

"We're not looking for anything," Matlow told me, "we'd just like to ask you a few questions, off the record. But if you don't want us to come inside, we can always take you downtown and put the same questions to you on the record."

This Matlow didn't fool around.

"Don't take me so seriously, I was just making a joke. Come on in."

They nodded. I had seen it their way, as they had expected. They entered the living room.

"Would you like a drink? Beer? Soda?"

Peterson shook his head and sat down on the sofa, in exactly the spot where Genie had humped Nick. Matlow sat next to Peterson. Both of them were stiff and businesslike. I tried to be casual, but the ominous vibrations emanating from those two made it difficult.

Peterson glanced around the living room as if to check on who else was home.

"My wife's at the hospital, if that's what you're interested in. I'm here alone with my daughter. She's upstairs asleep, so we'd better keep our voices down."

Peterson nodded.

"I'll let Detective Matlow tell you why we're here."

Matlow pulled out a small vinyl-covered notepad and reviewed his facts before speaking.

"Mr. Marcus, you have a brother named Joe, correct?"

I nodded.

"This brother of yours is president of the Federal Bank of Montserrat, the Los Angeles branch?"

I nodded again. The guy's tactics were obvious; he was trying to move from point to point until he built a case that would nail me to the cross. But which cross? And how was Joe involved? The situation appeared worse by the minute. I took another sip of scotch and tried to look calm.

"Your brother doesn't exactly have a background as a banker; how do you think he got that job?"

"I don't really know. I'm not that close to my brother. Why don't you ask him yourself?"

"We hoped you could help us; that's why we're here."

"My brother and I don't discuss business."

"What do you discuss?"

I stared at the two sour men. The question enraged me. Who the fuck did they think they were, asking me a question like that?"

"That's between my brother and me."

The two cops exchanged glances. I guessed that meant they were about to move on to plan B.

Matlow resumed his inquisition.

"Okay, we'll be honest with you, Marcus. Joe is in trouble. As you know, that's nothing new for your brother, except that this time the trouble is big. Interstate trouble. Federal offenses.

The Bank of Montserrat is a front. Your brother is involved in a scheme to defraud both other banks and innocent investors with phony loans, letters of credit, and offshore investment schemes. The FBI got a tip and we're trying to put together a solid case before more people get taken. Your brother is involved with some real clever operators. International types. Some of the cash they handle is laundered criminal money. Like in 'Mafia.' But so far they've been crossing their paperwork T's and dotting their I's, so we haven't been able to get enough facts to hand down indictments. That's why we're here; we'd like you to help us.''

"What exactly would you like me to do?'' I asked, in a tone of voice that made them think I would cooperate.

"We'd like to wire you. . . .''

"He means with a hidden microphone,'' Peterson interrupted.

"I know what he means, I watch TV,'' I told the lieutenant.

"We'd like you to just talk to your brother,'' Matlow continued, "about what he's really doing and who he's really involved with. It's the information we're after, not your brother. In fact, you'll actually be doing your brother a big favor because if we can stop them before they defraud more investors, Joe's going to be up for a lot less jail time, I can guarantee you that.''

"And if I won't do it?''

Matlow grinned pleasantly, as if none of us had a care in the world.

"Oh, we think you'll want to; you'll be doing both him and yourself such a favor. We're sure you'll help.''

What did he mean by doing myself a favor?

"Mr. Matlow,'' I said calmly, "you're asking me to betray a member of my family. Don't you think that goes against some basic human impulse? I mean, only a lowlife betrays his own family.''

"Mr. Marcus, it's very simple. You wouldn't be betraying him, you'd be helping him. If we put together a case and stop the scheme fast, the charges against Joe won't be that serious. But six months from now, after their scams are in operation, who knows how many years he might get. I don't see how cutting his jail sentence, in anyone's mind, could possibly be considered a betrayal.''

"Listen,'' I told them after thinking it over, "I'm just a druggist. I've got enough problems of my own at the moment without getting involved in my brother's. If you don't mind, I'd rather just stay out of it. I'm facing jail myself for defending my own pharmacy."

"That's why we figured you'd cooperate with us," Matlow told me. "Lieutenant Peterson told me how you felt about crime and the authorities' difficulties protecting innocent citizens. We figured you'd jump at the chance to help us, Joe, yourself, and society. Who loses? No one."

I stared Matlow straight in the eye.

"I have a lot of differences with my brother," I told him, "but I'm not going to be the one who gathers evidence to send him to jail. To you, it's just a case. I have to live with him as my brother for the rest of my life. I can't help you; sorry."

The two men sat quietly for a minute. They didn't seem upset. In fact, they seemed to have expected that answer. After another exchange of glances, Peterson took charge.

"We didn't really want to bring this up, but we know you've been talking to Joe lately. A lot of talking, I understand."

Matlow nodded in agreement. The discussion was about to turn nasty. I remained silent.

"I understand you have your principles," Peterson continued cheerfully. "In fact, I admire your principles. But sometimes principles have to be bent just a bit to accommodate reality, don't you think? I'd like to persuade you to soften your principles and help us."

The payoff was coming. Peterson didn't make me wait long.

"The reason Detective Matlow is here with me is because of a bizarre coincidence, the kind that we see all the time in my line of work. We do massive amounts of footwork, collect all kinds of seemingly unrelated information. We hear gossip, observe evasions, register confusions, and fill files with cross-referenced notes. Then, boom, suddenly everything comes together and makes sense, all neat and orderly like a Christmas package from the department store. Matlow has been tailing your brother for the last week trying to break the case, doing the hardest work of all, the three W's—watching, waiting, and walking. One day he follows Joe out of Los Angeles up to Santa Barbara, to the breakwater. Joe is waiting for someone. Who would it be but the ex-boyfriend of Genie, the girl whose life you thought you were saving in the drugstore. Detective Matlow follows Joe and some goon around for two days until their boat comes in. Then he calls for some help and uses a bit of technology to listen in on the conversation between Joe and this Nick character. That's when Matlow first hears your name being discussed. And blackmail. As well as shocking revelations concerning you and the underage girl. Like statutory rape. He hears about gun-wielding, potentially homicidal fathers. Drug payoffs for blackmail. Terrible things being done by decent, principled people like yourself. He heard threats made in your name. Hints of rape. Assault and battery. Sodomy. The list goes on. Your brother and his friend were engaged in a vicious little game. All in *your* name. As *your* agents. All this potential violence just to recover a few photographs. That's why Detective Matlow called me in. Our cases seemed to suddenly dovetail. It wasn't exactly what we were originally looking for, but then again, in this business, when you start something, you never know how it's going to turn out, do you?''

I took another drink of my scotch and didn't answer.

''We talked to Nick. You'll be pleased to know that what he gave your brother were really all the negatives and prints; Nick was that convinced by Joe's arguments. Without going into some secret tricks of the trade and explaining how he did it, let me just say that Detective Matlow found a way to get a quick look at the photographs. He was shocked at what he saw. Not that he hadn't seen it all before. And not that she isn't enormously attractive; I thought so myself from the beginning. But she's underage. A minor. In the vernacular, 'jailbait.' And her father is your friend and attorney. And you're a public figure, with a wife. A beautiful wife, I might add. And a daughter. Why would you do such a thing, I asked myself. Actually, it didn't matter. The fact is that you committed a crime both with her and in dispensing controlled substances without a doctor's instructions. The law tells me that, armed with these facts—and these are proven, undisputable facts—I must arrest you. This is my job.''

Here he paused for dramatic effect and turned to his accomplice.

''Am I correct in detail so far, Detective Matlow?''

''You might add,'' the FBI man noted, ''that I managed to copy a couple of Nick's pictures just to have something solid to show in court, if it comes to that. These are copies of my copies.''

Matlow passed me a small envelope containing photos of Genie and myself in the adult motel.

"You can keep them if you like," Matlow informed me.

I glared at him, enraged. These men, who were supposed to be on my side, were worse criminals than Nick. If only I had my gun, I told myself, I would mete out justice on the spot. But it was an empty threat; I couldn't kill them. Besides, being cops, they weren't the only ones with duplicates of the pictures. Given the way the system worked, I imagined that a hundred police bureaucrats had received copies of the pictures and were already whacking themselves off in their toilets to the images of Genie and me on that water bed. Killing the cops would do me no good; they'd just be replaced by others from the system. I would have to hear them out.

"You know, I thought about this for a long time. I have a lot of sympathy for you," Peterson continued. "The shooting in the store must have been a terrible trauma for you. I've see it happen to a lot of cops. Everyone is disturbed at having to take a life. No one's ever really prepared for it. The guilt is a great psychological price not many people understand. Between you and the girl, it must have created a deep bond; life and death situations do that. Then you were hit with that business from the ACLU and the indictments. I saw how angry it made your wife. You must have felt alone and abandoned. The only person who could possibly understand what you were going through was Genie. To me, such reasoning is natural. But could a jury comprehend it? Even if they could, what you did with Genie and Nick is illegal; they'd have to convict you. It does occur to me that it serves no one's interest to see you in jail. But as a cop, no matter how I feel about something, I have a responsibility to the law; I can't just throw evidence away and turn my back on a crime. That would make me an accomplice. So I talked to Matlow about it. I said to him, 'Ron, what if we get Marcus to help you out on the case with Joe and the Federal Bank of Montserrat? Couldn't we use that to justify convincing the D.A. not to press charges over the matters of Genie and the drugs?' He agreed. You help us, we help you. A feather in everyone's cap."

The scumbags had me trapped. As far as they were concerned my cooperation was an obvious, unquestioned fact, thanks to their clever presentation.

"How do I know you'll get the D.A. to drop the charges?"

"You'll have to trust us," Peterson answered.

Another liar and asshole that wanted me to have faith in him.

"You can get the D.A. to destroy all the evidence?"

"Sure," Matlow nodded.

Peterson seemed to agree.

"Actually," Matlow continued, "your brother will never know your role in the case; we'll use the tape you make just to get information. It's not admissible in court, anyhow."

Just like Richard Nixon's weren't. My brother was bound to find out the source of the information. In a bureaucracy the facts eventually leaked out; nothing could remain secret. So, as both of the cops knew in their hearts, they were lying to me. But they had the goods on me, no doubt about that. My mind was reeling. I needed time. Time had helped with Nick; maybe it would help with the police.

"I need to think about this," I informed the two cops.

"Of course," answered Peterson, grinning victoriously. "I understand completely. How about if we talk tomorrow?"

"Tomorrow?" I stalled stupidly.

"Yes."

"No," I said firmly.

"No?" asked Peterson, with a threatening tone returning to his voice.

"Tomorrow's a crazy day. I've got to go on TV with the mayor and debate the issue of crime and the role of the average citizen. Can you give me until the next day?" I couldn't believe I was suddenly welcoming my TV appearance.

"Hey, I heard about that," Matlow grinned. "I'm going to watch that one myself. I can't believe your jerk ball of a mayor, the liberal candy ass, was once a cop himself. And he favors citizens arming themselves and taking the law into their own hands. Unbelievable. Scares the hell out of me. Look what it's done to you." Matlow grinned at me, then turned to Peterson. "I'll go for giving him an extra day. Okay with you?"

Peterson nodded.

"We'll get in touch with you at the drugstore the day after tomorrow in the morning," Matlow informed me.

The two cops stood and I escorted them to the door.

"Working with us is the right decision, no question about it," Matlow told me with conviction, clearly enjoying his hold over me.

"Good luck with the mayor tomorrow," Peterson offered.

I said nothing. The two cops went outside, got into their

sedan, and drove off down the street. I shut the door, threw on the dead bolt, finished my glass of scotch, poured another one, flopped down in my wing chair, and tried to focus on my problem.

The only certain solution was, once again, suicide. All other choices seemed to offer only protracted suffering for everyone. It came down to the fact that there was no way I could betray my brother to the police, even to save my own skin. I couldn't do it. He was my flesh and blood. Beyond that, Joe had just put himself at risk to help me out—an act of heroic, unselfish love that, despite everything, moved me to unexpected heights of compassion and affection. What Joe did with his bank was between him and the law; as far as I was concerned my brother was my ally, to be defended to my death. My rational mind argued with this, bringing up example after example of betrayals Joe had committed against me in the past. But in my heart I knew the cops could torture me on the rack and I wouldn't rat against my brother.

The phone rang. I snatched up the receiver, certain it was Marilyn.

"Mi-chael," came the familiar voice of my mother. How did I get so lucky?

"Mom. Hi, how are you?"

"Michael, don't you call your mother back anymore?"

"Sorry, mom, it's been a hectic day. In fact, I can't even talk to you now. Let me call you tomorrow, okay?"

"That's why I telephoned, Michael. I want to know what time you're going to be on TV tomorrow. I want to watch. My friends want to watch."

Should I tell her that by tomorrow there'd be nothing to watch, that I'd be just a statistic in the suicide studies?

"Six o'clock."

"What channel?"

"Twenty-eight. Educational TV."

"What is that on my cable box?"

"Mom, you watch TV all the time. What do you think it is?"

"Six."

"Very good, you win the kewpie doll. Mom, I'll talk to you tomorrow after the show. Good-bye."

"Michael, you weren't going to tell me you were on TV were you? You know how I found out?" She waited for me to answer.

I said nothing.

"You don't want to know?"

"How did you find out, mom?"

"I was at the meat counter at Gelson's. Who was there but Mrs. Cotler, your attorney's wife. I recognized her from CBS, from when they interviewed her about her daughter. She told me about you and the mayor. I had to hear from a stranger, Michael. Your own mother had to hear her son was going to be on TV from a complete stranger. How can you do this to me, Michael? Don't you think I'm interested?"

"Mom, you have a very short memory," I told her angrily. "You weren't very happy that I shot that junkie, remember? You told me I was behaving like dad did when he had his 'episodes.' The mayor's putting me on TV to talk about the shooting. As far as I knew you didn't want to hear another word about it. So I didn't tell you, okay?"

"Michael," she addressed me as though I were four years old, "shooting a man is one thing; being on TV with the mayor is something else. You're my son. Of course I want to hear about it. What kind of a mother do you think I am? I just wish your father, may God rest his soul, were here to see his son on TV."

I, too, wished my father were there. As far as I could tell, he was the only person who might be able to think up a solution to my problem.

"Mom, since when do you want dad back? You didn't care what he thought when he was alive."

"Michael, he did have his good points. And he *was* your father, remember? He'd have been proud to watch you on TV. Who knows, seeing his son do well might have helped him behave better."

Mrs. Manipulation, that was my mother. She could distort any fact to suit her purposes. It was no secret where Joe learned that skill.

I don't know what possessed me to start talking to my mother about my father; it must have been a kind of psychic panic induced by my dilemma with the police. A question about my father and my mother had been running through my mind for several days, but it was something I would normally never have had the courage to ask. My mother was the only witness, and I doubted if she'd tell me the truth. But I felt I had to know.

"Mom, there's something I've been thinking about lately,

something personal. As one adult to another, if I asked you a question about you and dad, would you answer me honestly?''

"What is it you want to know?'' She sounded hesitant.

"Will you tell me the truth?''

"Michael, what are you talking about? I always tell you the truth.''

That was a lie if I ever heard one. Truth to my mother was a relative concept. She was a master of self-serving rationalization.

"I remember how much it hurt you when dad had those girlfriends. It hurt me too. I felt he betrayed all of us.''

My mother said nothing.

"I used to hear you argue with him about 'his girls.' Remember when you realized I understood what you were yelling about and you took me outside in the back yard by Joe's swing and explained to me about mental illness, schizophrenia, and dad? Do you remember what you told me?''

"What did I tell you?''

"You told me that his mental illness did something funny to him when he was around other women; the schizophrenia made him what you called 'over-sexed,' that around other women he lost control of himself, just like Chowder, our German shepherd, did around female dogs in heat. Was that really true?''

"Of course. Why would I lie about such a thing?''

"But you made dad sleep in his own bedroom. Alone. Why was that?''

There was a long silence on my mother's end of the phone.

"Why do you want to know all this, Mikey?''

"Mom, don't Mikey me; my name is Michael. I just want to know, that's all. I'm an orderly person; I like all the pieces of my life to fit together. You and dad were a puzzle to me and I'm still trying to make sense out of what happened while I was growing up. You must be able to understand that.''

"I do,'' she said after another long pause.

"So why the separate bedrooms?''

"Is this the question you wanted to ask me?''

"It's one of them.''

"What are the others?''

"Are you going to answer me or not?''

"Michael, in those days everyone slept in separate bedrooms. That was the fashion.''

"Mom, that's not true and you know it. You had a reason. What was it?"

"Okay. As you know, your father was a sick man. He tossed and turned all night and hardly slept. We decided his illness shouldn't keep both of us up. Doesn't that make sense to you?"

"Yeah, but he was only sick the last two years of his life; I'm asking about the twenty years before that when you slept in separate bedrooms."

"Michael, tell me, who is this talking to me, my son or the Los Angeles district attorney?"

"You told me you'd answer my question honestly. I guess you can't do it, can you?"

"How dare you talk to your mother like this, Mikey, you apologize to me right now. I demand it."

"If you can't answer me, you can't answer me; there's no reason I should apologize. Just don't tell me in the future how you always answer honestly, okay?"

There was another long pause in the conversation. When she finally spoke again it was a little softer, with a little more humility. We were getting closer to the real story.

"What I told you was the truth. Your father was a sick man for almost the entire time we were married. With his episodes. The cancer was something else. For twenty-two years I don't think your father slept more than three or four hours a night, tops. Was that supposed to mean that I shouldn't sleep for twenty-two years, too?"

"Mom, I lived in the same house with you, remember? I used to hear him arguing with you that he wanted to sleep in the same bedroom with you. That he missed you. Why didn't you give it a try? Maybe it would have helped him."

"Michael," she told me quietly, "you're a smart man. You understand many things I can't even pronounce. But there are some things you'll never understand. One of them is what it's like to live with an unfaithful husband. As you know, I don't believe in divorce. You get married, it's for life. I didn't believe in sharing myself with a man who fiddles around with other women. If your dad wanted other women, then that was all he was going to get. He made the choice, not me. He knew my standards. I made myself very clear to him."

Finally, there it was—my mother the hanging judge. My father

had loved my mother, of that I was certain. Yet for twenty-two
years he was excluded from her bed. No wonder he went crazy.

"You didn't mind sleeping alone for twenty-two years?"

"Of course I minded."

Then why did you do it?"

"Michael, today, from what I read in the magazines, everyone
has this idea that sex is everything. Well, I'm here to tell you
there are some things that are more important. A lot of things, in
fact. Your father behaved selfishly, like a child. He needed to be
taught what was good and bad. He learned. And he respected me
for what I did, believe me."

My poor father. I wished I had understood his dilemma years
before. Why had I listened only to my mother? Could it be that
my father was actually the saint in my family? He could have
divorced her, but he didn't. He could have turned Joe and me
against her; instead, he let us continue to believe in the sanctity
of motherhood. My father voluntarily took on the role of the bad
guy to preserve the idea of a family. Joe and I had been suckered
by our mother. I wondered if my brother knew the truth.

I was suddenly filled with an enormous revulsion for the
monster on the other end of the phone. At the same time I felt a
tremendous yearning, a great wish to see and talk to my father
once again. I wanted to forgive him. I wanted him to know that I
understood and loved him, and that I was sorry for judging him.
I wished I could have known him without all the anger I had felt
toward him while he was alive. The fact that my need for my
father was completely unrealizable made me very sad; the man
was gone. The only consolation was that after so many years, the
picture of my family finally made sense.

"I'm sure he did respect you for it, mom. Thank you for
telling me. I appreciate your honesty."

"I told you I'm honest; I'm glad you finally believe me."

"I believe you. Now I've got to go and work on my notes for
the TV debate tomorrow. Thank you for calling."

"You'll wear a nice suit, won't you Michael?"

"Of course, mom, good-bye."

" 'Night, Michael."

We both hung up the phone. Then I sat down in shock.
Everything that I had once believed about my life was now
twisted around backwards and upside down. All that made sense
was the .38 revolver in my drawer at the drugstore and how

delicious the barrel would taste as I placed it in my mouth, pulled the trigger, and blew all of my problems out of existence.

What stopped me was Rebecca. There was nothing worse that one could do to one's children than to kill oneself. I poured out another glass of scotch.

If I didn't cooperate with the police, they'd send me to jail and I'd lose everything. On the other hand, if I helped the police and Joe went to jail, then where would I be? I still would have lost Marilyn, and I would also have lost my sense of myself. I would be scum—a man who turned in his own brother to save himself. The only good part about this second course of action would be that in spite of losing Marilyn and my family, I would still have my business. But what value would it have to me? My exterior professional life would appear sound, but my interior emotional world would be empty and dead.

I wanted to call up Ed and ask his advice. When I tried to imagine what he would advise me to do about my situation (assuming the girl involved were someone other than his own daughter), I know he'd urge me to cooperate with the cops. His rationale would be that with or without my help, Joe was destined for jail.

I tried calling Marilyn. She was still "in surgery." No one could be in surgery that long; obviously she didn't want to talk to me. Didn't Marilyn know I needed to speak to her? I wanted to tell her how much I adored her and how much hope I had for our future. I couldn't understand how she could abandon me now, after I had been so honest with her. Throughout the night I kept trying her at the hospital, but she never would take my call.

Just before dawn, as the sky outside changed from foggy black to hazy grey, I had a strange experience. Maybe it was from the scotch, or perhaps it was brought on by the Ritalin I had taken to keep my mind clear. I heard a car pull into the driveway. I was sure it was Marilyn. Finally. I was so relieved. My wife was coming home to forgive me, to tell me she loved me, to commit herself once again to me and our marriage. I jumped from my chair and ran to the door, which I flung open. Outside I saw the car. It was an old Datsun—the paperboy delivering the morning *Times*. I shut the door, dejected, depressed, and discouraged. For a moment the excitement of Marilyn's return had cut through all of my confusion. That was when I had the idea.

It just came to me—a way out, perhaps the only one. It meant taking an enormous risk. I realized that blackmail could only exist where there were secrets. What I had to do was to shed my secrets and force the world to accept me on my own terms, as I was, just as I had tried to get Marilyn to do. My father had kept secrets. My mother still lived with secrets. My secrets gave the police power over me. Good or bad, I had to make those secrets public information. How this would affect Marilyn and my future, I had no idea. I did know that it was all I could do. I had to throw open my life to the world and, as the sun peeked over the horizon, I knew just how to do it.

49

Good ideas are supposed to be bulletproof. I was so convinced mine was in such a category that my despair lifted as the sun came up. Energetically, I began implementing the plan to extricate myself from my dilemma. I showered, washed my hair, shaved, and dressed in my most elegant suit. Then I awakened Rebecca, prepared her cereal, and waited patiently for Angie, the housekeeper, to arrive. Angie was right on time and she generously agreed to stay until nine o'clock that night so that I could get through my TV appearance. The hardest part of the morning was saying good-bye to Rebecca; if my plan didn't work, I might never see her again. Rebecca thought daddy was "very funny," kissing her, squeezing her, and behaving so emotionally over a simple departure for work. Angie, I'm sure, thought I was losing my mind. Maybe I was.

On the way to the pharmacy I stopped at Cedars to talk with Marilyn. As unbelievable as it seemed, she was actually in surgery, in the middle of a cesarean section which I could clearly watch through the operating theatre ceiling. I debated about scrubbing down and going in. But with a class full of students observing from the seats above, as well as a room full of nurses, the Ob/Gyn resident, and the anesthetist, Marilyn and I could hardly have a private discussion. All I'd do would be to anger her. I resolved to come back later.

I arrived at the drugstore to find Milt, Adam, and Harriet waiting for me outside the front door. Oddly enough, none of them seemed surprised that I was late. They simply and quietly mumbled "good morning" while I unlocked the front door. As soon as the lights were on and they went to work, I disappeared into my office to refine my plan.

Every half hour I called the hospital. But Marilyn was never available. At eleven, a familiar rapping sounded on my locked door.

"What?" I growled impatiently as I unlocked the deadbolt.

The door opened and Jerry bounded in, full of enthusiasm. He locked the door behind him.

"Good morning, good morning," he chirped.

I glared at him. "What do you want?"

"You, my friend, are talking to your own personal Santa Claus."

"Jerry, Christmas isn't for six more months."

"That's true for everyone else, but not for us. I just spent the morning down at the Bank of Tokyo talking to some friends of mine from Hong Kong. They've been following all the publicity about the drugstore and the robbery. And you know what? My idea about franchising was very appealing to them. Very, very appealing. In fact, Michael, they made a little proposal to me. A commitment. They want to back us to the tune of twenty pharmacies from Santa Barbara to San Diego. They put up the cash, they own forty-nine percent, and we call all the shots. What do you think of that, my friend?" Jerry flashed me his biggest shit-eating grin.

"Do they know about the TV debate tonight?" I asked.

"You bet they do; they're very impressed by you. They even talked to the mayor; he told them you've got a real future in politics."

"What do they think I'm going to say tonight?"

Hearing something odd in my tone of voice, Jerry looked at me more carefully.

"I'd assume they think the same thing I think—that you're going to talk about the robbery and citizens' rights. No?"

"No."

"But that's what the debate's about."

"That may be, but I have other plans. I'm afraid that what I'm going to say isn't going to inspire confidence in your investors."

"What are you saying, Michael?" Jerry was suddenly grim. "We're talking about money here. Big dollars. Lifetime security.

You'll have cash enough to build ten health spas if that's what you and Marilyn want. This is no time for funny business; my investors are serious men. What are you planning to say?"

"I'm going to tell the truth."

"What truth?"

"About Genie. Why I saved her from that junkie."

"And why was that?"

"Jerry, remember that little scene when Lieutenant Peterson was in here and I held the water pistol to your head?"

"Yeah?"

"You say a word to anyone about what I'm about to tell you and we're going to have a rerun of that scene, except with the real .38. Is that clear?"

"So what are you going to say?" My partner's voice was a mere squeak of its former self. He knew.

"You were right all along."

"About what?"

"About my interest in Genie."

"I was afraid of this."

"So was I."

"And that's what you're going to say on TV?"

"That's part of it."

"Terrific."

"Do you want to hear the rest of it?"

"Michael, everyone has his little affairs, but they don't go on TV and talk about it. Why are you being so naive?"

"You remember my brother Joe?"

"The hot-shot stockbroker?"

"Well, he's involved in some kind of new scam. The police want me to inform on him. They know about my affair with Genie. They have pictures of us together, highly incriminating photos. They told me last night that if I don't cooperate with them, they're going to arrest me for statutory rape and a few other prestigious charges. No matter what happens, it looks like an end to my career in the pharmaceutical business. And I don't think it's going to amuse your investors."

Jerry was uncharacteristically quiet. He was trying to figure out all the implications of my problem.

"What about your brother; is he guilty?"

"Who knows? Probably."

"Then what's the difference if you help them? If you don't, you're just going to hurt yourself."

"I'm not going to betray my brother."

"After all he's done for you; don't make me laugh."

"Jerry, I'm not asking your advice. As your partner, I'm just preparing you for what I'm doing."

"Can't you just get the flu and cancel out of the show? Think about it. Give yourself some time. You don't have to do this, it's crazy. You're going to ruin everything we've built over the years."

"I've already ruined it; I want to end the damage, here, today."

"Michael, if you go public with this, you're going to force the police to arrest you. Have you talked to a lawyer about this?"

"I don't think, given the circumstances, that Ed's going to give me the best advice, do you?"

"You need time here. Think this over. You're behaving too hastily. How can I get you some time?"

"You can't. I've made my decision. I'm going to do it."

"What about me?"

"What about you?"

"I'm your partner. You destroy your reputation and you destroy my investment. What do you think this place is worth if we don't have any customers? I mean, how many customers do you think are going to buy prescriptions from a man arrested for statutory rape?"

"That's a chance I'm willing to take."

"Michael, for god's sake, be reasonable. Don't destroy what's taken so long for you to build. Listen to me."

"My mind is made up."

"Just like that, you're going to destroy your life and business?"

"That's not how I see it; I think you'll understand better after the debate."

"You have more surprises?"

"Not as far as the business is concerned."

"There won't be any business after tonight."

"Jerry, I told you all this because I know you may be affected financially. I feel I have an obligation to you to let you know what I'm doing. What you tell the investors is your business. But I'm going on that show tonight and that's that."

"I think you've lost your mind."

"Okay, so I've lost my mind. Now I'd like to be alone, please."

"What about me, Michael?"

"What about you? You're a wealthy man. This isn't going to hurt you."

"It's certainly not going to help me. You're a god-damn selfish bastard, you know that?"

"I just thought you'd like to know my plans." I picked up my pen and returned to my legal pad.

"Fuck you, Michael. I'll see you later."

Jerry stormed out of the office and slammed the door. I locked it to prevent further interruptions.

By three-thirty I still hadn't been able to talk to Marilyn. Oddly enough, I interpreted the fact that she hadn't called me as a good sign. I knew that if she had actually made up her mind about what she planned to do, not only would I have heard about it already, I'd be unable to change her decision no matter how vehemently I disagreed with it. This meant I still had a chance.

Once again I drove to the hospital, hoping to plead my case in person. But again Marilyn was in surgery and unavailable. Either she had more cesareans that day than she normally had in a week, or she was simply ducking into other obstetricians' surgeries whenever she heard that I had entered the hospital. I left her a long letter telling her how much I loved her and pleading with her to watch me on the TV at six o'clock with the mayor. Then I had a bit of good luck. The nurse on duty was Edna, the very woman who'd admired the way I'd dealt with the junkie. I told her that I was going to be on the TV show with the mayor and asked if she'd please remind Marilyn to watch. Edna promised not only to sit Marilyn down in front of the TV in the recreation room, but to watch the show with her.

When I got back the pharmacy I had only twenty minutes to clean up before Ed arrived. And who should I find in my office waiting for me with a briefcase full of legal papers, but Jerry. He had to talk to me. I told him I didn't have the time. What I wanted to do was go over my notes for the debate. But Jerry was frantic and wouldn't leave until I'd heard him out. I gave him five minutes. First he attempted to talk me out of going on the show. Then he tried to get me not to mention the blackmail or Genie. When I refused, he did something I should have anticipated. He opened his briefcase and put an escrow contract in front of me.

"Before you destroy the business you can buy me out," he told me.

Jerry was prepared to sell me his forty-nine percent ownership in the drugstore for $400,000, triple what he'd paid to me five years earlier. The man was a pig, who obviously figured that after my television confession, the drugstore wouldn't be worth a plugged nickel. If I signed the escrow, no matter what the store ended up being sold for, Jerry would be guaranteed his money directly from me; I'd owe him. He couldn't lose. The fact that I might not have the money to pay him didn't seem to worry him. Nor did the outrageousness of his disloyalty in my time of crisis. He just wanted my signature on that contract.

Was $400,000 a fair price? I wanted to know how he'd arrived at that figure so quickly, but I didn't have time to hear an explanation. My priority was the TV appearance and freeing myself from the blackmail. If $400,000 would satisfy him and get him out of my hair, I'd sign. I couldn't see how he was going to collect, anyhow, given the fact I'd probably end up in jail. As I picked up my pen, Jerry opened the office door.

"Rhoda," he yelled into the pharmacy.

In walked his secretary, ready to notarize the escrow. Jerry had thought of everything. I signed. Jerry signed. Rhoda notarized. Jerry handed me a copy.

"Michael, skip that debate and I promise you I'll tear up this copy of the escrow in a second."

"No way," I told him as I locked both him and Rhoda out of my office.

Only ten minutes remained until Ed was scheduled to arrive. I was exhausted. Not only hadn't I slept in thirty-six hours, but I really had not gotten one decent night's sleep since the robbery. The Ritalin I had taken in the morning had worn off and my brain was beginning to feel cooked from fatigue. I went into my little bathroom, shaved, brushed my teeth, combed my hair, and reknotted my tie. My whole life was riding on a TV appearance and my energy level was at an all-time low.

Desperate situations cause desperate behavior. I slipped out into the pharmacy and cruised the storeroom shelves. Ritalin didn't seem to me to be up to the job, so I moved on to a couple of capsules of old reliable Dexedrine, washed down with thirty milligrams of Prednisone just to soothe my system with a flush of well-being—a speed and cortisone cocktail, my own invention.

At four-thirty on the dot, my office phone buzzed. Ed had arrived.

"Tell him I'll be right out," I said to Mary.

This was it, my last shot at life. I went into the bathroom and once again checked my appearance. Surprisingly enough, I didn't look too bad. The drugs had gone to work and were already beginning to soften the hard edges of my exhaustion. I brushed my hair, flashed my best talk-show grin, slipped on my suit jacket, and bounded out to greet Ed.

50

Moments later I was speeding toward Hollywood in the passenger seat of Ed's British racing-green XJ-S Jaguar. As he guided the powerful twelve-cylinder machine through traffic with the skill of a race driver, Ed held forth on the various techniques for a successful television appearance. I was more than happy to sit and listen. He had his plan for the debate and I had mine. There was little overlap. But it hardly served my interests, at this point, to tell him so.

We drove for miles with Ed lecturing and me pretending to be interested. Eventually, however, my state of mind became apparent. Ed stopped talking and studied me. He wasn't one for beating around the bush when he had something to say. His instincts led to the jugular. At that moment, so did mine. But I had no interest in bloodying anything until we were in public, at the TV station. My plan needed people around. And for that we were at least ten minutes away. I would have to stall.

"Michael, are you in some sort of trouble that I don't know about?" Ed asked.

"What do you mean?"

"You know god-damn well what I mean. I'm trying to talk strategy with you and you're off somewhere in never-never land."

"I'm just a little nervous. I've never debated on TV before."

"Michael, we're not in kindergarten here. You're talking to a man who's spent years in court asking questions of criminals, psychopaths, witnesses, and judges. Professional liars are my speciality. I'm like a bloodhound when I sense something is wrong; it's my daily work. One thing I know, Michael, is that you're lying to me. Why? What's bothering you?''

Obviously he didn't know about my relationship with Genie or he would have already confronted me. I still had some room to maneuver.

"It's that obvious?''

"It is.''

"I see now why you're so good in court. How'd you become so perceptive about this kind of thing?''

"Michael, god-damn it, this isn't the time to talk about that, what the fuck is wrong with you?''

"I'm afraid you're not going to like what I have to say.''

"Why don't you let me decide that, okay?''

I pretended to think about it before I spoke.

"You must see a lot of strange behavior in your line of work; people doing things that society as a whole doesn't approve of, right?''

"Yeah.''

"As you know, I've always been a guy who's tried to play by the book, be respectable, live by the rules, you know what I mean?''

Ed nodded.

"It's very hard when you live by one standard, keeping up an ideal, trying to really make your life mean something, when you suddenly feel impulses in yourself that conflict with your highest intentions and seem to pull you astray.''

"Michael, get to the point. We're going to be at the TV station in two minutes. What did you do?''

I just had to drag it out a little longer.

"It's about Marilyn. For the last six months, living with her has been like living with a stranger. My wife has become my roommate. To be honest with you, I've been very lonely. I used to think I could handle anything, but the loneliness has been more than I've been able to bear. Ed, I'm a man, with a man's needs; you understand what I'm talking about, don't you?''

Ed smiled broadly. Suddenly it all made sense to him. He was the Cheshire Cat, sympathetic and understanding of all human foibles, a man who didn't judge human behavior. Given his relationship with his own daughter, he was hardly in a position to judge.

"You're telling me you have a girlfriend.''

"I had an affair."

"Had?"

"Had."

"Why'd you end it?"

"Because I realized I loved Marilyn, in spite of our problems."

"Michael, you'll have to excuse me, but I still don't understand what's bothering you. Did I miss something you said?"

"Ed, yesterday I told Marilyn about the affair. Now she won't speak to me. She's spent the last twenty-four hours at the hospital. I'm afraid I'm going to lose her over this. It terrifies me."

"You told her? What are you, crazy?"

"I had to. I needed her to understand what her obsession had done to me. And I wanted her to forgive me."

"You couldn't have just bought her some flowers?"

"I don't understand."

"Michael, you're such a moral person. That's one of things I like about you. But you know, everyone has affairs. Everyone."

Ed flipped on his turn indicator and pulled the Jaguar into the parking lot of the TV station. Moments later we were out of the car, walking up the steps of the studio.

"Just relax and forget about Marilyn," Ed told me. "Your marriage is going to be fine. Marilyn loves you and will forgive you. Trust me; I know these things. Now, what you should be thinking about is the issue of crime in the community and the mayor's Community Watch plan. You're the star witness in support of his position. Remember why you're here."

I nodded and pretended to think about it as we gave our names to the uniformed guard at the door.

"Studio B is that way," the guard pointed, after affixing little name tags to our jackets.

Studio B was an old newsroom from the early 1950's when the now somewhat dilapidated public television station had been the West Coast broadcast headquarters for NBC. It had all the warmth and smell of a high school basketball court. The stage consisted of a carpeted platform supporting four chrome guest chairs, one leather host chair, and a five-foot rubber plant. Behind the stage, glued to the cyclorama, was an enormous Mercator Projection map of the world. Three video cameras stood by to record the proceedings. Technicians swarmed over the equipment, adjusting the lights, testing the microphones, and fiddling with the cameras.

Ed, who had obviously been here before, led the way to the stage manager and gave him our names. The stage manager ticked off our presence on his clipboard, then directed us down the corridor to the dressing room.

Hal Westheimer, the liberal Democratic candidate running against Mayor Malcolm, was already seated in the dressing room being groomed and made up for the debate. Westheimer looked very impressive in his charcoal pinstripe suit and pale blue shirt. The tan makeup applied to his face blended nicely with the muted colors of his clothing, providing a photogenic contrast with the touch of grey at his temples. Westheimer was in his mid-forties, neat, spare, and lean. I had seen him interviewed; he was full of ideas for the city. And for an ex-public defender, his ideas weren't too bad. What distinguished Westheimer from most liberal Democrats was his support of the police department. He championed a greatly enlarged force. I was sure he adopted this position only because Proposition Thirteen had forced the Mayor to come up with the Community watch concept as a result of the city's lack of funds to hire more cops. Westheimer capitalized on this in speech after speech and the police department supported him (unofficially, of course). How he would pay for the increased police protection was something I never understood. "The money was there if one concentrated on priorities," Westheimer claimed. He had been quoted as saying he "was strictly in favor of *professionals* enforcing the law, not home-grown vigilantes." By which he meant me.

Sitting next to Westheimer was Sam Grey, the ex-police chief of Sacramento, the expert behind the Democratic candidate's "Squash Crime" plan.

Ed, who knew both men, introduced me. They shook my hand politely, but I could see that they basically looked down on me as if I were some amateur piece of dirt accidentally blown their way by an irritating wind. Then we went to the opposite side of the room, where the makeup man began work on my face.

"They're afraid of you," Ed told me quietly. "That's why they were so cold; you've got them scared."

What can be said about logic like Ed's? He may have been right. But talk about scared; my whole life hung on the line. I wasn't there because of politics; my driving need was survival. Unlike Westheimer, I was facing humiliation, prison, and death and was enraged by his obvious contempt for me. I wanted him, along with Peterson and Matlow, stone dead. My sudden anger was good because it gave me energy. The trick, I knew, was to keep that emotion under control so I could remain effective on the show.

At fifteen minutes to air time, my makeup man finished. The mayor had still not arrived, which threw the stage manager into a panic. Unlike most TV shows, this debate was going on the air live. Without the mayor there was no show, and they had no one to put on in the mayor's place. I figures this was as good a time as any to finish the conversation I had begun in the Jaguar.

"Ed." I spoke quietly so no one would hear us. "What I told you in the car wasn't the whole story; there's more."

He moved closer, obviously interested.

"It involves you, too."

"How?" he asked uneasily.

"It's about you and Genie."

"What are you talking about?"

"You know exactly what I'm talking about."

"I do?"

"Yeah."

"Yeah, what?" he said, continuing to stonewall.

"I know something's gone on between the two of you that shouldn't happen between a father and daughter."

Ed stared at me. The look on his face made me wonder if he were packing his gun. I reassured myself that we were in a public place—with witnesses everywhere. There wasn't much he could do other than glare at me; even yelling would only call attention to information he wouldn't want overheard.

"Michael, what are you really saying?"

"I told you."

"You implied certain things. But I think what you implied is different from what you really mean, so why don't you try again?"

"You really want me to spell it out?"

"Yes."

"If the truth came out they'd send you to jail. Genie's a beautiful girl, Ed. But she's your daughter. You know the law."

"Is this what she told you, the vicious little liar?"

"No, she's the last person who'd admit to anything specific."

"Then why the hell are you accusing me? Have you gone crazy?" Ed hissed quietly through clenched jaws.

I kept close tabs on his hands; I wanted no gun play in this discussion."

"Ed, I saw it for myself; she didn't need to tell me anything."

Ed stared at me as if I were a lunatic.

"And how did you see it for yourself?" he asked sarcastically.

"Saturday night after your dinner party, at maybe three in the morning, you went into Genie's bedroom. You said you'd heard a noise. She said she had been having a nightmare. The real nightmare was the way you wanted to comfort your daughter. I know, Ed, because I was there, hiding in her closet. I saw it."

"What were you doing in her room in the middle of the night?" he asked after a long, anguished silence.

"The same thing you wanted to do."

Ed was so enraged that I know he would have shot me had we not been in public.

"How'd you get in the house?"

"How do you think?"

"I'm going to kill her."

"No you're not."

"I'm going to kill you."

"You're not going to do that either."

"I thought you were my friend. You spent the night in my daughter's bedroom. Both of you deserve to die."

"Ed, I knew this would upset you. But think about it reasonably. I'm no innocent, but I sure look like one compared with you."

"It's my word against hers, Michael. You don't have the evidence to prove what you're saying."

"I don't want to prove it."

"Then what do you want?"

"Two things. First, don't say a word about this to Genie. Leave her alone. Second, don't do anything to me for what I just told you. If you violate either of these conditions, the whole story, which is written down and stored safely in a vault, automatically goes public. Is that clear?"

"That's all you want?"

"That's it."

Ed was in great pain. He wanted to shout, to scream, to choke me, to murder me. But because he was in public all of his impulses had to be restrained and he just stared at me.

"How could you?" he growled.

"I could ask you the same question."

At that moment the dressing room door flew open and the

mayor charged in, followed by his army of media experts. The mayor carried himself like a winner; with his makeup already in place, he gleamed with self-confidence. Ignoring Westheimer, the mayor crossed the room to shake my hand, which boosted my confidence immeasurably.

"Michael, I can't thank you enough for helping me out like this. It's so good to see you again."

"Thank you, Mr. Mayor; I appreciate the invitation. As you know, I'd do anything for the good of the community."

The mayor grinned, slapped my cheek affectionately, and spoke to his aide.

"I can see he's going to do just fine."

The aide nodded.

"Michael, this is Chris O'Conner; he's head of my reelection campaign. I think he's someone you'll want to know."

O'Conner extended his fleshy hand, which I shook.

"Your speech at the chamber of commerce award impressed quite a few of us. But I guess Ed told you the reactions."

O'Conner glanced up at Ed, who nodded in spite of his anger.

"Okay, gentlemen," O'Conner told the mayor and me, "the way to view this show is as a sympathetic forum to present your ideas on community crime. The host, Alan Marshall, is on your side. The trick is going to be to stay calm, reasonable, and low-key and to let Westheimer argue himself into an intellectual corner."

The stage manager bounded in, all smiles.

"Five minutes everyone; take your places."

We stood. The mayor took me by the arm and led me out of the dressing room to my chair on the stage beside him. As we were fitted with microphones, Alan Marshall, the baby-faced host of the public affairs show, greeted the mayor, introduced himself to me, then sat down in the leather-covered host chair.

"Two minutes," yelled the stage manager.

Instead of being terrified, a strange calm descended over me. I don't know whether it was the drugs, exhaustion, or some emotional synergy of anxiety, desperation, and primitive survival instincts. My course of action was in motion and there was no way I could turn back.

"One minute," the stage manager called out.

The mayor reached over and put his hand on my arm, comforting me in the manner of an experienced father calming his son.

"Michael, the big trick on this kind of show is to say whatever you have to say as if you were just talking to a friend out there. We are all your friends here. And I know you'll do great."

"Thank you, Mr. Mayor."

"On the air," someone hollered.

We all faced the cameras.

"Five, four, three, two, one," went the stage manager's countdown.

"Good evening. Welcome to 'Topics of the Day.' I'm your host, Alan Marshall. The live topic for tonight is crime in Los Angeles, its causes and solutions. We have with us in our studio The Honorable Anthony Malcolm, mayor of Los Angeles. With him is Michael Marcus, the pharmacist recently in the news for successfully defending himself in a dramatic hostage robbery situation. With opposing views, on my right, we have Hal Westheimer, the mayor's Democratic opponent in the November election. With Mr. Westheimer is Sam Grey, the police chief of Sacramento from 1969 to 1975, who's been outspoken on the changing role of the police in contemporary society. Welcome gentlemen, and let's begin."

The show opened with the typically boring public affairs format; each candidate presented his position with a short, reasonable, positive, simplistic statement. We'd heard it all before. The mayor believed that crime was a community problem, not simply an isolated question of law enforcement. Crime was a symptom of society's troubles that could not be solved by simply paying more money to experts, like the police. What was needed, the mayor stated, was the daily involvement of each and every citizen. Westheimer disagreed violently, likening the mayor's position to that held by the sheriff of Dodge City in the old Wild West days. Westheimer tried to convince the viewers that only a massive increase in the size of the police force could reduce the onslaught of the professional criminal. To support the mayor, he claimed, was to support the era of the vigilante mob.

At this point the mayor called on me to relate to the viewers my own personal experience with street crime. The mayor specifically wanted to know what I thought would have happened in my situation if the city had a few more squad cars patrolling my area. Would that have done me any good, he wanted to know.

"Mr. Marshall," I addressed the host, "everyone else on the panel here is an expert and I'm just an ordinary pharmacist. But I have given the mayor's question a lot of thought and my answer is somewhat complex. I need three or four minutes, uninterrupted, to explain it. Can you give me that?"

Marshall was surprised by my direct request and looked to the other panelists. Westheimer and Grey seemed uncomfortable, but didn't object.

"Go ahead," Marshall instructed me.

It was my big moment. As the surfers say, I went for it.

"I used to find all this debate about crime, the number of police on the street and so forth all very interesting," I addressed Westheimer, as well as the host. "Until ten days ago when that junkie came into my store, stuck a pistol to the head of a young girl, and threatened to kill her if I didn't give him money and drugs. What I know for certain is that if the junkie had decided to kill her, twenty more police cars driving up and down my block wouldn't have been able to save her. For that I would have needed an armed guard in my store. Fortunately, I had one. Me. What city can afford to pay policemen to sit in every store?"

Westheimer and Grey looked unhappy with my remarks, but I continued before they could interrupt.

"The problem now is that I shot a man. It's tormented me ever since. Shooting a man is terrible, even if it's to save another person's life. And living with having shot him is even harder. I keep going over and over the idea that there must have been some better way, some nonviolent way. I didn't want to shoot the guy. I'm not a violent man. But when it came down to the girl's life or his, there wasn't any choice in my mind. More police in cars wouldn't have helped; it all happened too fast."

"I'd like to comment on that," Westheimer interjected.

"And I'd like to finish, please," I directed my remark to Marshall.

"Continue," the host replied.

"Thank you. The second point. Since the robbery, I've been the target of all kinds of cranks. Robert Allen's wife is suing me for shooting her husband. She's getting free legal help from the ACLU, while I have to pay thousands of dollars to defend myself. The district attorney's office is talking about prosecuting me for manslaughter and wrongful death if Mr. Allen dies. And all because I defended myself. The police haven't helped me, Mr. Westheimer. In fact, last night Lieutenant Fred Peterson, the detective in charge of my case, came to my house with an FBI agent named Ron Matlow and tried to blackmail me."

Everyone suddenly seemed to be holding their breath; there wasn't a sound in the studio.

"You see, the FBI thinks a relative of mine committed a crime," I continued, "but they can't prove it. While they were investigating my role in the robbery, they accidentally found out I was having an affair. Our noble police told me last night that if I wouldn't help them entrap my relative, they'd publicly reveal my affair, complete with their incriminating photographs, to my wife. Mr. Westheimer would like to increase the size and power of the police. It wouldn't have helped me in the pharmacy. But I'm sure it will help more of us get blackmailed. What I'm in favor of is the citizens being in control, not the local version of the Gestapo. When the police use the tactics of criminals, who do you go to for protection, Mr. Westheimer?"

The Democratic candidate just sat with his mouth open; he didn't know what to say. Nor did anyone else on the panel. They were stunned.

"As for my own behavior. . . ." I turned to the camera closest to me and looked straight into the lens. I tried to imagine that Marilyn was inside. "Marilyn, sweetheart," I addressed myself only to her, as if we were alone in a room, just the two of us together. Conjuring up her image worked, because I could literally feel her presence. "I know you're watching me. I know that what I've done has hurt you very much and I feel horrible about it. But I've told you over and over again that I love you. And I mean it. You're the only woman in my life. Since I confessed to you about the affair you haven't talked to me. I hope you'll forgive me, but this is the only way I know to reach you and clear the air between us. You know why I had the affair. And you know it's over. I'm telling you in this way because I want you to know, and I want the world to know, how very much I love you. The fact is that loving you means more to me at this moment than life itself. It would break my heart to lose you. Marilyn, darling, I'm asking you, begging you, please, forgive me and come back to me. I love you very much. Whatever it takes to work it out with you, that's what I'll do, I promise. Give us a chance, Marilyn, please."

My speech concluded, I turned away from the camera and back to Alan Marshall, the now dazed and stupefied host. I had done exactly as I had planned. I had made my proposal to Marilyn and offered her my unequivocal love. What she would do now was anyone's guess. The next move was hers. For the rest of the show, I said nothing. In fact, I hardly remember what the panelists discussed. I thought about Marilyn. Before the entire world I had renewed my commitment to her in what felt to me almost like a second marriage ceremony; the only thing missing was her "I do."

The other panelists treated my revelations like the proverbial hot potato. The subject and the way I had presented it had the potential of burning everyone, no matter how they touched it. Westheimer and Grey tried to steer the debate back to the statistical analysis of crime and the various methods other cities, notably Sacramento, had used to control it. But Mayor Malcolm brought the discussion back to me and my charges of blackmail by the police. The mayor promised to investigate, and thanked me for coming forward with the truth. He promised me "justice," which was all that I really ever wanted.

I wondered how Marilyn's surgeons reacted to my appearance. Would they still want to invest money if it meant being associated with me? If they chose to back out, which I could easily imagine them doing, it certainly wouldn't help Marilyn's enthusiasm for a reconciliation. As for Jerry's Hong Kong investors, I had made the speech that automatically set in motion the buyout of my partner. So much for franchising.

What concerned me was Rebecca. My hope was that she hadn't watched me on TV. But I knew that was unlikely. Whether she'd seen me or not, little Rebecca would inevitably have to face my confession if Marilyn took the hard route and insisted on a divorce.

My mother and her friends, well what can I say? My poor mother would never be able to set foot in public again. In her eyes, I'm sure I appeared as the living soul of my father. In fact, I wished my old man could have seen my TV appearance, not that it would have reformed him but it might have drawn us together—two fellow conspirators feeling their way through the painful adventure of adult life. My father had made a fool of himself in my eyes, many times. I had just done something that made his foolishness appear trivial by comparison. Whether the world perceived me as embarrassment or a hero, it didn't matter now; the die had been cast and no one could take the moment away from me. I had gone out into the water and ridden the wave.

In the dressing room after the debate, I was given a wide

berth. No one spoke as I removed my makeup. Even Ed, who had watched my performance on the monitor, sat stoically avoiding my glance, still too confused and angry to speak. I'm sure he felt that I had humiliated him with the mayor. For a brilliant, well-connected lawyer, Ed certainly looked to be in an uncharacteristic state of panic. Then Mayor Malcolm entered the silent dressing room, ignored Ed, and sat down in the chair beside me.

"Anthony," I heard Ed mumble to the mayor, "uh, listen I don't really know what to say. I had no idea he'd get so personal. If there's anything you want me to do, any statement you want me to make, you name it. If it'll help, we'll do it, I guarantee you."

The mayor didn't respond, but instead turned to me.

"Michael," he said, "I have to tell you, that was a remarkable performance. You have real courage. Honestly, I'm envious you were able to do that." The mayor faced Ed. "If what he said about the police is true, the city owes your client a full apology." He turned back to me. "You have it from me, Michael, I'm going to demand a complete investigation, and a report to me personally. We'll get to the bottom of this, once and for all. And I have to thank you. Not only did you prove my point about the necessity for community participation in crime prevention, but you showed Westheimer for the callous and insensitive opportunist that he is. You're a brave man, Michael. I hope your wife sees that. You can tell her that if she gives you another chance, which I sincerely hope, I'd like to have the two of you over to my house for dinner. It's not often I meet a man with your kind of backbone. I'd like to get to know you better."

The mayor extended his hand. I shook it.

"Thank you," I mumbled. "I was afraid I might have embarrassed you. But it was all I knew how to do."

The mayor shook his head, amused. "I meant what I said about the dinner, Michael. Call me when you can set a date."

"I will. Thank you."

The mayor departed, leaving me alone in the room with Ed and the makeup man. Westheimer and Grey had apparently left directly from the studio.

"I guess it didn't turn out so badly," I muttered, relieved.

Ed said nothing, stood up, then bolted from the room.

51

I arrived home in a cab from the TV studio at twilight on a beautiful summer evening. The lights inside the house illuminated the entire structure with a glowing comfort that seemed to promise a true and lasting peace. It was the perfect family scene with the exception of one jarring problem: the driveway was empty and my wife was obviously not home.

Unlocking the front door was very depressing. More than anything I wanted Marilyn to be inside, to greet me, to approve of me, to accept me, and to appreciate the action I had just taken.

"Daddy!" Rebecca called, running across the living room to embrace me as I entered.

"Hello sweetheart, how are you?"

"Daddy, Angie and I watched you on TV!"

"You did?"

I glanced at Angie, who was standing nearby. She avoided my eyes.

"If you don't need me anymore, Mr. Marcus, I gotta be going," she told me, staring at the floor. I had embarrassed her.

"I appreciate your staying late, Angie, thanks."

She grabbed her purse and headed for the door.

"That was some speech you made, Mr. Marcus. Good luck with Mrs. Marcus."

"Thank you, Angie."

" 'Nite Rebecca," Angie called, "see you tomorrow."

" 'Nite Angie," Rebecca yelled back.

Angie disappeared out the front door leaving Rebecca and me alone.

"So, what'd you think of Daddy on TV?" I asked my daughter.

"That was some speech, daddy."

"What does that mean?"

"That's what Angie said. She said it over and over. That was some speech your daddy made, some speech. Why'd she say that, daddy?"

304

"She must have liked what I said. Did you like what I said?"

"You were on TV, daddy, just like Big Bird." Rebecca pointed to the living room television console to further emphasize the point.

"Did you understand what I said, sweetheart?"

"Of course, daddy. You talked about the robber again. And you talked about mommy."

"That's right. Have you talked to mommy today?"

Rebecca nodded.

"Mommy called from the hospital right before the TV show."

"And what did she say?"

"She said she loved me and that she was very busy with a lot of work and missed me and not to worry, she'd be home after I was asleep.

"She said all that?"

Rebecca nodded with conviction.

"Anything else?"

She shook her head.

"No message for daddy?"

Again she shook her head.

"Becka, you have a very good memory, thank you."

"I'm happy you're home, daddy."

"I'm happy to see you too, sweetheart. Daddy told the mayor what a good little girl you were and the mayor wants to meet you."

"Who's the mayor, daddy?"

"He was the man sitting next to daddy on the TV."

She thought that over carefully before answering.

"Oh, that man. Daddy, I asked Angie and she told me to ask you. What's an affair, daddy?"

The question drove a knife right through my heart and jolted me years back to the day my hysterical mother first told me about my father's "girlfriend." I'll never forget the insane, overdramatic way my mother presented the situation. Although she knew my father had only gone out once with his lunch counter waitress, my mother had me convinced the world had come to an end; it was Auschwitz, Hiroshima, and brain cancer, all rolled into one. Compared with my father's crime, Attila the Hun was the world's sweetest guy. Such a memory convinced me to take a low-key approach with Rebecca.

"An affair is a special friendship, sweetheart. Sort of like what you have with Burke Gregory. You're special friends with him, but you still love mommy and daddy, don't you?''

"Oh," she said, "I'm glad you have a special friend."

"Thank you, 'Becka. But my special friend is gone and I won't see her again; I'll only see you and mommy. I love both of you very much, I hope you know that."

Rebecca nodded and gave me a big hug. I kissed her, lifted her off the floor while she squealed with delight, and whirled her overhead, near the ceiling. She always loved doing that; she said it made her feel like she was a bird, flying.

The phone rang. The only person I wanted to talk to was Marilyn. I set my daughter down, ran across the room, and snatched up the receiver.

"Hello?" I answered timidly.

"Is this Michael Marcus?" came the male reply.

"Yes?"

"This is Brad Hoftsteader from the *New York Times;* I wonder if I could ask you a few questions about your television debate tonight?''

"Sorry, but no."

I hung up the phone, ran to the kitchen, and turned on the answering machine. As I had expected, the phone rang almost immediately. It was the reporter again, trying to convince me to let him do the interview. I didn't pick up the phone; I simply turned up the volume monitor on the answering machine so that I could hear who was talking, in case Marilyn called.

Then I went back to the living room and played with Rebecca, who soon became tired and cranky. I carried her to bed where she made me sing "California Girls," which almost immediately sent her to sleep.

I went downstairs. The house was suddenly very large and terribly quiet. It was ten-thirty and Marilyn still hadn't called. She must have seen the television show or at least heard from other people about my performance. What did she think? Where was she? Why wouldn't she talk to me? I sat in my living room sipping whisky, passionately wishing for the sound of Marilyn's BMW pulling into our driveway.

Late into the night I must have fallen asleep, because the next thing I heard was an eerie echo of a car in the driveway. Feeling disoriented, I looked around the living room. Where was I? What time was it? What exactly was happening? Then I recognized the clunk of a well-made car door—a BMW, I prayed.

52

Familiar footsteps clicked over the concrete walkway outside the front door. I checked my watch. It was past three in the morning. Immediately I sat up and straightened my clothes. Then the footsteps stopped and I heard nothing for so long that I began to question whether I had ever heard anything at all. Perhaps it had just been a masochistic dream. But a sudden jangle of keys recharged all my expectations. The front door swung slowly open. Standing in the open doorway was Marilyn, who stared at me for the longest time as if she were still undecided about everything. Finally she stepped inside the house and shut the door.

Marilyn was tired; I could see that even in the dim light of the one living room lamp. But as I looked closer I saw much, much more. She exuded a vulnerability, an openness, a fullness, a kind of calm serenity that I'd never seen in her before. I couldn't quite put my finger on her new presence but it contained elements of shyness, a long absent softness, as well as a wonderful new sense of awareness, both of herself and me. I felt wired to her as if she had the power to nourish or destroy me by simple telepathic command. Yet she seemed hesitant and even a little nervous. To buy time, she brushed her long, black hair out of her eyes with a graceful stroke of her lovely, white fingers. I sat quietly, awaiting my fate.

"You know where I've been since the TV show?" she finally asked.

I shook my head; I had no idea.

"Driving."

I nodded. This impulse I understood.

"You know what I thought about while I was driving?"

Again I shook my head.

Slowly Marilyn began to unbutton her silk blouse. What I was witnessing was not the obsessed, controlling woman with whom I had lived for the past year or even the anxious, urgent lover I'd

experienced on the beach near Neptune's Net. As Marilyn
stepped out of her wool skirt and slowly, sensually began
slipping off her underwear, I saw a quality emerging that I had
absolutely never known in her. It was mysterious. It was elusive,
highly sexual, and very powerful. Marilyn wasn't hurrying. She
wasn't pretending. For the first time she was *real*. Somehow she
had tuned into the power of both her sex and her soul,
simultaneously, and that made her gentler, warmer, and openly
adorable. I was mesmerized. Naked, she walked toward me until
she was only inches from my chair. Then she knelt down, placed
her palms on either side of my face, and kissed me tenderly, just
for an instant.

"All I've been able to think about since I saw you on TV was
how much I wanted you. It frightens me, Michael. You frighten
me. What I feel for you isn't reasonable. I don't understand it.
For what you've done to me I have no doubt I should leave you.
But I don't want to and I can't. And it terrifies me. You're
making me break my own rules. How could you have said those
things on TV, Michael? In public. I never would have imagined
you'd do something like that. God, you can't know how much it
excited me to hear you tell the world that you love me. You're
crazy. And you're wonderful. And you scare me. And you know
what, Michael? It's you who excites me, not the man in the
cape."

I just stared at her and held my breath. I couldn't believe what
I was hearing; it was everything I had yearned for and more. I
wanted to talk, but there seemed to be no words perfect enough
to express my feelings.

Marilyn obviously understood because she reached down,
unzipped, then removed my trousers. An instant later she was all
over me with her hands, pressing, tickling, feeling, squeezing,
and caressing until the passion in me equaled the expectation in
her.

"Come, Michael."

She led me to the Indian cotton sectional sofa, where she
positioned herself facing the front door. I sat, lifted her by her
firm buttocks, and slid her down on my erection. Marilyn
squatted over me unself-consciously and began to thrust back
and forth, up and down, feeding the fire in herself. We moaned,
we sweated and pumped, we screamed with a salacious, energetic enjoyment I would never have believed possible.

My life had come full circle. Chaos had been kicked off by my watching Genie and Nick in this same spot, on this same couch, doing this same thing. Back then it had seemed another world, remote from my experience. I had craved passion; now I felt it. I had craved adventure; I now had that, too. Most of all I craved being connected to Marilyn, to life, and to feeling. I had wanted to take chances, to act with gargantuan vitality. I had all that now and more with my sensual, passionate, and beautiful wife. I held her close, feeling her responsive flesh under my hands, and believed for the first time in years that life not only offered incredible possibilities, but was alive with forgiveness, love and best of all, hope.

ABOUT THE AUTHOR

Born in Chicago in 1947, BRUCE GOLDSMITH has lived in Southern California since childhood. He received his B.A. degree from the University of Southern California. For the past ten years he has worked as a screenwriter; he wrote, produced and directed the TV film *Foreign Relations* with Judge Reinhold. *Strange Ailments; Uncertain Cures,* his first novel, has been sold to Paramount Pictures.

NERO WOLFE STEPS OUT

Every Wolfe Watcher knows that the world's largest detective wouldn't dream of leaving the brownstone on 35th street, with Fritz's three star meals, his beloved orchids and the only chair that actually suits him. But when an ultra-conservative college professor winds up dead and Archie winds up in jail, Wolfe is forced to brave the wilds of upstate New York to find a murderer.

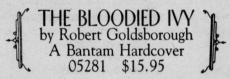

THE BLOODIED IVY
by Robert Goldsborough
A Bantam Hardcover
05281 $15.95

and don't miss these other Nero Wolfe mysteries by Robert Goldsborough:

☐ 27024 **DEATH ON DEADLINE** $3.95
            —FINALLY IN PAPERBACK!
☐ 26120 **MURDER IN E MINOR** $3.50

"A Smashing Success"—*Chicago Sun–Times*

And Bantam still offers you a whole series of Nero Wolfe mysteries by his creator, Rex Stout

☐ 24730 **DEATH OF A DUDE** $2.95
☐ 24918 **FER-DE-LANCE** $2.95
☐ 25172 **GAMBIT** $2.95
☐ 25425 **DEATH TIMES THREE** $2.95
☐ 25254 **FINAL DEDUCTION** $2.95

Look for them at your bookstore or use the coupon below:

Kinsey Millhone is . . .

"The best new private eye." —The Detroit News

"A tough-cookie with a soft center." —Newsweek

"A stand-out specimen of the new female operatives."
—Philadelphia Inquirer

Sue Grafton is . . .

The Shamus and Anthony Award-winning creator of Kinsey Millhone and quite simply one of the hottest new mystery writers around.

Bantam is . . .

The proud publisher of Sue Grafton's Kinsey Millhone mysteries:

"Ezell Barnes is in the front ranks of the new breed of inner-city Knight Errant."
—Loren D. Estleman
Author of EVERY BRILLIANT EYE

"The inner city is his oyster."
—*New York Magazine*

Easy Does It . . . His Way

Meet Ezell "Easy" Barnes. He's an ex-prizefighter ex-cop p.i. from the gritty streets of Newark, New Jersey. He's tough on crime, wields a wise sense of humor and occasionally thinks with his fists—sometimes that's all there's time for. Not far behind Easy you'll find his best informant—Angel the Sex Change, Newark's diamond in the raunch.

Be sure to read all of the Ezell "Easy" Barnes mysteries by Richard Hillary.

☐ 26470 SNAKE IN THE GRASSES $3.50
☐ 26666 PIECES OF CREAM $3.50
☐ 27172 PILLOW OF THE COMMUNITY $3.50

Bantam Books, Dept. BD27, 414 East Golf Road, Des Plaines, IL 60016

Please send me the books I have checked above. I am enclosing $_____ (please add $2.00 to cover postage and handling). Send check or money order—no cash or C.O.D.s please.

Mr/Ms _____

Address _____

City/State _____ Zip _____
BD27—9/88
Please allow four to six weeks for delivery. This offer expires 3/89. Prices and availability subject to change without notice.